PRAISE FOR
THE CONFIRMATION

The Confirmation sizzles with drama and is hard to put down. Ralph Reed is on his way to becoming the master of political thrillers.

—**Sean Hannity**, *New York Times* best-selling author and host of
The Sean Hannity Show

Ralph Reed has done it again! In *The Confirmation*, his follow-up novel to his 2008 debut novel *Dark Horse*, Reed has penned a rousing tale about all the intrigue behind the nomination and confirmation of a Supreme Court justice. Matters get even more complicated when some Iranian terrorists with nuclear materials threaten to blow up a major U.S. city.

As someone who has been at the epicenter of many of the most compelling moments in the nation's life over the past quarter century, Ralph Reed takes us behind headlines to the inner workings of the nation's Capitol. *The Confirmation* is a compelling and informative ride. Buy it, read it, and pass it on.

—**Richard Land**, president, Ethics and Religious Liberty Commission,
Southern Baptist Convention

With unforgettable characters and unpredictable plot twists, *The Confirmation* is a roller-coaster ride of a political thriller. Ralph Reed pulls back the curtain and reveals the secrets of how politics is really played. You won't be able to put it down.

—**Mark Levin**, host, *The Mark Levin Show*, and president of Landmark
Legal Foundation

Ralph Reed has nailed it in this fast-paced political thriller, showing all the nooks and dark corners where the best and worst takes place in America's Capitol. A great read.

—**Karl Rove**, former senior advisor and deputy chief of staff to President
George W. Bush

As a participant in Supreme Court confirmations as a member of the United States Senate, I know *The Confirmation* weaves a tale that, while fictional, is true. Ralph Reed shines a bright light on the backroom deals, special-interest-group pleading and the politics of personal destruction that plague judicial confirmations, but he does so in a way that is ultimately hopeful and inspiring.

—Former U.S. Senator **Rick Santorum** (R-PA)

Ralph Reed has done it again. I have been on the inside of Supreme Court Confirmation process. Ralph has written a novel that is more realistic than nonfiction. The spiritual dimension addressed in the book is compelling. This is a must read.

—**Jay Sekulow**, General Counsel
American Center for Law and Justice

PRAISE FOR
DARK HORSE

A spellbinding mix of suspense and intrigue . . . a timely account of the best and worst of American politics.

—**Sean Hannity**, *New York Times* best-selling author and host of
The Sean Hannity Show

Could be the best political novel of the (Reagan/Bush) era."

—*Tulsa World*

THE
CONFIRMATION

RALPH REED

THE
CONFIRMATION

A NOVEL

FIDELIS
BOOKS
NASHVILLE, TENNESSEE

978-1-4336-6924-8

Published by B&H Publishing Group,
Nashville, Tennessee

Dewey Decimal Classification: F
Subject Heading: ADVENTURE FICTION \ TERRORISM—
FICTION \ UNITED STATES. SUPREME COURT—FICTION

Author is represented by the literary agency of Alive Communications,
Inc., 7680 Goddard Street, Suite 200, Colorado Springs, CO 80920,
www.alivecommunications.com.

1 2 3 4 5 6 7 8 • 14 13 12 11 10

To Ralph, III

ONE

The president-elect stared into the mirror and struggled to tie the knot in his two-thousand-dollar silver Brioni tie as his fingers shook. He was surprised at how jumpy he was now that the moment he yearned for, dreamed of, and fought for his entire career had finally arrived. Satisfied at last with the knot, he gazed back at his reflection in the mirror. He noted with pleasure that his morning coat fit him snugly, the silvery tie and vest highlighting the streaks of grey in his wavy brown hair. The heels on his spit-polished alligator cowboy boots took his height to just over six feet. His steely blue eyes were open and inviting, reflecting his expansive mood.

Upstairs, an army of beauticians and hairstylists flown in from New York and Beverly Hills worked on the future First Lady's image. Rapid footsteps on the wooden floor above conveyed harried preparations. A dress assistant flown in by Oscar de la Renta, the design house providing two dresses for the inauguration, joined them. The entire production—hair, makeup, manicure, and wardrobe—was taking more time than landing the 82nd Airborne at Normandy.

The president-elect looked at his watch. His blood pressure spiked. They were supposed to be at St. John's Episcopal Church for the traditional prayer service in four minutes.

"Claire!"

No response. More frantic footsteps.

"Claire!"

"Coming!" came the cry from behind the bedroom door.

"Claire, we have to leave right now!" he shouted. "The president and First Lady will be standing outside waiting, and the whole world will see that I can't arrive at my own inauguration on time."

Bob Long, former governor of California, claimed the peak of American politics after winning the most bizarre presidential campaign in U.S. history. Defeated for the Democratic nomination at a convention tainted by corruption, he entered the race as an independent initially seen as merely a spoiler, and his candidacy caught fire with voters turned off by the partisan bickering in Washington. When no candidate won a majority in the electoral college, the election went to the House of Representatives. Long won an astonishing victory and became the first independent candidate elevated to the presidency in U.S. history.

Out of the fog of nerves and confusion, an advance man approached. "Governor, POTUS and FLOTUS are moving from the residence. ETA, three minutes," he said, using acronyms for the president and First Lady. "Should we tell them to . . . wait?"

Long looked at the advance man with a mixture of dread and panic. Then, as if on cue, Claire Long appeared at the top of the stairs, her hair pulled up, pearls the size of miniature golf balls on her neck, wearing a stunning royal blue dress with matching pillbox hat. "Well?" she asked triumphantly, spreading her arms. "Am I worth the wait?"

Long let out a long whistle. "You look just . . . incredible! You look like a modern Jackie Kennedy."

"Thank you, Mr. President," she said.

She glided down the stairs, chin held high, followed by a retinue for hair and makeup and brushed his cheek with her lips. That was when he caught the scent of vodka masked with expensive perfume. He shook it off. *Claire probably had a Bloody Mary with brunch to take the edge off,* he thought.

Long introduced himself to the makeup team enthusiastically. "You guys did a fantastic job. I love the hair. Which one of you is the hairstylist?"

"I'm a hair artist," replied a short woman wearing tight black jeans, a black T-shirt and reddish-purple hair.

"Forgive me," Long replied with a touch of sarcasm. "I didn't mean to give you a demotion. Of course you're an artist. And that goes for all of you."

They headed down the hall to the front door. "Hair artist, eh?" whispered Long. "I guess that means she's expensive."

"Not as expensive as me, honey," replied Claire.

The door opened and the Secret Service detail led the way to the waiting limousine. Long felt his heart rate quicken. It was all really happening.

ACROSS LAFAYETTE PARK, JAY Noble took a final sip of coffee as he finished a brunch fit for a king at the Hay-Adams Hotel. He downed an egg-white omelet, a plate of bacon (he was trying the low-carb thing), a bowl of fruit, and a syrup-drenched plate of French toast (okay, maybe not the whole Atkin's thing). His thatch of brown hair, combed more neatly than usual, had a telltale hint of gray at the sides, white hairs he gained as the architect of one of the most brutal presidential victories ever recorded. His high forehead, cherubic cheeks, and laconic posture telegraphed an attitude of smug satisfaction. Completely out of character for an aging political hack, he wore a tailored Hugo Boss suit. He held the china cup with three fingers. A fleet of waiters flitted around the table, the maître d' and manager did table visits, and other patrons craned their necks to see if it was really him. And why not? Jay was the political maestro who masterminded Bob Long's rise to the presidency.

"Not to pry, but why aren't you taking Lisa to the ball?" asked David Thomas, Long's campaign manager and recently named White House political director. He was referring to Lisa Robinson, the black-haired, angular beauty who ran the press shop in the Long campaign, and who recently jetted off to an exotic eco-resort in Mexico with Jay.

Jay let the dead air hang. Should he tell the truth or feed Thomas the same spin he gave everyone else? He chose the latter.

"It's complicated," he sighed. "Lisa's going to be White House communications director, and I'm the president's chief strategist." He shot Thomas a sly look. "Besides, I live by the rule that you keep your private parts out of the payroll."

Thomas, a born sucker for locker-room talk, smiled knowingly. "You're right. But it's still tragic," he said, shaking his head. "Lisa's hot—and smart."

"She's got the trifecta," Jay agreed. "Body, brains, personality." He let out a long sigh. "But there are plenty of other fish in the sea."

Jay was relieved that no one knew the truth, which was that he asked Lisa to be his date and she had turned him down flat. She needed to do her job, she insisted, and that meant being taken seriously by the press corps. They would "remain friends," she assured him. Pretending not to be crushed, Jay agreed. He had to admit she had solid instincts when it came to navigating negative press coverage. But a week later Jay read in the Style section of the *Washington Post* that Lisa was going with Senator Russell Evans of Tennessee, the fifty-four-year-old bachelor freshly divorced from the reigning queen of country music. Evans was one of the most notorious skirt-chasers on Capitol Hill, showing up at cocktail parties in DC with a different blonde on his arm every week. This was Lisa's idea of being taken seriously?

"So you're flying solo?" asked Thomas.

"No," replied Jay. He leaned back in his chair, trying to play it cool. "I'm taking Satcha Sanchez."

Thomas shot him a surprised look. "The Latina infobabe?"

"It's all part of my Hispanic outreach strategy," said Jay. He let out a rapid-fire, evil laugh.

Thomas chuckled. "You're too much." Jay waved for the check. As he signed the bill, he saw Thomas's eyes widen. "Well, what do you know . . . speak of the devil."

Jay turned around to see Satcha's five-feet-six-inch frame gliding across the room, hips swaying hypnotically, her hourglass figure wrapped in a fire-engine red dress with a plunging neckline. Her red lips formed an alluring smile, and her black hair with light brown highlights teased into an on-air bouffant that bounced as she stepped in Christian Laboutin heels. She carried a full-length mink coat over her arm.

"Subtle she is not," said Thomas under his breath.

The men rose from the table as Jay dipped his head in a gentlemanly bow. "You look *mahvelous*," he said to Satcha.

"Thank you, sugar," replied Satcha matter-of-factly. Her eyes sized up Jay's outfit. "Love the suit. *You are styling!*" A waiter appeared, pulling back Satcha's chair and holding her mink gingerly as though it were still alive. "Bottega loaned me the dress. If I decide to keep it, I can get it at a discount. But the mink is mine. Is it too much for television?"

"Absolutely not!" joked Jay. "It's positively understated."

Satcha shot him a sideward glance of mock disapproval. Her drop-dead looks and come-hither TV persona, spiced with a dollop of Latin sensuality, formed her into a symbol of Hispanic power. The ubiquitous Satcha was the empress of the Latino vote, her visage staring down from billboards and out

from magazine covers as she covered the campaign and moderated presidential debates for Univision. A Puerto Rican journalist of Cuban descent, she
started out in San Antonio as a meteorologist, then moved on to the Weather
Channel before hitting it big at Univision, garnering higher ratings than the
major networks in New York, LA, Houston, Chicago, and Miami. *People*
magazine named her one of the "50 Most Beautiful People." With Satcha on
his arm, Jay was guaranteed plenty of buzz, a play for Hispanic votes, and a
measure of sweet revenge against Lisa.

"Are you coming to the ceremony?" asked Thomas.

"No, I have to work," replied Satcha with a frown. "I'm anchoring the
inaugural coverage, and I stay on the air to cover the parade." She made a
face. "I just don't know if I can make myself sound interested as I announce
the marching band from Columbus, Ohio."

"You want us to help you get some senators and congressmen to stop by
the skybox so you can do some interviews?" asked Jay.

"That would be great!" Satcha's face lit up. "Get people close to Long. I
don't want anyone who is boring. I'm looking only for important people."

"You mean like me?" Jay asked, his face cracking into a smile.

"Not you, sweetie," she volleyed. "Univision signed off on my going to
the ball tonight, but if the suits think I'm getting too political, they will go
nuts."

"You mean you have to be careful about press coverage?" asked
Thomas.

"They won't leave me alone," Satcha sighed. "The only thing worse is no
one talking about you, right?"

Jay waved over the waiter, who returned and slid the mink on Satcha.
The power couple breezed from the lobby as the doormen held the door,
the frigid January air blasting through the entrance. More heads turned and
fingers pointed as they flew out of the hotel.

IN THE PRESIDENTIAL SUITE of the Willard Hotel, the Reverend
Andrew H. Stanton held court in a living room the size of a basketball
court, surrounded by the usual clutch of aides and hangers-on, gathered like
a highly compensated peanut gallery on a large sofa and several wing chairs.
Like any religious broadcaster worth his salt, Andy traveled with a posse
the size of a hip-hop artist. Today it included three ministry vice presidents

and their wives, several drivers, two security guards, Mrs. Stanton, Andy's four children and their spouses, and a press secretary. Also joining them was Ross Lombardy, Andy's political right hand. Everyone had VIP tickets to the inauguration and the balls, which Ross obtained by calling in every chit he had at the inaugural committee. Twenty-nine VIP tickets to the ceremony? No problem, Mr. Lombardy! After all, Stanton delivered an estimated thirty million evangelical votes to Long on election day. Ross also obtained parking passes, which was fortunate because the delegation required six SUVs just to drive the short distance to the Capitol.

"Can you believe they asked to see my prayer in *advance*!?" Andy fairly bellowed. "I'm not going to let some bureaucrat edit *my* prayer."

"I believe it, sir," replied Ross, whose day job was serving as executive director of the Faith and Family Federation. "They want to make sure it's politically correct."

"Meaning *what*?" asked Andy, his face twisted with righteous indignation.

"Meaning no J-word," said Ross. "God is good, God is great. But Jesus offends some people." He shrugged with a political operative's nonchalance.

"Too bad," shot back Andy, his blue eyes smoldering. "Jesus is my Lord and Savior. I'm not ashamed of the gospel." He enunciated each syllable.

The vice presidents grunted their approval with an "Amen."

"Can't you make it ecumenical?" asked Ross, pressing. "Why stir the pot?"

"You're the political guy; I'm the pastor. Leave the prayers to me."

"Then there's the Muslim thing," Ross coolly added. "We're in a global war on terror. Long's folks are spooked by anything that might be construed by the Arab street as relaunching the Crusades." Other than Long's inaugural address, Andy's prayer would be one of the highlights of the ceremony, seen or heard by over a billion people. It could spark an international incident if Andy "went Moses," as they liked to call it around New Life Ministries. Ross fielded several worried calls from the Long camp about Andy's prayer. He gave them all the same answer: no one would see or hear the prayer until Andy delivered it at the Capitol.

"Do you realize what today means?" asked one of Andy's obsequious aides. "You're the new Billy Graham."

Andy frowned, dipping his chin and clasping his hands firmly behind his back. "There'll never be another Billy. Besides, I'm controversial, too political, don't ya know."

"Billy prayed with presidents; Andy elects 'em," corrected Ross with a wicked grin. He turned to Andy. "Andy, you're Billy, Richard Daley, and Samuel Gompers all rolled into one."

Andy seemed momentarily taken aback by the comment. Then suddenly he broke into a little-boy grin and cackled with laughter, clapping his hands as he enjoyed the joke at his own expense. The posse, lined up on the couch like blow-up dolls, helmet hair frozen into place by too much hair spray, chuckled nervously. The comment struck close to home, but Andy's self-deprecating sense of humor gave everyone else permission to laugh.

The door swung open and a security guard stood at attention. "Reverend Stanton, time to go, sir."

Andy, followed in single file by the posse, headed out of the suite to an elevator.

SENATE MAJORITY LEADER SALMON Stanley strode through the Capitol Rotunda on his way to the inauguration of his sworn enemy wearing the plastic face of a defeated candidate. His puffy, white countenance masked the trauma beneath: resentment at Long's successful betrayal of the Democratic party and his preternaturally charmed rise, anger at the investigation of his campaign by a Republican Justice Department, and bitterness at the vicious attacks on his candidacy from the media. Still, Stanley was determined to grit his teeth and get through the ordeal, if only to deny his enemies the joy of his absence. But that didn't make it any more pleasant. Even though he claimed to have a hide as thick as an elephant, Stanley's wound went deep.

"We'll get through it fine," Stanley said in a hollow voice to his chief of staff, walking briskly beside him. "My father used to say, 'Son, when you get knocked down, get up, dust yourself off, and keep putting one foot in front of the other.'"

"You're a far better man than the one taking the oath of office today," the aide replied.

"Maybe," Stanley said. "Sometimes you just have to put the country first. John Adams left town rather than attend Jefferson's inaugural. Not me. I'm going to be on that platform when he takes the oath." He paused. "I'm not a quitter."

"Absolutely not," the aide agreed.

The rotunda was eerily silent save for the echo of their footsteps. A few stragglers passed awkwardly, averting their eyes. A security guard who normally waved at the majority leader simply looked away. Clearly, it was going to be a tough day.

"Will you go again in four years? I hope so." The aide turned philosophical.

"I don't know," said Stanley. "That's a long way off." Stanley turned to the aide with a twinkle in his eye. "The first step in a comeback is survival. And I am a survivor."

They walked down the stairs leading to the doorway to the west front of the Capitol. As he came down the stone passageway, the director of the ceremony greeted him and escorted him onto the sun-splashed stage where he was greeted by muffled applause from glove-handed admirers. He took his seat on the second row. It struck him that he would be sitting less than ten feet from Long when he ascended to the office they had both sought. He adjusted his scarf, checked the buttons on his overcoat, and braced himself against the cold.

TWO

At 11:30 a.m. the couples emerged from the White House and appeared on the North Portico, the mammoth and stately "front door" added in 1830 in keeping with the federal style of the time. They posed briefly for the cameras. The president then gingerly guided Claire Long to her car with an affectionate hand placed at the small of her back. The First Lady got in behind her. The president motioned for Long to get into the presidential limousine. He climbed in last. The secure package completed, surrounded by Secret Service agents on foot and surveyed by Navy Seal snipers perched on buildings above, the motorcade slowly inched down the driveway at a snail's pace.

For his part, Long was glad the show was finally on the road. The traditional preinaugural coffee in the Oval Office featured stilted chit-chat. The occasional pregnant pause spoke more than words, the chemistry between Long and the outgoing president awkward. And for good reason. After all, the president's handpicked successors were respectively dead and defeated. Vice President Harrison Flaherty was murdered by terrorists as he departed the Republican convention; his running mate, former Secretary of State David Petty, imploded in a sex scandal in the final days of the campaign. It was no exaggeration to observe that Long owed his election to an assassin's bullet and a rival's zipper.

As Long sat across from the president for the brief ride to the Capitol, it occurred to him that he was the last person on earth the president wanted taking his place—other than Salmon Stanley, whom they both despised. Long knew the president viewed him as the accidental president, a conniving opportunist who reached the White House by a maddening combination of cutthroat opportunism and dumb luck. He hoped their mutual hatred of Stanley would unite them in a partnership, if only based on shared disdain for their nemesis.

The president shifted to the edge of his seat, leaning forward from his torso. "Have you given any further thought to Iran?" he asked, the question landing like a howitzer.

I guess the small talk is over, thought Long. The president's steely eyes bore into him. He felt the walls of the limo closing in on him.

"The sanctions package before the Security Council is a start," Long answered haltingly. "If we could pass those, it could turn the screws. We can also interdict Iranian shipping."

The president frowned. "The Chinese are slow-walking it," he said, his irritation apparent. "They have the veto." He leaned forward, tapping his right index finger on Long's knee. "Iran is gaming us. If you want to stop the Iranians from getting a nuke, you're going to have to get more proactive."

Long was thunderstruck. He felt as though he was trapped in a metal tube falling to earth. A thought raced through his mind: *Thanks for the advice as you head out of town."* He reached for a question: "Is there a good military option?"

"Not really," the president sighed. "Unless you give the green light to the Israelis and that's complicated." He looked gravely into Long's eyes. "The CIA traced the funds from the terrorists who killed Flaherty to Iran through a bank in Caracas. They know we know. If we don't respond, they'll interpret your inaction as weakness."

"They'll find out soon enough that I'm not weak," Long replied firmly. Long agreed with the president on a theoretical level. He did not want a repeat of 2000, when the attack on the *U.S.S. Cole* in Yemen went unanswered.

"Salami is a lying, duplicitous terrorist and a cold-blooded killer," the president scoffed, referring to Mahmoud Salami, the president of Iran. "He hates Jews, hates Israel, hates Christians, hates America. I should have acted after the election when there was still time." The president looked out the window, his eyes searching. "But Petty convinced me it would be disruptive during the House election." His eyes returned to Long's. "Now I've left it to you."

"What about the mullahs?" asked Long. "Salami is just their puppet; he's a clown, and they hold the strings. Can we reach them through a back channel?"

"They're intimidated by Salami," the president replied. "He's a demagogue, and he has the radicals eating out of his hand. If you want him gone, you'll have to push him out." He leaned forward, his steely blue eyes unblinking. "Or have him removed from the picture."

Long could hardly believe his ears. *Was the president really suggesting that he have the president of Iran assassinated?*

The president read his facial expression. "Bob, we've been at war with Iran since they took our hostages in '79. They're bankrolling Hezbollah and Hamas. They tried to overthrow the Iraqi government. They murdered Flaherty. They'll have a nuke by the end of the year, maybe sooner. If you don't solve it, this will haunt your successors for the next fifty years."

"I said during the campaign that we can't allow Iran to have nuclear weapons, and I meant it," Long assured him, his gaze steady.

"Then may God be with you," said the president. "You'll have my support without reservation. I'll say something publicly if that will help."

"I appreciate that, Mr. President," Long heard himself say. *Start a war in the Middle East, check,* he thought. As he saw it, the president's sense of personal responsibility for avenging Flaherty's murder was eating him inside, and he was leaving office a tortured soul.

The president suddenly brightened. He glanced at his watch. "You'll be able to call me that for about fifteen more minutes," he joked. "Then it's all yours."

The presidential motorcade had arrived at the Capitol. Marine guards opened the doors of the limo. The couples emerged from their cars, the First Lady and Claire from one and the president and Long from the other, smiling and waving. A crowd of spectators behind police barricades on Constitution Avenue let out a loud cheer. Arm in arm, they walked up the steps into the Capitol.

IN ROOM 950 OF the Capitol Hill Hyatt, Senator Joseph Penneymounter, chairman of the Senate Judiciary Committee, lay with a woman young enough to be his daughter. He kept one eye on the nightstand clock as it ticked toward the ceremony.

"Sorry I have to run," he said as he slipped into his suit pants. "If I'm late, they won't seat me on the platform. I'll be in the nosebleed section."

"I'm surprised you want to go at all, given that it's Long," the woman replied.

"It's painful, but I don't have a choice. If I don't go, it will be a story." He turned back and smiled mischievously. "Call you later?"

"Sure," she said, sliding out from underneath the sheet. Penneymounter noticed how fit and trim her physique was as she slipped on a bathrobe. How he envied her youth. He glanced down at the paunch at his own midsection. *Age is a cruel thing*, he thought.

"Gotta run," said Penneymounter. "I have this room for another night, so you don't have to rush out."

"Another night?" she asked seductively, walking over to him and pressing up against his chest. "In that case . . . maybe I'll stay. That is, assuming you can handle me."

Penneymounter smiled. "What are you trying to do, kill me?"

"You'll die with a smile on your face," she said with a grin.

Penneymounter laughed as he knotted his tie. He opened the door slowly, checking to see if anyone was in the hallway, and walked briskly to the elevator. As he waited for the elevator to arrive, he looked at his watch. He had twenty minutes to get to his seat.

THE CHIEF JUSTICE OF the Supreme Court took his seat on the front row while the other members of the Court sat as a group to the right. One justice remained conspicuously absent. It was Peter Corbin Franklin, the eighty-eight-year-old senior justice and liberal lion of the Court. Some wondered: Was he boycotting the ceremony? Beset by old age and dementia, Franklin had taken to nodding off during oral arguments. His deteriorating mental state was an open secret among the media and Supreme Court watchers. But the feisty jurist, keeper of the progressive flame on the Court, had refused to resign his seat to prevent the outgoing Republican president to nominate a conservative to replace him. Long's election now made retirement even less likely. His absence would be a slap in the face at Long or a further sign of his declining physical condition; his presence in temperatures barely hovering above zero degrees Fahrenheit would say loud and clear that he planned to leave the Court only one way: feet first.

At ten minutes to noon, an ambulance pulled up to the east front of the Capitol. Lifted out of the ambulance on a stretcher and helped into a wheelchair by a team of paramedics was Peter Corbin Franklin. His withered frame was folded into a dark suit and a shock of white hair topped his weathered face. A wrinkled hand, twisted by arthritis and covered with blue veins and age spots, gripped a cane. The medics wheeled him through the Capitol. When he reached the stairs on the West Front, he insisted on walking and descended the steps with agonizing deliberation, balancing himself with the cane while he held onto the arm of the Marine guard who assisted him.

As Franklin struggled to his seat, people tried not to stare. But the sight of the frail and weak man, the liberal conscience of the Supreme Court who was determined to be present at the swearing in of the new president, was moving.

"Peter made it," whispered Salmon Stanley to a Democratic senator who sat next to him. "I'm so glad. Good for him."

"I hope he's going to be alright in this cold," the colleague replied.

"Me, too," said Stanley. "We need him healthy for four more years at a minimum."

"You mean until you're elected president?" the senator replied, jabbing the majority leader in the side with an elbow.

"Oh, you never know about things like that," replied Stanley. "It's a funny business."

"What better evidence is there than the fact that you and I are sitting here at Bob Long's inauguration, after you beat him in the primaries?"

"God help us," Stanley muttered.

ANDY STANTON ROSE TO give the prayer as everyone on the platform held their collective breath. As the most prominent evangelical leader in the nation, Stanton had led a flock of millions out of the Grand Old Party, helping deliver the presidency to Bob Long. His Norman Vincent Peale demeanor and aw-shucks Southern charm masked a Christian orthodoxy blended with rare political instincts. Even standing behind the podium, Stanton's six-foot-four-inch frame, which carried 224 pounds of the muscle and sinew of an aging Golden Gloves boxer, dominated the stage. At age fifty-six, his salt and pepper hair now showed more salt than pepper.

"Let us pray," Andy said as he bowed his head. "Father, we come before You today in a spirit of humility, gratitude, and repentance. Humility because we have too often followed our own ways and forsaken Your paths.

Repentance because our sins are legion, both as individuals and as a nation. Gratitude because of the blessings You have mercifully bestowed on us, an undeserving people." The wind blew the sheet of paper on which Andy had written his prayer, causing it to rustle in the microphone. "Forgive us. Heal our land, and grant us leaders of uncommon integrity and honor, who will walk humbly before You, seeking to do Your will and govern according to Your precepts."

Seated directly behind him, President-elect Long reached across his chair and grabbed the gloved hand of Claire, squeezing it firmly.

"We pray for our new President, Robert W. Long. We pray also for the members of the Cabinet, members of Congress, both House and Senate, the Supreme Court, and all those in authority," Andy continued in his booming baritone, which echoed down the Mall. "May they serve You and their conscience, not partisanship or political expediency." It was a veiled reference to Long's status as the only independent candidate ever elected to the presidency, beholden to neither party. "Turn the hearts of parents back to their children, the hearts of husbands back to their wives, the hearts of our leaders back to the common good, and the hearts of all of us back to You." Andy's breath fogged as he spoke. "Today, as we reaffirm the American experiment in self-government and celebrate the freedoms we enjoy, of which You are the Author and Protector, we ask for Your grace over our nation. Give us what we need, not what we deserve. We ask all this in the name of Jesus Christ of Nazareth, the *strong* Son of God, Savior of *all* mankind, and Lord of the nations."

Andy had punched the words "strong" and "all" for emphasis, so as to leave no ambiguity in his use of evangelical vernacular for the secular ear. As he turned, Long rose to greet him. Their eyes locked. Long shook his hand and whispered words of thanks.

After the Chief Justice administered the oath of office to Vice President Johnny Whitehead, it was Long's turn. He took his place to the right of the Chief Justice as Claire stood between them, holding the family Bible, which had once belonged to Long's grandmother.

"I, Robert Whitney Long, do solemnly swear," the Chief Justice began.

"I Robert Whitney Long, do solemnly swear," repeated Long, trying hard to concentrate on the words rather than on his rapidly beating heart, which pounded like a jackhammer in his chest. His mind raced, backward in time to his first race for the state legislature and forward to the challenges of the offices he was about to assume. He heard himself say, "And to protect and defend the Constitution of the United States, so help me God."

"Congratulations," said the Chief Justice firmly.

Long reached over and kissed Claire. She beamed. Army cannons boomed a twenty-one-gun salute, the percussions echoing off the Capitol with a ceremonial thud. A loud cheer rose from the throng that stretched out before him like a human carpet, from the Capitol all the way to the Lincoln Memorial. The Capitol Police estimated the crowd at more than a half million, the largest gathering ever to attend a presidential inauguration.

"My fellow citizens, today begins a new era in America," Long began. "It is a day in which there are no Republicans or Democrats, no liberals or conservatives, no blue states, red states, or green states. Today we are all Americans, and we stand united." It was a safe beginning, and the crowd dutifully applauded. "I did not seek this office to deliver more of the same to the American people. I came to bring honest change to the federal government. The people have spoken; they have demanded that Washington change, and change we must."

Sitting behind Long, Salmon Stanley clapped his hands silently, a look of barely disguised disdain on this face. But Long could not see him. His eyes drank in the view of the sun-splashed Mall, with the Washington Monument and Lincoln Memorial directly in front of him, the Jefferson Memorial and reflecting pool to his left. He was on a roll now.

"I assume this office beholden to no party or vested interest," he proclaimed. "Today we do not exchange one party for the other. We replace a tired and failed partisanship with a new era of seeking common ground for the common good." Members of the House and Senate sat impassively, their grey countenances decidedly unimpressed. Long knew they resented the fact that he had campaigned against them and everything they represented, denouncing business as usual in Washington. He was calling their bluff. Fight me, he seemed to say, and risk being drowned in a tidal wave of public disapproval. "The politics of the past, in which both parties vie for power while problems fester and people are disconnected from government, ends today. The founders' gave ultimate sovereignty to the people, not the powerful. It is they who must rule here, not the special interests."

Then Long delivered the money line. "To those who say that we cannot change the ways of Washington, to those who insist that the system is broken beyond repair, to those who claim that we are too divided, I say: we can overcome the challenges before us, for we are Americans." Loud and extended applause.

Long's speech, like most of the first inaugural addresses of his predecessors, focused on the domestic front, largely ignoring the world beyond America's shores. But Long's eloquence ignored a hard political reality: he had been elected by the smallest plurality of any president since Abraham Lincoln in 1860. A man without a party, he faced an openly hostile Democratic Senate and a skeptical Republican House. Could he succeed? Washington could be a petty and vicious place that took special pride in humbling those who rode into town on a white horse to tame it. Long was about to find that out the hard way.

THREE

Over at the Madison Hotel at Fifteenth and M Streets, in a room near the grand ballroom, a seemingly endless click line of tuxedo and gowned donors stinking of loud perfume and cologne snaked into the hallway, down the stairs and into the lobby. The money crowd had paid $5,000 a couple to have their photo taken with two of the biggest celebrities of Red State America: Reverend Andy Stanton and former U.S. Senator Keith Golden, the new attorney general of the United States.

Golden, a tall, earnest man with inviting eyes and a ready smile, sported a surplus of wavy brown hair, a fount of charisma and the political chops to help Long on the right. A graduate of the University of Virginia law school and a former U.S. Attorney, Golden had run for Congress sixteen years earlier against an entrenched Democrat and won, surprising everyone but himself. When the Democratic legislature carved him out of his district, he ran for the U.S. Senate, defeating another Democrat. After two terms, he lost a bitter campaign to a popular former centrist Democratic governor. But like a cat pitched off a roof, Golden had landed on his feet. Some attributed it to luck, others to Machiavellian maneuvering, still others to the favor of the Almighty. Whatever the truth, Golden was back, and he was hot.

Billed as the "Christian Inaugural Celebration," the black-tie gala included a five-course dinner that climaxed with flaming baked Alaska, an appearance by Vice President Johnny Whitehead (Jay Noble had deemed it too politically risky to send the president), entertainment provided by the nation's most famous contemporary Christian singers, and an open bar that sold soft drinks but no alcohol. After forty-five minutes, the last couple filed through the click line. Andy and Golden, facial muscles exhausted from constant smiling, stood like two department-store mannequins on their tape marks.

"Now what?" asked Andy to no one in particular. His staff stood around holding clipboards, wearing the pensive expressions of wedding planners.

"You hold here. We'll bring you out in a few minutes," said a staffer.

Stanton nodded. He clasped the attorney general by the arm and led him to a small table covered with a white tablecloth, a plate of mints, and a pitcher of ice water with glasses. Andy shot a look at his staff to leave the room, and they hustled out. The door closed behind them.

"Thanks for doing this," Andy said as he poured them both a glass of ice water.

"Wouldn't have missed it for the world," replied Golden, his puffy face a portrait of false humility and obsequiousness. The deep lines in his face and gray flecks in his hair gave him a look that was a cross between a distinguished public servant and a battle-hardened ideological warrior. "God works in mysterious ways, Andy. When I lost my Senate seat, I thought my political career was over." Andy nodded. "But God used my defeat to pave the way for me to be attorney general." He paused, his face like a flint. "Long would never have won without the voters you mobilized. Andy, I wouldn't be where I am without your ministry."

Andy's face broke into a proud grin. "It's just amazing, isn't it?" he marveled. "With five Supreme Court justices over the age of seventy-five and the war on terror still ongoing, you are in one of the most strategic positions on the planet."

Golden nodded vigorously. Andy pulled his chair closer, leaning into him.

"Keith, you're a modern-day Esther. God has elevated you to the position of attorney general for such a time as this. The future of the Supreme Court and the federal judiciary are in your hands." Golden stared back, his face blank. "But there's a flip side. As Mordecai said to Esther, if you are not willing to be used to deliver God's people, then He will raise up someone else who will."

Golden gulped. He took a sip of water.

"Long needs your help on court appointments." He shook his head. "I love him, but he's a former Democrat. I'm afraid our philosophy may not be in his DNA."

"I hear you loud and clear, my friend, and I share your concern," said Golden, confiding in Andy as a means to further bonding. "It's why I accepted Long's offer to be AG. But I told him I would only go to Justice if I had the lead on court appointments. He agreed." He bobbed his head in wonderment. "But I will say this: Long's judicial appointments in California were not that bad. He generally appointed centrists."

"That was then, this is now," Andy said, swatting aside Golden's assurances with a dismissive wave of his hand. "Washington ain't Sacramento." He spun a finger across the top of his glass, staring into the water as if in search of a hidden clue. "Keith, we're one vote away from overturning *Roe v. Wade*. When it comes to court appointments, it's going to be war. Anyone who thinks otherwise is deluding themselves."

Golden looked like he had been punched in the gut. The conversation had taken a quick turn into tricky rapids. "The president understands that," he replied noncommittally.

"He better," replied Andy. He stared blankly at Golden, letting the silence hang in the air. Although he was a preacher, Andy could negotiate like a Teamster, and he knew that whoever spoke next lost.

"My staff is assembling a list of judicial nominees that includes Republicans and some law-and-order Democrats," said Golden in a hushed voice. "It will include a lot of minorities and women. If we come out of the chute with a bipartisan group of judges that is heavily sprinkled with minorities, it will box in the Democrats." He grinned. "If they support our nominees, their base will be angry. If they oppose us, they tick off women and Hispanics."

"Sal Stanley won't care if Long's nominees have sex change operations," Andy deadpanned. Golden chuckled. "The big enchilada is the Supreme Court," Andy continued. "The pro-choicers will demand the defeat of any conservative. Stanley will lead the fight because he wants the liberal blogosphere's support if he runs for president again." He paused for effect. "Long's going to get a pick soon—very soon. He can't appoint a Souter type. Our people simply will not stand for it."

Golden crossed his arms, his body language defensive. "I hope you're right, but I'm not sure about that, Andy. We're hearing Peter Corbin Franklin and the other liberals are going to hang on for dear life to stop us from choosing their replacements, just like they have the past four years." He sighed. "So we may not have a pick for a while."

"You will," said Andy, his eyelids hooded. "Trust me."

"How can you be so certain?" asked Golden, his hand clawing for a mint.

"Because the Lord told me," said Andy without hesitation.

"That's a pretty good source you've got there," said Golden with a touch of humor.

Two knocks came on the door. A staffer with an earpiece and walkie-talkie stuck his head in the door. Stanton shooed him away with his hand. The door closed again.

Andy rose to his feet. Golden joined him. Their bodies were no more than six inches apart. "Keith, there's going to be a vacancy," said Andy. "Get ready to go to the barricades. Because if Long blows it, his presidency will be over." He tapped Golden on the chest. "And you'll go down with him, my dear brother."

"Thanks for the advice," said Golden. "I think."

The door opened again. "Dr. Stanton, the natives are getting restless," said the staffer, his face panicked.

"Coming!" exclaimed Andy with a touch of humor. "The attorney general and I were just discussing the weather." He laughed at his own joke. He put his bearlike arm around Golden and led him toward the door. Golden, his face pale, looked like he had just been hit by a truck.

"Ladies and gentlemen," an off-stage announcer intoned, "please welcome Dr. Andy Stanton and the attorney general of the United States, the Honorable Keith Golden!" Stanton and Golden plastered show-biz smiles on their faces and dove through the blue stage curtain, waving to the crowd as the ballroom exploded in a standing ovation.

OVER ON NORTH CAROLINA Avenue, three blocks from the Capitol, a very different party was underway. Billed as "The Inaugural Wake," it was the inside-the-beltway liberal counterparty to the Long celebration. While the Fortune 500 crowd polished off magnums of champagne over at the Chamber of Commerce building and the Faith and Family Federation put lipstick all over Keith Golden's collar, the Washington establishment of the Democratic party gathered for an alcohol-laced funereal affair in a redbrick, three-story prewar townhouse that was the home away from home of DC power broker G. G. Hoterman. (G. G. was currently separated from his wife as he tried desperately to save his marriage after an affair revealed by the investigation into the scandal that had sunk Salmon Stanley's presidential candidacy.) They deadened their pain with large quantities of vodka, beer, and wine and fortified themselves with a solemn oath to make Bob Long a one-term president.

In the basement at a makeshift bar, the chairman of the Senate Judiciary Committee ordered a second glass of red wine. He was among friends, and he was imbibing freely.

"Senator!" someone shouted from behind him.

Joe Penneymounter turned around to see a high-tech lobbyist who had once worked as legislative director for a colleague. He knew the face vaguely but couldn't quite place the name. "Is the Internet bill going to move in this Congress?" the lobbyist asked.

"Too early to tell," replied Penneymounter evasively. "We technically share jurisdiction. If the bill moves, it will come out of Commerce." (Translation: I'm your friend, but don't ask me to do anything to help.) He flashed a smile. "But I'm with you!"

"We know, and we appreciate it, senator," the lobbyist said.

"Consider it done," replied Penneymounter. He knew that this brief conversation, fully embellished and gilded with shameless exaggeration, would be billed to the lobbyist's client at the highest rate possible.

"Joe! Just the man I want to see!"

Penneymounter turned to see Christy Love moving across the room with singular purpose. Love, wearing a clinging black satin blouse and white flowing bell-bottoms, her black hair falling in tresses across her shoulders and back, moved like a puma. He braced himself for his encounter with the lobbyist-cum-grassroots agitator who headed Pro-Choice PAC.

"Christy!" Penneymounter called out affectionately, wrapping her in a warm embrace. "I sure hope you've got a plan to stop Long because no one else in town seems to."

"Oh, I have a plan alright," Love said with a purr. "But it means you're going to have to bust your rear end for the cause. I hope you're ready."

"I was born ready," he replied with bravado.

"What's your thinking on Long's court appointments?" she asked pointedly. "He's going to have some sooner rather than later, I fear."

"I'll work with Long when I can and oppose him when I must," said Penneymounter drolly. "The country wants bipartisanship right now, so I don't want to start off by launching a war on his nominees. I think I can influence him." He leaned into her, whispering in her ear. "Christy, he's really a Democrat. He only pretended to be an independent so he could beat Sal." Stanley was upstairs on the townhouse's main floor, so Penneymounter kept his voice down. "He's played the right-wing nuts for the fools they are."

"Come with me," Love replied, curling her arm through his. "We need to talk." She escorted him down a long hallway behind the bar. Their bodies brushed up against each other as they walked down the narrow, unlit hall. Penneymounter felt her hip bone against him, his elbow nudging her rib cage. Love led him into a back bedroom, flipped on the light, and closed the door.

"I hope no one starts a rumor about us," joked Penneymounter.

Love ignored the comment. "Joe, Long is not someone we can work with. He's sold his soul to the religious right." Her eyes bore through him. "Keith Golden's going to be picking the judicial nominees, not Long, because he's compiling all the lists of nominees. Andy Stanton has veto power."

"Not according to the president," replied Penneymounter confidently. "We have a deal. I agreed not to block Golden's nomination for AG as long as the White House clears appellate and Supreme Court nominees with me and the ranking Republican on Judiciary. If we both sign off, they are reported out of committee. If either of us objects, they never see the light of day." He smiled proudly.

"The White House agreed to that?" asked Love incredulously.

"Not the White House," Penneymounter answered. "The president. To my face."

"Well, I don't trust the man," said Love, placing her hands on her hips.

"Trust, but verify," smiled Penneymounter. "That's my motto."

"Long is a total charlatan and a fraud," Love shot back, her eyes aflame. "He'll be whatever he has to be, say whatever he has to say. No one else will tell you this because they haven't got the ovaries. But I'm your friend. Joe, you've lost major support on the left for giving Golden a pass. If you don't man up and fight Long, you can kiss our support good-bye in Iowa and New Hampshire." She paused. "Some people are even discussing asking Stanley to remove you as chairman."

Penneymounter physically recoiled, visibly stunned by Love's threat. Everyone in town knew he was planning to run for the Democratic presidential nomination four years hence.

"Christy, I can't believe this!" He screwed up his face. "I've been the best friend women have ever had in the Senate. *I* sponsored the Violence Against Women Act and got it through Congress. *I* got the Ledbetter bill passed. I carried *your* bills when no one else wanted them to see the light of day." The veins in his neck bulged. "You *know* that."

"It's appreciated, Joe. But then you gave Golden a pass."

"I've got bigger fish to fry," Penneymounter said dismissively. "Forget Keith Golden. My deal is with the president, and it will prevent him from choosing nominees that would be disastrous. You and your feminist friends should be thanking me, not reading me the riot act." His face brightened. "Besides, I didn't have the votes to defeat Golden. He's a member of the club—senators are reluctant to take on one of their own. You know that. So I negotiated away what I didn't have to gain something we need."

"A member of the *club*?" Love shot back sarcastically, her lips curled with contempt. "That didn't stop Sam Nunn from taking out John Tower. It didn't stop Pat Leahy from trying to block John Ashcroft. And you talk to me about the *club*? Joe, you've been inside the beltway too long. You didn't even put up a *fight*."

"Woah, hold on just a minute!" Penneymounter said, his voice rising in anger. "We wear the same jersey, remember? I'm on your team. I don't need any lectures about how to stop right-wing, extremist judges. I've done it my entire career, sister."

"Alright, then show me," Love said, throwing down the gauntlet. "There are sixteen vacancies on the appellate courts and thirty-four district court vacancies," Christy said. "Show me how many of those you can stop." She raised up on her heels, pushing her face into Penneymounter's until he could feel her breath on his chin. "And if there's a Supreme Court vacancy, who do you think Long is going to listen to—you or Andy Stanton?"

"The White House can't roll me, Christy." He let out an expletive. "Andy Stanton's a blowhard." His face hardened and his black eyes darted. "And you know why there are so many vacancies? Because *I* slow-walked Republican judicial nominees for *two years*."

"Bob Long will stab you in the back just like he did Stanley and the Democratic Party," Love fired back, blue veins in her neck showing through her fair skin. "When he does, you better fight him, or our members will not forget, and I assure you they will never forgive." She turned the knob on the door and disappeared.

Penneymounter stood there for a moment, pondering the ferocity of Christy's blast. He knew the pro-choicers hated Golden's guts, but Christy's attitude was borderline irrational. It would be impossible for him as the chairman of the Judiciary to deny a floor vote to all of Long's judicial picks for four years. He was going to have to disabuse the feminist crowd and the far-left blogosphere of this fantasy before things got even further out of control.

The fun had drained out of the party for Penneymounter. It was time to go. As he breezed through the living room on his way out the door, he was careful to make discreet eye contact with the woman staffer who was his surreptitious date. That was her signal to leave the party separately and take a taxi back to the Capitol Hyatt.

A NONDESCRIPT ADVANCE MAN wearing the official uniform of a dark suit and dark tie walked crossed the stage and placed a presidential seal on the front of the podium. The buzz of excited conversation filled the air. The crowd of more than three thousand people, bedecked in tuxedos and formal gowns, grew more anxious, the haute couture dresses of the women rustling as they pressed against the red velvet rope line. Secret Service agents took positions to either side of the stage. Above the stage, on a balcony elevated over the ballroom like a royal box at the opera house, the VIPs—elected politicians, bundlers, major donors, and lobbyists who masqueraded as power brokers—stared down at the scene as they heavily imbibed adult beverages and flashed their jewelry. At the bar in the VIP section, two bartenders worked feverishly to keep up with the demand for vodka cranberries and scotch and sodas.

In the back of the VIP section, hiding in the shadows, stood the darkened visage of Jay Noble. Other than the president, he was the man of the hour. Following the inaugural ceremony and congressional luncheon in the Capitol, he had headed over to the media skyboxes across from the White House to do a victory lap on the cable shows. He had then briefly joined the president and Claire Long in the family box during the inaugural parade, an honor accorded to few outside the immediate Long family.

Afterward, walking across Lafayette Park, he had been mobbed by the press and the great unwashed masses. At that moment it hit him like a load of bricks: he had become a political celebrity, and his life would never be the same. He had achieved the success and fame he had toiled for across two decades of smash-mouth, take-no-prisoners political combat. But now that he had arrived at The Show, Jay felt a flood of conflicting emotions and a broad continuum of ambiguity. He felt an emptiness, as though he had arrived at a banquet to find they were serving fast food. The reality of the achievement was not as satisfying as it had been in his imagination. Now, as the president made his final stop of the night at the California Ball— the hottest ticket at the inaugural—Jay was hiding in the shadows, pining for anonymity in his moment of triumph.

"Ladies and gentlemen, the president of the United States, Robert W. Long, accompanied by First Lady Claire Long!" came the announcement from off stage. "Hail to the Chief" blared from speakers, the crowd erupted in a cathartic roar, and Bob and Claire Long emerged from behind the curtain like Hollywood stars jumping off the pages of a glossy magazine. Long sported an Armani tuxedo, and Claire wore a glittering silver, off-the-shoulder Oscar de la Renta gown with a large black flower over the left side of her chest. Her strawberry-blonde hair was pulled straight back, highlighting her high cheekbones and blue eyes. She looked radiant, her skin kissed by the California sun, her feminine, sexy glow contrasting sharply with the pale, boorish formalism of her predecessor. Camera flashes from the paparazzi and the partygoers blinked like a sea of lightning bugs.

"We have been to eight balls tonight, but we saved the best for last," Long began to applause. "This is our last stop before we turn in, and it's a special one for us because it includes so many of our good friends from California."

"We love you, Mr. President!" someone shouted.

"And I love you right back." More scattered applause.

"Harry Truman once said if you want a friend in this town, buy a dog." (Laughter.) "Well, we have two dogs, so we're going to be just fine." (More laughter—isn't he a stitch!) "Seriously, so many wonderful people supported us and helped us in what was an uphill campaign. Not a lot of people gave us much of a chance, but you stood with us when tonight seemed like an impossible dream. Claire and I will never forget your friendship. We don't really need any new friends in Washington because we like the ones we have."

More applause and cheers. "Now, if you don't mind, I'd like to have one last dance with my bride." The crowd cheered. Camera flashes exploded as the band began to play. Long wrapped an arm around Claire's waist, grabbed her hand in his, and skillfully glided across the stage. Balloons dropped from a net above, creating a magical moment of seemingly limitless possibility.

"Mr. Noble, the president would like to see you," came the hushed voice from behind him. Jay turned to see an advance man. "Follow me." Jay quickly motioned to Satcha, who was being ogled by a corporate muckety-muck who had bought his way into the VIP suite with an obscenely large contribution. He grabbed her hand and pulled her along as he followed the advance man down a flight of stairs and into a service hallway behind the stage. Jay could hear the strains of violin strings as the president and First Lady danced. As they came down the hall, Jay caught sight of Lisa with Senator Russell Evans. He felt a pang of regret. Even the balm of Satcha's hot looks and celebrity did not seem to salve the wound.

"Hello, Jay," Lisa said, her eyes sizing up Satcha with undisguised curiosity. "Isn't this a lot of fun?" Lisa looked stunning, her black hair flowed down to her creamy white shoulders, the straps of her green sequined dress bringing out her hazel eyes.

"It is indeed," Jay replied. "Tomorrow comes the hard part."

"Sometimes I think anything will be a breeze after the campaign," said Lisa. She introduced him to Senator Evans, whose gleaming white teeth and jet-black hair seemed a tad too perfect.

The president burst through the blue curtain and bounded down the stairs behind the stage. He and Claire were effervescent.

"Jay, my main man!" the president shouted. He was jacked. "How did you convince such a pretty woman to be your date?" His eyes twinkled. He was in a great mood, flying high.

Jay was about to answer when Satcha jumped in. "Actually, Mr. President, I find that I'm only attracted to men of uncommon intelligence." She winked.

"I see," replied the president mischievously. "Well, I knew it wasn't his looks."

"She's only using me to get an interview with you," Jay joked.

"I am not!" said Satcha, her voice laced with mock indignation. "Well, I do want an interview. You should give me your first one-on-one, Mr. President."

"You have to convince Lisa," Long shot back playfully. "She's the gate-keeper." Jay knew the president was deliberately causing trouble.

Lisa flashed a fake smile. "I'd give you my card," she said. "But I don't have any yet."

"I know where to find you," said Satcha, her features hardening. "I'll let you get settled in and give you a call, maybe next week?" Her voice turned serious. "It would be a real statement if the White House granted its first broadcast interview with the president to Univision. We have more viewers than CNN or MSNBC in prime time."

"Satcha is indefatigable," said Jay.

"I'll just bet she is," said Lisa drily.

Long grabbed Jay by the arm and pulled him into a power clutch. Lisa chatted up Claire while Senator Evans fell headlong into Satcha's trance.

"So what are you hearing?" asked Long. It was one of his favorite conversation starters.

"Reviews of the inaugural address are very positive," Jay reported. "Marvin Myers said on the air that your election has ushered in a new era of reform. He compared you to Teddy Roosevelt. The sidebar story is Stanley blocking your agenda. The media is obsessed with the personal grudge narrative."

"Stanley was cordial but distant," said Long. "I'm going to need to charm him."

"I think we may just have to roll him."

Long nodded. "I think you're right."

"There's a flap about Stanton's prayer," said Jay. He noticed out of the corner of his eye that Senator Evans was undressing Satcha with his eyes. Jay thought, *the guy is shameless.*

"I thought Andy's prayer might cause a stir, but he brings a lot more than he takes away," said Long. "I don't think it's a big deal, do you?"

"No, sir," said Jay. "It's cable news trying to drive ratings. It's a one day story."

"We have to defend Andy."

"You bet," Jay agreed. "He delivered."

"Okay, talk to you soon," Long said, signaling the conversation was over. He and Claire, flanked by advance men and Secret Service agents headed down the hallway, with Lisa and Senator Evans trailing behind.

Jay slipped his arm around Satcha's narrow waist and spun her around, leading her back to the ballroom.

"I thought Evans was going to jump you," he said in a whisper when they were safely out of earshot.

"I couldn't believe it!" she gasped. "He asked me for my number."

"What!? With the president standing three feet away! I hope you didn't give it to him."

"What could I do? He's a United States senator," Satcha replied. "I gave him my office number. He'll go straight to voice mail." She paused. "He also pinched me."

Jay stopped dead in his tracks. "He pinched you? Where?"

Satcha stuck out her rear end, patting it with the palm of her hand. "My bootie!" she exclaimed.

Jay burst out laughing, clapping his hands together.

FOUR

The armored black Lincoln Navigator darted in and out of traffic as it headed north on Pennsylvania Avenue, running yellow lights and changing lanes before making a sharp turn on to Seventeenth Street and pulling into a back entrance to the White House. A guard opened the electronically controlled gate to the White House complex. The SUV, followed by a staff car carrying security personnel and a chaser car, inched slowly into the parking lot adjacent to the West Wing. Inside, a man wrapped up a call on one of the two secure phones he regularly worked from the back of the SUV. Finishing the conversation, he stepped out of the car and walked briskly across the pavement, head down. Climbing the flight of stairs in a slow jog, he disappeared into the Eisenhower Executive Office Building.

It was 7:37 a.m. when William Jacobs, director of the CIA, turned the knob on the door of his hideaway office on the third floor, which had no signage, and gathered his staff around him. A large, physical man with an awkward gait and penetrating brown eyes, he radiated brilliance and exuded discretion. Jacobs had come to his role as the world's leading spymaster via a circuitous path. After a stint as a naval intelligence officer, he spent ten years at the Defense Intelligence Agency before becoming disillusioned by the infighting among rival agencies. Retiring a jaded patriot, he took a cushy job at the Rand Corporation, where he wrote an article expressing doubt about Saddam Hussein's WMD program. When every intelligence agency in the world got it wrong about WMD stockpiles in Iraq, Jacobs was heralded as a prophet. The Senate refused to confirm a new CIA director unless Jacobs was part of a package deal as deputy director, and when he retired, Jacobs ascended to the top job. Long barely knew Jacobs, but with only fifteen days to assemble a government after his election by the House, he asked him to stay on. Jacobs, who lived by the rule that one never turned down the president, agreed.

Jacobs glanced at the wall clock. He was due in the Oval in ten minutes. He did a final run-through with his staff, methodically laying pages of the President's Daily Briefing (PDF), the Bible of the Agency, out on the desk. The unpretentious surroundings—plaster walls, historical prints, government-issue furniture—gave no indication that they were reviewing the most sensitive material in the entire government for the leader of the free world on his first full day in office.

"We're about to drop the hammer on him," Jacobs said. "Expect objections because it's going to be unwelcome news." His eyes scanned the room. "Let's be ready for push back."

"Sources," replied one of the briefers. "How do we know? Can we be sure?"

"Precisely." Jacobs liked to quiz his staff, pushing them. "What's our answer?"

"Multiple sources, tested with sound methodology by our best analysts," replied the briefer. "Stress the variegated nature of the evidence: satellite photos, captured telephonic conversations, verified reports from foreign clandestine services, solid interpolation of the data, and humint," he said, referring to human intelligence.

"He'll ask if this is the Cuban missile crisis or Colin Powell at the UN," deadpanned a second briefer.

Jacobs stared back. "Can you blame him?" he asked. "After Iraq, we've got a high bar to clear." His eyes surveyed every face. "Is everyone absolutely confident about this? If not, speak now or forever hold your peace." Jacobs knew that once his shadow crossed the threshold of the Oval Office, there was no turning back. A tense silence hung in the air as his probing eyes scanned every face. No one said a word.

"We've got it right," said one of the briefers at last.

"Alright," said Jacobs. "Grab your jockstraps and let's go."

BOB LONG HAD ENTERED the Oval Office at 7:00 a.m. sharp and slid into the chair behind the large *HMS Resolute* desk that was the centerpiece of the room. The decoratively carved oak desk had been used by Franklin Roosevelt, John F. Kennedy, Ronald Reagan, and George W. Bush. A gift to the United States from Queen Victoria in 1880, it had been fashioned from the timbers of a British ship abandoned at sea in 1854. After a U.S. navy captain returned it to Great Britain, it was decommissioned with the desk built from its wooden remains. A symbol of the close relationship between England and America, it was best known for the trapdoor on the front, which John F. Kennedy Jr. had once crawled through as a little boy, captured by White House photographers at the height of Camelot.

In the few hours between the preinaugural coffee and the parade, workers had replaced the carpet (Long had selected the royal blue with a beige trim), the drapes, the furniture, and the paintings on the wall, and switched out the desks. On the walls hung portraits of Washington, FDR, and Reagan, signaling Long's independence and the bipartisan spirit of his administration. Long marveled at the transformation of the room and the efficiency of the White House staff.

Three soft raps on the door. "Mr. President, Director Jacobs is here," said his assistant.

The president nodded firmly. "Send him in."

Jacobs walked across the room in long strides and shook the president's hand firmly, making eye contact. Accompanying him was the briefer who would actually conduct the PDF review, chief of staff Charlie Hector, and national security advisor Truman Greenglass. Jacobs sat down in the chair to the president's immediate left, Greenglass to the right, and Hector and the CIA briefer took chairs directly across from the president. Long's desk had not a scrap of paper on it. Jacobs handed him a brown booklet labeled "TOP SECRET/EYES ONLY."

The president began to flip open the book. Jacobs held up his hand to stop him. "Mr. President, before we begin, I'd like to tell you a story."

"Sure," Long replied, perplexed but curious. "Go ahead. I like stories."

"When Franklin Roosevelt sat in that chair in this very office," Jacobs began, "a group of Princeton scientists asked Bernard Baruch to hand-deliver a letter to the president from Albert Einstein. In it Einstein warned that Nazis scientists were conducting experiments to unlock the power of the atom for military purposes." Long listened intently, his eyes unmoving. "FDR launched the Manhattan Project, and we got the bomb first." Jacobs leaned forward. "If Roosevelt had not acted, the Nazis might have won the war."

Long nodded slowly. He swallowed hard.

"Mr. President, the information we are sharing with you this morning is as critical to our national security as Einstein's letter to FDR." Jacobs had a reputation as a no-nonsense, low-key DCI. He was not known for hyperbole or melodrama. The tension in the room thickened. Jacobs turned to the CIA briefer and nodded.

"Mr. President, if you turn to the first article in your book, you will see that we conclude with a high degree of confidence that Iran has now weaponized a nuclear device." He paused, letting the blow sink in. "I won't regurgitate the entire document. The high points are: Iran has had some twenty-five thousand centrifuges producing highly enriched uranium for three years. We assess that they have had enough for a nuclear weapon for about a year. What they have lacked was the technical ability to create a chain reaction leading to an explosion. Until now."

"How did they get that?" asked Long.

"They acquired it from a highly placed scientist in the North Korean nuclear program."

"A North Korean version of A. Q. Khan," said Jacobs.

"He was the Pakistani scientist who sold nuclear secrets to Lybia," noted Greenglass.

"I know," said Long. He was growing testy.

"We assume North Korea is behind the technology transfer, but that is conjecture to some extent," said the briefer. "Proliferation is a cancer. Once it's out of the bottle, it's hard to get it back in."

"How do we know about the North Korean connection?" interjected Hector.

"The German intelligence service intercepted communications between the North Korean black marketer and his Swiss middleman," replied Jacobs. "We worked with the Germans to get the Swiss engineer's bank records and computer files. We have everything—hard drives, wire transfers, e-mails, documents, you name it. It's open and shut."

Long let out an expletive. His eyes focused on the PDF.

IRAN HAS OBTAINED A NUCLEAR WEAPON

We assess with a high degree of confidence that after years of pursuing a uranium enrichment program with dual use capability, Iran has now obtained a nuclear weapon. It has done so by indigenously producing sufficient weapons-usable fissile material and by obtaining from a rogue North Korean scientist the capability to explode a nuclear device.

Combined with Iran's long-range missile capability, specifically the Shahab-4, which has a range of two thousand miles, allowing it to strike Tel Aviv and many major cities in Europe, Tehran's nuclear weapons pose a grave and immediate threat to Israel, Europe, and possibly the United States.

We are unable to judge whether Iran's nuclear weapons program is primarily offensive or defensive in nature. It is plausible that Iran views it as a nuclear deterrent to an Israeli or U.S. attack. Iran may also see nuclear weapons as vital to achieving its clearly articulated goals of being a dominant Middle East power and having the capability to strike Tel Aviv.

Tehran views its nuclear weapons program as critical to achieving its regional and global foreign policy aspirations. For that reason we judge that it is unlikely that international pressure will be sufficient to persuade Iran to dismantle its nuclear weapons program.

Long scanned the document hurriedly as the conversation around him faded in and out of his hearing. The frightening truth? He did not feel entirely prepared on his first day on the job, after an exhausting two-year presidential campaign that had ended just two weeks ago, to process this body blow. Through a tangle of conflicting emotions—frustration at the CIA for ambushing him, anger at his predecessor for leaving it for him, and self-pity that it was now his problem—Long felt the full weight of the presidency fall on his shoulders.

"Mr. President?" asked Jacobs.

"Yes?" Long replied, snapping back to attention.

"Do you have any further questions?"

Long looked back at him nonplussed. "Yes," he said, visibly uncomfortable, shifting in his chair. "What do we do? I mean, is this a fait accompli, or are there any actionable options?"

"Mr. President, that is not the function of the CIA," Jacobs said, throwing a polite brush-back pitch. "Our job is to provide sound intelligence to you and other clients in the government. What comes next is up to you after consultation with State, Defense, NSC, and the Joint Chiefs." He paused. "That's the law."

Long frowned. Typical, he thought: the CIA drops a live grenade on the table and then runs for cover. The Agency had practically invented the CYA maneuver.

Greenglass jumped in. "Bill, I think what the president is asking is, what's the next step? We need to inform the American people and other governments. How much of what we know can we say publicly?"

Jacobs stared Greenglass down, his gaze steady. "I don't do PR. But this is as solid a case as I've seen in my thirty-four-year career. The evidence is from many sources, including electronic surveillance, foreign clandestine services, and human sources."

"Slam dunk?" asked Hector, a wicked smile curling on his face.

Jacobs said nothing. He didn't think it was funny.

"Keep digging," the president said firmly, appearing to regain his balance. "And check in with Mossad. They're going to be players. Israel's not going to take this lying down."

Jacobs appeared to flinch. "That's what worries me, Mr. President. Israel is our ally, but they're a tricky customer." He paused. "We will touch base with them—with appropriate caution."

Long smiled knowingly. "Truman will reach out to his counterpart as well. We need to decide whether it is in our interest for the Israelis to take some action, and if so, what. But in the end they are a sovereign nation. We can't tell them what to do."

The president's words hung in the air. Was he talking about a military strike? The meeting ended without a clear answer. Jacobs and the CIA briefer left, accompanied by Greenglass. Hector closed the door and approached the desk, his face drained of color. Long turned in his chair to face him. He wore a shell-shocked expression.

"There are two people I want to see," said Long. "Yehuda Serwitz and Sami Saad." He had named the Israeli and Egyptian ambassadors to the U.S. "Get them in here."

"Done, sir. I'll also organize a Principals meeting," said Hector.

Long let out a long sigh. "We're not in Kansas anymore, Charlie."

LISA ROBINSON STOOD BEHIND the podium in the White House briefing room, her hands grasping its edges, knuckles white. The White House press corps had applauded when she entered the room, but now the fireworks had started. They peppered her with hostile questions, interrupted her answers, and generally caused a ruckus. It was 1:07 p.m. on her first day as the president's communications director, and the honeymoon was officially over.

"Reuters is reporting that during their ride to the Capitol yesterday, the former president urged Long to retaliate militarily against Iran for its alleged role in the assassination of Vice President Flaherty. Can you confirm that?" asked UPI.

"I'm not able to comment on that report. I don't have a readout of the conversation on the trip from the White House to the Capitol," Lisa volleyed back.

"Did they talk about Iran at all?"

"That's just not something I'm going to be able to comment on," Lisa said, fouling off the follow-up. "There have been numerous conversations about a range of foreign policy issues during the transition. Those included conversations at the staff level, as well as between the president and the then president-elect."

"I'm talking about in the car between the outgoing president and Long—"

"I've already told you I don't have a readout." Lisa's mind raced—how did Reuters know about such a conversation? Who was talking?

"Can you get us a readout?"

"Don't hold your breath," Lisa deadpanned. The press corps chuckled.

"Lisa, the Anti-Defamation League sent a letter to the White House today criticizing Andy Stanton's prayer at the inaugural. They say the prayer was 'intolerant and exclusionary,'" said CBS News. "They're asking for a formal apology from the president."

"There is a long tradition of inaugural prayers invoking the deity," Lisa replied. "Dr. Stanton's prayer was entirely consistent with that tradition."

"So you're rejecting the ADL's demand for an apology?"

"I have not seen the letter, so I can't comment directly on that. I would point out that the benediction was delivered by a rabbi. A Muslim imam delivered the prayer at the congressional luncheon." Lisa paused, letting the point sink in. "The inaugural was an ecumenical moment that embraced Americans of all faiths."

"The Saudi foreign minister has issued a statement condemning Stanton's claim that Christ is—" He flipped open his steno pad, scanning the page. "Quote, 'Lord of the nations,'" fired Knight-Ridder. "He says it's highly offensive. Do you really want to offend one of our most important strategic partners in the Middle East?"

"Dr. Stanton was speaking in his capacity as a minister of the gospel," Lisa responded. "He does not speak for the U.S. government."

Dan Dorman, the new White House correspondent of the *Washington Post*, hung back like a jackal in the weeds. Slumped in his chair on the second row, reading glasses perched on the end of his nose, the matted grey hair on his balding head twisted in an unkept tangle, he prepared to pounce.

"Is the president concerned about the rioting in Gaza? Palestinian protesters are burning him in effigy," Dorman said provocatively. "This prayer has sparked an international incident. Is it worth damaging America's standing in the world to pay back Andy Stanton for his support of Long during the campaign?"

Lisa's eyes shot darts and her face hardened. She and Dorman had developed a famously strained relationship during the campaign. In fact, she hated him. For his part Dorman reveled in her disdain: it had been a major career enhancer.

"I disagree with the premise of your question," Lisa shot back. "The inaugural was a moment of national unity that reflected the many faith traditions of the American people: Christian, Jewish, Muslim, and Hinduism."

"Hinduism?" Dorman asked sarcastically. "What about the riots? Aren't you concerned that this is inflaming anti-American sentiment on the Arab street?"

"As we made clear during the campaign, the president is fully committed to the creation of a Palestinian state at peace with Israel. If you have more specific questions about the incident in Gaza, you should direct them to the State Department," Lisa replied coldly.

"You're dodging a question about civil unrest that threatens the entire peace process."

"*Dodge* is your word, not mine," Lisa said, spitting out the words, the muscles in her jawbone tightening. "I'm not going to speak for the diplomats. As I have already stated, Andy Stanton does not speak for the U.S. government, and he does not direct our foreign policy, including policy in the Middle East."

"But you gave him a platform, and he has offended one billion Muslims and the entire Jewish community. Isn't that a problem?"

"Dan, I've said all I have to say on this. The inaugural was an ecumenical event that included invocations of the Deity by representatives of every major faith." She looked directly at Dorman, lecturing him like a schoolmarm. "Maybe some have a problem with the freedom of expression of religious beliefs we enjoy in America. We do not."

"Thank you," said Hearst Newspapers, the senior member of the press corps, signaling that the briefing was over. Lisa closed her binder and stepped from the podium, heading back to her office in the West Wing. She reflected that after all their hard work on Long's inaugural address, it was as if the president had never said a word. The entire news cycle was lost because of six words in Andy Stanton's prayer. It was a total nightmare.

IT WAS APPROACHING 6:00 p.m. when Jay Noble walked into the United Airlines first-class lounge at Dulles International Airport, waiting to board a flight to Rome. While all of his friends were settling into the West Wing, Jay was getting out of town. He had put Satcha on an airplane to LA that morning, and now he was free as a bird. The inaugural behind him (what a pain that had been!) and the new administration in place, the painful truth was he was no longer needed. He was a political strategist, not a government employee. The only thing he knew how to run was his mouth. Some thought him crazy for passing up a chance to work in the White House. But Jay knew 1600 Pennsylvania Avenue was a government-run insane asylum surrounded by an iron fence. Besides, he had no interest in working eighteen hours a day for 135 grand a year. As much as he hated leaving his friends behind, he was cashing in by hanging a shingle as the hottest political strategist on the planet. His first client was Lorenzo Brodi, the mayor of Rome and candidate for prime minister of Italy, a center-right candidate who wanted to model himself after Bob Long.

With time to kill before the flight, Jay went to the bar and ordered a Bloody Mary, then walked to a deserted corner of the lounge and pulled up a chair, occasionally glancing at the television set while he scanned his BlackBerry. The talking heads on cable had been screaming about Stanton's prayer all day. At moments like this, Jay reflected, everyone read their cue cards like B-grade actors in a bad movie, faces contorted, fingers jabbing, voices raised, tempers flaring. It was all for show, a charade to drive ratings. Jay was firing through his e-mails when he heard the familiar voice of Ross Lombardy of the Faith and Family Federation crossing swords with the executive director of the American Civil Liberties Union.

"Bob Long turned his inaugural into a political payback to the religious right, and he staged a sectarian religious service," said the ACLU spokesperson, leaning into the camera. "It violated the separation of church and state and runs counter to Supreme Court rulings."

"Are you going to file a lawsuit?" asked the anchor, eyebrows arched suggestively. His eyes danced with barely restrained joy. *Please say yes,* his eyes seemed to plead.

"We're keeping all our options open. That includes litigation," said the ACLU.

"So you're not ruling out suing the president of the United States?"

"No. Or Andy Stanton. They are both complicit in what is clearly a violation of the constitutional separation of church and state."

The anchor spun in his chair. "What say you, Ross? The ACLU is threatening to sue your boss. Are you going to let them get away with that?"

Ross folded his arms across his chest confidently. "First, the Supreme Court decision that he's referring to is *Lee v. Weisman*, which involved a high school baccalaureate service, and it turned on the allegedly compulsory nature of a prayer," he said. "An inaugural ceremony is not a school event, attendance is voluntary, and prayers have always been offered, going back to the first inaugural of George Washington. There's no case here."

"But the charge is that the prayer was sectarian, claiming Jesus Christ is Lord and Savior," the anchor intoned. "Didn't Reverend Stanton go too far at an official government occasion?"

"That's why we have a First Amendment," Ross shot back. "You don't need a First Amendment to defend noncontroversial speech. You need it to defend unpopular speech." Ross jabbed the air with his finger. "Remember, Andy was speaking in his capacity as a minister of the gospel, not in his capacity as a political figure. The Constitution guarantees freedom of speech, including religious speech by a minister or rabbi."

Jay fired off a quick e-mail to Ross Lombardy. "Great job on TV, pal. Talked to POTUS last night. Behind you 100 percent." Jay was not going to let any sunlight come between him and Stanton. He knew mentioning the conversation with the president would send warm fuzzies throughout Lombardy's body and would be duly passed on to Andy.

His Blackberry vibrated. He glanced down and noticed the prefix of the phone number indicated the call came from the White House.

"Jay, it's Lisa. Do you have a minute?"

"Sure. What's up?"

"Charlie Hector thinks we should release a statement making it clear Andy spoke for himself, not the administration."

"What!? Is he out of his mind?" Jay blasted into the phone. He looked around, lowering his voice to a whisper. "You tell Charlie he wouldn't have his job without the Faith and Family Federation. We've been in office for twenty-five hours, and we're already going to kick one of our best friends in the teeth?"

"Jay, it chewed up half the press briefing. It's a feeding frenzy," Lisa explained. "The State Department is going bats. Their phones are ringing off the hook with angry calls from Arab ambassadors. There are riots in Gaza and Beirut. They're burning American flags."

"Those are rent-a-riots. They're bought and paid for by Iran," Jay said dismissively. "Lisa, we can't let a bunch of quiche-eating diplomats in pin stripes over at Foggy Bottom run the government. This is a test of whether or not the president has got a spine. If we throw Andy to the curb, he'll never forgive us and we'll look weak."

"Look, this is not my decision," said Lisa. "I just wanted to give you a heads-up. If you want to stop it, you better call Charlie right away."

"I'll call him." He shifted topics. "By the way, it was great to see you last night. Evans seems like a good guy." It was faint praise. Jay chose not to mention that the senator had asked Satcha for her phone number before pinching her on her rear.

"He's nice," Lisa replied in a hollow voice. "Looks like you didn't need me to come with you to the ball after all." She was twisting the knife.

"What, Satcha?" asked Jay. "Oh, that's just business. Satcha wants an interview with POTUS, and I want the Hispanic vote." He chuckled. "Like all relationships in Washington, we're both using each other."

"That's pretty cynical."

"No more than being on the arm of the most eligible bachelor in the Senate," said Jay with a sarcastic laugh. "I thought you were in charge of the press, not congressional liaison."

"Good-bye, Jay." Lisa hung up abruptly. Jay felt slightly guilty about saying such a hurtful thing, but Lisa could have been his date and had rejected him. Rather than be honest about his hurt feelings and be vulnerable, he was hiding behind the same toughness that had already contributed to the breakup of his two marriages.

Jay suddenly felt empty. He couldn't wait to get on the plane and leave everything behind—the phoniness of DC, his feelings of uselessness now that the campaign was over, and most of all, Lisa. He picked up his garment bag, slung it over his shoulder, and headed to his gate. With his free hand, he speed-dialed Charlie Hector's number on his BlackBerry. He had to stop the nervous Nellies at the White House from throwing Andy Stanton under the bus.

FIVE

Jay never saw the interior of the Rome airport. As soon as his plane landed, an attractive brunette airline employee escorted him to a VIP lounge, where he munched on bacon-wrapped figs, drank espresso, and killed time while he cleared customs. He had no checked luggage—he had not checked a bag in years. The same woman then led him to a metal door that led directly to a back stairwell, where they descended into a cavernous garage. Slightly groggy and jet-lagged, Jay's eyes fixed on a driver wearing a black suit and tie.

"Your car and driver, Mr. Noble," the woman said, smiling. "He will take you to your destination."

Jay made a pistol with his finger and pointed it at the driver, who nodded. "Bonjourno," said the driver, greeting him in Italian.

Jay grunted in acknowledgment, embarrassed that he knew no Italian. It struck him that he was now in charge of winning a hard-fought prime minister's race and spoke not a word of the country's native language. In fact, he knew nothing about Italy. But that was beside the point. He was the most sought-after political strategist in the world, and people like Lorenzo Brodi were prepared to pay big bucks to have Jay whisper in their ear. The Italians were paying Jay an eye-popping fifty thousand euros a month, which translated into nearly ninety grand in U.S. dollars. (This did not include Jay's share of the media buy, which was 5 percent, and would earn him another two million dollars.) Besides, Jay reasoned, he was a quick study and could easily fake it when he didn't know what he was talking about. When all else failed, he figured he would entertain them with war stories from the Long campaign. That always worked like a charm.

Jay slid into the backseat of the black Mercedes sedan. The driver closed the door behind him and sped away. Jay flipped through a briefing book that had been assembled by his assistant that included basics on Italian demographics, election results, and news clips from newspapers and Web sites, all translated into English. *There is no substitute for good staff work,* he thought. Having slept only fitfully on the plane and still exhausted from the inaugural, he dozed off.

He woke thirty minutes later to the rattling sensation of the car flying across the cobblestone side streets of Rome. He marveled at the car's tight suspension: his body felt almost glued into his seat. Jay saw the massive dome of St. Peter's basilica to his left. The driver made a right, and they drove through what appeared to be a high-end shopping district. As the car moved through traffic, Jay made out the signs on the stores: Gucci, Versace, Ferragamo, La Perla, Armani, Prada. The display windows were works of art, some of them featuring live models. Glamorous, exquisitely clad Italian women with money glided by wearing high heels, designer sunglasses, and attitude. Jay felt very fortunate to be in Italy.

The car climbed up a steep hill and pulled up to the Hotel Hassler, at the top of the Spanish steps, which would be Jay's home away from home during the campaign. He walked to the front desk, flashed his passport, and attempted to give the clerk a credit card.

"All charges are taken care of, Mr. Noble," the clerk said with a smile. He motioned over a bellman, who relieved Jay of his garment bag and accompanied him to the elevators. They rode to the top floor, where the bellman placed the electronic key in the latch and opened the door of his suite. Jay could hardly believe it. The apartment stretched across the entire front and side of the hotel. It included a spacious den with a wet bar, a large bedroom, a master bath with whirlpool, a study with a desk and book-lined shelves, and a wraparound balcony overlooking a garden terrace to the right and a breathtaking view of Rome in front. Jay walked out on the balcony and soaked in the view. A thought entered his mind: *good Italian wine, great food, gorgeous women, and politics. What more could an aging political hack ask for?*

After a hot shower and a power nap, the car picked up Jay and whisked him to a restaurant on a narrow street near the House of Deputies building. An eager and solicitous aide escorted Jay to a private room in the back of the restaurant, opening the door to reveal Lorenzo Brodi sitting in the semidarkness at a table surrounded by a clutch of aides, his beefy hand rubbing a piece of bread in a small dish of olive oil and peppercorn. Brodi bolted from his chair and hurried across the floor, greeting Jay with a wide grin and a vigorous hand pump.

The first thing Jay noticed about Brodi was how white his teeth gleamed against his dark skin. Brodi was not a tall man, but he presented a commanding presence with a compact, muscular body and a deep tan that bespoke health, wealth, and power. With his jet-black hair combed behind his ears, shoulders back and chest jutted, he exuded the charisma of a movie star.

"Mr. Mayor, pleasure to meet you," said Jay by way of greeting.

Brodi replied enthusiastically in rapid-fire Italian. An aide translated to English. "The mayor says, 'So this is Bob Long's brain that I have been hearing so much about.'"

"Not the brains," Jay corrected him. "The muscle."

As the translator began to speak, Brodi waved him off. He raised his right arm and made a show of flexing his bicep, saying, "The muscle! Tough guy!" He pointed at his arm. They all laughed.

"That's right," said Jay smoothly. "I take care of the president's friends as well as his enemies. And from now on I will do the same for you." He knew that any prospective client or donor was a sucker for any line that celebrated his notorious killer instincts. Jay was used to being seen as the cleaner, cleaning up other people's messes and leaving no fingerprints.

Brodi rattled off a response, punctuating his speech with animated hand gestures. The aide translated for Jay. "The mayor says he has far more enemies than Long, and he wants you to take care of all of them."

Jay stared back at Brodi as the smile had drained away from his face. "Tell the mayor I look forward to it," he said.

IN A THREE-STORY PREWAR townhouse on C Street, two blocks from the Supreme Court building, the live-in nurse for Justice Peter Corbin Franklin prepared lunch. She ladled chicken noodle soup into a bowl. Using a knife, she methodically cut the bits of chicken and the noodles into smaller pieces because Franklin had difficulty chewing his food. A registered nurse who specialized in home care for geriatric patients, she had worked for Franklin since the death of his wife six years earlier. But the job was getting more difficult. As his health had deteriorated and his dementia advanced,

Franklin had taken to occasionally showing up at work wearing a suit coat, dress shirt, and tie with pajama bottoms, face unshaven, visibly disoriented. One day he had gone to work and sat at his desk for half an hour, buzzing absent staff and growing increasingly agitated. He wandered the halls, angrily demanding to know where his staff was. A security guard had sheepishly explained to Franklin that it was Sunday and everyone had the day off. After that sad episode, Franklin's colleagues implored his nurse to move into his townhouse to keep a closer eye on her patient.

Lunch was a daily ritual with an unchanging menu. She stirred the soup with a spoon and placed two crackers (no salt) on top. Exactly two crackers—never more or less or she would hear about it. She placed a single scoop of chicken salad, the Justice's favorite from the corner deli, on the side. She walked down the hall toward Franklin's private, sun-lit study. He preferred to take his lunch there while he read the newspaper and listened to classical music. A folded copy of the *Washington Post* sat on the tray.

The instant she entered the room, she saw Franklin slumped across his desk, body motionless, one hand clutching reading glasses, the other hand reaching for his right temple. She dropped the tray, its contents shattering on the floor. She rushed to Franklin and quickly checked his vital signs. With her index finger at his neck, she felt a faint, irregular pulse. His breathing was labored. She quickly surmised that he had suffered a coronary episode of some kind, or perhaps a cranial thrombosis. She picked up the phone and dialed the number of the medical team at the Supreme Court.

"I need an ambulance for Justice Franklin stat," she said hurriedly. "He is unconscious and in severe distress. Please hurry!" She glanced back at Franklin. Every minute was critical if they had any chance of saving his life.

PHIL BATTAGLIA AND CHARLIE Hector walked down the narrow hallway leading to the Oval Office. Battaglia, who had served as Long's counsel in the governor's office in California and during the presidential campaign, was only midway through his second day as White House counsel. He was still unpacking boxes. This was his first meeting with the president.

Checking through the peephole on the door to the Oval Office, Hector rapped on the door before entering. They walked in together, signaling that something important was happening. Long's eyes seemed to ask, "What's up?"

"Phil has some disturbing news," Hector said.

"You've been on the job for one day and you already have disturbing news? What is it?" asked Long.

"Mr. President, Peter Corbin Franklin was found unconscious in his home about thirty minutes ago," Battaglia reported. "He's been rushed to GWU hospital. He's in intensive care. There's no official word, but it looks bad."

Long was thunderstruck. "Was it a stroke?"

"We don't know yet," said Battaglia. "But given his age, that's not a bad guess."

"He didn't look good at the inaugural," said Long.

"No, sir, he did not," Battaglia agreed. "He's really gone downhill since his wife died. He looked terrible. Just terrible."

"Now what?"

"We wait," said Hector. "Health bulletins are provided by individual justices, not the Supreme Court. It's basically up to Franklin's doctors and family to release information on his condition. Unless and until we receive word, we should not comment."

"Even if he's incapacitated?" asked Long, pressing the point.

"Yes," said Battaglia. "Frankly, Mr. President, his clerks have done the heavy lifting for years. They write his opinions. Unless he resigns or dies, there's no vacancy."

"What if he's a vegetable?"

"Doesn't matter. Constitutionally speaking, it's a lifetime appointment," Battaglia explained, his hands cutting through the air like a prosecutor making a point. "If the prognosis is that he can recover, they could hear cases with only eight justices present and hold any cases in abeyance decided by a tie vote. But if he's in a coma, I would think there will be a fair amount of pressure on his family to have him resign."

"I think we stay as far away from this as possible," Hector said.

Long stared back impassively. "What if he ends up like Ariel Sharon did? People who have had a stroke can live for years."

Hector appeared visibly uncomfortable. "We cross that bridge when we come to it. For our sake, let's hope that doesn't happen."

Long nodded, his mind racing. "What if he doesn't make it? Are we ready?" He leveled his gaze to Battaglia.

"I can't say definitively that we are, Mr. President," said Battaglia. "People are still moving into offices. Golden's top deputies at Justice are not confirmed, and they can't legally do their jobs until they are. We're working on a preliminary list of judicial nominees, but it's not ready for you just yet."

"Well, get it ready," ordered Long. "Let's accelerate the process. Get on the phone with Golden and get things moving. Because if we have a vacancy, I want to move quickly. You know what LBJ said: if you send a bill up to the Hill and it just lays there, it stinks up the place. The same is true with a judicial nominee. Speed is essential."

"Yes, sir," said Battaglia. They turned to go. Battaglia spun on his heel as if he had forgotten something. "Any guidance for me on the list?"

"All other things being equal, I'd like a woman or a Hispanic."

Battaglia nodded and turned to leave again.

"And Phil—"

"Yes, sir?"

"Get me a memo on what happens if a Justice is incapacitated," Long said. "I'd like to know all my options." He leaned forward, lowering his voice as if trying to avoid being overheard. "And Charlie, very delicately find out what you can about Franklin's medical condition. I don't want to be flying blind."

Battaglia and Hector left, closing the door behind them. As they walked back to their offices, they uttered not a word; the only sound made was their shoes on the carpet. Battaglia had been struck by how anxious Long seemed to replace Franklin—maybe too anxious. If Long wanted to know his options if Franklin did not die, it could only mean one thing: he had not ruled out trying to force out the eighty-eight-year-old in the case of incapacitation. That meant impeachment. Battaglia shuddered at the thought. It would spark a firestorm on Capitol Hill.

IT WAS TWO O'CLOCK in the afternoon, and Andy Stanton was due in the radio studio in an hour. Ross Lombardy knew that he would be at home doing show prep. Ross was one of only a handful of people with his private number. Andy answered on the first ring.

"Andy, did you hear the news?"

"What?"

"Peter Corbin Franklin had a stroke."

"Wow, this is big," Andy said excitedly. "I *told* you there would be a Supreme Court vacancy, didn't I?"

"Not yet, Andy. Franklin's unconscious, but he's alive."

"I don't see how he can live for long. Did you see him at the inaugural?"

"No, I didn't. But this is eerie, Andy. You called it!"

"The Lord called it. God told me before the election there would be a vacancy on the Supreme Court early in the next term," Andy said. "I told Long. He didn't believe me."

"I bet he believes it now." Ross marveled at the way Andy said God had spoken to him as casually as if he had talked to the guy at the car wash.

"We need to handle this with caution," Andy said, his voice grave. "Get out a statement that says we're praying for Franklin's recovery. I can hide behind that. We don't want to do anything that sounds political."

"If you ask people to pray that Franklin recovers, your listeners will be angry at you," Ross interjected. "If you ask people to pray that he's replaced, you'll spark a media firestorm while we're still in the middle of the flap over the inaugural prayer."

"I'll be careful. I've done radio for a while, remember?" He paused. "So I guess I should check in with Golden?"

"No, absolutely not," Ross said a little too sharply. "If you call the attorney general now, you can count on him being asked at some point if he ever spoke to you about a possible vacancy. There's only one good answer to that question: no."

"Too late," Andy replied. "I already talked to him about it at the inaugural."

"Terrific," groaned Ross. "What did you say?"

"I told him the Lord has spoken to me and showed me there would be a Supreme Court vacancy very soon. I told him he was a modern-day Esther. I said the future of the republic was in his hands and he better not blow it."

Ross almost fell out of his chair. "What did he say?"

"He just stared at me."

"I'll call Keith's chief of staff," said Ross. "I'll tell him we will be passing on some names for consideration." He paused, shifting gears. "By the way, how are you holding up under all the attacks about the inaugural prayer?"

"Holding up?" chuckled Andy in a low rumble. "Brother, I'm positively *blessed*. My TV show has the highest ratings in the history of the network. My ratings are up 25 percent!"

Ross laughed and hung up the phone. As he glanced out his window at the sprawling campus of New Life Ministries, row after row of Georgian brick buildings and hundreds of cars stretching across acres of parking lots, he marveled at Andy. Many people thought he was a right-wing crank, and more than a few considered him a nut. But in Ross's view he was neither. Andy simply operated on a different plane. He heard things that others did not hear, saw things others did not. He was an evangelical Rain Man. Of course, Andy was wrong as often as he was right. This was one time Ross hoped he really had heard from God.

SIX

Keith Golden slid into the chair at the head of the long table in the stately conference room just off his private office on the fifth floor of the Robert F. Kennedy Center, the massive building at Pennsylvania Avenue and Tenth Street that served as headquarters for the Department of Justice. As attorney general, he presided over the largest law enforcement agency in the world, a sprawling, global behemoth that included the FBI, the federal prison system, one million inmates, 124,000 employees, and agents all over the world. With Peter Corbin Franklin's stroke, his priority had become singular: identify and recommend a Supreme Court nominee to the president.

Golden's inner circle was solidly and reflexively conservative, an insular collection of ideologues and loyalists who shared his commitment to reshaping the federal judiciary, most of whom had been with him for years. To them Franklin's stroke was a personal tragedy but also the opportunity of their careers. They had no intention of blowing it. Golden leaned forward, placing his hands palms down on the table, immediately getting down to business. "Charlie Hector called. The president wants to meet with me and Battaglia no later than the day after tomorrow to discuss judicial nominees."

Art Morris, who headed the Office of Legal Counsel and was one of Golden's closest aides, raised his eyebrows and let out a long sigh. "That's a tall order."

"We've got biographical backgrounders on the top candidates," reported his chief of staff, a longtime aide in the Senate who had followed him to Justice. "We did that during the transition. But a thorough vetting yet of all their articles, speeches, and legal opinions will take weeks."

"We don't have weeks. We have two days," shot back Golden. "I want a fifteen- to twenty-page memo on each of them, with a two-page executive summary so the president doesn't have to read the entire document." He took a swig from his Diet Coke. "I want analysis of every word they have ever spoken or written. Every case they've ever been involved in. I don't want to leave a stone unturned."

"What about candidates with a thin paper trail?" asked Morris.

"Don't sugarcoat it," Golden answered firmly. "We stress to the president that if someone has left no footprints in the snow, there's usually a reason." He tapped the table with his knuckles. "No surprises."

"In other words, no Souters," chuckled his chief of staff.

"No more Souters," repeated Golden, referring to former Justice David Souter, appointed by George H. W. Bush and viewed as a stealth nominee who ended up greatly disappointing conservatives. "Not on my watch." He paused. "Charlie said the president wants a close look at women and Hispanic nominees."

"We have five or six," said Morris. "The best by far is Marco Diaz."

"He hasn't been on the DC Circuit long," noted Golden.

"Nineteen months. But he's terrific. It would be nice to send the second Hispanic Supreme Court nominee in history and watch Stanley and Penneymounter flail around."

"I like it. What about women?" asked Golden

"We have two solid candidates and one not so solid," said Morris. "The best, at least in terms of optics, is Yolanda Majette, an African-American woman who is chief justice of the California Supreme Court. Her father was the former state chair of the NAACP."

Golden's eyes lit up. "Did Long appoint her?"

"No, but he will know her. She's stellar."

"We're getting press calls asking if we're preparing to transmit names to the White House," reported the chief of staff.

"Tell them it's business as usual," said Golden. He raised his voice and craned his neck as if to imitate a press spokesperson. "Reviewing judicial candidates is standard at the start of every administration. There is no connection whatsoever to Franklin's medical condition."

"But we can always hope," joked Morris.

"Ross Lombardy called," said the chief of staff, changing subjects. "He wants to give us some names."

"Get them from Andy's legal eagle, not Lombardy." Golden's eyes widened and his face lit up. "By the way, Andy got in my face at the inaugural-—backstage at the Faith and Family celebration—and told me that God had told him there would be a vacancy very soon." He shook his head in wonder, chuckling. "I don't know if he's a prophet or clairvoyant."

"Don't you know Stanton's got a direct pipeline to God?" laughed Morris. "Either that, or Mars."

Golden rose from his chair, signaling the meeting was over. "Gentlemen, organize your team and make assignments." He smiled wryly. "I recommend you order in some pizza because I suspect you'll be pulling some all-nighters."

CHRISTY LOVE PUT DOWN her ever-present can of Diet Dr. Pepper and rapped on the table. The casual conversations wafting through the room abruptly stopped. The lawyers—she called them her hired guns—sat around the conference table, yellow legal pads open, pens poised, earnest expressions on every face. The communications and political staff lined the wall in chairs. They were puffed up like blowfish, ready to attack. The tension in the room was thick. Everyone's adrenal glands were wide open.

"Okay, folks, this is the real deal," Love announced grandiloquently, hands on hips. "This is not a drill. Justice Franklin is in our thoughts, and we hope he pulls through. He's tough, and he's gotten through worse than this before. But should there be a vacancy, as much as we hope there won't be, we have to be prepared for the mother of all confirmation battles." She looked around the table. "Is the press release out yet?"

"Done. We shot that out fifteen minutes after the AP bulletin on Franklin," answered the communications director, beaming. "We've got more than two hundred press calls. You have interviews lined up with NBC, CNN, Fox News, and the BBC."

"CNN is setting up in your office now," Love's assistant reported.

"Good," said Love. "The message is: we hope there won't be a vacancy, but if there is, we're ready. The stakes could not be higher, and if the Long administration tries to play politics with the Supreme Court, we will oppose them with every resource at our disposal."

"We're locked and loaded," said one of the lawyers.

Christy shot him a withering look. "Off message. This is Pro-Choice PAC, not the NRA, for crying out loud!" The room broke into nervous laughter at Christy's trademark cutting wit.

"The Faith and Family Federation issued a release saying that Franklin was in their prayers," offered someone in the back of the room, sarcasm dripping from his voice.

"Gag me," said Love. "Stanton makes me want to puke." She turned to her lead staff attorney. "Do we have the legal research on all the likely candidates?"

"We do," the counsel reported to the group. "We have dossiers on all of the candidates. We're more ready than we've ever been."

Love nodded approvingly. "People, there's no margin for error," she warned. "Bob Long won the White House with the religious right and angry white males. It's payback time." She paused, surveying every face. "We're the only thing standing between the American people and the shredding of the Constitution." Her eyes sparkled with intensity. She clapped her hands together twice. "Let's get to work and fight for women's rights like our whole lives depended on it. Because they do."

The room broke into loud applause. Someone let out a shrill whistle. Love was head coach, field general, and attack dog all rolled into one: a Doberman in designer heels. She and her team had drawn a line in the sand: they would stop Bob Long from putting a right-wing extremist on the Supreme Court or die trying.

THE MEDICAL TEAM AT George Washington University gathered in a small office steps, from the ICU, studying pictures from the MRI and the CT scan of Peter Corbin Franklin. Twenty minutes earlier they had finished three hours of emergency surgery on the justice, during which the surgeons inserted a stent at the base of his brain stem to relieve pressure caused by the bleeding in his skull. The lead surgeon pointed to various regions of the brain with his index finger as they talked in hushed voices. On the positive side, there was no sign of a tumor or growth in the brain. But the shaded areas on the MRI were the telltale signs of a massive cerebral hemorrhage. The bleeding in the brain had done extensive tissue damage, and the GWU hospital surgical team knew it was irreversible.

"He has massive intraparenchymal bleeding," the lead doctor said.

"Do you think it affects the medulla?" asked a member of the surgical team.

"Yes. We don't know if it caused damage to the vagus nerve. The immediate objective is to stop the bleeding. We won't know his true condition until he stabilizes. Then we'll see if he can breathe without assistance."

"It looks like classic CAA," said a GWU professor of medicine who was consulting with the surgical team. One of the surgeons arched his eyebrows in curiosity. "Cerebral amyloid angiopathy," the professor continued. "It's a weakening of the blood vessels in the brain that makes the victim especially prone to cranial bleeding."

The lead surgeon nodded. That ruled out blood thinning medication, which made recovery even more unlikely. The realization deepened the already sober and determined mood in the cramped office.

"He may not regain consciousness," said another doctor. "If he does, it's questionable whether he'll be fully cognizant."

The lead doctor frowned to signal his disapproval. The rest of the trauma team greeted this statement with silence. The reality of Franklin's precarious condition was something only to be spoken of in hushed whispers.

A male nurse wearing a green smock stuck his head in the door. "Doctor, phone call," he said to the lead surgeon. "It's the White House."

"The White House? What in the world would they want from me?"

"I don't know, sir. It's the operator. Line two."

The lead doctor looked at his colleagues, shrugged his shoulders, and picked up the phone. The voice on the other end said, "Doctor, thank you for taking my call. This is Charlie Hector, calling from the White House."

"I know who you are," the doctor replied coldly. "What can I do for you, Mr. Hector?"

"We're getting press inquiries about Justice Franklin's medical condition. Obviously, I don't want to pry or violate the confidentiality of the doctor-patient relationship. But we are trying to be responsive to the media, so I was wondering if you could provide us with any guidance in a general way on the Justice's condition. Or I can just keep this conversation confidential."

"I'm afraid I can't tell you anything at this time," the doctor said, swatting aside Hector's empty caveats.

"Well," said Hector haltingly. "In that case, do you have any plans to hold a news conference or issue a statement? An awful lot of rumors are flying around on the Internet. It might help."

"Mr. Hector, my only focus is on taking care of Justice Franklin," said the doctor, his voice distant. "I don't have anything to report at this time. When we do, we'll inform the public, and you'll find out when everyone else does."

"I know you'll handle it in a thoroughly professional way," said Hector, his voice hollow.

The doctor hung up the phone with a thud. He turned to his colleagues. "I can't believe the chutzpah of this White House," he said through clenched teeth. "It's just beyond the pale."

"Who was that?"

"Charlie Hector doing his best imitation of the Grim Reaper."

"We need to release a statement and throw a wet blanket on the death watch," urged one of the doctors. "Things are spinning out of control. There are two dozen camera crews outside the emergency room entrance."

"We have to tell the truth, but it needs to be positive enough to force the White House and the media to back off," said the lead physician. The doctors appointed a committee of two to work with the hospital's public relations officer to draft a statement. The two doctors who drew the short straw headed down the hall toward an elevator.

The lead surgeon padded back into the ICU, still wearing his green surgical gown, and stopped at the foot of the bed of Peter Corbin Franklin. He stood there silently, staring. Franklin's frail body was twisted at an impossible angle, legs pulled up to his abdomen, his right hand involuntarily forming a claw. Tubes came from every part of his body, extending from his nose, chest, and mouth. The repetitive beep of an EKG echoed in the background. Franklin's pale, drawn face resembled a death mask. His mouth agape in a silent scream, he wore a stricken expression, black eyes unseeing. Even if he lived, he would never again be the brilliant legal mind with a rapier wit that had once enraptured audiences and intimidated lawyers at the Supreme Court. Worst of all, Franklin was now a pawn in a larger political chess game. They wouldn't let the poor man die in peace.

SEVEN

Jay Noble used a wooden spoon to shovel shellfish and pasta onto his plate from a large bowl at the center of the table.

His hosts brought him to La Terraza, a trendy restaurant around the corner from the Piazza Navona. The restaurant pulsated with energy, waiters carrying tables over their heads and setting them down to accommodate new arrivals, wine stewards floating in and out brandishing expensive bottles of wine, and loud, animated conversation filling the courtyard. Handsome couples, walking arm in arm, arrived in a steady flow. Jay's party had already downed plates of caprese, bruschetta, and calamari. Now they were on the main course, a steaming confection of linguine, crawfish, prawns, and eel. The ever-present maître d', who impressed Jay as having the managerial acumen of a CEO and the charisma of a pop idol, kept a close watch on their table. Even halfway around the world, Jay was a VIP.

"So tell me the truth," Jay asked his hosts. "Do you guys eat like this every day?"

"In Italy," one of them explained, "food is not just for nutrition. It is . . . how you say?" He drew his fingers together as though holding a pinch of salt. "The essence of life."

"That's food?" Jay replied with a smirk. "I thought that was sex."

Jay's hosts exploded with laughter. "That, too!" one of them exclaimed.

"So where does politics fit in?" asked Jay, taking another bite from a prawn lathered in sauce. "In Italy is it primarily a sport or deadly serious?"

"We've had forty-two governments since World War II," one of his hosts said, swirling red wine in the bottom of his glass. "We burn through prime ministers like the French do their mistresses." More laughter. "So I would say politics is a sport."

"We're getting ready to win big," Jay said, "and when we do, we will build the most durable governing coalition of your lifetimes. A center-right coalition with a third or more of the seats in the House of Deputies from Brodi's party will be unshakable. The left-wing parties will be irrelevant." He paused. "We did it in the U.S. We can do it here." They all nodded. Jay knew what they were thinking: *are we paying this guy enough?*

Jay's BlackBerry vibrated. He glanced down to see the number of Marvin Myers, the media Big Foot who wrote the leading syndicated column in America, carried in four hundred newspapers, and also hosted a ratings-grabbing Sunday show. Jay was a key source for Myers. He held up his index finger and excused himself from the table.

"Jay," came Myers's smooth drawl. Jay was surprised how clear the connection was. "What's the White House thinking on the Peter Corbin Franklin situation?"

Jay walked to the front of the restaurant, where a large refrigerator displayed fresh seafood, salmon, shellfish, eel, and trout. The smell of dead fish filled his nostrils. "Marvin, I'm sorry, but I'm out of the country. What's up with Franklin?"

"He had a stroke," said Myers, surprised that Jay was out of the loop. "He's in intensive care at GWU hospital. From what I hear, it's bad, as in he's not likely to go home."

Jay almost dropped his phone. "I can't believe it."

"The hospital issued a statement saying he suffered a cerebral hemorrhage," Myers reported. "They claim his condition is not life-threatening. That doesn't really add up."

"No, it doesn't. He was in bad shape *before* this happened."

"A clerk for another justice told me Franklin's in a coma and is brain dead. If that's true, it's going to require some kind of resolution, isn't it?"

Jay suddenly felt nauseous from the overpowering smell of dead fish. Myers was on the case and was about to write one of his agenda-setting pieces that would have all of Washington talking. Jay stalled him. "Let me see what I can find out."

"I'd be eternally grateful." Myers reloaded. "If Franklin isn't coming back, Long will have an appointment. I'm trying to get a feel for who might be on the short list."

"You might check in with someone at DOJ," suggested Jay. "Do you have good sources over there?" He wanted to pacify Myers without being the source on something as sensitive as Long's short list for the Supreme Court. That was a little too hot to handle.

"Jay, I have sources *everywhere*," Myers said with characteristic aplomb. "Don't be disappointed, but you're hardly the only person I'm talking to."

"How well I know that," Jay said, laughing. As he talked, a tall Italian woman with dark skin and a mane of black hair breezed by, towering in six-inch heels. She wore a black ribbed turtleneck sweater, a snug-fitting black leather jacket, and designer jeans into which it appeared she had been poured. As she passed, Jay noticed a tattoo just above the shoe line on the top of her foot. He was liking Rome more with each passing day; it was a little like LA, only with history and culture.

"Where are you?" Myers asked, interrupting his thoughts.

"I can't say," Jay said. "I'm working on a campaign outside the country."

"Really?" said Myers. "I'd like to write something on it."

"Not yet, Marvin. Give me some time to get my feet on the ground. I'll help you on the Franklin story, but I need you to sit on this one for a while."

"Alright, but pay attention to Franklin. This one could get sticky."

Jay hung up, disturbed by Myers' call. His head was swimming. If Franklin died, Sal Stanley, still bitter from losing the election and pining for revenge, would do everything he could to kill Long's Supreme Court nominee in the Senate. The scary thing was the White House wasn't ready; it was all happening too fast.

Jay returned to the table and poured another glass of red wine, which he suddenly needed to deaden the shock of Myers's news. His eyes followed the black-haired beauty as she sat down at a table with a grey-haired man old enough to be her father, wearing a striped shirt unbuttoned to his navel, with gold chains hanging from his neck. Jay just shook his head: wasn't this the way it always was?

THE PRESIDENT LEANED BACK in an easy chair in the solarium, unwinding on the second floor of the White House, his feet up on the table. He was deep in conversation with Gerald Jimmerson, the Republican

Speaker of the House. Jimmerson, a small, intense bantam rooster of a man, led the fight against Long when the election was thrown into the House of Representatives. When members of his own party bolted to Long, Jimmerson suffered an embarrassing defeat from which he was only now recovering.

The two men needed each other. Jimmerson needed Long's supporters to join forces with the Republican Party or at least view it favorably. Long needed Jimmerson to pass his domestic agenda so he invited Jimmerson over to talk shop. He was love-bombing him.

"Gerry, I want to put the campaign behind us," Long said. "You did what you had to do. I respect that. I don't hold it against you."

"Well, that's certainly comforting to know," Jimmerson said with a grin. "Because if you did, we'd have a hard time working together."

Long flashed a relaxed smile. "You went after me pretty hard."

"I supported the nominee of my party. I felt obligated. "

"I didn't feel obligated to support my party's nominee," Long chuckled.

"And I don't think poor Sal has gotten over it yet." He leaned on the arm of his chair, almost touching the president. "But one thing you'll learn about me soon enough, Mr. President. I'm a bottom-line kind of guy. If I'm against you, I'll tell you to your face. I won't say one thing to you here and then go back to the Capitol and stab you in the back."

"I appreciate that." He patted Jimmerson on the arm. "You and I can do business together."

"After eight years of a Republican administration that was devoid of ideas and politically all thumbs, I'm glad to have a president who listens." He paused. "But I have to be up front with you. I won't be for your health-care plan. In fact, I'm going to fight you tooth and nail."

"Why? There's no net increase in federal expenditures under my plan," Long protested. "All I do is shift money from Medicaid and Medicare to cover the uninsured."

"Mr. President, it's government-run health care. Your plan has employer mandates, which is a hidden tax on small business," Jimmerson said. His face broke into a crooked grin. "I'm going to have to nail you on this one."

Jimmerson's face turned serious. "What's your thinking on the Franklin seat on the Supreme Court? What are you going to do, or do you know yet?"

Long held his cards close. "Not really. I don't think he's likely to return to the Court. But until he either comes back or resigns or passes away, all we can do is sit here and wait."

"I'm not particularly in a waiting mood," Jimmerson shot back.

"Meaning?"

"We can impeach him."

Long was shocked. "You're going to impeach a guy who is comatose? Come on!"

"I don't see why not," Jimmerson said, his gaze steady. "If Franklin doesn't recover, you have a coequal branch of government rendered inoperative. The Judiciary Committee can move an impeachment resolution based on his inability to carry out the duties of his office. It's a simple majority vote on the floor and I've got the votes." He read Long's surprised expression. "If the man can't function, he's got to go. Simple as that."

Long's face went white. He shifted uncomfortably in his chair. "Why make your guys walk the plank? The Democrats in the Senate will never vote to remove him."

"Maybe they do, maybe they don't," Jimmerson volleyed back. "Either way, I win. If Stanley and Penneymounter keep a vegetable on the Court, they look like fools." He crossed his legs and opened his hands wide. "How can you defend that?"

"I hear you. But impeachment . . ." Long's voice trailed off. "That's risky. Just ask the Republicans who impeached Clinton. That didn't turn out so well."

"This isn't Clinton dropping his trousers with an intern. It's Woodrow Wilson," Jimmerson said. "Franklin is paralyzing an institution of government because he's unable to function. " His eyes bore into Long. "The question is: can I get your support?"

Long threw up his hands as if trying to calm a bucking horse. "Gerry, I can't go there. I'd burn so many bridges in the Senate I will never be able to get a nominee confirmed." He crossed his legs and rested his hands in his lap, assuming a thoughtful pose. "But if I can't help you, I'll try not to hurt you."

Jimmerson nodded slowly. "I appreciate that," he replied. "But once the shooting starts, no one is going to be able to remain neutral. And that includes you."

Long was stunned by the audacity of Jimmerson's plan. He was beginning to think the man was unhinged. First vowing to block health-care reform and now this? He realized Franklin's status would not be his alone to resolve. Republicans in the House, led by Jimmerson doing his usual Braveheart routine, were plotting to impeach an eighty-eight-year old stroke victim. If Jimmerson went through with his threat, it would start a constitutional showdown.

THE HEAD NEUROSURGEON AT George Washington University entered the family waiting room down the hall from the ICU and closed the door. He turned to face the three children of Peter Corbin Franklin and their spouses. His black eyes were hooded, his facial expression solemn, his hands stuck in the pockets of his white coat.

"As I told Peter Jr., on the phone yesterday, your father suffered a catastrophic brain hemorrhage," said the surgeon. "The bleeding caused swelling of the brain, compressing both cerebella. The damage is extensive. We controlled the swelling with medication and a stent at the base of the brain, which drains fluid from the brain. So far it's working. But if the brain continues to swell, it will press down on the stem, affecting motor functions like breathing and circulation."

Franklin's daughter Janet's eyes filled with tears. "So he can breathe and his heart is beating, but beyond that he's not there."

"He has no cognitive brain function. It is highly unlikely he will regain consciousness. But we want to make him as comfortable as possible and hope for the best."

"What are our options, doctor?" asked Peter Jr.

"You can wait for an infection to take him or his heart to stop. That could take days, months, or years. Or you can choose to remove his feeding tube."

"Thank you. Can you give us some time alone?" asked Peter Jr.

"Of course." The surgeon turned and exited the waiting room. The children sat in silence for a moment, absorbing the blow.

"Dad's gone. His body is still here, but he's not," said Janet.

"He wouldn't want to go on like this," said her husband.

Peter Jr. rose from his chair and leaned against the wall. "You didn't know my father very well if you think that," he said. "Dad loathed Bob Long and Andy Stanton and everything they stand for. Believe me, if he had to stay alive on a respirator, he'd do it to keep Long from replacing him."

"This isn't about the Supreme Court. It's about our father," said Terry, the youngest of the three children.

"The heck it isn't! This is all about the Court," fired back Peter Jr. "Dad loved this country, and he stood for a set of principles. He wouldn't want to quit, not with Long appointing his successor."

Silence hung in the air. "You're right. Until Dad goes on his own, we have to honor him by hanging on as long as we can," said Janet.

Peter Jr. glanced at Terry. He silently nodded.

"Ending Dad's suffering is the easy way out," said Peter Jr. "But it's not how Dad lived his life, and it's not how he would want to die. You know Dad. He's going to go out swinging." They all smiled knowingly. "Hell will freeze over before I stand idly by and let Bob Long nominate his replacement."

AT 7:45 A.M., THE president's legal team gathered in the Roosevelt Room, across the hall from the Oval Office. The agenda: review the top candidates for the Supreme Court, narrow the list to those the president would interview, and discuss strategy for confirmation. No one knew if Franklin would live or die, but it was important to be ready. Everyone was a little jumpy.

The door opened and the president walked in. He sat down as a steward brought him a cup of coffee in a china cup bearing the presidential seal. He was all business.

Long asked Keith Golden to begin.

"Mr. President, we've presented you with memoranda on eleven top candidates," Golden began. "Some of them have been on lists in previous administrations so they're known quantities. Anyone on an appellate court—there are four in this group—has already been confirmed. They've been to the dance."

Battaglia noticed the president had not opened the briefing book containing the memos. It gave all the appearance of a backhanded slap at Golden.

"It's not the dance. It's more like triple-A ball," Battaglia corrected. "A Supreme Court confirmation is a different ball game. Just because someone had a smooth confirmation to a circuit court does not guarantee them one for the Supreme Court."

"Agreed," said Golden curtly. "But they've cleared an FBI background check and have been vetted."

"Okay," said Long. "Give me the best and brightest."

"Robert Hillman on the DC Circuit is first-rate," Golden said. "He graduated first in his class at Yale Law, clerked for Scalia, and served as solicitor general. He's the gold standard."

Long nodded.

"Hillman is Bork redux," Battaglia objected. "It'll be a holy war. The Democrats hate his guts. He'll be a very tough sell."

"Anyone who is a strict constructionist will engender fierce opposition," fired back Golden, clearly irritated with Battaglia's second-guessing. "I served on the Judiciary Committee. I know Penneymounter. He's running for president, and he'll never support your nominee."

"I don't care about Penneymounter," said Long. "But we have to pick off some red-state Democrats to win." He took another swig of coffee, his eyes leveled at Golden. "Keep going."

"Marco Diaz, also on the DC Circuit, is solid," Golden continued. "University of Chicago law, assistant attorney general, former district court judge. Great narrative. His father came to the U.S. from Mexico and turned a used car lot into the largest Hispanic auto dealership in North America. Diaz turned down offers from blue-chip law firms to return to the barrio."

"Upside: solid guy, good record, Hispanic," interjected Battaglia. "Downside: he's only been on the DC Circuit a short time."

Long let out a long whistle. "He sounds great. Who else?"

"We have four women on the short list. The two strongest candidates are former Congresswoman Susan Cunningham, who currently sits on the Florida Supreme Court, and Yolanda Majette, African-American chief justice of the California Supreme Court."

"I know Yolanda. She's impressive," Long replied. "Can she handle the scrutiny of a Supreme Court confirmation?"

"She's tough," offered Battaglia. "Penneymounter will have a hard time attacking her."

"Alright, let's take a vote," Long said. "Who's your top choice?" Everyone appeared stunned that Long was putting them on the spot. "Let's go around the table."

"Bob Hillman," said Golden. "He's the best. It's not even close."

Art Morris, assistant attorney general in charge of the Office of Legal Counsel had said nothing during the meeting. He kept his head down, taking notes. "Mr. President, you won't find a more brilliant nominee with a better judicial temperament than Judge Hillman."

"Phil?"

"Majette or Diaz, in that order," said Battaglia. "I don't think we can ignore the fact that there is only one African-American and two women on the Court right now. There is currently no Hispanic. If you get a vacancy, it's an opportunity to capture the country's imagination."

Long nodded. "You guys meet with the top candidates very informally. This won't rise to a presidential decision unless and until there is a vacancy." He took a final swig of coffee. "Focus on anything personal that could be a problem. I'd prefer not to have any surprises."

"We'll do a full GI track exam on all of them," assured Golden.

When the meeting broke up, Battaglia approached the president. "Can I see you for a moment?" he said in a half whisper. The president put his arm around him and walked him across the hall to the Oval, leaving Golden and his aides behind. He closed the door.

"I spoke to the chief justice," said Battaglia.

"What did he say?"

"He told me Franklin's chances of recovery are zero. He's being kept alive on a feeding tube. According to the chief, the family is in denial, and they won't pull the plug because they don't want you to appoint his successor."

"Unbelievable," said Long. "He could live for years."

"The chief says he strongly opposes Congress's removing Franklin," said Battaglia. "He views it as a separation of powers issue. But for the same reason he does not want to take Jimmerson on publicly."

"That's great," said Long. "We've got a split court, a comatose justice, a renegade Speaker of the House, and the chief justice has a fit of integrity. I wish he would go public and oppose impeachment. We need someone to stop this."

"Instead we're going to be subjected to the Gerry Jimmerson show, with Andy Stanton leading his army on the Capitol, followed by a show trial in the Senate," Battaglia muttered.

Long rolled his eyes. "I tried to charm Jimmerson, but he's a maniac." He sighed. "He thinks if he impeaches Franklin the conservatives will turn out and vote Republican next year. I told him I couldn't back him but I'd stay out of it, which I viewed as doing him a favor, but he wasn't really pacified."

"He's willing to tear the country apart for his own partisan gain," said Battaglia, his tone of voice disgusted. "It's pathetic."

"Oh, well, thanks for the update. Keep me posted."

Battaglia turned to go. He hoped the shot at Stanton had worked. In his mind ideologues like Golden and Stanton were parasites trying to hijack the administration. Battaglia went along with using the wing nuts to get elected, but he had no intention of letting them run the government. This was a battle for the soul of Long's presidency, and Battaglia had no intention of giving up without a fight.

EIGHT

The Lincoln Town Car carrying Andy Stanton and Ross Lombardy pulled slowly through the iron gate at the entrance to the White House complex and inched up the driveway to a reserved parking spot next to the West Wing. Andy sat in the back, bouncing his knees like a little boy, rubbing his hands together, giving rapid-fire instructions to the driver. Nervous energy flowed from every pore of his body. And why not? He was about to meet with the president of the United States—who he had helped to elect—and give him his recommendations for appointment to the Supreme Court. Andy had built up a lot of political chits with Bob Long, and he was now calling them in.

Andy, accompanied by Ross and a security guard, walked through the narrow doorway leading to the West Wing lobby and approached the guard at the security desk, announcing his arrival. Ross took a seat on the couch below the oversized clock in the lobby, which seemed designed to advertise the exaggerated importance of time and space in this hallowed real estate. Andy, unable to suppress his excitement, remained standing, admiring the full-length portrait of George Washington. Truman Greenglass, national security advisor, came down the hall from the Oval Office and greeted Stanton with courteous but restrained professionalism.

David Thomas, White House political director, came out of the Roosevelt Room, apparently leaving a staff meeting. His earnest posture, schoolboy baby face, and flame-thrower intensity radiated energy. "Dr. Stanton, how are you?" he asked solicitously, pretending to be surprised to see him. In fact, the entire building was on full alert. Even the cooks in the White House mess knew that Andy was in the building.

"I'm *wonderful*," Andy fairly gushed. "How are you?"

"Oh, holding up, you know," said Thomas with false humility. "I'm glad to see you here." He cupped his hand to his mouth. "Not everybody is glad you're here. But I am." He winked knowingly.

Andy forced a smile. Was it a veiled shot?

"So you're meeting with the president?"

"Yes!" Andy said a tad too enthusiastically. "Should be any minute now."

"Great. Have a good meeting. Ross, why don't you come with me, and we'll catch up while Andy's in with the boss." Thomas and Ross headed across the alleyway to his office in the Eisenhower Executive Office Building.

"Dr. Stanton, the president will see you now." Andy turned to see the president's assistant, a pretty, well-groomed woman in her fifties, smiling invitingly. She walked down the hall with him, exchanging small talk, and then opened the door. The president stood in front of a wing chair before the fireplace, which had a crackling fire. Charlie Hector stood in front of one of the couches to the side.

"Andy!" the president greeted him. "Come on in! You know Charlie."

"Of course," replied Andy. He greeted Hector, and the president waved to him to take the chair next to his. They engaged in some banter about the news of the day. Then Andy quickly got down to business. He was not a man to mince words.

"Mr. President, my listeners and viewers are very concerned about the appointment of justices to the Supreme Court."

"I know," Long replied. "It was one of the biggest applause lines I had on the stump."

"Peter Corbin Franklin being in a coma has piqued a lot of interest in who you might nominate should there be a vacancy." He paused. "We are praying for his health and well-being. But my nephew, who is on the staff of the teaching hospital at Johns Hopkins, tells me it is highly unusual for someone with his injury to live."

The President stared back impassively.

"Mr. President, I believe you will get at least one and maybe two Supreme Court picks. The future of the country is at stake. Evangelicals voted for you in large numbers in no small part because of your conservative judicial philosophy."

"Andy, let me stop you there," said Long firmly, holding up the palms of his hand. He quickly took charge of the conversation, guiding it circuitously so that he was both responsive and opaque. "I've told Golden, Phil, and the folks in OPP that I don't want them to yield one inch on my pledge to appoint judges who share my philosophy and have impeccable credentials. It's going to be rough sledding with Penneymounter in charge of Judiciary. But I have told them not to change a single thing in selecting judges." He had used the acronym for the Office of Presidential Personnel, which handled presidential appointments throughout the government.

Hector sat silently, taking notes.

"That is great—just great," said Andy enthusiastically, his face beaming. "Your stand on judges was critical to your winning evangelical votes. I brought something for you that I hope will be helpful. The dean of my law school put together a dossier of leading candidates for judicial appointments," Andy explained. "They're available for a full range of positions, from district court all the way to the Supreme Court." He smiled proudly. "These folks are solid citizens with impeccable credentials."

"Good for you," replied Long as if he were praising a student who had completed his homework.

Andy extended the slim bound volume toward the president, offering it to him. Long physically recoiled, eyeing it as though it were a shrapnel grenade about to explode. Hector jumped forward, snatching it out of his hands.

"I'll pass this on to Phil Battaglia and his team," said Hector curtly as he flipped through the pages, feigning interest.

"Anything else on the personnel front?" asked Long, quickly changing the subject. "I assume you were happy with our appointments at HHS."

"Yes," replied Andy. "There is one other thing that is important, not just to me, but to the entire faith community. That's the commissioner of the IRS."

The president nodded.

Andy lowered his voice. "Within ten days after I let Petty have it in the last campaign, the IRS showed up at my doors and launched an audit of my ministry."

The president chuckled and shook his head. "I'm sure that was purely a coincidence," he said sarcastically.

"We think Bill Diamond was behind it," Andy said, referring to the former vice presidential chief of staff and senior advisor to the president in the previous administration. "They wanted to punish me for not supporting the Republican ticket. And not just me. They parachuted IRS audit teams into every major conservative evangelical ministry in the country."

"What are they looking for?" Long asked.

"Anything that might trip me up." His eyes widened. "The first thing they asked for was my personal expense reports, as well as documentation of any personal use of the ministry plane by me or my family. It's a witch hunt." He leaned forward, lowering his voice again. "I've had twelve agents on the grounds of my ministry for four months. The lead agent showed up wearing an ACLU membership pin on his lapel."

"Good night!" said Long, astonished, casting a glance at Hector. "You've got a dozen agents working right out of your headquarters?"

"No, we built a special place for them," Andy said grinning. "We brought a double wide trailer onto our campus, and we put them in there."

Long barely suppressed a chuckle. He shot a glance at Hector, who smiled. "Andy, in my experience, you don't want the commissioner. You want the head of the exempt division."

"Fine," said Andy. "I'll take the head of the exempt division."

"Get some names to Charlie. He'll work with OPP." Andy was beginning to get the distinct impression that Hector was running the White House, not the president. It was another nonresponsive answer. Unfazed, he plowed ahead.

"Mr. President, I just returned from Israel. I met with the prime minster and foreign minister. There is grave concern there about Iran."

"I know," Long said, his face projecting worry. "Salami has gamed the UN and the IAEA for years. Now the gig is about up. If we don't do something, Israel will."

"Iran with a nuclear weapon would be a disaster."

"We can't let it happen," said Long crisply. "That's our policy. The question is, what's the best way to proceed. Invading Iran is not an option. Our forces are already stretched thin in Afghanistan and elsewhere."

"What if Iran invades Iraq?" asked Andy.

"Why would they do that?" asked Long, a surprised look on his face.

"It's in the Bible," Andy replied, not missing a beat. "Isaiah 13 predicts the Medes will turn Babylon, which is now Iraq, into a wasteland. The

Medo-Persian Empire arose in what is now modern-day Iran. The rise of Salami and a nuclear Iran represent the second fulfillment of that prophesy, the first being Cyrus of Persia." He looked at the president, his eyes unblinking. Hector's legal pad fell from his lap to the floor. He reached down to pick it up.

Long looked as though someone had hit him in the head with a brick. "Iran has funded splinter Shiite militias in Iraq. But they've never amassed troops on the border. If they did, we would do whatever was necessary to defend Iraq."

"I'm not a military strategist; I'm a pastor," Andy demurred. "But Iran will move against Iraq. It's only a matter of time. Israel will strike Iran unless we act soon. And Russia, which is selling antiaircraft defenses to Iran, has said that if Israel attacks, they will move in to protect Iran. It's all lining up into a situation prophesied in Ezekiel 38."

Long's eyes widened. After a long pause Hector jumped in.

"I don't think it's a good idea for us to work this into the president's State of the Union address," Hector deadpanned.

Andy broke up with laughter. "No, this is just between us." He cocked his head. "Mr. President, would you mind if I prayed for you?"

"I'd be honored, Andy."

Andy reached over and put his hand affectionately on Long's shoulder as Long closed his eyes tightly. Hector bowed his head. "Lord, I thank You so much for President Long, for what he means to America and what he means to the entire world. I thank You for his leadership, for his character, and for having a heart for You." The president sat completely still, not moving a muscle. "I pray for strength and wisdom as he seeks to do Your will. Surround him with godly men and women who will give him wise counsel. Grant him supernatural understanding as he makes the hard decisions for our country. Bless him, Lord, and his family and his administration."

Long and Hector raised their heads and opened their eyes. "Thank you, Andy," said the president, patting him on the arm. "You're a dear friend."

They stood up and Long took Andy around the room, pointing out the portraits of Lincoln, FDR, and Washington he had hung on the walls. There was also a portrait of Big Bear Lake, which roughly approximated the view from Long's weekend cabin in the mountains that he would now rarely see. Andy paused to admire a bust of Winston Churchill. The president's assistant knocked gently on the door. Andy shook the president's hand and left. The assistant closed the door behind him. They looked at each other, eyes wide.

"Boy, Andy's a little nutty, isn't he?" asked Hector, breaking the silence.

"Andy may be a nut," said Long with a sigh. "But he's *our* nut."

A GROUP OF REPORTERS huddled together against the cold wind at the "stake-out" location, which was marked by a thicket of microphones in the West Wing driveway. Word had spread to the press corps that Andy was in the building, and a small media horde had gathered, hoping to liven up the day by stirring up still more controversy after the flap over Andy's prayer at the inaugural. As Andy and Lombardy emerged from the building, the reporters snapped to attention. Andy walked casually to the microphone, placing his hands behind his back.

"I had a very good meeting with the president," he began. "It was really a courtesy call, if you will. He's a good friend, and it was an honor to spend some time with him today. He is in great spirits, he's upbeat, and he's excited about doing the job the American people sent him here to do."

"Reverend Stanton, did you discuss Peter Corbin Franklin's medical condition?" asked Reuters.

"Very briefly," Andy replied. "I told the president that we were praying for Justice Franklin."

"So you did discuss Franklin—and did you give the president your advice on what to do if there is a vacancy on the Court?"

"I don't advise the president," said Andy firmly. "I'm a pastor. I prayed for him."

"You prayed for him?" asked the Associated Press, sensing a headline.

"Yes."

"What did you pray about?"

"None of your business," said Andy with a smile. The reporters chuckled. "I prayed that God would help him deal with all of you." More laughter.

"You worked hard to elect President Long, turning your back on the Republican Party in the process, and you would like to see the Supreme Court overturn *Roe v. Wade*," said McClatchy News. "You expect us to believe that you weren't here today to call in your chits and remind the president of his commitment to appoint a conservative to the Court?"

"Well, first of all," replied Andy, a look of bemusement crossing his face, "I didn't turn my back on the Republican Party; the Republican Party turned its back on us. In the last election the GOP ticket forsook the moral values that had attracted millions of evangelicals to its banner, including the issue of life. As for judicial appointments, the president's stance on judges was a major factor in winning evangelical support in the last election. I fully expect him to fulfill his commitment to appoint judges who will interpret the law, not legislate from the bench."

"Did you say that to him today?"

"Yes." Ross Lombardy flinched slightly behind Andy at this acknowledgment.

"What did he say in response?"

"I don't discuss what the president says to me in private. But President Long is a man of integrity. I believe he will govern exactly as he pledged he would during the campaign, and that includes in the area of appointing judges."

"So you're satisfied he will appoint Supreme Court justices to your liking?" asked the *New York Times*.

"Not to my liking," corrected Andy. "Consistent with the commitment that he made to the American people. They elected him."

"Some people say you elected him," shot back UPI, chuckling.

"Those people are wrong," said Andy. "I supported Bob Long in my capacity as a private citizen. But he won the election on his own."

"Did the president express any regret to you today about the controversy over your prayer at the inaugural?" asked the *Christian Science Monitor*.

"Honestly, it didn't come up."

"Surely you regret the embarrassment you've caused the administration, and the riots you have caused in the Middle East?" asked the *Washington Post*.

"I regret if anyone was offended, but I am a minister of the gospel. I believe that Christ is the Savior of all mankind, and it is my job as a pastor to say so," said Andy. "What I really regret is that Islamic extremists have tried to turn my prayer into an expression of U.S. government policy, which it was not, in order to stoke hatred against the United States among Muslims. That is unfortunate."

"Thank you all very much," said Ross firmly into the microphone as the reporters shouted more questions. He had had enough, and he clasped

Andy by the arm and guided him down the driveway to the Town Car that was warming up on the curb. They both got in the back seat and closed the door.

"Well?" asked Ross, eyebrows arched. "How did it go?"

"I think it went as fine as it could," said Andy, looking slightly crestfallen. "We prayed together. He's with us on judges. I don't think he'll let us down. But he didn't show his hand. He kept his cards close to his vest." He turned to Ross, looking directly into his eyes. "He's the president now, Ross. He's surrounded by people who didn't elect him and by forces he doesn't control. I don't even know if he realizes it. The one-worlders, the bureaucracy, the State Department." He frowned. "I'll probably never meet with him alone again."

Andy and Ross rode to the airport in a silence broken only occasionally by gossipy asides. Like the rest of the world, they were spectators now. They had little choice but to wait for word of Peter Corbin Franklin's fate, and for Long's much-anticipated nomination of a replacement.

NINE

"Who leaked this?" asked Long, his voice raised, his face flushed, the veins in his neck bulging. Long rarely blew his top, but when he did, the effect was volcanic. Behind his back the White House staff called these his "Crazy Eddie" moments.

"I don't think it came from here, sir," replied Charlie Hector, who stood in front of the president's desk stoically absorbing the blast. "Only two people at NSC had access to it, Greenglass and his deputy. I think it was the CIA."

"Why in the world would Jacobs do that?" Long asked.

"To force your hand," said Hector matter-of-factly. "CIA tells you that Iran has a nuke. In their mind we slow-walk it so they tell the world. Now we have to act."

"Get Greenglass in here," Long ordered. "I want someone hanging by their fingernails for this."

Hector opened the door a crack, stuck his head out, and asked the president's assistant to buzz Truman Greenglass. Three minutes later Greenglass appeared at the door.

"Yes, Mr. President?" He looked warily at Hector slumped in a chair, looking like a punching bag. Long was visibly agitated.

"Get in here, T. G.," Long said curtly. Greenglass took the chair on the right side of the president's desk. Long looked him up and down. "Do you think there's any chance that someone in your shop leaked this story about Iran to the *New York Times*?"

"No, Mr. President," Greenglass replied. "The reporter called me and asked me to be a confirming source, which I declined to do. By the time they talked to us, the story was already written. This definitely came from somewhere outside the White House."

The president frowned. "Charlie thinks it was CIA."

"Makes sense. And probably high up."

"Jacobs?"

Greenglass shrugged. "I doubt it. He's too much of a patriot."

"We need to take them down a notch," Long said firmly. "I mean, when has the CIA ever been right? They put Saddam Hussein in power in Iraq in 1953. They botched the Bay of Pigs. They said the Soviets were a major threat two years before the Soviet Union collapsed, and they were dead wrong about WMD in Iraq."

"No one wants to take them on," said Greenglass. "The corporate culture at Langley goes back to Wild Bill Donovan and the OSS. It's a bunch of Ivy Leaguers playing spy games. Crossing them is dangerous."

"The problem is this could dominate the news cycle for days. Jimmerson's going to be all over cable calling on us to take military action against Iran," Hector said in disgust. "Talk radio will erupt. Everyone will genuflect to the Israel lobby, demanding action."

"Well, we can't confirm this report," Greenglass warned. "It compromises sources and methods and puts you in a box, Mr. President."

"Change the subject, then. Make the *Times* the issue," suggested Hector. "Irresponsible journalism, anonymous sources, endangers national security—"

"Unpatriotic," snapped Long.

"All the above. I'll make sure Lisa is loaded for bear for the press briefing," said Hector.

"Gentlemen, we're sleeping with the enemy." Long's eyes blazed as he tapped the desk firmly with his index finger. "Langley's a snake pit. The joint chiefs aren't much better. They're cutting the legs out from under us."

"The bureaucracy is fighting back," said Hector.

"This isn't normal bureaucratic infighting, Charlie," Long seethed. "I have no problem with internal dissent. But selling out the country by compromising its intelligence-gathering capability is unacceptable."

"I think we should say that."

"You bet we should. And you tell Golden to look into what we can do within the chalk marks to plug these leaks. That includes a grand jury issuing subpoenas to reporters."

"I hope we don't end up with the *Times* reporter on a hunger strike in the DC lockup," said Greenglass.

"Judith Miller, call your office," interjected Hector.

"If that's what it takes, so be it." The president glanced away, staring out the window at the Rose Garden. "T. G., call Jacobs right now. Tell him I want the person who did this escorted out of Langley by security."

Hector exited the Oval Office and headed back down the hall to his own office, head down, wheels turning, his thoughts a jumble. People passed him in the hallway, but he never made eye contact. The thought entered his mind: he wished he could go back to being just a member of Congress. What an easy job that had been compared to White House chief of staff. Now in addition to managing the president, he had to deal with the fallout of a national security leak without committing Nixonian excesses, and find a conservative Supreme Court nominee confirmable by a Democratic Senate.

"Buzz Lisa and ask her to come to my office, stat," he said gruffly to his assistant and closed the door behind him.

LISA ROBINSON WALKED INTO the White House briefing room at 12:30 p.m. and stepped to the podium. Every seat was filled, and an unusually large crowd of reporters lined the walls. The networks turned on their cameras as print reporters pulled out their tape recorders and flipped open steno pads. Rumors had flown all morning that the White House was going to take on the *Times* in a frontal assault. Everyone waited for the fireworks to begin. "I have a statement and then I'll take your questions," Lisa began. She cleared her throat. "There is a report in the *New York Times* today based on unnamed, anonymous sources claiming to relay information contained in the Presidents Daily Brief, a summary of intelligence provided to the president by the CIA. This administration has a strict policy against commenting on leaks of classified material. We will neither confirm nor deny this story. But if someone did provide the *Times* with information contained in the president's brief, it is a felony and a serious breach of the law and our national security. The *Times's* decision to print this story was reckless and irresponsible. Journalists do not surrender their citizenship or its obligations when they obtain a press badge." Someone in the back of the room let out an audible gasp. Lisa paused, leveling her gaze. "Any questions?"

"So you're not disputing the story. The CIA has informed the president that Iran has a weaponized nuclear device?" asked CNN.

"I cannot comment on the president's classified daily intelligence briefings."

"The Israeli ambassador told Reuters today that unless the United States acts militarily, Israel may be forced to take action on its own," said CBS News.

Lisa arched her eyebrows. "Is there a question there?"

"The question is, how do you react to Israel threatening to act unilaterally?"

"I have not seen the ambassador's statement. Israel is a sovereign nation. We do not tell them what to do. Besides, I don't do hypotheticals."

"The IAEA is shortly going to issue a report on Iran's uranium enrichment program, and the preliminary indications are that they will say their investigation is basically stalled due to Iran's lack of cooperation. What are your hopes for additional sanctions by the UN? Or is military action the only remaining option?" asked the *Washington Times*.

"Well, the IAEA report only serves to underscore that Iran is refusing to cooperate with the international community. I don't really have an update in terms of additional sanctions. As you know, the secretary of state is in the Middle East as we speak and is seeking to resolve this situation by the diplomatic process underway, not by military action, which is the choice of last resort," Lisa replied. "But as the president has said, all options are on the table."

"Lisa, how would you characterize the U.S. relationship with Iran after this revelation?" asked the *Washington Post*. "Is it belligerent? Would it be fair to characterize Iran as a belligerent nation vis-à-vis the U.S.?"

"As the President has said in the past, it is a very difficult and tense relationship."

"That's it?" shot back the *Post*. "Isn't this a virtual declaration of war by Iran?"

"I'm not going to label it based on an unconfirmed press account that relied on anonymous sources," said Lisa, taking another dig at the *Times*. "Iran's nuclear ambitions and its unwillingness to live up to its obligations under the Nuclear Non-proliferation Agreement is destabilizing to the region and the world. That's where we are right now."

The *New York Times* correspondent had heard enough. "You seem to be saying that any media outlet that reports on what our government has learned about Iran's nuclear program is committing treason. Is that your claim?" asked the *Times*.

"You're trying to put words in my mouth," Lisa fired back. "I said it was reckless and irresponsible. If the story was based on the president's daily brief, providing that information to anyone—including a reporter—is a felony."

"Is the administration planning to prosecute the source or the reporter?" asked UPI.

"That question should be directed to the Department of Justice."

"But you don't rule out prosecuting reporters who publish such material?"

"I have already noted that to provide such information is a serious violation of the law, but we do not comment on criminal investigations, hypothetical or otherwise, from this podium." Frustrated, the press corps peppered Lisa with hostile questions for another twenty minutes. She never budged. The parlor game in Washington shifted from who might replace Peter Corbin Franklin to who was willing to risk a prison sentence to force Long's hand on Iran.

IT WAS 9:52 ON Sunday morning, and the Speaker of the House strolled into the Fox News green room on Capitol Hill, a large cup of Starbucks in his hand, his features hardened like a marble statue. He had already been slathered in makeup, his helmet hair blasted with hair spray. He ignored the spread of bagels, danish, and fresh fruit on the table. Like a boxer in training, Gerry Jimmerson disciplined his appetites in pursuit of a bigger prize, this one on the set of Marvin Myers's highly rated public affairs show, Washington's version of must-see TV. Jimmerson was wired: he took a swig of the Starbucks, the double shot of espresso hitting his bloodstream. His press aide sat on the couch monitoring the television set, his posture reflecting the low morale of a man who knew his boss wouldn't listen to his advice, so why even bother?

The floor director entered the room. "Mr. Speaker, we're ready for you on the set."

Jimmerson followed him to the cavernous set, its thermostat set to the temperature of a meat freezer. Marvin Myers shook his hand but otherwise ignored him, his eyes glued to blue index cards that contained his questions. After the theme music and a program opening rolled on video, the floor director counted down with his fingers and then pointed at Myers.

"Joining us now is the Speaker of the House, Gerald Jimmerson. Mr. Jimmerson, welcome back," Myers said with hollow hospitality.

"Thank you, Marvin, it's good to be here," Jimmerson said.

"The chairman of the House Judiciary Committee, Sam Manion, announced this week that he will hold hearings on the condition of Supreme Court Justice Peter Corbin Franklin," Myers began. He went straight for the jugular. "Do you support this move?"

"Well, first of all, Marvin, Justice Franklin is in all of our thoughts and prayers," replied Jimmerson in his disarming Tar Heel drawl. "His condition is serious. We pray for his full recovery." He paused, his face etched with concern. "But if he does not recover and were to remain in a comatose state, it has the possibility to render an entire branch of our government incapable of functioning. I think that is an appropriate issue for the committee to look at."

"What do you say to the critics who charge this is simply a predicate to removing Justice Franklin from the court?"

"No one wants that, least of all me. But as long as Justice Franklin remains in a coma, the Supreme Court cannot fully conduct its business. Cases on appeal will be in a permanent state of limbo." He made animated hand gestures to drive home the point. "Justice delayed is justice denied, Marvin. People seeking redress before the federal courts need to know that their cases will be heard and adjudicated without unnecessary delay."

"So if Justice Franklin does not recover, you don't rule out removing him by impeachment." Myers phrased the explosive words as a statement, not a question.

Jimmerson visibly flinched. "I'm not going to prejudge anything until the Judiciary Committee does its job first," he said, scrambling for cover. "That's why Chairman Manion is holding hearings. But without addressing the Franklin situation directly, as a general matter, the removal of a judge who cannot perform his or her duties is well within Congress's purview."

Myers nearly came across the table. "But a Supreme Court justice has never been impeached. Aren't you concerned about a backlash?"

"No, I'm not," shot back Jimmerson. "First, while it is true that no Supreme Court justice has ever been impeached, that is only because they resigned prior to the Senate's voting to do so, as was the case with Abe Fortas in 1969. I will defer to Chairman Sam Manion—"

"But you appointed Sam Manion. He is one of your closest allies in the House," interrupted Myers. "Do you expect anyone to believe that he is acting contrary to your wishes?"

"Sam Manion is his own man," said Jimmerson with a smile. "He's no wallflower." He took a sip of water from a blue coffee cup, staring down Myers. "I have great respect for Chairman Mansion and the members of the House Judiciary Committee, and I think the committee process should proceed without interference from either side."

"But just to be clear, Mr. Speaker," replied Myers, "you have no objection to removing Justice Franklin if it is determined that he is incapacitated?"

"Marvin, I'm not going to speculate about that. We all honor Justice Franklin's service. Right now the best thing we can all do is pray for his recovery," Jimmerson said firmly. "But at some point the wheels of justice cannot grind to a halt because of one justice's medical condition. I think everyone agrees on that."

"Thank you, Mr. Speaker." It took every ounce of self-discipline Myers possessed to keep from letting out a victory yell on the air. Jimmerson had walked right into his punch. The next morning every newspaper in America would lead with the screaming headline: "Jimmerson Refuses to Rule Out Removal of Ailing Franklin." Every one of those hundreds of stories would credit the news to his program. Myers still had the mojo, which was why he was the unquestioned king of the Sunday shows.

TEN

Jay thought he might bake to a crisp in the red Fiat convertible with the top down and the sun blazing overhead as they pulled off the main highway and crunched over the gravel of a long driveway, a trail of white dust rising behind. Deftly guiding the steering wheel with the palm of his hand, the driver steered the car through acre after acre of sun-baked vineyards, pointing at various wineries. The car lurched from side to side, the tires occasionally spinning on the gravel.

"This is the shortcut!" the guide shouted.

Jay Noble wondered if Guido, his guide for the day, knew where he was going. They had been careening across the hills of Tuscany for almost two hours, gazing at the breathtaking scenery, and there was still no sign of the famous Fellissi winery. Guido, a thin, hyperkinetic man in his mid-thirties with an expansive face, sunken cheeks, penetrating eyes, and a crew cut that made him look a little like a character actor in a prison film, entertained Jay with a running monologue on the Tuscan wine country and his philosophy of life, which could be summed up crisply: eat, drink, and be merry.

After a final sharp right turn down a driveway, they pulled up to the Fellissi winery. It was both charming and imposing, a large house with several out buildings, a courtyard, and a garden, all surrounded by vineyards for as far as the eye could see. Jay stepped out of the Fiat and stretched his legs, inhaling a deep breath. The smell of jasmine relaxed him. The view from the yard was enchanting, miles of vineyards and wheat fields as far as the eye could see, the faint outline of the spires of San Gimignano in the distance.

Mauro Fellisi came down the stairs of his house in a welcoming gait, speaking loudly to Guido in rapid-fire Italian. He wore blue jeans, scuffed work boots, a white T-shirt, and a blue flannel shirt over his bulky frame. His bulging belly and too-small head stood atop long, spindly legs. His skull was deeply tanned, his bald head fringed with white hair.

"Bonjourno!" he shouted before asking a question in an agitated manner.

Guido smiled. "He wants to know where we have been," he said with a wink.

Guido introduced him as the famous political strategist for President Bob Long. Jay stood there in the 100-degree heat, grinning sheepishly. Mauro greeted him like a long-lost friend, shaking his hand firmly and kissing him on both cheeks. Mauro's farmer's tan and calloused hands betrayed a life spent working the Tuscan soil, his deep blue eyes and shy manner reflecting the genius of one of Italy's most famous vintners.

More rapid-fire Italian, followed by a wave to the main building of the small winery.

"We eat first!" Guido translated. "Then he will give you a tour of the winery."

They walked into the basement of the home, which resembled a sunken warehouse, surrounded by gigantic oak barrels large enough to hold a small family, all filled with aging wine. A large table, covered with a checkerboard tablecloth, was spread with cheese, sausage, bread, and caprese. They each pulled up a chair. Jay noticed there was one empty seat.

"Gabriella!" called out Mauro.

Jay turned around to see a gorgeous woman in her early thirties gliding toward him wearing snug jeans and a ribbed, sleeveless T-shirt, black belt with an oversized silver buckle that pinched her slim waist, and black wedges. She seemed to move in slow motion. With her volleyball-player legs, long neck, high cheekbones, espresso eyes, Midlothian abdomen, and flowing brownish-blonde hair, she struck Jay as a flesh-and-blood pallet of Italian womanhood. The Tuscan sun had toasted her shoulders and arms to a deep brown. Small dots of sweat beaded on her nose and neck. Jay felt his legs go rubbery.

"You friend of Guido," she said warmly in broken English. She smiled, revealing perfect white teeth that gleamed against her tan.

"Yes," replied Jay.

"I am Gabriella," she said. "Welcome."

"Well of course you are," he exclaimed. He motioned to the lunch await-ing them on the table. "Perfecto!" Gabriella laughed at his attempt at Italian. Jay extended his hand, and she shook it. Her skin felt soft in Jay's hand. Mauro and Guido grinned.

"Eat! Eat!" she ordered, and the men sat down. With the help of a middle-aged woman with a shock of dark hair and weathered skin, Gabriella brought the first course to the table, a heaping bowl of pasta.

"Who is the other woman?" asked Jay out of the corner of his mouth to Guido.

"Mauro's live-in girlfriend. She and her teen-age son live here with Mauro. His wife passed away about five years ago."

"And Gabriella is his daughter?"

"Yes," replied Guido. He read Jay's look. "*Very* single," he chuckled beneath his breath.

Mauro made a big production of bringing out the first bottle of wine for lunch. He started with a 1999 Brunello, pouring it into a glass, swirling it in the bottom, breathing in the aroma, and then taking a sip, letting it run across his tongue as he tasted it. He nodded with approval, then began methodically to pour it into each glass around the table. He and Guido exchanged words that appeared to be related to the quality of the wine.

"This is the first of several bottles," Guido warned. "So pace yourself."

Jay swirled the wine himself and drank from his glass. The taste was smooth and musky, with a hint of oak. As Mauro rattled on, Guido trans-lated, giving Jay a crash course on the art of growing the Montelchino grape. To qualify as a Brunello, Guido explained, the wine had to be made from only a select grape and age for five years. The acres that could grow the proper grape were limited, so by definition a good Brunello was limited in supply.

Jay was far more interested in Gabriella than the wine. She was ach-ingly attractive, and he found himself smitten and distracted, unable to stay focused on the conversation. Her tom-boy personality only made her more compelling. As the daughter of one of the wealthiest land owners in Italy, she was well connected—not just in Italy but in America. Jay soon learned that among those who regularly visited and were investors in the Fellissi winery were Rupert Murdoch and Warren Buffet. Gabriella had vacationed on Larry Ellison's yacht. She oversaw the business side of the winery.

"I've seen you on television before," Gabriella said, her eyes twinkling with mischief.

"Here in Italy?" asked Jay, surprised.

"No, in the States. I was there during the campaign."

"I hope I didn't say anything stupid," Jay said with a smile.

"Oh, no," Gabriella replied. She flashed him a smile. "You're cuter in person."

Jay felt a sudden rush of excitement. Was she flirting? "I'll take that as a compliment."

"I'm cuter in person, too, don't you think?" asked Guido, happily joining the conversation.

Gabriella smiled and reached over to pat Guido on the cheek. "Yes, my darling, you are much cuter in person."

"He doesn't look cute to me," joked Jay. "He looks like a stray dog."

"I'm not supposed to look cute to you," fired back Guido. He laughed. "If I was, that would sure make headlines in the States, no?"

"How odd you should come here, of all places," said Gabriella, her gaze fixed on Jay.

"I came halfway around the world. I thought it was to run a campaign. But I think it might have been to become friends with you and your father," said Jay. He hoped the line wasn't too corny. Gabriella smiled, raising one eyebrow suggestively.

The wine flowed easily as Mauro's girlfriend brought the entrée of wild boar and fresh baked vegetables. Mauro complained that the first bottle had the taste of cork. No one else had noticed, but Mauro replaced it with a 2003 Brunello, which was fabulous. Later he switched to a 1995, and then finally to a 1999 Reserve, made from the finest grapes of the harvest, personally selected by Mauro. By now the entire party was having a good time, laughing too loud and too long at one another's jokes. Jay found himself laughing even harder when they said something funny in Italian, even though he didn't understand it.

"So what brings you to Italy?" asked Gabriella. "Running one country isn't enough for you?"

Jay burst out laughing. He leaned into her, putting his finger over his lips. "Don't tell anyone," he said in a half whisper, giggling. "After this, it's on to Great Britain!"

"No, the food there is *terrible*," she protested, her mouth forming a pout. "Do France next! I'll visit you in Paris. I'll show you the best restaurants and the finest wines." She waved her hands in the air as she spoke. "I will help you take over Europe, one country at a time!"

Jay could hardly believe his ears. He began to feel warm and tingly all over. Was it the wine, or Gabriella? He suspected it was a bit of both.

"Gabriella does business all over Europe," Guido said. "She is beautiful, of course." Gabriella blushed. "But her beauty is deceiving. She is a very savvy businesswoman."

"I have no doubt," said Jay, taking another sip of wine. Gabriella smiled.

After lunch, topped off by grappa (a 100-proof port made from the fermented skins of grapes) and a cup of espresso, Mauro and Gabriella escorted Jay through the winery, showing him the oak casks, the vineyards, and the bottling operation. He slapped down a credit card and impulsively bought $5,000 worth of wine, letting Guido and Mauro choose the cases. By now he was flying high, intoxicated by Gabriella's presence and the Fellissi empire.

As they walked back to the car, their shoes crunching across the gravel, Guido asked, "Why don't you ship one of the cases of reserve to Jay in Rome? He's there for the month to work on the Brodi campaign."

"Si, si!" said Mauro.

"Only if Gabriella personally delivers it," said Jay with a sly smile.

"Sure," Gabriella said. "But you have to share some with me."

"Absolutely!" Jay exclaimed. "I have a suite at the Hassler. Come and visit."

"Don't let her anywhere near Brodi!" joked Guido. He repeated the line to Mauro, who rolled his eyes and guffawed. Brodi was a notorious skirt chaser.

Gabriella gave Jay her card and scribbled her cell number on the front, saying something about having to be in Rome the next week. They all exchanged hugs and pecks on the cheek, and Jay, with two bottles of reserve for the road compliments of Mauro, climbed into the Fiat. As they pulled away and screamed down the road, Guido turned to him, wagging his finger.

"You are a bad boy!" he shouted gleefully, banging the steering wheel with the palm of his hand. "You were shamelessly chasing Gabriella!"

"Was it that obvious?" Jay asked. He furrowed his brow. "Oh, well," he said.

CONGRESSMAN SAM MANION OF Iowa sat in a small anteroom filled with government-issue couches and chairs that resembled a no-money-down furniture showroom. Glasses on the end of his nose, dark circles enveloping his tired eyes, his thinning brown hair combed and sprayed without a strand out of place, he resembled a trial lawyer awaiting a jury verdict. He sat on the couch, legs crossed, telephone cradled against his shoulder as he scanned notes in his hand. A staff aide sat across from him, leaning on the edge of his seat, chewing on his fingernails.

"Mr. Speaker," Manion said into the receiver. "I've got the votes. Wanted to let you know where we stood. Just waiting for the green light and we pull the trigger."

"So were you able to pull over a Democrat?" asked Gerald Jimmerson in his silky Southern baritone.

"Not a one," Manion replied with a chuckle. "Mr. Speaker, this is the most ideologically polarized committee in the House. I'm not gonna get a Democrat. Not now, not ever. I had to hold the hands of my squishy Republicans just to get a majority."

Jimmerson laughed knowingly. "It would have been better if we could have gotten at least one D. I guess they're not going to carry our water on this one."

"Nope," agreed Manion. "They're in the bunker. It's going to be like the Clinton impeachment all over again. The Democrats are playing to their base, and we're giving our guys a backbone transplant so they'll do the right thing."

Jimmerson sighed. "Well, if you've got the votes, I say we go."

"Consider it done, Mr. Speaker." Manion hung up the phone and looked directly into the eyes of his staff aide. "That guy has got the gonads of an elephant."

"So he wants to jump without a single Democrat?"

Manion shot him the weary look of an abused understudy. "He'd run over his own mother if he had the votes to do it." They both laughed.

There were two quick raps on the door. Another aide stuck his head through the door. "Mr. Chairman, we're ready."

"Showtime!" said Manion. He walked out of the anteroom, crossed a narrow hallway, and walked through an open door into the cavernous hearing room of the House Judiciary Committee. It was in this very room in the Cannon House Office Building that the Judiciary Committee had passed articles of impeachment against Richard Nixon in 1974. It was the same room where House Republicans passed two articles impeaching Bill Clinton on a straight-party vote during the Monica Lewinsky scandal in 1998. As he stepped through the door and into the blaze of the television lights, Manion heard the rustle of the press corps, the explosion of still cameras, and murmurs from the assembled throng. Cable newscasts broke away from regular coverage to broadcast the proceedings live.

Manion sat down in his chair at the center of the dais and raised his gavel, ceremonially banging it with authority. "This meeting of the committee will please come to order," he said firmly, his voice booming over the sound system. "I have a brief statement, and then I will ask the ranking member of the other party to make his statement. Each member of the committee will then have five minutes to make their own statement before we proceed to a final vote." He paused and looked around the committee room, glancing down each end of the dais, then quickly snapped his head back to the papers he held in his hand.

"This committee has before it one article of impeachment of Supreme Court Justice Peter Corbin Franklin," Manion began. "On January 22 of this year, Justice Franklin suffered a cerebral hemorrhage that left him in an irreversible comatose condition, incapacitating him and thereby rendering him unable to carry out his duties as a member of the highest court. Under Article Three, Section X, the House is empowered to impeach and the Senate to remove a judge so incapacitated."

"Lies! Lies!" shouted a protestor from the back of the room. "Peter Corbin Franklin lives!" The wild-eyed, slightly disheveled woman wearing thick glasses had stripped off her overcoat to reveal a yellow shirt with the slogan "Stop the War against Women" emblazoned in black letters. Two muscled Capitol police hustled her toward the door. She began to kick and squirm as she shouted. "Stop the lies!"

Manion banged the gavel three times. "Spectators will refrain from outbursts or any other disruptive activity, or they will be removed."

The protestor shouted still louder. The members of the committee watched with bemused expressions on their faces. The Capitol police dragged her from the room, her limp legs dragging behind.

"Few members of the Court have served with such honor and distinction. No one has ever brought more passion and intelligence to the cause of justice than Justice Franklin," Manion continued. "But the fact is his medical condition is grave. I regret that none of his doctors chose to appear before this committee. But the expert testimony we heard from other witnesses made clear that the stroke he suffered was massive and incapacitating. None of us on either side of the aisle have asked for this sad duty. But it is a duty we cannot shirk, and we cannot deny. There are times in public life when we must choose between what is politically expedient and what is best for the country. This is one of those times. Therefore, I will reluctantly and sadly vote for the article of impeachment removing Justice Franklin."

Manion turned to the ranking Democrat on the committee, a bespectacled and fiery liberal from Boston, Massachusetts, Alan Freedman.

"Mr. Chairman, fellow members of the committee, ladies and gentlemen, what is occurring here today is a disgrace. It is an affront to this body, the Supreme Court, the separation of powers, and the Constitution itself." Freeman spat the words in an agitated squeak, rising slightly in his chair in righteous indignation. His voice quavered with anger. "On the basis of highly speculative testimony from doctors who had never treated or examined Justice Franklin, this committee is rushing in an unprecedented action to remove a member of the Supreme Court. This is a kangaroo court, Mr. Chairman." He held up a sheaf of papers, waving them in the air. Still camera shutters exploded to record the scene. "I hold in my hands affidavits from some of the leading brain surgeons in the country. They all say that a patient in Justice Franklin's condition could recover from his condition and return to this position on the court. He deserves the benefit of the doubt." He turned to Manion, his eyes shooting darts. "Today's action will be viewed by future generations as one of the darkest days recorded in the history of the Congress."

Loud cheers erupted from liberal partisans who had packed the hearing room. Manion sat impassively, his face expressionless, his eyes stone cold. He had the votes, and their venting meant nothing. After two hours of pontificating and finger-pointing, much of it heated and emotional, the

committee voted twenty-three to nineteen to send the article of impeachment against Peter Corbin Franklin to the House floor. All the Republican
members of the committee voted for it; all the Democrats voted against it.
Manion had done his job, but a nagging doubt gnawed at his gut: was he the
next Peter Rodino or the next Henry Hyde? Was he striking a blow for the
Constitution, or was he on an errand, however vaunted its motive, that was
doomed to fail? He feared it might be the latter.

ELEVEN

G. G. Hoterman's Falcon III banked as it descended to two thousand feet and made its final approach. G. G. glanced out the window at the seemingly endless expanse of turquoise water rippling beneath the sun and the white beaches of the islands. A massive hulk of a man, he resembled a human bowling ball sheathed in a custom French-cuffed dress shirt from Charvet's and a four-thousand dollar tailored suit. He felt a sudden jolt of adrenalin—or was it the three cups of coffee and two Diet Cokes he had sucked down during the flight? G. G. was about to meet Stephen Fox, the Internet billionaire, at his seaside compound in the Turks and the Caicos, where Stephen escaped when he got bored of his Newport Beach mansion or his 140-foot yacht, which he kept docked in Bermuda. Fox was one of G. G.'s "angels," a multimillion dollar donor to Democratic causes and a client of G. G.'s law and lobbying firm, Hoterman and Schiff.

It was a dicey time for both men. G. G. had barely dodged indictment in the Dele-gate cash-for-votes scandal that torched Sal Stanley's presidential campaign and might yet send his political consigliere Michael Kaplan to prison. Fox, meanwhile, was under investigation by the Federal Trade Commission, the IRS, and two separate divisions of the Justice Department. The public integrity division was still looking into Fox's contributions to the qualified 501c4 that had allegedly paid bribes to delegates in the Dele-gate scandal; the antitrust division had sued Wildfire.com, the Internet giant acquired by Fox's private equity firm, alleging that it had improperly discriminated against competitors in its online advertising business. Fox lived perpetually in the fast lane, veering into gray areas that constantly attracted the attention of regulators. He hired gumshoes and private eyes to dump-ster dive and dig up dirt on competitors and retained an army of lawyers to sue his many enemies. Sometimes he put a law firm on retainer just so they wouldn't sue him. Stephen and G. G. lived in the rarefied world where business intersected with hardball politics, where destroying one's foes was blood sport, and where politics was just another means to the ultimate end of making the almighty buck.

That went double when it came to their relationship with the opposite sex. Fox was on wife number three, the beautiful and ravishing Felicity, who sat on numerous charity boards, raised millions for the arts, and seri-ally decorated homes in Bermuda, Manhattan, Silicon Valley, Switzerland, Aspen, and the Turks and Caicos. G. G. was on his second mistress, the striking Deirdre Rahall, who had departed his law firm in disgrace when she and her brother were implicated in Dele-gate. She had testified before the federal grand jury investigating the scandal and became tabloid fodder and cable news candy after being romantically linked to G. G. She sat across from G. G., her blonde hair cascading across her shoulders, her trim figure folded into the seat, legs crossed, wearing a Lily Pulitzer pink-and-green skirt with a white blouse and pink heels. Also on board was Christy Love, clad in a Bebe T-shirt, skinny jeans, and a blue-and-white spectator jacket. As chair-woman of Pro-Choice PAC, Christy was one of the most important women political leaders in the country.

After the plane taxied to a stop in front of the nondescript FBO, they cleared customs and deplaned, loading their luggage into the trunk of a Mercedes sedan that drove them to Fox's compound. After a two-mile drive, they pulled up to the deceptively inconspicuous front door. A butler wear-ing a white coat with gold trim and white polo shorts opened the door and escorted them to the beach, where Felicity and Stephen were having a drink at the poolside bar under a thatched roof.

"G. G., you made it!" boomed Stephen. He caught sight of Deirdre and Christy and his face lit up. "I hope you're going to introduce me to these beautiful women!"

"These are my DC power chicks," joked G. G. "Meet Deirdre Rahall, who was most recently at my law firm, and Christy Love, the most powerful woman in Washington."

"I am not!" protested Christy. She leveled her baby blues at Stephen, shaking her head. "Don't believe a word he says," she said with a faint Long Island accent.

"Don't sell yourself short," said Stephen as he walked toward Christy, greeting her with a peck on each cheek, his hands grasping hers. "Your reputation precedes you." He glanced up and down approvingly at Deirdre before kissing her politely. "Deirdre, so glad you could join us." He glanced at G. G. "It sure relieves me from having nothing but G. G.'s fat frame to look at!" Everyone laughed nervously while G. G. cracked an embarrassed grin. Stephen then pivoted in the direction of Felicity, who had walked around from behind the bar. He put his arm around her narrow waist. "Meet my wife Felicity."

As usual, Felicity looked like a million bucks. She wore a sleeveless teal, turtleneck, ribbed sweater; black pants with aqua threading that made her look even taller than her five feet, eight inches, black zippered Dior heels; and a stunning five-carat David Yurman black onyx and diamond necklace with matching earrings and popcorn bracelet. Felicity shook everyone's hands. "Welcome to our little paradise," she said.

"It really is," said G. G., stepping forward and putting his hands on his hips, gazing out over the Caribbean. "What a wonderful respite from Washington."

"Especially with Bob Long in the White House," said Stephen.

"Tell me about it," muttered Christy, her voice laced with disgust.

"Don't ruin dinner by talking about Long!" ordered Felicity. "I've got a great meal planned. Save the politics for after-dinner drinks and cigars."

Over a round of incredibly strong margaritas, the conversation flowed easily with talk centered on children, careers, and travel, avoiding thorny topics like Dele-gate or G. G.'s wife throwing him out of the house after learning about Deirdre in the newspaper. After watching the sun set over the ocean, they walked to a candlelit glass-and-cane dining room table. The chef presented a sushi tuna appetizer that featured soy sauce flowing down a waterfall powered by a small electric motor. The sauce flowed into a small dipping bowl.

"I didn't eat like this growing up in south Alabama!" joked G. G.

"Wait until you see the entrée," said Felicity. "This chef is an *absolute genius*. He used to work at our favorite restaurant in Manhattan. We liked him so much that Stephen hired him."

Felicity appeared oblivious to the fact that most people didn't hire help from five-star restaurants to cook for them at home. Stephen just smiled awkwardly.

The main course did not disappoint: thinly cut slices of seared Kobe beef that melted in their mouths. Then came a key lime pie presented with a mango puree and splayed kiwi fruit with whipped cream. Felicity made a big deal of calling their chef to the table, where everyone applauded and showered him with compliments.

After dinner the women chitchatted over decaf coffee while the men retired for cigars. Stephen signaled G. G. to walk with him back to the thatch hut by the beach.

"Cigar?" he asked.

"Sure. What are we smoking?"

"Aroma de Cuba. It's a turn-of-the-century cigar made famous by Winston Churchill. It's my favorite cigar right now," said Stephen. They both lit up and took long drags, the lit ends glowing in the dark. Stephen shifted gears. "Well, we lost the election, in spite of our best efforts. Stanley blew it. He should have put Long on the ticket. Fortunately, we still have the Senate, where we have an outside chance of blocking Long's agenda. I know you didn't come here to take a dip in the ocean. So what's the strategy and how can I help?"

G. G. leaned in close, holding his cigar to the side, and raised his chin, blowing a whiff of smoke into the air, where the wind took it. "Stephen, we can end Long's presidency in its first year. Peter Corbin Franklin is not going to make it. Long's going to nominate a right-winger to pacify the Federalist Society crowd. If we can beat him, it will be Long's Waterloo."

"No question. But Franklin is still on life support."

"The House is going to impeach Franklin," Hoterman said with clinical detachment. "The Senate won't go along. Once he dies, whenever that is, Long will appoint a strict constructionist in the model of Scalia, Roberts, or Alito." He took a puff from the cigar and exhaled. "That's where we come in. We have to defeat the nominee, or the court will overturn *Roe*. This is like taking down Bork under Reagan. Let's face it, Reagan never really recovered. Everyone remembers Iran-contra, but it was really defeating Bork that signaled the end of the Reagan era."

"I agree with your analysis 100 percent, and I agree we have to stop Long," said Stephen. "But when it comes to his Supreme Court nominee, I have a problem."

G. G. felt his stomach tighten. He had been counting on Stephen for a million dollars. He tried to maintain his composure. "What problem?" he asked.

Stephen lifted his cigar and took a long puff, the ash turning bright orange. "We lost the Wildfire antitrust case before the DC Circuit in a split decision. We're appealing to the Supreme Court."

"Sure, I know," said G. G. "We're working the Democratic state AGs and lobbying the Judiciary Committee members on the Hill, remember? I'm all over it."

"I know what you're doing. So you understand this is a pending legal issue. The largest investment of my equity fund is at stake." He lowered his voice. "We're reaching out to Golden to see if we can settle." Stephen turned toward the ocean, his eyes staring into the blackness. "Franklin is a New Deal liberal. I did everything I could to beat Long, but ironically his nominee will be more pro-business than Franklin." Stephen shook his head, laughing. "So the guy I tried to beat could end up saving me billions of dollars."

"But are you sure you need the vote of Long's nominee?" asked G. G. hopefully, watching desperately as Fox's contribution went down the drain.

"We don't know," Stephen said. "But we can't take any chances. Wildfire's ability to innovate and utilize personalized and predictive consumer data to drive online advertising will be destroyed. My investors will be out twenty-two billion dollars." He looked into G. G.'s eyes. "That's a lot of money, pal."

G. G. kept his game face on, but inside he was reeling. He had come to view Fox as an ATM—insert card, enter password, take cash. "I don't see that as a problem," he said smoothly, unflappable as always on the outside. "We just have to make sure that whoever Long picks to replace any extremist we defeat is good on antitrust."

Fox shot G. G. a withering look. "That's quite a bank shot when the future of my equity fund is on the line."

"Okay, okay," Hoterman said, reading Stephen's doubt. "Just give us an initial contribution to do the polling, focus groups, and oppo research and prepare the ground game. We won't use anything you give toward any negative ads against Long's nominee until we run it by you first."

"How much?" asked Stephen.

"One million."

"Alright," Stephen said. "But no paid ads."

"You have my word," G. G. said smoothly. In reality he would use it for whatever he wanted.

Stephen started walking slowly back to the house. "Deirdre seems very nice," he said, changing the subject.

"She is," said G. G. His separation from Edwina was an awkward topic. He was not surprised that Fox had raised it first—he had not wanted proactively to mention the fact that his marriage was on the rocks. He had hoped to pretend that his relationship with Deirdre was purely professional. Clearly Stephen was not fooled.

"G. G., you've never told me how to live my life, and I've never told you how to live yours," Stephen said quietly, his voice barely audible above the ocean breeze and the crash of the waves on the beach. "I'm the last person to judge anyone. Heck, I'm on my third marriage."

G. G. shot him a knowing glance.

Stephen grabbed him by the shoulders and pulled him close. "But if you can, try to make things work out with Edwina. I walked away from two marriages before I married Felicity." His face glowed, the moon's rays illuminating his features. G. G. saw his face etched with emotion. "I love her, and we have a terrific marriage. But I'm telling you from firsthand experience, the grass is never greener on the other side. All the problems you're dealing with in your current marriage will follow you."

"I hear you," G. G. said noncommittally. "But I'm not sure I can. I don't think Edwina will take me back. And I love Deirdre."

"I understand," said Stephen. "It may well be that you can't reconcile with Edwina. But take it from me, if you marry Deirdre, she'll be your wife. You'll have all the issues with her, plus all the issues with children and your first family following you. And Deirdre will be just as crazy as Edwina." He screwed up his face. "They're all crazy, don't you know that?"

G. G. laughed. "I'm afraid I do," he said.

They walked up the beach, sand pushing between their toes, and rinsed their feet off at a shower station before reentering the house. G. G. was stunned by the emotional force of Stephen baring his soul. Fox had it all: gorgeous wife, homes on every continent, jets and yachts at his beck and call, and billions of dollars. But he was still haunted by his failure to build a lasting relationship with the wife of his youth. It frightened G. G., for he saw his own future in Stephen's pain.

"SENATOR!" SAID BOB LONG into the telephone with theatrical bravado. "I understand you wanted to talk about something." He glanced across the desk at Charlie Hector, who had put the call on his schedule, and winked.

"Yes, Mr. President, I did," said Joe Penneymounter, the edge in his voice evident. "I hope you'll forgive me for being direct, but I think it's only right that I tell you where I stand on the Peter Corbin Franklin situation."

"Sure," said Long. "I appreciate it. What's on your mind?"

"Well, a lot, actually. First, the House impeachment resolution is going nowhere in the Senate. I don't think there are forty-two votes. It's dead on arrival."

"Mmmmmm," Long replied.

"Second, I frankly view this whole thing as a dangerous infringement on the separation of powers," Penneymounter continued, the words tumbling out on top of one another, his voice rising. "This is an attempt by the Congress to reconstitute the highest court in the land by legislative fiat. It's the worst case of court-packing since FDR in 1937. I feel like I'm living in a Third World country. This is America, not Venezuela, for crying out loud."

"I hear you, Joe," said Long sympathetically, trying to placate him. "I warned Jimmerson. When we met here at the White House for what was supposed to be an informal get-together, he gave me a heads-up about all this, and I told him there was no way on God's green earth that the Senate would act on an impeachment resolution."

"Gerry could care less. He's *glad* it's going nowhere. He's *thrilled* that he can play to his religious right base and take no responsibility for the outcome."

"Well, why don't you just say that?"

"I *am* saying that," Penneymounter protested. "But it doesn't matter. Even though a resolution removing Franklin will stink up the Senate like a mackerel in the moonlight, we'll still have to hold hearings and a trial. It will chew up valuable time on the calendar. Your lower court nominees will languish." He paused, clenching a verbal fist. "That's why I need you publicly to oppose the impeachment resolution, so it never gets out of the House."

Long shot forward in his chair, giving Hector a surprised look. "I don't know if I want to jump into that briar patch, Joe. It could have the opposite of the desired effect."

"Let me be a little clearer," Penneymounter said, the edge in his voice growing sharper. "If you don't distance yourself from Franklin's removal, I'm not going to be able to spend my political capital on your judicial nominees. Our agreement to report any judicial nominee to the floor that has the support of me and the ranking member will be null and void." He reloaded. "And even worse, I'll be forced by my own troops to oppose any Supreme Court nominee you might send up to replace Franklin."

Long was stunned by Penneymounter's threat. The phone line was silent for a full six seconds. "I hear what you're saying about impeachment," Long said at last, his voice betraying his anger. "But my nominees shouldn't be the innocent victims in a shooting war over Franklin's impeachment. That's just no way to run an airline, Joe. If you want to pay back Jimmerson, do it with some pet project he wants. And I don't see the point in rushing to judgment on a Supreme Court nominee that hasn't happened yet. There's no vacancy."

"Mr. President, Jimmerson is about to impeach a man whose only crime was to suffer a stroke. You can't outsource this issue to Jimmerson and Andy Stanton. You're the president. We need you to lead."

"I will, but I can't tell the House what to do any more than I can you," said Long curtly.

"Well, that's your decision," said Penneymounter. "But at some point you're going to have to come out of the Rose Garden and take a stand."

It was a cheap shot, and Long bristled. "I'm going to lead," he vowed. "But I'm not going to jump into the middle of a food fight. This is the kind of partisan politics the American people are sick and tired of in Washington." He tapped the desk with his index finger for emphasis. "And if you make my judicial nominees pay a price, you're tangling with *me*. I'm not going to be able to take that lying down." He bit off the syllables of each word.

"I know that. I don't want to do this at all, but I will, Mr. President, *I will*," said Penneymounter, not giving an inch.

"Thanks for calling, Mr. Chairman," said Long coldly. He slammed the receiver down with disgust and looked at Hector, eyes aflame. "That weasel threatened me."

"What did he say?"

"He demanded that I come out against Franklin's removal or he would slow-walk my lower court nominees and oppose my Supreme Court nominee."

"He's playing with fire," said Hector. "He's totally out of control."

"I agree," said Long. "This is a declaration of war. I had a deal with the guy! His word is worthless." His eyes bore into Hector. "I won't forget that."

"I think he wants out of the deal and is using Franklin as a convenient excuse," said Hector. "He's under major pressure from the far left. Franklin is a fig leaf."

Long shook his head. He was learning the hard way that the old partisan habits in Washington died hard. Jimmerson was taking the Republicans in the House off a cliff, and Penneymounter and Sal Stanley were doing the same with Democrats in the Senate. Part of him wished Peter Corbin Franklin had never had a stroke in the first place, while another part of him wished he was already dead.

TWELVE

A crowd of two hundred people sat patiently in their chairs in the East Room, awaiting the arrival of the First Lady. It was her first solo public appearance since moving into the White House, and there was a great deal of buzz connected to the event. Fairly or unfairly, Claire Long had developed a reputation during the campaign as the Ice Lady: the fiery strawberry-blonde with a chip on her shoulder who hated her husband's enemies and liked more than the occasional glass of wine on the campaign plane. She had made no attempt to disguise her contempt for Sal Stanley, who stole the Democratic nomination from Long, and she had lashed out at more than a few reporters that she viewed as unfair in their coverage of her husband. Her coming-out party as First Lady was designed to soften her image.

The occasion was an event honoring women business leaders. Several female corporate CEOs sat on the front row in pastel power suits. The made-for-television sign on the podium read, "Women Growing Our Economy." It was a safe debut for Claire, and the East Wing staff had made sure there was a full entourage of reporters, including *People* magazine and *Entertainment Tonight*, both of which had been offered print and broadcast interviews.

"Ladies and gentlemen, please welcome the First Lady, Claire Long," intoned an announcer over the sound system. Fashionably late, Claire Long entered from the back of the East Room and walked up the center aisle to a standing ovation. She bounded up on stage exuding confidence, wearing a smart St. John green jacket and black skirt with black heels. But as she stood to the side listening to a glowing introduction by the former CEO of a technology firm, she seemed to wilt, and she appeared disoriented as she approached the podium.

"Thank you so much," she said slowly, her face resembling a plastic mask, her hands gripping the podium as the dead air hung. Her speech was slightly slurred. The press corps knew instantly that something was awry. "But you shouldn't cheer me. Save your applause for my husband. He's the important one. I'm just a famous housekeeper." Nervous titters from the audience. Claire patted her heart. "But you touched me . . . you really moved me."

Cards on the podium contained Claire's speech, but she ignored them. Instead, she rambled, at times endearingly, but mostly incoherently. "Women are the backbone of our families, and yes, our businesses. If it weren't for women, our economy would grind to a halt. Come to think of it, the *world* would grind to a halt!" She let out a nervous too-loud laugh. "Bob is like most men. He doesn't like to admit it, but it's true, isn't it?" Scattered applause—they were trying to throw her a lifeline.

The speech had turned into a train wreck. "Most of you might not know it, but I have reviewed and edited every major speech Bob has given in his career," Claire bragged. "Of course, he doesn't always listen." Nervous titters. "And that's when he gets into trouble!"

Standing against the wall and watching all this was Lisa Robinson, who wanted to sink into the floor, her face frozen, arms crossed, clutching a legal pad so hard her knuckles turned white. She knew the entire press corps was watching her. Improvising, she called over the CEO who had introduced Claire. They huddled in a power clutch under the horrified gaze of members of the audience.

"Get her off the stage . . . *now!*" whispered Lisa out of the side of her mouth.

"How?" asked the CEO, clearly distraught.

"I don't *care*. Just get up there and *do* it."

The CEO stepped gingerly on to the stage as if she were tiptoeing across a minefield, a nervous smile on her face. Claire either did not see her or ignored her.

"You know that old phrase, behind every successful man is a strong woman?" she asked, her face twisted in sarcasm. "The truth is *beside* every successful man is an equally successful and accomplished woman." She wagged her finger. "And never let the men forget it."

Lisa looked down at the floor. She could no longer make eye contact with the press. The CEO moved in closer to Claire, who finally noticed her.

"Is my time up already?" she asked to nervous laughter that mixed relief with tragicomedy. "But I haven't gotten to the part about how the majority of men die within eighteen months of their wives dying." Audible gasps filled the air. "They can't even face life without us." The CEO grabbed her by the arm and escorted her gently off the stage, walking her down the center aisle to relieved applause.

Lisa bolted for the door. She knew the video of Claire's meltdown in the East Room would be on the Internet within ten minutes. They needed to come up with an explanation—fast.

Dan Dorman of the *Washington Post* ambled over, bald pate gleaming under the TV lights, wearing a wicked grin. He physically blocked Lisa's exit. "Alright, no spin," he said accusingly. "Is she drunk?"

"Dan, she's tired," Lisa said, thinking on her feet.

"She sounded tipsy." He glared over his glasses at Lisa with a look that seemed to say: *If you lie to me, I'll make you pay.*

"I *said* she's tired, Dan. Now please get out of the way. I have a meeting." Dorman reluctantly stepped aside and Lisa blew by him. She hoped there was a way to contain the carnage, but she knew the video of Claire would lead all the cable shows and light up YouTube. Lisa had to alert the president and Charlie Hector right away. The White House was about to go into damage-control mode.

AT A BACK TABLE in the dining room of the Willard Hotel, three blocks from the White House, four people huddled at a power breakfast. Stephen Fox cut into eggs Benedict while he plotted his next move in the Justice Department's antitrust case against Wildfire.com. Joining him were G. G. Hoterman; antitrust litigator Amy Thornton from the white-shoe law firm Powell, Murphy, and Weiss; and Frank Gross, head of corporate security for Wildfire.com.

"Peter Corbin Franklin's been in a coma for ten weeks," said Fox wearily. His long, gun-metal gray hair, penetrating blue eyes, and perma-tan gave him the appearance of an older male model. "He could live for years. The vacancy is hanging over this case like a guillotine. The question is: when does the blade drop?"

It was a startling analogy when referring to the comatose Supreme Court justice. Thornton visibly winced as she took a sip of coffee. Gross showed no emotion, his poker face expressionless.

"I always say that we solve our client's problems—just not too quickly," joked G. G., his blue Hermes tie and matching suspenders highlighting his blue pin-striped suit. "But this is getting ridiculous. We could be left dangling for a year or two." He turned to Amy. "Amy, is there any way we ask the Supremes to kick this back to the appellate court and have the case reheard en banc?"

"We could, but that motion will never be granted," said Amy as she daintily spooned oatmeal with blueberries. With dark brown hair, doeish brown eyes, porcelain skin, and a petite figure (her brown Dior ensemble was a size two), Amy's China-doll visage masked the killer instincts of a seasoned litigator. She was one of the most skilled lawyers in the country, taking five cases all the way to the Supreme Court and winning them all. She had never lost a case.

"Why not?" asked Fox. "This case has the entire technology sector in limbo."

"Because the Supreme Court wants it," answered Amy matter-of-factly. "They never ruled on Microsoft or Google. Google dodged a lawsuit by making concessions to the FTC when it acquired Doubleclick. Microsoft settled its browser war case with DOJ. So this case is the biggest antitrust case dispute since the breakup of AT&T to go to the highest court."

"Any chance they'll hear it with only eight justices?" asked Fox.

"Possible but unlikely," said Amy. "We're not forcing the issue because we're not sure we have the votes. We're far better off waiting for Franklin's replacement."

Stephen frowned. "The analysts are pounding our stock. The one thing Wall Street hates is uncertainty."

"We should try to settle," offered G. G. "After all, Golden is the new sheriff in town, and he's a pro-business Republican. He doesn't want bureaucrats deciding what advertisements Wildfire runs on the Internet."

"I agree, and we're trying. The problem is, I'm viewed by the Long crowd as having been in the tank with Sal Stanley," said Fox. "I don't know if Bob Long's Justice Department wants me to make a boatload more money so I can give it to guys like you trying to defeat them, G. G."

"Anything is doable in this town," said G. G. "Let's hire Fred Edgewater, Long's pollster, to do a research project on Internet advertising and privacy issues. Have Fred give a briefing to the White House technology advisor. Then we do a high-level bank shot from the West Wing to Justice, saying, 'The president would like this case to go quietly into the night.'"

"Will Fred do it?" asked Fox.

"I think so. Assuming the price is right."

"How much?"

"I'd guess 250." Everyone knew he meant a quarter of a million dollars.

Fox nodded, nonplussed. It was pocket change, given Wildfire's valuation.

"We should hire someone close to Golden," suggested Amy. "Work it from the DOJ side. I know some people we could bring aboard."

"Just keep G. G. out of camera range," said Stephen, chuckling.

G. G. smiled. "Long hates me. But Penneymounter and I have been friends for twenty years. I helped Joe on his first Senate campaign. Two years ago, at his request, I went to Stanley and lobbied him to name the only person senior to Joe on the committee as the new chairman of Rules. Joe owes me big time. And he's interested in this issue."

Amy raised her eyebrows. "Penneymounter might be with us? That would be big."

"G. G.'s portfolio is black ops," said Fox, his voice lowered to a rumbling baritone. "I don't know how he gets things done, and I don't want to know."

"Things just magically happen," said G. G., waving his fingers in the air like a magician making an imaginary dove fly out of a handkerchief. "They appear out of thin air. No faxes, no e-mails. No paper trail."

Frank Gross had remained silent up until now. A former FBI agent with twenty years in corporate security, Gross had the clean-cut intensity of a Marine, the bulk of a longshoreman, and the discretion of an assassin. His black hair combed perfectly, he seemed to be the only man on the planet who still used Brylcream.

"G. G. and Amy, I'm going to send one of our technicians to your offices later in the week to install encryption software for your e-mail," Gross said. "From now on we think it is advisable that all e-mail sent between Wildfire employees and you two needs to be encrypted."

"But my communications are privileged," said Amy, her voice betraying concern.

Gross's gaze cut right through her. "If anything goes wrong, we simply can't count on your firm not waiving that privilege. Our competitors don't like the idea of our winning this antitrust case. They will stop at nothing. So we can't take any chances."

Amy nodded. They rose from the table and walked out of the restaurant, strolling through the lobby and making small talk. Gross excused himself, heading to the elevator. Once outside, Amy peeled off, hailing a taxi.

G. G. glanced up Pennsylvania Avenue and saw the Capitol dome glowing under the morning sunrise. It was a cool, brisk morning, and the crisp air invigorated him. "Not that I really care, Stephen, but why are we encrypting our e-mail?" he asked Fox.

"Get in," said Fox, pointing to his Town Car.

G. G. waved to his driver to follow Fox's car, and he slid into the backseat next to Fox. Stephen reached over and pressed a button on the console, raising the dark glass partition between them and the driver.

"Frank is extremely capable . . . and discreet," Fox said quietly, his tone grave. "He's a professional. He's going to be overseeing some aspects of our operations, and we don't want them compromised in any way."

"What kind of operations?"

"You don't want to know."

"Just be careful, Stephen," warned G. G. "We can probably still settle with DOJ. I don't want us to do something stupid."

"We're not going to do anything stupid," Fox replied. "You do what you do. Frank will do what he does."

"That guy gives me the creeps."

"Guys like Frank are cut from a different cloth." Fox turned in his seat to face G. G. "Don't worry. Pretty soon Peter Corbin Franklin will be gone. Long will appoint a new justice, and we will get our day in court."

The car pulled up in front of the large building off Seventeenth Street where Hoterman and Schiff had its offices. Fox's driver jumped out and walked around the front of the car, opening the door for G. G. He stepped out and stood on the curb, watching Fox's car drive off.

JEFF LINKS, BOB LONG'S pastor, was on a golf course in Laguna Niguel when his cell phone buzzed, and the White House operator announced that the president was on the line. He broke away from his foursome and walked alone up the fairway.

"Jeff, it's Bob Long," came the voice on the line.

"Bob, it's great to hear your voice," said Jeff.

"Jeff, I need your help on something." Long wasted no time getting to the point.

"Absolutely. Just say the word."

"Well," Long began slowly, a hint of embarrassment in his voice. "I'm usually the one helping others and not making a call like this asking for help myself. But Claire has been drinking too much. I'm not saying she's an alcoholic, but she has not been able to work this out on her own. Maybe I've just been too busy to confront her. Maybe I just didn't want to create a major conflict. But she had a couple of drinks before a speech she gave today and it was obvious. It's leading all the newscasts."

"How is she?" asked Links.

"She's embarrassed and distraught, as you can imagine," Long replied. "I've only talked to her briefly. She's blaming herself and taking it hard. But when I asked her if she thought she had an alcohol problem and needed help, she said no."

"That's not unusual," said Links.

"Jeff, the upshot is, if she doesn't get help, there could be more episodes like this. I think we need to do something," Long said. "Claire respects you. She'll listen to you. Can you come out here and talk to her?"

"Of course," said Links. "I'll be on the next airplane."

"Should I tell Claire that you're coming?" asked Long.

"Yes, but only to talk to her. Don't let her think that this is a full-blown intervention. That might put her on the defensive. We have to get her help and soon."

"I agree 100 percent," said Long. "I'm really worried about her." Long's voice caught, and his eyes filled with tears. He could hardly believe that he was conspiring with his minister to get his wife emergency medical help.

"Bob, I've dealt with these kinds of situations many times," said Links. "I know a place that can do a world of good for Claire. It's an inpatient clinic that treats this problem from a Christian perspective."

"I trust your judgment, Jeff. I need help, and I didn't know who else to turn to."

"I'll help you, Bob. Believe me, I'm glad you're doing this. It takes a lot of courage to do what you're doing," said Links. "I'll be there no later than tomorrow."

"God bless you, Jeff," said Long. "Thank you so much for your help."

Long hung up the phone. He knew Claire was going to be livid when she found out that he had been plotting with Jeff behind her back. But she had left him no choice. Her alcohol problem was no longer just threatening their marriage and her health; it was threatening his presidency.

THIRTEEN

The House of Representatives chamber crackled with tension. Not a single seat was empty. Staff lined the walls, spectators swelled the galleries, and a long line of those waiting to get in snaked through the Capitol and out into the parking lot. Just five months after the House had elected Bob Long as president by a single vote, the wounds from that ugly battle still raw, its members prepared to vote on the impeachment of a Supreme Court justice for the first time since 1805.

Sam Manion, chairman of the House Judiciary Committee, wrapped up his speech. His message was joyless and pedantic, a thoroughly boring recitation of the Constitution, the separation of powers, and the founders' conception of impeachment. Everyone heard; no one listened. They had already decided how they would vote, and the rest was noise.

"The Chair recognizes the gentleman from North Carolina!"

Gerry Jimmerson strode to the podium in a confident gait. There had been some discussion within the GOP leadership as to the advisability of the Speaker addressing the chamber at all, but his forward-leaning posture indicated it would have taken a pack of wild horses to keep him out of the well. To say that Jimmerson was a lightning rod was being charitable. He was the chief bogeyman of the left, vilified by the liberal commentator and blamed by the Democrats for railroading the resolution to the floor. But Jimmerson was not easily intimidated. Indeed, he seemed to revel in their hatred.

"Fellow members of the House," Jimmerson began, his voice strong and resonant. "I come before you today not as a North Carolinian, not as a Republican, not as a Southerner, not as a conservative. I come before you as an American." Members were taken aback. Jimmerson, whose encyclopedic knowledge of American history was legendary, had invoked Daniel Webster's peroration from his famous speech that led to the Compromise of 1850. Jimmerson paused, letting the drama build, surveying the anticipatory expressions on the faces of his GOP colleagues and drinking in the disdain of the Democrats, who watched him through narrowed eyes.

"No matter which way each of us votes today on the question before us, no one is happy about casting this vote," he continued. "Least of all me."

The Democratic side of the aisle erupted in sarcastic guffaws. None of them believed that Jimmerson, the ultimate practitioner of slash-and-burn politics, regretted his vote to remove the most prominent liberal voice on the Supreme Court. Jimmerson ignored them, his head turned away, chin raised, black eyes unblinking.

"That's what leadership is about," Jimmerson said, his voice booming, echoing off the walls and ceiling. He rose up on his toes and pointed to the four lawgivers whose statutes ringed the corners of the chamber. "Moses, Washington, Aristotle, and Jesus Christ—they are the models of justice upon which our nation was founded. They knew that respect for the rule of law is the foundation of civil order, and when it breaks down, chaos is inevitable." He cast the impeachment of Franklin as a matter of patriotic duty. "If the highest Court in the land is paralyzed or hopelessly deadlocked, the rule of law will collapse."

"The issue before us is not a single case, though the cases pending before the Supreme Court are among the most important in our lifetimes. The issue before us is not a single justice, though Peter Corbin Franklin is one of the most distinguished and accomplished jurists to ever sit on the Court." Jimmerson paused, his voice falling to a whisper. "The issue before us, ladies and gentlemen of this House, is justice itself and the rule of law." He pointed his finger for emphasis, jabbing the air. "No matter how much we may honor an individual justice, they like all of us, must yield to the demands of the law. I urge this House to do its duty." He lowered his head and closed his eyes for a moment, seemingly emotional, though everyone knew it was an act. "Reluctantly, sadly, and with a heavy heart—but do . . . . its . . . duty. May God bless this House, and may God bless these United States of America."

Republicans leapt to their feet. The Democrats sat impassively, their faces frozen, staring at Jimmerson with hatred. They despised everything that Jimmerson, in their eyes, symbolized: partisanship, cynicism, political calculation, the abuse of power. No matter. Jimmerson's whips had counted 230 solid votes to impeach Franklin, twelve more than they needed.

FRANK GROSS PARKED ON a side street near George Washington University hospital. He wanted no security cameras in the parking lot to record his coming or going. He glanced at his watch: it was 4:50 p.m., and the guard would be changing in ten minutes. Wearing green chinos, work shoes, and a denim oxford shirt, he looked like any visitor stopping by to see a family member. He walked into the hospital lobby and headed for the elevator, keeping his head down and his feet moving. Through decades of security work, he had learned to carry himself with the confidence of someone who belonged, above all, to move quickly and avoid eye contact.

Getting off the elevator on the fifth floor, he ducked into a restroom and closed the door to the far stall. He methodically removed his outer clothes and placed them in a plastic bag, stripping down to a green hospital orderly uniform that he wore underneath. He clipped on an employee identification card. He walked back to the elevators and, after looking in both directions, opened the door to a service area, dropping the plastic bag containing his street clothes down a garbage shaft.

Walking down the hallway, he felt his heart rate quicken. This was the moment of maximum danger. He could be seen, captured by video cameras, or stopped by security. But he knew the route well, and he knew the patterns of the DC police officer who guarded the hospital room of Peter Corbin Franklin. He knew when he came on duty, when he took his lunch break, and when he relieved himself or visited the vending machines in the break room.

It was 5:42 p.m. when the cop left his station. Gross moved quickly, stepping into a room and disconnecting the EKG from a patient, setting off an alarm at the nurse's station. As hospital personnel hustled to the patient's aid, Gross went down a side stairwell to the fourth floor. The lead nurse left her station to check on the patient. As she reconnected the EKG machine, Gross moved down the hall to another stairwell and walked back up to the fifth floor. Reaching the door, he opened it and looked both ways. All clear.

He stepped across the hall to Peter Corbin Franklin's room. It was dark and quiet, with a fluorescent light on over the bed. Franklin looked like a sack of bones underneath the sheets, and Gross guessed he now weighed no more 110 pounds. An intravenous drip emptied into a vein in his right arm. Gross moved quickly. He opened the valve of the drip, pulled a syringe out of his pocket, and pressed down the plunger, inserting a burst of air into the tube. Closing the valve, he put the syringe back in his pocket and exited the room.

As he headed back to the elevators, the DC cop passed him, carrying a Diet Coke in one hand and a package of mini doughnuts in the other. They briefly made eye contact. A wave of fear passed through Gross: had the cop made him? There was nothing left to do but keep moving. He took the stairs down to the first floor, passed through the lobby, and walked out the front door. Turning down the side street, he looked around to make sure no one else was watching him. He got into his car and pulled away. He dialed a number on his cell phone. "It's done."

"Did anyone see you?"

"I don't think so," Gross lied. "I passed a DC cop in the hall. That's it."

"You're probably alright," replied the person on the other end of the line. "But just to be safe, lay low."

THE AIDE IN THE Speaker's office hung up the phone, her hand shaking as she scribbled a note on a piece of paper. She bolted from behind her desk, nearly tripping over a trash can, and stumbled down the hall to the Speaker's private office, her dress heels clicking on the white marble floor. Gerald Jimmerson was meeting with a group of utility executives.

The aide quietly opened the door and walked wordlessly to the Speaker. Jimmerson kept one eye on a television set in the corner tuned to C-Span and the vote proceeding on the House floor. She passed him the note. Jimmerson opened it and read its contents, his face going white. He immediately rose to his feet.

"Gentlemen, forgive me, but I'm needed on the floor," he said with a start. He quickly pumped hands around the coffee table. "Please forgive me for having to duck out. I'll try to rejoin you, but you are in able hands." He nodded to two aides and turned on his heel to go.

After the door closed behind him, one of the aides leaned over and picked up the note. It read: "AP News Alert: Peter Corbin Franklin Dies."

ON THE HOUSE FLOOR, word of Franklin's death spread rapidly, sparking pandemonium. Panic-stricken Republicans scrambled to change their votes to "present"—they didn't want to be seen as kicking a dead man. Democrats buzzed with energy, pointing accusing fingers as the Republicans' votes kept changing from green to amber on the display board. Whips for both sides darted in and out of the aisles.

Sam Manion stood in the midst of the chaos looking as if a grenade had just gone off in his foxhole. His colleagues came up to ask him what should be done. His face ashen, he mumbled that he didn't know.

An aide appeared at his side. "The Speaker would like to see you in the cloak room."

Manion hurried off the floor and found Jimmerson standing in a circle of worried members of the GOP leadership. "Franklin has died," said the Speaker. "He must have passed as we were giving our speeches."

"Good God," said Manion.

"How much time is left?" asked Jimmerson.

"Two minutes," answered a staffer.

"Alright," Jimmerson began, taking charge. "Can we stop the vote?"

"Stop the vote?" asked Manion, incredulous. "I don't think so."

"We can do whatever we darn well please," Jimmerson fired back. He tapped Manion on the chest. "When we get inside a minute, move to suspend the rules. After that motion passes, we'll pull the resolution from the floor."

"But that takes a two-thirds vote," Manion objected. "It'll never pass."

"Just *do* it, Sam," sputtered Jimmerson, highly agitated. Everyone filed through the door of the cloakroom and onto the floor.

When the Democrats caught sight of Jimmerson, they smelled blood. "Shame! Shame!" shouted several Democratic congressmen, pointing accusingly as they shouted.

"Mr. Speaker, I seek recognition for the purpose of a parliamentary inquiry," said the ranking Democrat on the Judiciary Committee.

"The chair recognizes the gentleman from Michigan."

"I note that the members on the other side of the aisle are changing their votes from yes to present and now to no," he said with a smirk. "I wonder if given the fact that they have preoccupied the House with this charade and now have egg on their face, if they wouldn't feel more comfortable under the circumstances simply abstaining."

Laughter rumbled up and down the Democratic side of the aisle. Republican members hurled insults and shouted catcalls at their tormentors. In the press gallery reporters sat on the edge of their seats, scribbling notes, their eyes on high beam, unable to believe what they were witnessing.

"The gentleman from Michigan's inquiry is not of a parliamentary nature," the presiding officer said. He raised the gavel and banged it three times. "The House will come to order! Order in the House!"

The Democrats ignored him. "Shame! Shame!"

"Mr. Speaker, I move that the resolution before the House be placed on the table," said Manion into a microphone on the floor.

"Cowards!" shouted the Democrats.

"The gentlemen from Virginia has moved that the resolution be tabled. All those in—"

"Mr. Speaker, this motion is out of order!" screamed the Democratic floor manager.

"—favor, signify by saying aye."

"Aye!" shouted the Republicans.

"All those opposed, signify by saying nay."

"Division of the House! Division of the House!" The Democrats demanded a roll call on the motion.

"The ayes have it. The resolution is put on the table."

Boos filled the air as Democrats joyfully vented their outrage. By now they were performing for the cameras. Out in the hallway members from both sides held dueling news conferences beneath a blaze of television lights. Reporters flitted between them, dutifully recording the charges and insults that each side hurled at the other.

Gerald Jimmerson decided it was time to make his exit. He had nothing to gain from remaining in camera range. He ducked into the cloakroom. A harried press aide approached.

"Marvin Myers says he's writing his column, and Joe Penneymounter gave him a quote saying you are abusing your office to trampling on civil rights." He paused, gulping. "He compared you to George Wallace."

Several members stood around, transfixed. They seemed to flinch as Jimmerson stood there, a smoking volcano about to blow.

"He said *what?!*" Jimmerson shouted. His eyes darted around the room. "He compared me to *whom?*"

"George Wallace, sir."

Jimmerson's face went beet red. The veins in his forehead began to pro-
trude. "You tell Myers that I said that is the most despicable, dishonest, dis-
ingenuous smear I have heard in my political career. It is beneath contempt."
He turned on his heel and began to march away, then wheeled around and
pointed at his press aide. "Tell him to quote me on that!"

IT WAS A LITTLE after 6:00 p.m. when G. G. Hoterman climbed on to the
treadmill at the Washington Sports Club next to the Ritz Carlton down-
town. It was all part of his losing battle with his weight, a battle he had been
fighting for three decades, ever since the two-a-days of his college playing
days gave way to the sedentary lifestyle of a Washington lobbyist. *Too many
steaks, too little exercise,* thought G. G. He began moving his legs in a brisk
walk, flipping the television built into the treadmill to MSNBC. But when
he saw the News Alert logo at the bottom of the screen, he almost fell off
the treadmill. "Justice Peter Corbin Franklin Dead" read the headline. The
female anchor delivered the news in a grave tone of voice. "After suffering a
stroke from which he never regained consciousness, leaving him in a coma
for the past four and a half months, Peter Corbin Franklin died last night
from heart failure," she said. "One of the greatest progressive champions
and among the most celebrated liberal icons in the modern history of the
Supreme Court is gone. President Long will now make arguably the most
important decision of his young presidency: whom to nominate to replace
Franklin."

Hoterman slowed down the treadmill and reached for his BlackBerry,
dialing Christy Love's office number. She answered on the first ring.

"I assume you heard about Franklin," said G. G., his breathing
heavy.

"Yes," answered Christy in a stricken voice. "We all knew this day was
coming. But it still hits you like a ton of bricks."

"Poor Franklin is spinning in his grave at the thought of Long picking
his successor."

"That may be why he hung on as long as he did."

"What's the game plan?" asked G. G.

"I'm jumping on a strategy call in ten minutes," said Christy.
"Preliminarily, I expect Long will move quickly. He's had plenty of time to
get ready."

"I agree," said G. G. "I think he'll wait until after Franklin's funeral, at least for appearances sake."

"I'd say we have five to seven days tops," said Christy. "And if he picks who we think he will, there'll be plenty to work with. We've got enough research to fill a small warehouse."

"Who do you think it's going to be?"

"Majette or Diaz."

G. G. dialed the treadmill down until it was barely moving. "The first African-American woman or the second Hispanic," G. G. replied. "Brilliant."

"Bingo," said Christy. "Majette is from California so it's home cookin' for Long. The Diaz play is so cynical that it's obvious. It's a twofer: energize social conservatives and make a play for Latinos."

"What have you got on them?"

"Between us? Enough dirt to fill a dump truck," said Christy.

"That's very encouraging to hear."

"We're going to need some more dough," Christy added, moving in for the kill. "The other side will be well funded."

"Absolutely. I'll help you," said G. G. "How much do you need?"

Christy thought a second. "Five million." She paused, letting the blow sink in. "That's just to start. I'll need twenty million before it's over."

"Get me a budget," said G. G. crisply.

"You'll have it by COB tomorrow at the latest."

G. G. hung up the phone and dialed up the treadmill, quickening his pace. Over the noise of the treadmill motor, the voices of the cable chatter faded into background noise. A jumble of unanswered questions filled G. G.'s head. How had Franklin died? He suspected foul play. His mind raced back to his conversation with Fox the previous day and his expression of confidence that Franklin would soon be gone. A shudder went through him.

ANDY STANTON SAT IN the chair in his dressing room just off the set of his television show as a female makeup artist wiped his face with a hot washcloth. He had been taping some promotional spots for his next prime-time special. She occasionally paused to look in the mirror to check her handiwork. Stanton paid no attention. He was engrossed in the Associated Press copy announcing Peter Corbin Franklin's death.

The phone in the dressing room rang. It was Ross Lombardy. The makeup artist handed Andy the phone.

"Ross, I told you Long would have a Supreme Court appointment in his first year as president," said Andy with characteristic self-assurance. "The Lord told me."

"You heard Him alright," Ross agreed, suck up juices flowing. "Did you hear about what just happened in the House?"

"No, what?" asked Andy.

"They were literally voting on Franklin's impeachment when the news broke about Franklin dying," related Ross. "The Republicans immediately tabled the resolution. The Democrats are livid. They have still refused to leave the floor. Jimmerson ordered the clerk of the House to turn off the air-conditioning and the lights, but they still won't leave."

"The Democrats are holding a sit-in in the dark in the House chamber?" asked Andy in an excitable squeal. "Brother, you can't make this stuff *up!*"

"They're lighting candles and singing 'We Shall Overcome,'" chuckled Ross. "It's total chaos."

"Jimmerson has all the subtlety of a sledgehammer," said Andy, his voice dripping with contempt. "He tried to play hardball with us during the House election of Long and that totally backfired. Now he's overplayed his hand on Franklin." Andy thought Jimmerson had grown increasingly erratic, lurching from crisis to crisis with no strategic plan. It made Andy's ties to the Republican party, already frayed from his endorsement of Long, weaken further.

"Well, at the end of the day, it's a blessing in disguise," Ross replied. "We couldn't be against impeachment, given where our base is, but we didn't have the votes in the Senate. It was like the Clinton impeachment only we were trying to remove a grandfather in a coma. What a mess."

"This is for all the marbles, Ross," Andy continued, barely pausing to breathe. "Long's got the chance of a lifetime with this appointment. This is for *Roe v. Wade*, the sanctity of marriage, tort reform, the right to pray in school, the future of the family. It's everything we've worked for over four decades."

"No question," said Ross. "But it's not going to be a cakewalk with Penneymounter and Stanley already sharpening their knives."

"By the way, did you get my list to Golden?" asked Andy.

"He's got it."

"Any feedback?"

"Not yet, but I'll check back in with his chief of staff," promised Ross.

"No more Souters," said Andy. "I told the president that when I met with him in January."

"I remember well. Let's hope he listened."

Ross hung up the phone and felt a surge of energy go through him. He had a front-row seat to the most important Supreme Court pick in two generations. Long's pick would be Bork cubed. This time, Ross vowed silently to himself, they would win.

FOURTEEN

"Mrs. Long?" asked the woman at the door, her manner pleasant but professional.

"Yes," replied Claire.

"Dr. Kelly will see you now."

Claire rose from a straight-back chair in the airy, brightly lit lobby painted in pastel colors on the campus of Hope Ranch, the rehabilitation and wellness center outside Phoenix she checked into the previous night. Secretly ferried from Camp David by helicopter to Andrews Air Force Base, she transferred to a government Gulfstream V for the long flight to Phoenix, arriving at a little past 10:00 p.m. After a night of tossing and turning in her private room (fresh roses on the bedside table, her own private sitting room, a spacious bathroom with marble floors and Jacuzzi), Claire awaited her introductory counseling session. In rehab speak, it was her "initial consultation."

Vanilla-scented mood candles flickered on the coffee table, a Spanish guitar strummed softly on the sound system, and hushed voices and forced smiles of Hope Ranch employees greeted patients (in rehab speak, "residents") at every turn. To Claire, it was fingernails on a chalkboard, sensory reminders of a bad dream in which she awoke to find she was an inmate in an asylum.

Don't they know I don't belong here! The words echoed in her head in a silent scream. *I am not an alcoholic!* Through a maze of jangled nerves and jumbled emotions, her overriding feeling was pure anger. She was mad at Bob for overreacting to the East Room mishap, angry with the media for portraying her as a drunken witch and the latest poster child for alcohol-laced bad behavior, and angry at Jeff Links for deceiving her and selling her down the river. Once again Bob's political career came first, and once again Claire was being sacrificed on the altar of his ambition.

Hope Ranch had a strict policy of confidentiality. But Claire knew it would not spare her from public scandal. It was only a matter of time before tabloid helicopters buzzed overhead, telephoto lenses poised.

Mostly she felt suppressed anxiety (sheer terror better described it) at confronting the demons that had hounded her for years, snapping at her heels until they finally brought her to this antiseptic hell masquerading as a $25,000 a month resort for drunks, druggies, and losers. Consumed by an overwhelming sense of guilt and fear, Claire followed the woman down the hall to the office of Dr. Jack Kelly.

She half expected a male version of Nurse Ratchet. But Kelly was so understated as to be unimpressive, greeting her with a smile that crinkled the crow's feet around his eyes and gave his brown eyes a soft glow. Dressed in blue slacks and a white button-down shirt, he appeared to be in his mid-sixties, with a shock of whitish hair, but his manner was that of a young, energetic man. He motioned Claire to a simple leather couch while he sat across from her in a chair, crossing his legs and placing his hands on his lap, a model of empathy.

"Claire, welcome. I guess we should start with why you are here," Kelly said. A manila folder sat on his lap, and Claire assumed it was her patient records.

"Yes, I've thought about what I would say about that," said Claire, her voice halting and nervous. "The short answer is my husband and pastor made me come." Her barely concealed hostility curled her red lips, her face hard and brittle.

"Does that make you angry?"

"Not really angry," she lied. "I'm past anger. Upset, maybe."

"So you don't think you should be here?" Kelly asked.

"No."

"And if someone were to ask you if you were an alcoholic, what would you say?" asked Kelly, putting his hand on his chin, drawing her out.

"I would say no."

Kelly nodded as if he had expected the answer before he asked. "And why would you say no?"

"Because I can quit any time I want to," replied Claire.

Kelly flashed a knowing smile. "That is a common misconception about alcoholism," he said. "But in reality, whether or not someone can stop drinking has little or nothing to do with whether he or she is an alcoholic." He leaned forward, his eyes steady. "In fact, as strange as it sounds, alcohol itself is not the problem. It's simply the medication people use to treat the deeper problem."

Claire rose from the couch and walked to the window, gazing out at the desert. It was beautiful: rolling hills of sand, brush, and cactus, bathed in the morning desert sunlight. She turned back from the window. "Doctor, with all due respect—"

"Please, call me Jack. I got over being impressed by my medical degree a long time ago."

"Alright, then. Jack, that's nonsensical. If someone can quit drinking any time they want and they don't need alcohol, how can they be an alcoholic?"

Dr. Kelly went to a whiteboard on the wall. He drew a circle and divided it into six sections. Above it, he wrote "Emotions/Feelings." In the six sections, he wrote *Love, Joy, Peace* followed by *Fear, Anger, Depression*. He tapped the three sections in which he had written the negative emotions.

"Have you ever heard the phrase, 'I need a drink'?"

"Sure."

"Ever say it yourself?"

"Of course."

Kelly walked back to his chair and sat down. "That's fine. It's a common phrase, thoroughly embedded in our culture at this point." He pointed back to the lower half of the circle, where he wrote *Anger, Fear,* and *Depression*. "But alcoholism is about these negative feelings. It actually has little to do with alcohol. Chemicals such as alcohol, prescription medication, or illegal drugs are simply the thing outside themselves people take to cope with and manage negative feelings. They don't know how to deal with negative emotions, and rather than process them, they medicate themselves. It doesn't have to be alcohol."

Claire crossed her arms and nodded. "How about Diet Dr. Pepper?" she asked.

Kelly smiled wanly. Claire was toying with him. It was a self-defense mechanism, they both knew. "I suppose one can be addicted to caffeine from coffee or soft drinks but not in the way that I am talking about," he said. "The point is, someone who can't deal with negative feelings becomes dependent on a chemical to make them feel better. With continued usage over time, there is a biochemical reaction in the brain to the alcohol. Without realizing it, they cannot function without it."

"That's not me," said Claire firmly.

"You've never had a drink to make yourself feel better?"

"Sure, doesn't everyone?" asked Claire. "Why else do people drink?'

"Because they like the taste. Such as a fine red wine."

Claire shot Dr. Kelly a disbelieving look. "What if I simply don't agree that I'm an alcoholic and I decide to leave?"

"You can choose to do that," Kelly answered. "But I think you should ask yourself whether everyone else who suggested you come here is wrong." He reloaded, crossing his legs. "Tell you what: give it three days. If after three days you have not learned something about yourself and how to deal with negative feelings, there's the door." He pointed to the door of his office. "I'll even drive you to the airport. But I predict you'll learn a lot and it will greatly benefit you and make you a better person."

Claire found herself lowering her guard. Was it a trick? "Just three days?"

"Three days. But there are two rules."

Claire arched her right eyebrow. "And what are those?"

"First, no alcohol. Not even a sip. Second, you have to attend the group and individual sessions." He paused. "That's all. Do you want to give it a try?"

Claire mentally reviewed her options. She figured if she gave it three days and it was a dud, she could call Bob and Jeff, and they might let her come home. "Alright," she said with a hint of resignation. "Three days, but that's it."

BOB LONG SAT AT the head of a green tablecloth-covered table and talked health care, jobs, and taxes with a group of business leaders in Akron, Ohio. In White House lingo, it was a "message event," the latest in a mind-numbing string of public appearances by the president designed to sell his health-care plan, which was on life support in the Republican-controlled House and buffeted by grassroots protests from the very right-wing activists who voted for him six months earlier. The VFW center in Akron was filled to capacity with two thousand screaming and angry citizens, and another thousand milling around in the parking lot, holding up handmade signs and gesturing to the cameras.

Long prowled the stage like a lynx, his eyes intense and deep blue. He seemed to feed off adversity (including the marital trauma roiling his personal world, still unknown to the outside world). His chief domestic policy initiative lay in shambles, his as-yet-unnamed Supreme Court nominee awaited a hostile U.S. Senate, and his wife was in rehab. Yet a strange calm enveloped Long. He wielded the microphone like a saber, his rhetorical flourishes and charisma giving him a Luke Skywalker glow. The local congressman was still on the fence, and the White House hoped a presidential visit might sway him. But the offer backfired. Still blaming Long for the attempted impeachment of Franklin, the congressman blew off the event. It was a slap in the face.

After fielding tough questions from the audience and parrying with the business leaders, Long exited through a blue curtain. David Thomas slid up beside him, walking rapidly.

"Is this doing any good?" Long asked.

"Yes, sir," replied Thomas. "It'll dominate the local news. The Cleveland nets and Fox carried it live." He used communication-shop shorthand for the network television affiliates.

"I don't know," Long sighed. "It's hard to break through when the House is impeaching a comatose Supreme Court justice. What a sideshow that is."

Long reached the limousine, where a line of greeters, local dignitaries and elected officials who had supported him or he was wooing, awaited. Long worked each one, hand on shoulders, eyes glued to each face, as the official photographer snapped away. Then he climbed into the back of the limo.

Long looked at Thomas's face. His expression was noticeably strained.

"What is it?" asked Long.

"Mr. President, Justice Franklin is dead," said Thomas softly.

Long's face fell. He had expected the news for some time but the gravity of it still rattled. "Poor old guy," he said. Then suddenly his face cracked into a grin, and he let out a low rat-tat-tat chuckle. "You've got to hand it to Franklin. He stabbed Jimmerson in the back as he walked through the pearly gates, didn't he?"

"That he did, sir," said Thomas, enjoying the irony.

"Serves him right," said Long, his face animated. "Impeachment was a boneheaded move from the get-go. I warned Gerry, but as usual he wouldn't listen." He paused, looking out the window as the car emerged from the parking garage into the blazing sunlight. Protestors shook angry fists and waved wilted signs. One read: "LongCare = Socialism."

Long shook his head in detached wonderment. "Socialism? What planet are these people from?" he muttered. "I cut taxes six times when I was governor of California. Does that sound like socialism to you, David?"

Thomas answered dutifully. "No, sir."

Long picked up the phone from the console next to him, and a White House operator appeared on the line as if by magic. "Get me Phil Battaglia, please." As he waited, the president cupped a hand over the receiver. "Do you realize that I can get someone anywhere in the world on the phone, anytime I want? Last week I got a letter from a woman in Alaska complaining about the Small Business Administration. I was on Air Force One, and I asked them to get her on the phone." He snapped his finger. "They had her on the phone in less than a minute. All I knew was her name!" Long's face lit up. "Big coverage in the local papers: 'President Calls Local Woman Who Wrote White House.'"

Battaglia came on the line. "Hello, Mr. President."

"David just told me about Franklin. It's beyond bizarre," said Long.

"Unbelievable," said Phil. "It happened in the middle of the impeachment vote. The House is in chaos. Jimmerson has snapped." He let out a guffaw. "You should see him! He looks like he's not taking his meds."

"This helps us, don't you think?"

"I do," replied Battaglia. "We've triangulated Jimmerson and the far right and Penneymounter and Stanley and the far left, who are demanding that you appoint a liberal. You're the only adult in the room. You look like a leader among Lilliputians."

"Well, I hesitate even to say this, but the health-care bill probably won't make it out of the House," said Long. "We need a victory. I was trashed for not taking sides on impeaching Franklin, but now we're above the fray."

"Exactly, sir," agreed Battaglia.

"I don't see any reason to wait any longer," said Long. "My sense is that you and Golden have vetted candidates."

"We're ready, sir."

"Get me a memo tonight or tomorrow. If it's ready tonight, send it up to the residence."

"Done."

"Good," said Long briskly. "Bring in the top candidates over the weekend. We'll do it in the living quarters. Make sure they are not seen by anyone." Long leaned forward in his seat as he issued rapid-fire instructions. "And Phil?"

"Yes, sir."

"No leaks. Loose lips sink ships."

Long hung up the phone and turned to Thomas. "Strap on your helmet, pal. We're about to go twelve rounds with Sal Stanley and Joe Penneymounter wearing brass knuckles."

Thomas's face twisted into a wicked grin. "I relish the prospect, sir."

Long gazed out the window into the middle distance, deep in thought. A strange mixture of dread and anticipation filled him. If he selected a conservative, he was assured a Bork-like confirmation fight. But if he picked a moderate, the right would erupt in protest. No matter what he did, the White House was in for the fight of the decade. All they could do was climb into the bunker and ride out the artillery barrage.

IN A FORTUITOUS TWIST of timing, the White House chose the afternoon after Peter Corbin Franklin's death and the House's botched impeachment attempt to announce Claire had checked into rehab. Lisa Robinson argued they should release a statement. Hector blew his top, arguing it made the president look cold and distant at a time of familial upheaval. Hector lost. The White House released a brief statement at 3:22 p.m.: "Claire Long entered an inpatient facility for treatment for dependency on alcohol. Like millions of other families who have dealt with this issue, the Longs ask the media to respect their privacy and ask for the prayers of their friends and the American people. The president has never been prouder of Claire and hopes her courageous decision will encourage others to seek help."

There was only one problem: the press was in full-blown revolt. They demanded Lisa appear before the cameras to comment on Franklin's death and Claire's status. The press shop decided to feed the beast before they were torn limb from limb.

At 4:08 p.m., Lisa walked into the briefing room, lips pressed into a thin line of lipstick, face etched with strain. "The president has sent a letter to the children of Peter Corbin Franklin expressing his deep condolences upon the death of their father. The letter reads in part, and I quote, 'The principles for which your father stood throughout his life will inspire future generations of Americans, and his example of being a voice for the voiceless will long endure. His service for the least among us will always be honored and will now be greatly missed by our nation.'" She paused, looking up from her notes. "I'll take your questions."

The room exploded in raised hands and shouted questions.

"Lisa, why weren't we told the First Lady checked into a rehab facility until thirty minutes ago? What were you trying to hide from the American people?" asked Dan Dorman, chief attack dog of the *Washington Post*.

"The decision about when to inform the public was made out of an abundance of caution due to security concerns and to protect Mrs. Long's privacy."

"How much of this is related to her performance at the women's business forum when she appeared to be under the influence of alcohol?" asked *Politico*. "Has Mrs. Long become a liability to her husband?"

"This was a personal decision. Politics played no role whatsoever."

"Will you be announcing where Mrs. Long is receiving treatment?" asked the *Washington Times*. "One unconfirmed account reports that it is Hope Ranch in Phoenix."

"That decision will be made by the Long family, but as of now . . ."

STANDING IN FRONT OF the television in the private anteroom just off the Oval Office, Long stood with his arms crossed, watching the news briefing. Charlie Hector stood silently at his side, his face a study in punch-drunk exhaustion, common among occupants of the West Wing.

"We can't let Lisa take these bullets," Long said quietly. "This is my storm, not hers."

"You mean you want to go to the briefing room . . . right now?" asked Hector.

"Yes," Long said firmly. "This is my wife they're attacking. I have to defend her."

"You're preaching to the choir, Mr. President," Hector replied. "I told you my position before. But if you walk in there now, you're jumping into a shark tank. They smell blood."

"I'll take my chances," Long said. "Let's go."

The door to the Oval Office flew open, and the president and Hector walked briskly down the hall and turned toward the elevator to ride down to the basement, drawing the surprised stares of passing staff as Secret Service agents scrambled to keep up.

THE PRESS WENT SLACK-JAWED when Long walked into the briefing room. At first Lisa did not notice him. Then, reading the faces of reporters, she became flustered, glancing at the president, unsure of what to do next. Bailing her out, Long approached the podium.

An aide affixed the presidential seal to the podium. Then, without a note or apparent mental calculation, Long spoke firmly into the microphone. "I have been in love with my wife Claire for thirty-two years. I love her, and she loves me. She is my best friend. In those three decades, through raising four children, and countless campaigns, I have never been more in love with her or been more proud of her than I am right now." Everyone sat in respectful silence. The only sounds were *click-whir-click-whir* of still cameras and roller pens flying across steno pads. "The decision Claire has made was not easy. The price of admitting you have a problem can be high in our gotcha culture, especially for someone in the public eye. That is why I have so much respect for Claire. She has my full support, my prayers, and, most importantly, my unconditional love." He paused, his eyes misting. "Our marriage has never been stronger. Claire will be a better person, and we will be a stronger couple because of her decision. I know the American people will support Claire, as they have in everything else we have dealt with as a family."

Long leaned forward, inviting eyes and body language soliciting questions. It was Long's unique political skill: taking a liability and turning it into a positive.

"Mr. President, I know this is a difficult topic," said NBC News. "But Scottie Morris, your media consultant, was arrested for cocaine possession during the presidential campaign, and you said at the time you were oblivious to the fact he had a drug problem." Long stared back, keeping his composure. "Your wife has entered a rehabilitation center for alcoholism. I'm wondering if this hasn't forced you to consider whether you may have been so self-absorbed that you may not be aware of the personal struggles of those closest to you?"

Lisa stood ten feet away, arms across her chest, glaring at the NBC reporter. But Long shook it off. He seemed to understand that like a karate chop, the question could be turned back on the person who struck the blow.

"It's a fair question, and one that I have asked myself on more than one occasion in the last forty-eight hours," replied Long, impressing the press corps with his capacity for introspection and self-awareness. "Look, alcoholism doesn't just claim one victim. There are many victims. Just as alcoholics can be in denial about their problem, so, too, can family members and loved ones. That may have been the case for me. Because I have always admired Claire's strength, I didn't want to admit that she should get help." Long spoke in a strong voice, looking directly into the camera, ignoring the reporters. "The first step to recovery is admitting you have a problem. That's true not only for Claire but also for our family." He shifted his weight, placing an elbow on the podium, suggesting an intimate aside. "One thing I can assure you, we are together on this as a family. We're going to confront it, beat it, and heal together."

The press corps was thunderstruck. Long took a vicious shot and returned the volley with greater force.

"Mr. President, how much of this was precipitated by Mrs. Long's recent appearance before an audience of women business leaders at the White House, which was universally interpreted as a flop due to her apparently being inebriated?" asked Reuters.

Long seemed to stiffen a bit. "Claire and I discussed it. She was upset by some of what you all reported, which was very hurtful. But we both understand that the presidency is a fishbowl, and everything we say or do is fair game." He widened his eyes for emphasis. "We get that. Let me say this: Claire is a fabulous First Lady. She has done her job with grace and dignity. Her decision was based solely on what was best for her health and recovery."

"How long will Mrs. Long stay at the rehabilitation center?" asked AP.

"We don't know the answer to that at this point," Long replied deliberately, punctuating the last three words with pauses: "at . . . this . . . point."

"Weeks? Months?"

"Whatever she and her doctors agree on," Long said with a shrug. He smiled, breaking the tension. "We want her back as soon as possible. But we want her to stay as long as she needs to for successful treatment. That's the most important thing."

"Mr. President, on a different topic, Supreme Court Justice Peter Corbin Franklin has died, and you have expressed your condolences to his family," said Fox News. "Can you give us a sense of how soon you will arrive at a replacement?"

"No, I can't," Long fired back. "I spoke with Peter Jr., Justice Franklin's eldest son, today. I told him we were saddened to learn of his father's death and his family was in our thoughts and prayers. I think for now we should honor the memory and service of Justice Franklin. I will submit a nominee for the Supreme Court to the U.S. Senate after an appropriate period of deliberation and consultation."

"Do you have a short list yet?"

"If I did, I wouldn't tell you," said Long with a grin. The press corps chuckled.

"Mr. President, you refused to take a position either way on the impeachment of Justice Franklin as he lay comatose in a hospital," said Reuters. "Do you regret remaining neutral given the circus that unfolded in the House of Representatives? Don't you bear some responsibility for the poisoned and partisan atmosphere?"

Long nodded. "It's a fair criticism. First of all, I never believed the Senate had the votes needed to remove Justice Franklin. Perhaps I would have taken a different position if there had been, but now we will never know." He tapped the podium like a professor with his index finger. "This dispute involved the other two branches of government. Respect for the separation of powers required me to refrain from any action that might prejudice my selection of the next justice if and when there was a vacancy. I know a lot of politics was involved here. But I had to put the Constitution first."

"Thank you!" shouted Lisa from the corner of the stage.

Long caught a glance of Lisa out of the corner of his eye. "Thank you all very much, and let me again thank the American people for their prayers for Claire and our family." The media horde leapt out of their chairs to hurl more questions, hoping to catch Long at a spontaneous moment.

"Is Marco Diaz on your list?"

"What is your reaction to the impeachment vote in the House?"

"Joe Penneymounter says he won't hold a hearing until after the Court is in session!"

Long ignored them, turned on his heel, and exited through the narrow doorway leading to the Oval Office. Lisa Robinson, Charlie Hector, and a trail of aides followed him.

On the front row Dan Dorman of the *Washington Post*, turned to a colleague, whispering in her ear, "Nukes in Iran, a health-care bill going down the tubes, a Supreme Court vacancy, and the First Lady in rehab. If the Long presidency were an IPO, its stock would be in a free fall."

"Yeah, but you gotta give him credit for one thing," replied the colleague.

"What's that?" asked Dorman.

"He isn't boring. The Longs sell a lot of newspapers."

Dorman flashed a wicked grin. "For that we are eternally grateful."

FIFTEEN

Gabriella Fellissi breezed through the lobby of the Hotel Hassler, a bottle of Fellissi Reserve under her arm, Gucci shopping bag in her hand, flicking back her sun-streaked mane of brown hair with her other hand. Every head turned reflexively. And why not? Gabriella was dressed to kill: black skinny jeans, Dolce and Gabana leopard-spot tee, tapered leather jacket, Chanel sunglasses, Gucci purse, and matching leopard-spot Mahlano Blahniks. She asked the concierge to call Jay's suite and announce her arrival.

"Yes, Ms. Felissi," replied the concierge dutifully. Gabriella wore fame the way she wore her designer jeans: effortlessly. "Mr. Noble, Ms. Felissi is here."

"Tell him I brought the wine," she said playfully.

"She brought the wine, sir," said the concierge as ordered.

When Jay stepped off the elevator less than a minute later, Gabriella stood before him, hand resting on jutting hip, sunglasses resting on her flowing hair, head cocked and wearing a mischievous smile. Jay tipped the bellman to bring up the case of wine and invited Gabriella up to his suite. Was it too forward to invite her to his room? He hoped not. Jay grabbed a wine opener and two red wine glasses, and they walked out on to the veranda. He opened the bottle and poured a small amount gingerly into one glass. He lowered his nose, breathing in the aroma, then taking a sip.

"Incredible," he said.

"Let it breathe," instructed Gabriella. "When the oxygen hits the grape, the flavor will come out like a bouquet." She bunched her fingers and then spread them, imitating a blooming flower.

"Sorry I don't have a decanter," said Jay.

"No, it's fine. The glass works."

They swirled the wine in the bottom of their glasses, alternately inhaling the smell through their noses and taking deliberate sips. An hour later, when Jay opened the second bottle, the sun was going down over the Roman skyline, and the mood grew more relaxed. The conversation flowed easily. Gabriella slid her chair closer, and her long, slender fingers occasionally brushed against his arm or knee when she made a point. Jay felt a jolt of sensual tension every time she touched him, however briefly. They were talking about business and politics since the election in Italy was now only eight days away, but their eyes spoke of deeper yearnings, helped along by the wine.

Jay held his glass aloft, gazing at the rust-tinged, scarlet color of the liquid illuminated by the sinking sun. "Look at that!" he exclaimed in wonderment. "It's almost brown. I've never seen red wine with quite that color before."

"It is the grape," said Gabriella, leaning over to gaze at it from Jay's angle. Her breath tickled his neck. "The Sangiovese grape in the Montalcino region has more character than a merlot or a cabernet. For the reserve, it is selected from Papa's very best grapes, handpicked by my father, from a seventy-five-year-old vineyard with soil that produces the smallest number of grapes per plant, of the highest quality." She crossed her arms proudly. "After that, we age it in oak barrels for three years and then in bottles for eighteen months." She gazed down at her glass, spinning the wine in the bottom. "The year 2003 was very good."

"I had no idea the process was so complicated," said Jay, amazed. He turned to Gabriella, their faces a hands-length away. The thought entered his mind to kiss her. But he was leaving Italy in a week. This was no time for romantic complications.

"Have you had dinner?" asked Gabriella, as if reading his mind.

"No, not yet."

"What is it with men? You never eat!"

Jay thought: *Me? You must live on celery to be able to pour yourself into those jeans.* But he bit his tongue.

"Come on, I will show you a place," she said, gathering up her Gucci bag and curling her arm through his. They rode down the elevator to the lobby and out into the driveway, where the valet had her black Porsche 911 up front. Jay had a car and driver but thought it would be more fun to ride in Gabriella's Porsche. Besides, he liked the idea of her being in charge of the evening's itinerary. A mile later they pulled up to another hotel, the Molvano, which Jay did not recognize. They rode the elevator to the roof.

"You will like this," Gabriella said with girl-about-town assurance. "It is a magnificent restaurant and then becomes a club at night." She winked. "It gets wild later."

"Sounds like my kind of place," said Jay with a smile.

It was ten o'clock when they were finally seated. The maître d' escorted them to a table against the rail with a view of the illuminated dome of the Pantheon, with St. Peter's in the background. They ordered another bottle of wine and ate ravenously. Gabriella ate like a horse, ordering a beluga caviar appetizer and lobster pasta. Jay had calamari and fried eel simmering in olive oil pulled out of a pan thirty seconds earlier.

The waitress brought them a dessert menu. Gabriella ordered the chocolate soufflé.

"Bring two spoons," she said.

"Fattening him up before the kill?" the waitress asked with a smile.

"Yes," replied Gabriella, winking.

Jay felt a tingle go through his body. He was a little tipsy and was losing control of the situation. Jay knew he was being followed by U.S. reporters in Italy, so he tried to keep a low profile. But he found Gabriella irresistible, and he had lost count of how many glasses of wine he drank. Was it the wine, Gabriella's looks, or was he simply catching an Italian babe on the rebound from Lisa Robinson and Nicole Dearborn, the girlfriend who turned out to be a mole for Sal Stanley? Probably all three, he surmised.

"Can I ask you a question?" Jay asked.

"Sure, what?"

"Were you ever a model?"

Gabriella blushed. "How did you know?"

Jay slapped the palm of his hand down on the table. "I knew it!" He paused. "How did I know? Are you kidding? You're freakin' gorgeous."

"Not really. I didn't have what it took," Gabriella demurred. "I only dabbled in modeling. I always wanted to be a businesswoman and grow the family business."

"I want to see your portfolio!" exclaimed Jay.

"My stock portfolio?" she asked quizzically.

"No, your modeling portfolio," Jay laughed. "I want to see the photos!"

"Okay," said Gabriella, then, in a soft whisper: "But I'll have to remove the lingerie shots,"

"Don't you dare!" exclaimed Jay.

"I have to tell you something," said Gabriella in a low voice as she sipped a cappuccino. She paused, looking both ways, and then leaned in closer. "I was married before."

Should he tell her? He decided honesty was the best policy. "Me, too," he said. Gabriella's eyes widened. Jay held up two fingers.

"Twice?" said Gabriella, relieved. "Wow. That makes me feel better." She wriggled out of her leather jacket. Jay tried not to stare. "Maybe the third time is the charm, no?"

"I'm hoping," said Jay. "I haven't met the right person yet."

"You will," said Gabriella. He wondered if she meant he already had.

They mangled the chocolate soufflé beyond recognition. Jay noticed the restaurant was taking on the look of a club, with lights, thumping music, swirling bodies, and tables moved out of the way. Gabriella grabbed him by the hand and led him to the dance floor. She seemed to glide across the floor, lost in a trance, her body moving to its own internal gyroscope as she swayed her hips and rocked her head. She was mesmerizing. Jay, trying to disguise his awkwardness, glanced around and tried to imitate others' movements.

After a couple of songs, Gabriella excused herself to use the restroom. Jay went over to the bar. As he leaned against the rail of the bar, he felt someone pinch him from behind. Shocked, he wheeled around to see an Italian version of the Upper West Side party girl. She was Twiggy on speed, blondish-brown hair with highlights falling down her neck and shoulders, looking like a raccoon with heavy mascara, sheathed in a tight purple dress, black leggings, and spiked-heel Gucci boots. The place was a meat market.

"What are you doing with Gabriella?" she shouted over the loud music. "She's crazy, you know." She put her finger to her head and twirled it.

"Well, so am I," Jay volleyed back. "So we'll make a fine pair."

She handed him her card. "When you get tired of her, which won't be long, call me," she said, disappearing into the crowd. Jay looked down at the card. It was printed in Italian on the front and English on the back. Flipping it over to the English side, it read: "Lolo Luigi," and underneath a decidedly amorphous job title: "Massage Therapist, Spiritual Counselor, Artiste."

Gabriella reappeared, and Jay quickly shoved the card in his pocket. He felt slightly guilty about keeping it, but he was flattered by the party girl's attention. The truth? The attention made him feel better about himself, affirmed him. They went back to the dance floor and slow-danced, their bodies touching and swaying, occasionally raising their arms and clasping their hands. When the song ended, they made their way back to their table.

"I need a shot," said Gabriella. "Jay, will you have some grappa with me?"

"Sure," said Jay. He was game. At that moment Jay would pretty much do whatever Gabriella suggested.

The waitress brought a bottle of grappa, and Jay and Gabriella did a shot. Then another. Then a third. Jay was beginning to feel woozy. They danced some more. He wondered how much more of Gabriella he could handle.

It was now approaching 4:00 a.m., and the dance floor empty except for a few stray couples lost in each other's gaze. Jay waved for the check and handed the waitress his credit card. When he opened the bill, it was 650 euros, close to nine hundred dollars. Who cared?

After signing the check, Jay helped Gabriella into her jacket, and they headed to an elevator, the door held open by the maître d'. When they reached the lobby, Jay saw her Porsche on the curb, the valet standing at attention. As they stepped out through the revolving door, Jay saw shadowy figures in the bushes out of the corner of his eye. Suddenly there was an explosion of flashes. The paparazzi! Panicked, Jay dove into the passenger side while Gabriella jumped in the driver's seat and gunned the engine, pulling away.

"It's the paparazzi. They are the dregs of the earth," said Gabriella as she threw the stick shift into second gear, roaring down a cobblestone side street.

"How did they know we were there?"

"Someone tipped them off."

Jay looked out the window to see a motor scooter to his right wedged in between the Porsche and the wall of the alley, the photographer wielding his camera like a gun, blazing away in a string of flashes. There could not have been more than two inches between them and the scooter as they flew down the alley going at least thirty kilometers per hour.

"Grab my cell phone out of my purse!" shouted Gabriella over the roaring engine.

Jay fumbled around in her bag. She dialed a number and spoke in rapid-fire Italian. She hung up.

"Who was that?"

"My friend with the Rome police. He's setting up a checkpoint outside the Hotel Hassler to block the paparazzi."

"I don't believe this," said Jay. "They haven't bothered me once."

Gabriella shot him a look. "Darling, that's because you haven't been with me," she said. "Welcome to my world."

The Porsche flew down past the Spanish Steps and up the cobblestone road to the top of the hill, where a police car parked sideways and two wooden temporary roadblocks had been erected. A white-gloved policeman held up his hand as Gabriella slowed the car and rolled down her window. He waved them through, stopping the paparazzi and ordering them to leave the area. They spun around in their scooters and shot down the hill, looking for an alternate route. Gabriella pulled up to the Hassler and came to an abrupt stop. Jay could smell the burning oil from the revving engine, which purred as the car sat in neutral.

"Would you like to come upstairs for a drink?" asked Jay. It was the best line he could muster in his frazzled state.

"I'd love to," said Gabriella, her eyes yearning. "But I really have to go."

Jay was crestfallen. "Not even one little drink?"

"I can't." She glanced back and looked out the rear windshield. "The paparazzi will camp out and shoot pictures as I go in and out, and they'll report what time I leave."

"Okay, I'll talk to you tomorrow."

Gabriella kissed him softly on the cheek. "It's taking all the willpower I have to let you go," she said. "But I need to leave."

Reluctantly Jay got out of the car. As he turned to leave, Gabriella rolled down the window on the passenger door. "Jay, I had a wonderful time."

As Jay walked through the lobby, the concierge gave him a knowing glance. "Graci," said Jay, referring to the roadblock.

"My pleasure, Mr. Noble. Have a good evening," replied the concierge.

Jay stepped on the elevator and pressed the button to his floor. He glanced at his watch. It was nearly 5:00 a.m. He had a strategy meeting for the Brodi campaign in three hours. It was eight days before the election, his candidate was in a race too close to call, and he had spent the night clubbing with one of the most eligible bachelorettes in Italy. Jay shook his head, becoming angry at himself. He couldn't handle another failed romance. What was he thinking? He stumbled to the bedroom, kicked off his shoes, and fell face forward. He needed to get at least a couple of hours of sleep.

YOLANDA MAJETTE, CHIEF JUSTICE of the California Supreme Court, walked across the lawn of Oxford University, where she was enjoying a European vacation that masqueraded as a summer graduate seminar in legal theory. It was an unusually springlike day, the sun breaking through the clouds, the grass and trees lit up in bright shades of green. Glancing at her cell phone, she noticed she had a voice mail. Because the court was not in session, she rarely received phone calls, checking in with her office sporadically. To her surprise, the message was from Attorney General Keith Golden.

Though out of the country, Majette had learned of Peter Corbin Franklin's death. Her mind raced. Why else would the attorney general be calling? Her fingers shaking, heart rate quickening, she dialed the number. Golden's assistant put the call through to him.

"Madame Justice, how are you?" Golden asked brightly. "I hope I'm not reaching you at a bad time. Your office said you were overseas."

"Yes, I am," Majette answered. "I'm in England, teaching a seminar at Oxford."

"Well, I certainly hate to interrupt what must be a wonderful respite from the daily grind of the court," Golden said empathetically. "But I wonder if you could come to Washington." He paused. "As soon as possible."

Majette felt a burst of adrenalin. "I . . . I'm sure I can," she heard herself say. Her mouth suddenly turned to cotton. "If you don't mind my asking, does this have anything to do with a court vacancy?"

"Keep this between us, but yes," said Golden. "I'd like to meet with you to discuss it. The president would like to visit with you as well. Yolanda, we're interviewing potential candidates, and we're moving fairly fast."

"Alright," Majette replied, trying to stay calm. Her heart pounded through her chest. "I'll have to cancel my seminar for day after tomorrow."

"I understand. Just don't tell anyone there why," Golden cautioned. "Maybe you can arrange to come down with a bad cold."

"I think I'm feeling a cold coming on even as we speak."

"My staff will arrange the logistics. We'd like you to be on the first flight to Dulles or BWI. Don't fly into Reagan. There's too much of a chance you might be recognized."

"I see." Majette realized this was not a drill. She was under serious consideration.

"Other than your husband, tell no one about this. That includes parents, in-laws, children, former law partners, close friends. No one."

"I understand."

"See you tomorrow." She heard a click as Golden hung up.

Majette placed her cell phone in her lap, stunned. She looked around at all the students and faculty as they hurried by to their next class, oblivious to the lightning bolt that just hit her. She was on the short list for appointment to the U.S. Supreme Court. Majette, whose father pastored an AME church and whose uncle was a prominent pastor in Jackson, Mississippi, had sensed from her childhood that someday God would call her to a high place. Was it coming true? She excitedly dialed her husband's cell phone number to tell him the news.

SENATOR JOE PENNEYMOUNTER BARRELED through the Senate Democratic cloakroom like a man on a mission. His face like a flint, his longish grey hair swept back behind his ears, his blue suit pinched at the waist, he walked in long, purposeful strides. Bodies parted like water before him. He walked to his desk on the Senate floor and clipped a microphone to his coat pocket.

"Mr. President, distinguished colleagues," he began in a firm baritone. "With the death of Peter Corbin Franklin, our nation has lost one of the greatest champions of civil liberties to ever sit on the U.S. Supreme Court. It now falls to the Senate to decide his replacement. The framers of the Constitution never intended for the U.S. Senate to be a rubber-stamp of presidential prerogative. Advice and consent is a solemn duty, and it is one we all take seriously. The Senate is coequal in this responsibility with the president."

Having fired his initial salvo asserting senatorial privilege, Penneymounter went for the jugular. "During his campaign Bob Long appeared before the religious right at Trinity University and pledged to appoint justices in the model of Alito, Roberts, Scalia, and Thomas. He vowed to nominate judges who would merely interpret laws as passed by legislators, not engage in what he called 'judicial activism.'" Penneymounter assumed a professorial pose, reading glasses perched on the end of his nose, his jowly face stretched into a fleshy scowl.

"These are code words, Mr. President!" he thundered. "Everyone knows what the president meant when he promised to nominate only judges guided by judicial restraint. These are code words for outlawing the right of women to reproductive choice, impinging upon the personal freedom for gays and lesbians, defending powerful corporate interests, and turning back the clock on two generations of civil rights for minorities." His body coiled with energy as he raised his right arm high to punctuate the point. "With this vacancy on the Supreme Court, we could soon have a majority of justices hostile to a woman's right to choose. And make no mistake, Mr. President: more than *Roe v. Wade* hangs in the balance. Three generations of progress for civil rights are in danger."

Desks began to fill with Democratic senators as word rifled through the Capitol that Penneymounter was unloading on Long. The press gallery also filled with reporters, their eyes dancing with glee, their fingers flying across the keyboards of their laptops. Spectators in the gallery could hardly believe their luck. Everyone knew if Penneymounter had the floor, fireworks would light up like the fourth of July.

"The question, Mr. President, is: which of his conflicting promises will President Long keep?" Penneymounter asked, leaning forward in a satirical bow, hands on hips. "Will it be his promise to Andy Stanton and the far right to pack the federal courts with clones of John Roberts and Sam Alito? Or will it be the oath he took to uphold and defend the Constitution of these United States?" He paused, turning a page slowly in his stack of papers. "I hope and pray President Long will honor the oath of his office. But I fear the worst. I worry that in almost canine obedience to the sectarian, fundamentalist faction of his third-party movement, he will shred the Constitution and its protection of reproductive freedom, the cherished right to privacy, and the sanctity of our homes and bedrooms."

PHIL BATTAGLIA SAT IN his cramped West Wing office, glowering at the television set, his arms crossed over his chest. An aide rapped on the open door and stuck his head in. "It's Attorney General Golden."

Battaglia picked up the receiver. "Are you watching Penneymounter?" he asked. "The guy is melting down before our very eyes."

"He's channeling Howard Dean. The only thing missing is the scream."

Battaglia chuckled. "He's trying to define the nominee before we have even selected them."

"No question. Do you think it'll work?"

"It could," Battaglia replied. "It worked with Bork. It almost worked with Thomas. It backfired during the Roberts confirmation." He sighed. "I think it depends on the nominee. If there's no paper trail and no skeletons, I think we win."

"I agree."

"Speaking of which, did you reach Majette?"

"Yes," said Golden. "She was at Oxford. She's flying in tomorrow. I'll meet with her, then she'll visit with the president first thing Saturday morning in the living quarters."

"She's solid. The president knows her and likes her. I hope this doesn't leak."

"She's under strict orders to tell no one beyond her husband," said Golden.

"I'm just glad I don't have to decide," said Battaglia. "We can't screw this up."

"That's why he's the president and we're not."

"This is really for all the marbles, isn't it?" asked Battaglia.

Golden paused, measuring his response. "Yes, it is."

"Let's just make sure we don't blow it."

"We won't, Phil. We won't."

Battaglia hung up the phone. The Supreme Court nomination was like a gift coming so early in Long's young presidency. Win or lose, Battaglia thought, the outcome would likely define Long's tenure.

SIXTEEN

The staff wheeled a birthday cake the size of a Yugo into the East Room. Long stood before it beaming, crow's- feet crinkling, blue eyes twinkling with satisfaction, a rubbery smile stretched ear to ear. The official occasion was Vice President Johnny Whitehead's seventy-fifth birthday. Since Whitehead's age was the butt of jokes from late-night comics, the communications shop decided to hang a lantern on the problem and throw a big party. It was classic Long strategy: turn your weakness into a strength and your opponent's strength into a weakness. The room was filled to capacity with White House staffers, lobbyists, political grunts, major donors, and campaign volunteers. A bluegrass band from Whitehead's native Kentucky jammed on stage, a squat man dressed as Colonel Sanders in white suit and goatee roamed the floor, and a line of cloggers dressed in rustic mountain outfits performed. The press stood on a riser, their faces twisted with contempt.

The crowd whooped and hollered as the cloggers left the stage. Long walked to a small podium to loud applause. He stood before the towering cake bearing the vice presidential seal, painted in gleaming blue and white icing (the colors of Whitehead's beloved University of Kentucky) and topped with authentic Kentucky bluegrass, reveling in what Jefferson called the "splendid misery" of the presidency. Jaunty and confident, he placed one hand on the podium and put the other in his pocket, loose and at ease.

"I promised the vice president we wouldn't put candles on the cake for each year," Long joked to warm laughter. "I didn't want him to strain his lungs by trying to blow them all out. So Johnny, you only have seven and a half candles—one for each decade!" More laughter. "Come on up here and say a few words, and I mean a very few words, so we can give these folks some birthday cake."

Whitehead ambled to the podium wearing a crooked grin. He seemed not to mind being the sidekick to Long's comic routine. John Nance Garner famously called the vice presidency not worth a bucket of warm spit. Not for Johnny Whitehead. He was retired and forgotten when the phone rang and Long gave him a chance to get back in the game. For Johnny, being veep was like winning the lottery every single day.

"They say age is just a state of mind, and I know what they mean," he began, smiling in anticipation. "After all, I'm only eleven years old in dog years." (A roar of laughter.) "Take off some of those candles!" he joked. Long stood to his side, clapping and stage-laughing. Wheeling to face the cake, Whitehead blew as hard as he could, straining to reach the last candle, which continued to flicker against the force of his blast. Inhaling, he blew again, snuffing it out. The room erupted in applause.

The celebrants formed a receiving line that snaked through the East Room. Each guest shook the vice president's and the president's hands.

Ten minutes into the receiving line, Chris Calio, Republican congressman from New Jersey, approached Whitehead. "Did you hear Penneymounter's speech on the Senate floor today?" he asked, grimacing. "He's a *disgrace!*"

"No," Whitehead replied, his face expressionless. "I try not to pay any attention to Joe."

Long leaned over, joining in the fun. "Who did you say you were avoiding, Johnny?"

"Joe Penneymounter," said Calio, relishing his face time. "He accused you of shredding the Constitution and said you had a canine obedience to Andy Stanton."

Long put his arms around Whitehead and Calio, forming a huddle. "Penneymounter is an insufferable *blowhard*," said Long, spitting the words through clenched teeth. "He calls me up and drones, blah, blah, blah." His eyes widened. "He's TOTALLY IRRELEVANT."

Standing in the back of the room, Lisa Robinson caught sight of an ABC News camera crew swinging its directional mike to the president. She knew Long's comments would be posted on abcnews.com within minutes. She bolted down the hall to warn Charlie Hector. As her stomach did flips, she wondered: *What are we going to do about this flap?*

JAY STROLLED THROUGH THE long, frescoed and high-ceilinged lobby of the Chamber of Deputies building known as the transatlantico, or ocean liner, where members of parliament and influence peddlers gathered informally on couches and chairs between votes. His appearance caused heads to turn and conversations to fall to a muffled whisper. Jay's status as the imported political genius from America was legendary, his every move fueling gossip, most of it urban legend. At the bar Jay ordered his third shot of espresso and a pastry to jolt him out of his hangover and sleep-deprived exhaustion. His head spinning from the combined effects of the grappa and espresso that rolled around in his stomach like battery acid, he departed the lobby and climbed a flight of stairs to a conference room. Fashionably late, he pulled up a chair at the opposite end of the table from Lorenzo Brodi.

Fred Edgewater, who Jay had pulled into the campaign (for a cool quarter of a million euros, plus expenses), fired up his laptop and walked through a PowerPoint presentation. He reviewed the latest tracking numbers in a dull, flat monotone. Ice in his veins, showing no concern as he described Brodi's falling numbers, Fred delivered the shocking news: Brodi's twelve-point lead over the incumbent prime minister had evaporated. For Brodi and his political team, it was a punch in the solar plexus. They were tied, and Brodi's negatives had spiked six points from a barrage of negative ads. When Fred finished, Brodi sat stone-faced, lips pressed together, eyes smoldering with frustration.

"I thought you were two wizards who elected Long in America!" bellowed Brodi. "How did I drop twelve points in two weeks?!" He got up from the conference room table and paced back and forth before walking over to the breakfast spread and grabbing an apple impulsively, taking a large bite. He chewed it, the juice forming beads on his lower lip. "My message is not getting through." He pointed at Jay accusingly. "You are not getting my message across to the people."

"Perhaps our American strategist is too busy chasing Italian women," said one of Brodi's advisors with a wry smile. He slid a copy of a Rome tabloid splashed with the photos of Jay and Gabriella leaving the club the night before across the table. Brodi glanced down at the front page, the veins in his temple protruding. Jay thought his head might explode.

"I thought that was my job," he said sarcastically. Brodi was notorious for his not-so-secret romantic assignations, causing frequent heartburn for his political advisors, not to mention his wife. The wild parties at Brodi's Lake

Como estate were notorious, and he sprinkled his coalition's electoral list with "Brodi's broads," as the press called the models and busty game-show hosts who campaigned in short skirts and plunging blouses.

All heads turned to Jay. He had hoped the tabloids would sit on the photos of him and Gabriella for at least a day or two. Angry with himself and bored with Brodi's pity party, he leaned forward, rounding his shoulders as he prepared to deliver what he called his "candidate smack down" lecture.

"Let me tell you something, Mr. Mayor. Fred is neglecting corporate clients who are paying him millions of dollars to help you as a personal favor to me," Jay fired back. "He called Long's precise margin of victory when every single published poll was wrong. So you better listen to him." He leveled a steady gaze at Brodi. "You are a coronary patient flatlining on the operating table. Fred and I are trying to save you—" He spun in his chair and pointed at Fred. "And you're criticizing us because we're trying to turn around your candidacy?!"

An aide translated Jay's rant to Brodi, whose eyes widened. No one ever talked to Brodi like this. Jay was trying electroshock treatment.

"And let me tell you, Mr. Mayor, It's going to get worse before it gets better," Jay said. He paused, allowing the dead air to hang and let the point sink into Brodi's thick skull. "Sir, you are going to lose this race unless we do something dramatic and do it right now." He rose from his chair, steadying himself with a hand on the table. "Why? Because against my advice, you tried to protect your lead and run out the clock. Now we're in the fight of our lives. We are done trying to win pretty. You now have only two options: win ugly or lose."

Everyone stared back at Jay as the translator rattled off Italian to Brodi and his aides. Finally Brodi raised his palms. "What do you recommend we do?"

"Take the bark off Flavia," answered Jay, referring to Flavia Porro, the incumbent prime minister. Jay's eyes scanned the table as a few of Brodi's advisors recoiled at his gruesome imagery. "Porro's education minister ordered austerity cuts and furloughed teachers, eliminated teaching assistants, and closed schools," Jay said. "Isn't the head of the teacher's union supporting us?"

"Yes," said one of Brodi's aides. "He's endorsed the mayor."

"I don't want his endorsement," Jay answered, his tone dismissive, as if he were talking to a child. "I want *chaos*! I want teachers picketing, schools padlocked, parents protesting in front of shuttered classrooms, children wandering the street." Jay's eyes were wild, his gestures animated, his voice raised to a shout. "I want television coverage of people standing outside empty classrooms shouting Porro's name like a curse word!"

Brodi turned to one of his aides. "Can that be arranged?" he asked.

"We'll have to give the teacher's union some love," answered an aide.

"Porro was health minister in the previous government, right?" Jay asked. He was on a roll. "He privatized nursing homes. Those contractors, who are also his biggest contributors, are under investigation." Heads nodded; the investigations had uncovered evidence that elderly patients were neglected and died, with one patient left sitting in a wheelchair with bedsores, languishing in his own feces for days. "Hang it around his neck like a burning tire. We need an ad with a memorable phrase, something that rhymes in Italian: Porro Hides, Seniors Die."

"Porro fare uno scherzo, un quanti mororio," said one of the Italian advisors.

"What does it mean?" asked Jay.

"Porro played a joke while seniors died," said the translator. "It's a play on words. Like Nero fiddled while Rome burned."

"It doesn't quite work," replied Jay. "I need something punchy." He pointed to the translator. "Come and help me with the Italian." He turned to the media consultant, who he despised. "I want that ad up by tomorrow morning. Not by 10:00 a.m. or noon—by 7:00 a.m." He glanced around the table. "Who's reaching out to the teacher's union guy?"

An aide to Brodi raised his hand. Jay nodded. "Tell him the classrooms will be reopened and the teachers rehired."

"Where are we going to find the money to do that?" asked the aide.

"What do I care?!" Jay exploded. "Find the money or you'll lose the election."

The meeting was over. Edgewater packed up his laptop as Jay walked over to Brodi. Leaning in, he whispered: "If you do exactly what I say, you'll win by three to five points. You can thank me later."

"Si," said Brodi. "Now I know how Long won. You are an evil genius."

"No," said Jay corrected him. "Long won because he was the better candidate. And that's why you're going to win."

Jay headed for the door, the translator in tow, Edgewater galloping behind in rapid-step, Brodi's advisors chagrined and white-faced.

"That was a performance worthy of an Academy Award," joked Edgewater. "You almost reduced the mayor to tears. I'd say it was above even your high standards."

"Sometimes a candidate needs a wake-up call like a sledgehammer upside the head," replied Jay with a smirk. "I don't think we'll be hearing any more whining from Brodi for a while."

As they headed down the stairs to find a private office, Jay's BlackBerry vibrated. He pulled it out of his pocket and checked his e-mail. It was a *Wall Street Journal* news alert. The headline read: "Long Calls Chairman of Judiciary Committee 'Irrelevant Blowhard.'"

"What!?" said Jay aloud. He stopped on the staircase and scrolled through the story. He could hardly believe his eyes. Allowing a boom mike to get so close to the body was a cardinal sin. While Jay was in Rome clubbing with Gabby and saving Brodi's campaign, the Long presidency was imploding.

SEVENTEEN

Claire sat out on the veranda of her cabana at Hope Ranch soaking in the sunset as dusk settled over the desert, bathing cacti and rock formations in a pinkish orange glow. She drank a cup of herbal tea and read one of the books that Dr. Kelly gave her. It was her homework. The phone in her room rang, and she walked back in and picked it up.

"Hi, honey. I just wanted to check in and see how you are doing," came Bob's voice.

"I'm doing well," said Claire with a relaxed sigh. "The therapy aside, it's been great to get away and think and relax. It's really beautiful here in the desert. I needed the time away."

"I know you did," said Bob empathetically. "We've both had a rough few years, I think you especially. Too much campaigning."

"Yes," said Claire.

"The demands of my political career required too much from both of us," Bob continued. "And the children." He paused. "Claire, I want to apologize for having the wrong priorities for so many years. I demanded that you and the kids take a backseat to my political ambition. I wasn't there for you, and you had to turn elsewhere for emotional comfort. I see that I bear a lot of the blame for what you have gone through, and I'm very sorry."

"It means a lot to me that you would say that," replied Claire, her eyes filled with tears. She was floored by Bob's admission. "I'm sorry, too. I think both of us needed to make changes. I'm really working to make the changes I need to make."

"Me, too," Bob said, his voice scratchy. "I miss you so much."

"I miss you too," said Claire. "But I hope you understand that I need to stay here for a while. I need time. I know it would be better for you if I came back now, with the media feeding frenzy, but I want to make sure that when I do come back, I'm the person I'm supposed to be."

"I agree. Stay as long as you need. I don't want you to feel any pressure at all to come back until you're ready. I mean it."

"Okay."

There was silence on the phone line for ten seconds.

"I love you," said Bob. Tears filled his eyes.

"I love you, too," said Claire through sniffles. "We're going to get through this."

"I know."

"Is Consuella taking good care of you?" Claire asked, referring to the housekeeper in the living quarters.

Bob chuckled. "Like a mother hen. She lays out my clothes in the morning. I'm not sure she realizes I've been dressing myself for more than a half century."

"She knows you need looking after," said Claire. "Well, I have to go to dinner. I'll talk to you tomorrow."

Claire hung up the phone and stood in the middle of her room. She glanced outside through the window. There was only a faint line of red where the sun had been just a few minutes earlier. For some reason she could not explain, she felt like praying. She got down on the floor facedown, her head nestled in her hands.

"God, I've tried to run my life for too long, and all I've done is mess it up," she prayed slowly, her voice halting, searching for the words. "I can't do it anymore. I'm tired. I can't believe I ended up here, but I did. Please help me. Help me." She began to weep.

BERT STAMPONOVICH WAS A bulldog of a litigator and one of the leading election law and tax lawyers in the nation. His job was to keep Andy Stanton out of hot water with the IRS and the Federal Election Commission, as well as defend him against an endless string of lawsuits. An ideologue and political combatant, Stamponovich was chief counsel to Gerry Jimmerson as well as two dozen other Republicans in Congress, whom he billed over one million dollars a year. He was also general counsel of the American

Justice Foundation, the right's answer to the ACLU. No boardroom lawyer, he argued three cases successfully before the Supreme Court, including the landmark decision that gutted McCain-Feingold restrictions on campaign issue ads by outside groups like the Faith and Family Federation.

Andy joined the conference call with a loud "Hello, dear brothers!" after Stamponovich and Ross Lombardy had killed some time with political gossip.

"Bert, what's the word?" asked Andy. It was his normal bird call.

"Ran into Golden yesterday at the White House," reported Stamponovich, fulfilling the two-pronged objective of providing information and underscoring his importance in DC.

"Yes?" asked Andy expectantly. "Did he tip his hand at all?"

"I asked him if we were going to be happy. He said, 'I hope so.'"

"That's not good," said Ross.

"No, it's not," continued Stamponovich with clipped efficiency. "Keith holds his cards close to the vest, but we're good friends. He said his top two candidates are Hillman and Diaz, in that order, but Long wants a woman."

"So do I," said Andy. He paused, rolling the idea over in his mind. "It's easier to confirm a woman. But I don't know why these guys are always playing identity politics. Did we get any black votes because Bush 41 appointed Clarence Thomas. Heck no!"

"My concern, Andy," Stamponovich drawled, "is that the woman he's leaning toward is Yolanda Majette."

"Remind me who she is again?" asked Andy.

"She's the chief justice of the California Supreme Court," chimed in Ross. "Long knows her. African-American, attractive, articulate, smart. Basically centrist like Long. Not a liberal, but not one of us."

"The California mafia is pushing her hard, starting with Battaglia," said Stamponovich.

"She's a moderate?!" shrieked Andy, his blood pressure spiking. "Where is she on the moral issues? They don't call California the land of fruits and nuts for nothing."

"No core convictions that I know of," answered Stamponovich. "When the California Supremes ruled on same-sex marriage, she voted to uphold the marriage amendment, but her dissent argued that the gay couple suing lacked legal standing. She pointedly did not join the minority opinion that same-sex couples have no right to marry under the California state constitution."

"Good grief. That's unacceptable, my dear brother," muttered Andy.

"Totally," said Ross firmly. "If Long nominates Majette, it'll blow up in his face like a shrapnel grenade in his Partridge Family lunch box."

Andy giggled morbidly. He found Ross's bizarre analogies to be a source of constant amusement. "All of the above," he said. "Bert, you stop Majette right now. We need a full court press on Golden."

"I don't think Golden's the answer, frankly," said Stamponovich. "He may have been promised control of judicial nominations, but that's not how it works in the real world. This is being run out of the West Wing. Battaglia's driving this train."

"He's no friend of ours," said Ross.

"No one's our friend, Ross. Haven't you figured that out yet?" joked Andy.

"Phil's a problem," said Stamponovich. "He's a technocrat who doesn't care about ideology. Second, he's part of the California mafia, so he's biased for Majette."

"Should I call the president?" asked Andy. "He owes me."

"Big time. But we won't be able to pull that off without it being staffed," Ross warned. "Hector will want to know what the call's about; we can't tell the truth and we can't lie."

"Forget Hector!" bellowed Andy. "Who is *he*? I don't need his permission to talk to the president! I can call Long any time I want."

"Let me try something first," suggested Stamponovich, scrambling for an alternative to Andy's calling Long. "I'm on a daily judicial strategy conference call with the Federalist Society, Right to Life, Heritage, and the bloggers. We can start a firestorm in the blogosphere, and that will give me an excuse to call Hector."

"We can also slip the mickey to Marvin Myers," said Ross. "This is cat-nip for him. I can see the headline now: 'Evangelical Groups Shoot Down Majette Trial Balloon.'"

"Good idea," said Andy. "Myers is a pit bull."

"Bert, you call Hector and I'll call Jay," said Ross. "Jay gets it. He still talks to the president almost every day."

"He's in Italy running the Brodi campaign," said Stamponovich, chuckling. "I think he's got his hands full."

"He can multitask," said Ross, chuckling.

"Somebody better tell Jay to get in the game, or Bob Long's gonna be a one termer," said Andy, the octave of his voice rising with anxiety. "We'll look like idiots if he picks Majette. Our troops will turn on us. We'd have to oppose her or remain neutral at best."

"We're on the case, Andy," said Ross smoothly, trying to calm down his increasingly agitated boss. "Majette will be in the trash bin by the time Bert and I get done."

Andy laughed. He got a big kick out of it whenever Ross started trash-talking about how many bodies he was going to pile up.

JAY'S RENTAL CAR SHOT up a narrow road that skirted craggy rocks in the mountains over Carmignano, seventeen kilometers east of Florence, and he tried to stay focused as he drove past five-hundred-foot drops with only a chain-link fence separating him from certain death. Carmignano began as a medieval outpost of the Florentine army, and a mountaintop fort still intact served as a lookout for invading Siennese armies. The Medicci family summer palace was just across the valley. The Fellissi family's summer villa was on top of the mountain right next to the ancient fort. Arriving at last, Jay pulled up to an iron gate, dialed a number into the intercom, and announced his arrival. A housekeeper buzzed him in.

"Miss Fellissi is down by the pool," said the housekeeper, her disapproving eyes surveying him up and down.

Jay walked around the villa to find Gabriella reclining in a lounge chair in a yellow string bikini that left little to the imagination, the straps down off her shoulders, her arms, legs, and abdomen glistening with tanning oil. She flipped lazily through a fashion magazine. Tanned body wrapped in yellow, she looked like a human Brach's candy.

"Jay, *bonjourno!*" she called, waving. "I see you found it alright."

"*Bonjourno.* I'm just glad to be alive after that drive up the mountain," laughed Jay. "This is not an easy place to get to."

"But worth the effort," she replied.

"Unbelievable," said Jay. He gazed out over wheat fields and vineyards that stretched for kilometers. The cupola and bell tower of the Doma in Florence were faintly visible through the mist. "This has got to be one of the most incredible views in Italy."

"Glad you like. This villa has been in our family for five hundred years," said Gabriella matter-of-factly. "Except the pool. I made Papa build it a few years ago."

The housekeeper brought out a tray with assorted cheeses, ham and sausage, a garden salad, fresh olives, and a bottle of red wine. Jay noticed she was sizing him up warily. He surmised he was the latest in a long string of male suitors.

"Come. Eat," said Gabriella, putting a fishnet wrap-around skirt on her narrow hips. She seemed to float to the table, long legs gliding, hips swaying. "We're having dinner tonight in Florence. My driver will take us so we don't have to worry about how much we drink." It was typical Gabriella, making plans without consulting Jay. "Then I take you to the place with the best gelato in Italy."

"I've already been to about ten places that allegedly serve the best gelato in the world," said Jay with a smile.

"Trust me. This is the best of the best." She smiled. "After dinner I usually come back here and swim under the stars," she said with a suggestive lilt in her voice. "You can join me if you like," she said, winking.

"But I didn't bring my bathing suit," said Jay.

"You won't need it, sugar," said Gabriella, not missing a beat.

"In that case skip the gelato!" They both laughed. Jay cut into the huge sausage with a knife, slicing it into thin wafers to have with the cheese. "What about tomorrow? I know you have the entire weekend planned already."

"Tomorrow big!" said Gabriella. "We are going to Sienna for the running of the horses. It is, what do you call it? A mob scene. My family rents an apartment overlooking the Piazza de Campo, and we throw big party."

"The horses run around the square, right? It's a little like our Kentucky Derby."

"No mint juleps or big hats," Gabriella said, giggling. "Red wine and short skirts."

Jay's BlackBerry vibrated. He glanced down at the number. It was Ross Lombardy.

"I better take this," said Jay. "Last call of the weekend, I promise—unless it's Brodi."

"Always working," said Gabriella, her lips forming a pout, shooing him from the table with a wave of her hand. Jay walked past the pool to the sloping lawn, standing on the rock wall at the edge of the property to give himself some privacy.

"Ross, my main man," he said affectionately. "What's shaking?"

"Sorry to bug you in Italy, Jay," said Ross apologetically.

"How do you know where I am?"

"The *New York Times* did a big write-up about you helping Brodi," said Ross. "Said it was a test of whether you could replicate the Long coalition in Europe. They had a picture of the chick you're seeing over there, the wine heiress. . . . She's hot!"

Jay glanced at Gabriella, chatting on her cell phone in rapid-fire Italian, gesturing with her hands. "Yes, she is," he sighed.

"I know you're in the weeds with the Brodi campaign, but I need your help on something. It's pretty important not only to us but for Long."

The truth? Jay was barely involved in the Brodi campaign anymore, having stepped aside (partially pushed) after the latest blowup over strategy. Tired of dealing with advisors who resented his input, sick of Brodi's ego and ingratitude, done with being harassed by the press, Jay was mailing it in. No matter. The final TV ads were on the air, and Jay was now licking his wounds with Gabriella. Besides, Brodi could not afford to fire him, and he had already pocketed his two million euro consulting fee.

"Sure, fire away, buddy. What can I do you for?"

"We're hearing rumors that the president is looking at Yolanda Majette for the Supreme Court pick," said Ross. "She's not a conservative. Andy's so mad he's about to clear a McDonald's parking lot with a machine gun. He wants to call the president directly and urge him not to pick Majette."

"Ouch," said Jay. "We don't want *that*."

"No," said Ross gravely. "But if it's Majette, we go to Defcon 5. Her decision in the California marriage amendment case is a big problem." He paused, loading. "Jay, we can't support her. And we might have to oppose her."

Jay gulped. "I'm familiar with the marriage case," he said. "I was in California at the time. Some have interpreted her ruling on the gay couple's standing as an unwillingness to make the right call on the merits. But she's a jurist, not a legislator, so she rules based on the law. If that's giving indigestion to some of your friends, let's figure out a way to fix it."

"I don't think we can. The marriage case is on its way to the Supreme Court. The next justice is the deciding vote. Majette's unacceptable to our people."

"Look, the president is committed to appointing judges who interpret the law, not legislate from the bench," replied Jay, rattling off his talking points, brain on autopilot. "We're willing to listen to objections to Majette, but they have to be based on the facts."

"Jay, I'm your friend," said Ross, going for the knockout. "I can't sell her and neither can Andy. If she's the nominee, you can count us out."

"I got that already," said Jay impatiently. He glanced over at Gabriella, who was chewing a bite slowly, arms across her chest, D&G sunglasses on the end of her nose, disapproving eyes cutting through him. If he didn't end the call soon, the midnight swim was off. "Ross, the president holds Majette in high regard. She's a woman of deep Christian faith. I know her, and I'm confident she'll be a solid vote. But I'll weigh in and report back within twenty-four hours."

"Thanks, man," said Ross, the hostility draining from his voice. "You're the greatest. My only regret is that you're not in the White House where you belong."

"I wouldn't wish that on my worst enemy, dude," said Jay. "I'm a political hack, not a White House aide."

Jay hung up and walked back to the pool, his mind a jumble. Pausing on the stone steps, he gazed at the breathtaking vista of the Tuscan countryside, the Medici summer palace across the valley, row upon row of vineyards, and Florence nestled among the hills in the distance. Impulsively, the thought occurred to him to buy a villa with the Brodi campaign fee and hang out in Italy for a while. But another thought jarred him: while he was drinking wine, playing tourist, and swimming with Gabriella, the coalition he had painstakingly built to elect Long was unraveling. If he didn't do something soon, Long's presidency might be on life support.

EIGHTEEN

Keith Golden dreaded making the call but felt he had no choice. After two meetings in the Oval with the president (who remained studiously opaque) and a flurry of calls with Hector and Battaglia, it was clear the Supreme Court pick was going sideways. Leaks out of the West Wing indicated Long (the scuttlebutt Battaglia was behind it) was leaning toward Yolanda Majette, Golden feared Long was about to commit political suicide and that he might be collateral damage. Nominating Majette would ruin Golden's street cred on the right.

The president came on the line. "How's my top cop?" he asked. "What's on your mind, General?"

As usual Long cut to the chase. Risking alienating the president, Golden dove in. "Mr. President, I know you're high on Yolanda Majette. She's an outstanding jurist. But I wanted to convey a few concerns."

"Sure, Keith," said Long, his voice suddenly drained of enthusiasm. "But if you're worried about the California marriage case, she's got an answer for that one."

"I've got no issue with that," answered Golden. "Andy Stanton's going to be bent out of shape, but her ruling was perfectly consistent with solid judicial temperament."

"I agree," said Long. "So then what's the problem?"

"As the first African-American woman on the court, she would be a historic pick, no question," Golden said, pouring a little honey on the dirt sandwich. "I just don't want her to be your Sotomayor. Mr. President; she's not as well versed on constitutional doctrine."

"Mmmm-mmmm," said Long.

"She has no background on the federal courts," Golden continued. "She was a state superior court judge, which is a political appointment, so her facility in constitutional law is limited. In a confirmation hearing she'll get asked really tough, probing questions." He paused, weighing his words. "Sir, I recommend we give her an interim step by putting her on the Ninth Circuit. Let her season a bit, and then she'll be ready for the next vacancy."

"What if I don't get another appointment?"

"There's no way to know, but I wouldn't let that drive your decision, Mr. President. You don't want to operate on an artificial deadline."

"I don't disagree with that," said Long, his tone noncommittal.

"Mr. President, if you try to make a quarter horse jump a six-foot fence, there's a danger it will break its leg," said Golden. An experienced rider, Golden loved horses.

"You're right," said Long. "But I'd rather have a mule that can plow a straight row than a show horse who looks good in the stable and can't run worth a lick. I think Majette is a quick study and can get up to speed quickly."

"Frankly, I'm actually less concerned about her on the Court than I am about her ability to get through the confirmation process," said Golden. "She's going to be pressed on her views on constitutional doctrine. It's not like cramming for a final exam in law school. Sir, my guys are concerned that she's not ready."

"Well, I really appreciate the input, Keith," said Long, his voice flat. "What I need to know is, can I count on you to be on the team?"

Golden was taken aback. On every question, it seemed, Long cared less about arriving at the right decision and more about who was on the team once the decision was made. "Mr. President, you'll have no stronger advocate. I'll make my best case on the inside, but once we walk out the door, no one will defend your nominee more forcefully than me."

"Good," said Long. "Let's talk more often."

Golden hung up and gazed longingly at a photo of himself in a power clutch with Long in the Oval. The picture mocked him. Phil Battaglia's physical proximity and close relationship with Long had trumped Golden's title. Despite Long's promises to the contrary, Golden had been reduced to being a spectator as the future of the Supreme Court hung in the balance.

JAY SAT HUNCHED OVER a utility table, his unblinking eyes scanning a computer screen in the count room at the Brodi campaign's makeshift headquarters. He and the campaign high command gathered in a suite at the Hotel Nationale, just across the piazza from the Chamber of Deputies building, where Frank Sinatra once crooned at the bar and where members of parliament hung out and drank with reporters and lobbyists. As returns filtered in from across Italy, the result was no surprise to Jay: the race was too close to call.

Chewing on his fingernails and downing one cup of espresso after another, chased with an occasional Pellegrino and lime, Jay was wired from a combination of caffeine and stress-induced anxiety. The campaign had ended in a barrage of negative ads never seen in the modern political history of Italy. There were rumors of payoffs to trade union chiefs, and Jay knew some of them were true. Big Feet reporters from the States were following the election with a ferocious interest, praying Jay stumbled.

"Where are the remaining Rome wards!?" Jay asked of no one in particular.

One of Brodi's insufferably obsequious aides appeared at Jay's side, black hair slicked back, two days of beard growth flecking his face, shiny Italian suit cut trim. "Don't worry, Americano," he said in a patronizing tone. "This is Italy. We are holding back our vote so Porro can't steal the north." He smiled.

"So you're telling me that we're stealing it so he won't?" asked Jay, incredulous.

"Not stealing exactly," replied the aide. "But we want to make Porro go first."

Jay calmed down but only a little. His BlackBerry's inbox filled with e-mails from reporters in the U.S. looking for the inside scoop. He ignored them. Finally a little after 11:00 p.m., the totals from the all-critical Rome suburbs came in, and Brodi's narrow lead widened. Jay allowed himself a broad smile. With only urban precincts remaining to be counted, Brodi was all but assured the premiership. Someone opened a bottle of champagne and began to fill glasses.

"Who's going to call Brodi?" asked Jay.

"You should, Jay," said the campaign manager. "Your ads did the trick."

"Me? Absolutely not!" Jay objected. His relationship with Brodi had been a roller-coaster ride, alternately tempestuous and collaborative. He knew Brodi resented his dependence on Jay even as he admired his American *wunderkind.* Ignoring his protests, someone handed him a phone. The line was already ringing to the phone in Brodi's suite.

"Sir, you've going to make a great prime minister," said Jay into the phone when Brodi answered. He smiled and gave a thumbs-up to the rest of the team. Everyone applauded. "No, sir, I see no reason to wait for Porro to concede. It's over." He paused. "See you in ten minutes." He hung up. "The mayor wants to go ahead and give his victory speech."

They all stuffed into a small elevator and jumped into waiting taxis to head over to the victory celebration at the Exelsior Hotel. For Jay it was Groundhog Day: another brutal campaign, another bloodletting, another near-death experience dodged. Only now the highs were no longer so high. Still Brodi's victory showed that Jay still had his mojo. He was also 500,000 euros richer; his win bonus was payable within ten days. That brought his total to $2.8 million for eight weeks of work—assuming one could call his Italian adventure work.

They pulled up in front of the Excelsior and quickly encountered a mob that filled the street, crammed the lobby, and snaked out of the ballroom. Someone grabbed a policeman who acted like a cow-catcher, pushing bodies to the side. News photographers recognized Jay and began to snap photos. As they walked into the ballroom of the Excelsior, Brodi was already on stage, soaking up the wild adoration of the crowd. He clutched his wife's hand (she stood beside him despite rumors of infidelity and embarrassing revelations about the parties at his Lake Como villa), and together they celebrated vindication.

"Brodi! Brodi! Brodi!" the crowd chanted. Little Italian flags chopped the air.

As Jay arrived backstage, his BlackBerry vibrated in his pocket. Hiding behind the curtains, hand cupped over his other ear to block out the crowd noise, he took the call.

"Congratulations, my American top gun," came Gabriella's husky voice.

"Thanks," replied Jay, trying to block out the raucous celebration. "It was ugly, but a win is a win."

"This calls for a proper celebration, no?"

"Sounds like a plan," replied Jay. "Just tell me where and when."

"W-e-l-l," replied Gabriella, drawing out the word. "I fly to Paris tomorrow morning for an industry show. We're unveiling a new vintage. It's a big deal." She paused for a beat. "Why don't you come? We can celebrate with a long weekend in grand Paree."

Jay knew he should get back stateside and help out on health care and the Supreme Court pick. But when it came to Gabriella , Jay's judgment was nonexistent.

"I only have two questions," replied Jay. "When do we leave, and what do I wear?"

"I'll pick you up in front of the Hassler at 10:00 a.m. Bring some casual clothes and a suit for dinner. I have a couple of official functions, but otherwise we're free to do whatever we want."

"Whatever we want?" said Jay.

"You won't be disappointed," said Gabri. "I know how to have a good time in Paris."

"I'm beginning to think you know how to have a good time anywhere," said Jay.

Gabriella let out a throaty laugh. "I don't have a lot of use for Brodi, but I'm happy for you. Congratulations, baby. See you tomorrow."

Jay hung up and peeked back around the curtain to see Brodi gesticulating wildly, waving his arms, whipping the crowd into a frenzy. Our guy may be a demagogue, he thought, but at least he's better than the other guy. Then it hit him: he had not even bothered to bring a nice suit to Italy. His closet at the Hassler was filled with a political consultant's uniform: khakis, jeans, and blazers. He wondered where he could find a new suit in Rome in the middle of the night.

THE PRESIDENT STRODE DOWN the colonnade leading from the Oval Office, shoulders thrown back and arms swinging at his side, a sprightly spring in his step, his Supreme Court nominee glued to his side. The press snapped to attention. Who was the person with him? Necks craned. The dark complexion and statuesque height gave it away. It was Yolanda Majette! To the surprise of virtually everyone, Bob Long had stared down the right-wing poo-bahs at the Faith and Family Federation and the Federalist Society and nominated a centrist from the Golden State in his own image. And the cherry on top was Majette would be the first African-American woman ever to sit on the Supreme Court. It was an electric moment.

Long and Majette walked down the steps leading to the Rose Garden, their earnest expressions telegraphing the gravity of the moment. Long stepped to the podium and half smiled; Majette stood behind him. Seeing her regal beauty and stately poise on stage after days of speculation and handicapping came as a bit of surprise. Her milk-chocolate skin, jet-black hair, high cheekbones, feline eyes, and athletic frame made her look like Noami Campbell crossed with Condoleezza Rice. No shrinking violet, she wore a fire-engine red Chanel dress with black trim, black buttons, a wide black belt that pinched her thin waist, and red pumps.

Long glanced down at the blue index cards bearing his remarks and then glanced up at the press, savoring the moment. He loved surprises. As when he selected Johnny Whitehead as his running mate, Majette was not only a complete surprise but a stroke of genius.

"No greater responsibility befalls a president than to nominate justices to the Supreme Court," Long began. "It is the forum of last resort for those seeking to protect their rights under the Constitution. Throughout our history the Supreme Court has passed judgment on the most central and contentious issues facing the American people. This is a decision I made after seeking bipartisan input from a wide range of people."

By protocol congressional leaders from both chambers sat on the front row. Chief among them, wearing strained poker faces leaking emotions ranging from begrudging admiration to abject hatred, were Salmon Stanley and Joe Penneymounter. The chairman of the Senate Judiciary Committee, in particular, looked as if he had just been punched in the gut. He slumped down in his chair, legs crossed, hands clasped on his knees, looking pale and wan.

Long launched the opening salvo on what promised to be the vigorous marketing by the White House of Majette's compelling personal story. "I wanted someone with outstanding professional qualifications. But I also wanted someone with a heart who could bring wisdom and compassion to the court, as well as respect for the rule of law, and the intellect to translate the hopes and aspirations of average Americans for social justice into an enduring body of constitutional jurisprudence." He flipped over a card, plowing through the talking points. "I found that person in Yolanda Majette. The daughter of a Methodist preacher who grew up in the shadow of segregation in George Wallace's Montgomery, Justice Majette knows the sting of discrimination, the humility of social ostracism, and the vital role of the judiciary in redressing injustice." The whir and clicks of still cameras echoed across the lawn.

"Justice Majette has enjoyed a legal career of remarkable distinction. She graduated from Harvard Law School, where she was the first African-American woman elected to the law review, and served her country as an officer and judge advocate in the U.S. Army. She taught constitutional law at the University of California and was elected as a superior court judge." Majette stood to the side, stoic and humble as Long recounted her many achievements. "Appointed to a vacancy on the California Supreme Court, she was elected in her own right with a margin of 68 percent of the vote." Long raised his head, his face filled with mirth. "I never got that margin in four campaigns for statewide office." (Laughter, scattered applause.) "On California's highest court she has been a model of fairness, judicial temperament, and achieving consensus. I am proud to nominate her to the U.S. Supreme Court and will transmit her name to the U.S. Senate for confirmation."

Majette shook Long's hand and stepped confidently to the podium. Her back straight, shoulders square, chin high, she was a picture of America's possibility. She clearly grasped that her nomination symbolized the twin and tortured destinies of race and gender in the nation's history. Her physicality, striking appearance, and poise spoke preternatural toughness, an inner core shaped by the experience of growing up black in the segregated South. At five feet ten inches in her heels, she stood almost as tall as Long. She was a living metaphor for the old anthem of the civil rights movement: "We Shall Overcome."

"Mr. President, thank you for the great honor of this nomination. It is a long way from the white clapboard church my father pastored in Montgomery, Alabama, to the White House," she said as Long smiled proudly. "I stand before you today not only as a judge but also as my father and mother's daughter, a soldier, an educator, and a woman of color whose country has afforded me unimaginable opportunities." The enraptured press corps gobbled it up. This was no Al Sharpton in pumps. "If anyone doubts that in America anyone can rise as high and as far as their talents will carry them, today is a reminder of the great promise of our country."

Long began to tear up. Even the normally cynical reporters were moved. Majette was speaking not just for minorities but for all Americans.

Her success was *their* success, and her accomplishments were the nation's accomplishments.

"Should I be fortunate enough to be confirmed as an associate justice of the Supreme Court, I will seek to ensure the law embodies that same promise of equality, opportunity, and liberty for all." She glanced in Long's direction. "Thank you again for your confidence, Mr. President. I look forward to meeting with individual senators and confirmation hearings as soon as they can be arranged."

Long and Majette stepped gingerly from the podium and walked back to the Oval Office. They took no questions.

All eyes turned to Joe Penneymounter. Doing his best not to look outmaneuvered, he pumped hands, slapped backs, and grasped the arms of senators and congressmen, all for the benefit of the cameras. Would he launch an all-out attack on Majette or take a pass on what was an unquestionably inspired selection, both a minority and a woman? No one knew, least of all him.

NINETEEN

Ross Lombardy was in his hotel room at the airport Radisson in Orlando preparing for a rally and fund-raiser when Long made the announcement in the Rose Garden. As he watched it on television, he was overcome with nausea. It was a total betrayal. Three minutes after the news conference ended, the phone rang. It was Andy, and he was puffed up like a blowfish.

"Brother, Bob Long stabbed us right between the shoulder blades," said Andy. "He's no better than the Republicans."

"I'm in a state of shock," said Ross. "How could the guy be this dumb? We elected him. Now he gives us this?"

"Sin can be forgiven, but stupid is forever. I won't support him for reelection," Andy said. "I got a call from a friend of mine who pastors one of the biggest churches in the country. He said Long's going to bring God's judgment down on his administration."

Ross was more interested in whip counts in the U.S. Senate than hellfire-and-brimstone jeremiads. The evangelicals had already divorced the Grand Old Party. Now Bob Long was leaving them at the altar.

"We can't support Majette," said Ross. "But I think you need to be careful. Stay above the fray."

"Stay above the fray!?" bellowed Andy. "We put twenty-two million votes in Long's back pocket, and he has betrayed everything he stood for during the campaign. We have to make an example out of him, just like we did Petty. I'm going to unload on him!"

Andy was in the midst of what vice presidents at New Life Ministries referred to in hushed whispers as one of his "Dennis Hopper moments." At times like this Ross longed for a tranquilizer gun. "I don't recommend that, sir," he said.

"Why not?" asked Andy.

"I don't believe in putting the general out on the point where he can get shot," said Ross.

"Meaning what precisely?"

"Let our friends in the Senate take the lead," said Ross. "It's time they started earning their keep. If they want our support in the next election, they need to show some guts."

"The honorables are profiles in cowardice. Who will do it?"

"Tom Reynolds. He's ambitious, and he'll do anything to separate from the pack."

"Or get on television. The guy is a shameless camera hog."

"And in this case that works in our favor."

"Alright," said Andy, sounding chastened. "But I can't guarantee I won't say something on my radio show. This is the biggest story in the country, and I can't just ignore it."

"Why don't you book Reynolds on the show and let him say it?"

"Call him and see if he'll come today."

"Will do, Andy." He paused. "You want to fly above the battlefield like a blimp. Between Penneymounter on the left and us on the right, we can take down Majette without your becoming a lightning rod in the process."

"Lightning rod? Are you kidding? I'm the lightning *bolt*."

Ross hung up the phone and walked out on the balcony, his legs rubbery, his head spinning, watching the cars whizzing by on Interstate 4. He drew in a breath of hot, humid air. It reached his lungs but seemed to carry no oxygen. He was physically sick. Jay Noble shafted him.

THE PRESS JAMMED INTO the office of Senator Preston Smith of Alabama, arch conservative and a junior member of the Judiciary Committee. Beneath his good ole boy charm and country lawyer exterior simmered white-hot ambition. Sheathed in an off-the-rack blue suit with a red-and-blue rep tie and button-down dress shirt, he smiled awkwardly under the television lights, his doughy face and chipmunk cheeks glistening. His pale skin looked bleached, and his high forehead was topped with a wave of jet-black hair.

Yolanda Majette sat beside him in a straight-back chair, hands clasped in her lap, legs crossed, a tremulous smile on her face.

"Senator, how concerned are you about the allegations regarding Judge Majette's husband's law practice?"

"I'm looking forward to talking to the judge about her judicial philosophy," said Smith, his voice a monotone, swatting aside the question.

"Are you going to ask her about her husband's firm making millions off clients with cases on which she ruled?"

Smith just kept right on smiling.

"Judge Majette, Christy Love with Pro-Choice PAC has called for you to withdraw your name from nomination? Any comment?"

Majette's face hardened but she betrayed no emotion.

"Thank you!" shouted a press aide. He spread his arms, gently prodding reporters and photographers out of the room. The door closed. Only four remained: Smith, his chief of staff, Majette, and Don Kottkamp, a former senator turned lobbyist that the White House recruited to escort her to meetings with senators.

"Judge, how are you holding up?" asked Smith.

"I'm pretty immune from the hoopla," said Majette. "I'm so busy getting ready for the confirmation hearings and meeting with folks like you that I don't pay a lot of attention."

"Good for you," said Smith. "Judge, I'm particularly concerned about what I see as an overt hostility toward religion by the courts. Take the war on Christmas. You've got courts pulling down crèches and nativity scenes, or requiring that atheist exhibits be displayed next to Christmas trees. It's total nonsense."

Majette nodded sympathetically.

"How do you feel about the federal courts driving faith in God out of the public square?"

"I believe there is an appropriate role for the public expression of faith," said Majette noncommittally. "The jurisprudence in this area is complex. The Supreme Court, as you know, has generally taken a positive view of free speech, including speech with a religious content, such as Bible clubs meeting in public schools. It has taken a dimmer view of official actions by public officials, such as the posting of the Ten Commandments in a courthouse."

Smith looked bored with the first-year law school lecture. He crossed his legs and frowned. "What's your view of the *Lemon* test?" he asked, referring to the Supreme Court's *Lemon v. Kurtzman* decision in 1971 involving state aid to parochial schools.

"Senator, as one justice has observed, the *Lemon* test is a lemon," Majette said, as if reading a cue card. The room fell silent. Kottkamp shifted uncomfortably in his seat.

"Can you be more specific?"

"I don't know that I can address that with greater specificity," said Majette haltingly. "The 'lemon test' has not provided a consistent standard to guide local communities in making decisions involving the establishment clause. But how I would rule on a specific case would depend on the facts."

"Have you given any thought to what might be a different constitutional standard?" asked Smith helpfully.

"I'm sure there is one," Majette replied. She looked as if she were reaching for a lifeline. "There is, of course, the . . . the compelling state interest standard."

"I see," said Smith. "The *Lemon* test says government can't be excessively entangled with religion. I don't even know what that means. Do you?"

Majette looked sucker punched. "Establishment clause jurisprudence is an area of law replete with vagaries and permutations." She glanced at Kottkamp, who nodded and smiled.

They chatted amiably for about half an hour. After Majette departed, Smith closed the door and turned to his chief of staff.

"Could you believe that?" asked Smith. "I hate to say it, but she's a quota appointment, pure and simple. She's Souter in pumps."

"It's scary," the aide replied.

"If I hadn't been sitting here, I don't know that I would believe it myself," Smith said. "I tried to help her out, but it was hopeless. Does Long really want to give her a lifetime appointment to the Supreme Court?"

Smith walked briskly to his desk and picked up the phone. "Charlie Hector, please. Tell him it's Senator Preston Smith." He tapped his foot and compulsively rearranged papers on his desk. He knew Hector; they had served together in the House.

Hector came on the line. "Senator, how are you?"

"Charlie, Yolanda Majette just left my office. We talked for thirty minutes. She's a very attractive woman with a compelling personal story. I know this was a courtesy call, but I have to be honest with you, I don't know if I can support her. If I had to decide now, I'd vote no."

"I'm sorry to hear that, Senator. What can we do to improve her performance?"

"Charlie, it's not her performance that is the problem," replied Smith. "It's her knowledge of the law. She didn't seem to know what the *Lemon* test was. Every first-year law student in the country knows that. She's asking to be confirmed as a justice of the Supreme Court for crying out loud."

"I'm sure she knows what it is."

"I just asked her! She gave me gobbledygook. Come on, Charlie. Throw me a bone."

"I'm sorry the meeting did not go well, Preston, but I assure you, she'll know the *Lemon* test upside down and sideways by the time of her hearings. Don't make a final decision until after the hearings. All I ask is that you keep your powder dry."

"I will," said Smith. "But if she's doing as poorly with the other members of the committee as she did with me, I'm gonna be the least of your problems."

"Thanks for the heads-up. I'm on it."

Smith hung up the phone and looked at his aide.

"Well?" asked the chief of staff.

"I think I got his attention," said Smith.

CHARLIE HECTOR SAT IN the back of a nondescript Town Car, or at least as nondescript as a limo could be flying through flashing yellow lights at 5:30 a.m. on Rock Creek Parkway. There was no traffic at this early hour. Under the glow of a reading light, Hector studied the front page of the *Washington Post* like a coroner examining a cadaver. It was going to be a rough day. Dan Dorman served up another one of his head shots: a two-thousand word hit piece on Yolanda Majette's husband, whose law practice catered to clients with cases pending before the California Supreme Court. The eighteen-point headline read: "Majette's husband's firm paid millions by clients with cases before her."

Hector's heart sank as he read the jump page. It was a toxic journalistic stew: an anonymous source here, blind quote there, the implication of a conflict of interest, and the proverbial goo-goo quote from some mouthpiece at Common Cause claiming that the whole thing raised "troubling questions demanding answers before Majette can be confirmed." Just great, thought

Hector with disgust. It was all part of a deliberate effort by Pro-Choice PAC and liberal groups to slow down Majette's nomination so reporters could dig up more dirt. Dorman was acting as Joe Penneymounter's stenographer.

The basic facts were simple enough. Clients hired Majette's husband or other attorneys and lobbyists at his firm to make their case, often on matters unrelated, at times that coincided with disturbing frequency to their cases being heard by the California Supreme Court. In one case Charles Majette joined the board of directors of a hospital shortly before Majette voted to overturn a lower-court malpractice judgment against the hospital's anesthesiologist. She previously addressed why she did not view the case as a conflict, pointing out the malpractice suit was against the physician, not the hospital, but the optics were bad.

Hector put down the paper and looked at the buildings and street lights whizzing by. He felt his stomach tighten. The beating had begun. He hoped Majette had a thick skin because she was going to need it.

TWENTY

Joe Penneymounter dropped the *Washington Post* on the coffee table in his spacious, sun-splashed office in the Russell Office Building. A blue and gold carpet that featured an outline of the state of Minnesota lay on the floor. Slumped in chairs and sprawled on the couch were key members of his Judiciary Committee staff and outside advisors on judicial confirmation strategy. They wore their best game faces. Everyone was ready to go to war.

"Well, the *Post* piece is the opening gun. Start your engines," Penneymounter said.

"We already have, Senator," said Christy Love. She leaned forward to pour cream in her coffee, Penneymounter's eyes following her every move. Gorgeous as always, Christy positively glowed in mauve eye shadow, reddish-purple lipstick, and a touch of rouge, looking a bit like a china doll, creamy skin flawless after a recent exfoliation. "We've e-mailed the *Post* story to two million activists and asked them to sign a petition calling on her to withdraw. My statement is plastered all over the *Huffington Post,* and I'm doing press interviews all day."

"I'm glad Majette's taking on water. But I wonder: do we want her to go down?" asked Penneymounter's chief of staff. A legal pad rested on his lap, his sleeves rolled up to the elbows, tie loosened, head cocked in smart-guy bravado.

"Good point," said Penneymounter, perched on the edge of his chair, pointing his finger dramatically. "Majette's not my cup of tea, but she may be the best we're going to get from this president. Frankly, she's no Scalia or Thomas, which is why Andy Stanton is ticked."

"It's an open question as to whether we'd be better off with her or what's behind door number two," agreed Love. "But it's theoretical. If only to weaken Long, we need to defeat her or die trying."

"I'm going to be asked about the *Post* story," said Penneymounter. "Any thoughts?" Camera crews were already gathered in the hallway outside his office, hoping to catch the senator on his way to the Senate floor.

"I'd pull the punch a little bit," said the chief of staff with clinical detachment. "Dorman did the dirty work for you. Say you're concerned about alleged conflicts of interest and say the committee will look into it thoroughly."

"You don't want to come off sounding like you've prejudged the situation. You don't want to be the bad guy," agreed Love.

"Christy, I'm *already* the bad guy," said Penneymounter with a chuckle.

"The key is to defeat Majette by any means necessary," said Christy. "We have the opportunity to strangle Long's presidency in the crib."

It was a startling metaphor coming from the leading pro-choice lobbyist in the nation. Everyone licked their lips at the prospect of paying Long back for bolting their party and rushing into the arms of the far right. Their hatred of Long bound them in an almost tribal loyalty.

"Defeating a Supreme Court nominee isn't easy," said Penneymounter, reaching for a candy from a bowl in the middle of the table. He unwrapped it, popping it into his mouth. "If we could do it, it would cripple Long. Health care's going down. If Majette is voted down or withdraws over these ethical issues, what can he point to as an accomplishment?"

"Forget about Majette," said Natalie Taylor, the striking Judiciary staffer who had remained silent until then. "I think she'll withdraw within two weeks."

"Really?" asked Love, stunned. "Why?"

"Dorman's piece is just the beginning," said Natalie. "There's more."

"What else?" asked the chief of staff.

"More clients, more conflicts for her husband and his law firm," said Natalie. "The *New York Times* is all over it. And from what I'm hearing from friends on the minority staff, she's not doing well in her one-on-ones with Republican senators."

"That kills her," said Penneymounter firmly. "If the Republicans cut her loose, she's done."

"Stick a fork in her," said Christy. "But I'm not sure. I think we have to assume the Republicans stick with her." She locked eyes with Taylor, who was one of Penneymounter's favorites. "The conflict of interest charge may not have legs. After all, Majette's husband can just resign from the firm, and the problem goes away."

Natalie shrugged. "We'll see. But I hear there's more to come."

Penneymounter rose from his chair, signaling the meeting is over. "Keep hammering away, Christy. We wouldn't be where we are without you."

"Mr. Chairman, when I take aim, I put metal on the target," said Christy. She rose from her chair and shook Penneymounter's hand, their faces inches apart, grins plastered on their faces, mutual political love oozing from every pore.

"Remind me never to be on your bad side," joked Penneymounter. He turned and headed for the door, opening it to the outer office, where the press waited.

Penneymounter's press secretary raised her arms over her head, trying to calm the mob. "The Senator is going to make a brief statement."

A hush fell over the reporters as they elbowed for position.

"The story in the *Washington Post* this morning raises serious questions about Yolanda Majette's nomination to the nation's highest court," Penneymounter began, a grave expression on his face. "I am concerned about possible conflicts of interest involving Judge Majette and her husband's law firm. If individuals with cases pending before the California Supreme Court hired her husband or his law firm and either expected or received favorable treatment from Judge Majette, those are serious allegations." He glanced down at the piece of paper in his hand, then leveled his eyes at the cameras. "I will not prejudge this matter. But the committee will thoroughly look into this issue and leave no stone unturned." Finished with his statement, Penneymounter folded up the piece of paper and placed it in his pocket.

"Thank you very much. That is all!" shouted the press secretary.

"Senator, do you believe these revelations about her husband's lobbying, if true, are disqualifying?" asked *Politico*.

Penneymounter ignored the question. More shouted questions followed, again to no avail. In the shadows Christy and Natalie stood side by side, both looking like models in their form-fitting outfits and designer heels, arms crossed, wearing satisfied expressions. They were having fun.

Penneymounter shot them a smile and winked in their direction, then turned and headed for the elevator.

JAY STEPPED OUT ON the terrace of Gabriella's suite at the Hotel Ritz, just off the Place de la Vendome. He could see the gold-gilded dome of the Hotel des Invalides and the Eiffel Tower in the distance. Gabriella reached into the ice bucket and picked up the bottle of Dom Perignon, pouring into a fluted glass.

"To Paris," she said. They clinked glasses. "And to victory."

"Let me see your watch again," he said.

They went to the Cartier store that morning and Gabriella fell in love with a diamond-studded, eighteen-karat white gold watch. Impulsively, Jay bought it, putting $35,000 on his American Express card without so much as a thought. What did he care? He could buy one every single day for a month and still have money from his Brodi campaign fee left over. Gabriella extended her wrist. Jay held her hand, turning it so the diamonds sparkled.

"I love it," said Gabriella, gazing admiringly at the jewels that studded the bracelet. "Every time I look at the time, I'll think of you and this moment."

"That was the idea," said Jay. He glanced out at the Parisian skyline, letting out a satisfied sigh. "What a perfect way to celebrate Brodi's victory. I never thought it was possible to so thoroughly relish the victory of such an egoistic oaf."

"Enjoy it while you can, cowboy," Gabriella said, turning up her champagne glass to take a sip. "Brodi will screw it up soon enough."

Jay laughed. "They all do," he said. "That's why I get paid the big bucks."

Gabriella glanced at her watch, this time reading the time. "Mama mia, it's six o'clock! I have to shower and put my dress on," She quickly ushered him to the door. "Shooh, shooh!"

Jay headed down the hall to his room and changed into the black Prada suit Gabriella had persuaded him to buy. The store manager promised to finish the alterations that afternoon and deliver the suit to his hotel room at the Ritz. Jay stood before the mirror, turning in different directions. He hardly recognized himself. He tried his best to suck in his gut, which hung out over the waistband. The suit and hand-stitched Italian shoes cost him four thousand euros.

Half an hour later Jay sat in the bar of the Ritz working his way through a second glass of champagne, this one with a dollop of orange-raspberry sherbert floating on top. When Gabriella appeared at the door, he almost dropped his glass. Her hair was piled up on her head, accentuating her espresso eyes, curving eyebrows, Roman nose, and full lips. She wore an off-the-shoulder, full-length black gown with a white choker halter by John Galliano, huge diamond earrings, diamond bangles, her new Cartier watch, and a matching white Chanel purse.

"Magnifique!" Jay exclaimed. He could hardly believe she was really his date.

"Thank you, darling," said Gabriella. "You look terrific. I *told* you that you would look great in Prada."

Jay silently demurred. He hoped Gabriella's fashion sense would not affect his entire wardrobe, or he'd be hooted out of DC. But for tonight, who cared if he looked like Austin Powers in a Beatles suit? *Anything for Gabri,* he thought. Holding hands, they walked through the lobby, Gabriella drawing stares, and stepped outside to their waiting car and driver.

"Grand Palais, s'il vous plait," Gabriella instructed the driver. She turned to Jay. "The reception is around the corner. These are trade ministers, industry executives, celebrities, and the usual European political muckety mucks. Just smile and be Jay Noble."

Jay laughed. "That's pretty much all I do these days."

The car shot past the Elysee Palace, the presidential residence, which had blue European Union flags fluttering next to the French flag because the French president currently occupied the rotating EU presidency. As they zipped down a side street and turned on to the Champs Elysee, Jay could see the Arch de Triomphe lit up. He leaned forward like a tourist.

"It's beautiful at night," said Gabriella. "Other than Rome, this is probably my favorite city in Europe."

"It really is something," Jay agreed. "I love Paris already."

The car made a left on Winston Churchill Boulevard and pulled up in front of the Grand Palais, the iron and glass Beaux-Arts structure built for the 1900 World's Fair. It was bathed in white light, its glass panels reflecting the glare, its grounds crawling with French police. The bronze statutes at each corner of the top of the building and French flag in the center were lit up with white spotlights. The street was blockaded, and soldiers paced back and forth with machine guns. Gabriella gave her name to a policeman, who checked it against a list and then waved the car through.

After ninety minutes of schmoozing, Gabriella decided to make a fashionably early exit. She grabbed Jay by the hand and led him back to the car. She rattled off the street address for the restaurant. He nodded and pulled out, making a right on to Franklin D. Roosevelt Avenue.

"Did you pick a restaurant on a street named after a U.S. president just for me?" he asked.

"No, I picked it for the food, silly."

The car pulled up in front of Laserre. The doorman directed them to an elevator, which they rode to the second floor. As soon as the doors opened, Jay felt transported to another planet. Glittering glass chandeliers hung from the ceiling, giving the room a white glow. On the tables in the dining room, bone china shimmered, and gold cutlery gleamed in the light. Orchids lined the shelves of the barriers surrounding the main dining area, paintings by French masters hung on the walls, and the ceiling was covered with an Impressionist-style painting of nudes in an idyllic garden. In the corner a pianist incongruously played Disney songs, which Jay found odd. He made out the chords to "Beauty and the Beast." *Even in France you can't escape American commercialism,* he thought.

The maître d' escorted them to a corner table. After ordering another glass of champagne (Jay's fourth, and the night was still young), the head waiter did a table visit and made a big production of greeting Gabriella, kissing her on each cheek. They chatted amiably in French as Jay smiled, understanding not a word. As the head waiter handed them menus, Gabriella held up the palms of her hands.

"Reme, we don't want to see a menu tonight," she said. "Tell the chef to fix us a tasting menu. Surprise us."

Reme smiled. "Certainement, mademoiselle et monsieur." He bowed and left the table.

Within minutes another waiter brought them a large glass filled with lobster bisque topped with a scoop of caviar. The first course: pumpkin soup served slightly above room temperature. Just as Jay spooned a bite of the soup, the roof of the restaurant began to open. Stars twinkled against the dark canopy of sky, green ivy hanging from the edges, a cool summer breeze rushing in through the opening.

"I've never seen a restaurant where the roof opened," said Jay.

"That's because you've never been to Laserre, dahling."

"What else are you going to show me that I've never seen before?" asked Jay.

Gabriella said nothing in reply, giggling as she licked the spoon of the last drop of beluga caviar.

TWENTY-ONE

Phil Battaglia sat in his office on a Saturday morning hunched over his computer, burning through his e-mail. The White House was in the bunker: the wing nuts were in full-blown revolt over Majette. Battaglia was a one-man PR shop, love-bombing the Federalist society types, assuring them he had known Yolanda Majette twenty years and knew her to be a woman of faith, integrity, and judicial restraint. There was only one problem: Battaglia had no credibility with the right. In fact, they blamed him for Majette being chosen in the first place.

His deputy stuck his head in the door. "Marvin Myers is on the phone."

Battaglia raised his eyebrows. Marvin was a size fourteen Big Foot. If he wandered into the Majette story, it could be bad. He picked up the receiver.

"Good morning, counselor," said Marvin, his voice syrupy, his manner disarmingly ingratiating. "I wanted to ask the one person who would know: will Majette make it?"

"Yes," said Battaglia. "We've seen no slippage at all in her support in the Senate." It was a lie, but Battaglia told it convincingly. "Penneymounter will put up a faux fight for the media and his base, but he'll let her go because he's worried about who's next. And he should be." He paused. "The president is totally committed to Judge Majette's confirmation."

"You say Penneymounter should be worried," said Marvin, sniffing around like a blood hound on the scent. "So you're telling me the other names on the short list were more conservative than Majette?"

Battaglia realized he tipped his hand. He had to avoid being fingered as the source for this nugget. He could see the headline now: "White House Counsel Warns More Conservative Nominee Likely if Majette Is Rejected."

"Marvin, I didn't say *that*," Battaglia said, backpedaling. "The president laid out a clear standard for his judicial nominees during the campaign, and he's not going to deviate from that standard, come what may."

"Methinks thou doth protest too much," Myers chuckled, toying with his prey. He paused. "If Charles Majette lobbied for Wildfire, that would be a problem, wouldn't it?"

"Off the record, that depends," Battaglia replied guardedly. The White House was still trying to reconstruct her husband's billing records; the firm was not being entirely cooperative for fear of leaks. "To my knowledge, he did not. Others did work for Wildfire, not on the antitrust case, by the way, but on other matters. Charles never did."

"What if I told you internal records show otherwise?"

Battaglia felt a sudden palpitation in his chest. "I'd have to know more."

"I've got the evidence in my hands. Frankly, it's pretty damning."

"I'd be careful, Marvin. Billing records are funny things. Remember Hillary Clinton during the Whitewater scandal? I'm not saying Charles Majette's firm padded their hours, but it's been known to happen. In the absence of work product, you've got nothing."

"I didn't say the proof came from the law firm," fired back Myers, holding all the cards. "Obviously I don't have a response from Majette or her husband yet, which is why I'm calling you. But assuming the evidence is solid and with the Wildfire case pending before the Supreme Court, it would be a serious issue, wouldn't it?"

"Let's dispense with the twenty-one questions, Marvin," said Battaglia, growing visibly impatient. "What have you got?"

"Read my column tomorrow."

Battaglia's throat constricted, his pulse quickened, and the blood rushed to his head, an involuntary physiological reaction to danger. "Marvin, we've gone over it with a fine-tooth comb. Be careful. Someone at Wildfire may not want Majette ruling on the antitrust case. I wouldn't put it past someone to pass off fake documents as real."

"I think you better watch *your* step," said Myers, puffing up like a poison toad. "Charles Majette's story does not square with my information."

"Alright. Get me what you've got, and I'll look into it."

"I can't do that."

Battaglia nearly blew a fuse. "You're going to write a story about alleged internal documents smearing Charles Majette and not let me see them so I can react?"

"My source gave me the documents on the condition that I not release them."

"That ought to tell you something, Marvin. For all I know, they're forged."

Myers ignored the comment. "Are you going to give me a comment or not?"

"No. You'll get a call from the press office," said Battaglia. He had no desire whatsoever to be in the story. "Write whatever you want, but know this: hell will freeze over before she withdraws."

"Can I quote you on that, maybe as a senior administration official?"

"No." Battaglia hung up the phone. He looked at the wall. The photos of him with the president were moving, their outlines hazy. Myers did his homework, and if he claimed to have something this damaging, it was usually reliable. Battaglia hoped Yolanda could survive the blow. He had pushed hard for her. If she went down due to poor vetting, he would take a major hit. He buzzed his deputy.

"Get Majette on the phone. Now."

IT WAS NEARLY 10:00 p.m. on Saturday night when Charles and Yolanda Majette walked into their hotel room after a quiet dinner on Maryland's Eastern Shore. They jumped in the car that morning and drove to get away from the media scrutiny, the clutch of reporters who maintained a vigil outside their DC hotel, and the unrelenting pressure. They hoped the time away would give them a respite from the madness.

Yolanda's cell phone rang. It was Phil Battaglia.

"Yolanda, I'm very sorry to bother you on a Saturday night, but we have a new development, and we need to fashion a response pretty quickly."

Majette's knees buckled. She grabbed the nightstand by the bed to stabilize herself. "What is it?" she asked.

"Marvin Myers claims he has documents proving Charles did work for Wildfire," said Battaglia. "We told him that was not the case. But we need Charles to search his memory and recheck his files to be sure."

Yolanda turned to Charles, the look of shock on her face conveying more than any words could. "What now?" he asked.

She pulled the phone from her mouth. "Phil says Marvin Myers is writing a column claiming you did work for Wildfire."

"That's absurd!" He grabbed the phone. "Phil, this is Charles. I never lobbied for Wildfire. I never made a single phone call or had a single meeting with a legislator or regulator. *Not one.* Myers is lying."

"One of our sources at the firm says he heard it was consultation between you and another lobbyist in the firm that turned up in a billing record," said Battaglia. "If that's true, someone in the firm is trying to drop a dime on you. Any idea who that could be?"

Charles sat down on the bed, his mind churning. "There was a woman paralegal who did some work with me. She hated Long because he flip-flopped on same sex marriage. She mentioned it more than once. But I can't believe she'd leak firm records to a reporter."

"Believe it," said Battaglia. "Trust me, when the stakes are this high, people will do anything. Including forging documents and violating attorney-client privilege."

"She could have been doing research on Wildfire, then putting it on my work sheet."

"We'll do some checking on our end. If you think of anything else, let me know ASAP. You can reach me through the White House switchboard."

Charles handed the phone back to Yolanda. "Phil, what are we going to do?" she asked plaintively, her voice quavering with fear.

"Hang in there," said Phil, trying to buck her up. "I know this is tough, but it's part of the confirmation process. There's a lot of fog, a lot of rumors. We'll see what Myers has when his column runs. I doubt it's a game changer."

"Thanks, Phil," said Yolanda. She sounded beaten down.

Battaglia hung up the phone. He wondered: *Was it really worth this for a seat on the Supreme Court?*

G. G. HOTERMAN AND Deirdre were hiding out at Higher Ground, his weekend home in the Adirondacks, enjoying a brilliant summer morning. The June bugs were gone so he was taking a late breakfast on the deck overlooking the lake, its glassy surface reflecting the morning light. But as soon as he fired up his laptop and pulled up Marvin Myers's column in the *Washington Post,* his day was ruined. G. G. tore into a piece of French toast as his eyes scanned the copy, letting out an expletive. Myers never let an opportunity pass without taking a gratuitous shot at him. He picked up his cell phone and dialed Stephen Fox.

"Stephen, have you seen Marvin Myers's column?"

"Afraid so," said Stephen, who paced the sundeck of his yacht in the British Virgin Islands. "Myers is a piece of human garbage. Can you believe he called my VP for communications at 5:30 p.m. for a comment? The piece was already written!"

"The guy's a slug," said G. G. "Did you see where he fingered me as the guy who hired Majette's husband's firm? Pathetic."

"What a joke!" shouted Stephen into the phone, working himself into a froth. "So what if you recommended state lobbying subcontractors. That was your job. Big deal!"

"It's standard operating procedure," said G. G.

"It was brilliant to hire Majette's husband's firm, G. G. My only regret is that we've now lost a valuable relationship. They did terrific work, and now we have to cut them loose."

"I just hope they don't find out we hired law firms with ties to judges everywhere," said G. G. "California is just the tip of the iceberg."

"Tell me about it. Eliot Spitzer, call your office," said Stephen, referring to the former New York AG and governor who had been a constant thorn in the side of Wildfire. Fox hated Spitzer so much that he threw a party when he flamed out in a call girl scandal.

"I'm still stumped as to how Myers got his hands on the billing records."

"We think it was probably a rogue employee in the accounting department."

"What! You mean we fragged ourselves?" asked G. G., incredulous.

"It looks like it," sighed Fox. "We have a lot of gay employees, as does every technology firm in Silicon Valley. We provide health-care benefits to their partners. They were livid about the way Majette ruled on the marriage amendment."

"Sure, and who can blame them? But to leak proprietary information and put Wildfire in the crosshairs in order to sink Majette is beyond disloyal. It's a fireable offense."

"It may well come to that, but we have to proceed with caution," said Fox. "Given everything that is going on, if we fire a gay employee, there will be a rent-a-riot on the campus of Wildfire and all kinds of negative press." Stephen shuddered at the prospect. He changed topics. "Do you think Majette will survive?"

"I don't know," said G. G. "We need to see how senators react." He stretched and yawned. "Ironically, it may be better now if she goes down. Because if Majette is confirmed, now that this is out there, she might have to recluse herself from the antitrust case."

"Get our lobbyists on high alert. We need to be ready for whatever happens."

"Already on it," said G. G. "I have a conference call for my team in thirty minutes. We work 24-7, including holidays."

"I knew it," said Fox with a satisfied chuckle. "That's why I never complain when I get one of your absurdly high bills."

As Hoterman hung up the phone, Deirdre walked out on the deck wrapped in a black silk kimono-like bathrobe with the hemline at mid-thigh, carrying a bowl of blueberries and skim milk with a mug of hot chamomile tea. She sat at the picnic table on the deck, folding one leg underneath. "Who was that?" she asked.

"Stephen Fox. Marvin Myers just outed us in his column for hiring Majette's husband to do some consulting for Wildfire."

"Ooooh! That hurts!" she exclaimed, eyes widening. "Who was the bonehead who came up with that stupid idea?"

"Me."

"Oh," said Deirdre sheepishly. "Stephen isn't upset, I hope."

"Are you kidding?" laughed G. G. "He thought it was brilliant. And you know what? It worked . . . for a while."

TWENTY-TWO

It was mid-morning when Jay dragged himself out of bed, showered, and ordered room service. As he ran a brush through his wet hair, he noticed an envelope shoved under the door. Hotel bill, perhaps? Curious, he picked it up. To his shock, inside was a fax of Page Six from that day's *New York Post*, sent by his assistant. "Jay Noble Does Paris," screamed the headline. "The City, Not the Bimbo." The *Post's* dispatch brimmed with snarky detail. "Gabriella (no last name necessary) wore a stunning black dress by designer John Galliano that had jaws dropping and tongues wagging. After a reception with international glitterati at the Grand Palais, the power couple headed to the tony restaurant Laserre, where they dined on Iranian caviar, foie gras, and wild duck. Gabriella picked up the $1,200 tab. Afterward they decamped to the Ritz bar for drinks, where witnesses reported the love birds canoodled until 3:00 a.m."

Canoodled! Jay was incensed. The tab was $1,500, the caviar was Russian, not Iranian, and Jay bought dinner. He sighed with disgust. At least they didn't know about the Cartier watch he dropped thirty-five grand on for Gabriella. He tossed the fax aside.

A room service waiter arrived and set out breakfast on the small table on the balcony. Over café au lait, croissants with jam, and a cheese tray, Jay tried to distract his mind by reading the *International Herald-Tribune*. But the paper carried two stories from the *New York Times* chronicling the sinking political fortunes of Bob Long. As if that were not enough, the lead editorial dismissed Majette as Clarence Thomas in pumps and an embarrassment to her race, scolded her husband for trying to cash in on his wife's judicial career, and called on Long to withdraw her name.

Jay was relieved he was not in DC. He imagined his friends at the White House dealing with this crap. Just then his BlackBerry vibrated. He wondered who could be calling . . . it was 5:00 a.m. on the East coast. He answered to hear the authoritative baritone of Charlie Hector.

"Jay, I wanted to give you a quick heads-up," Hector said, getting right down to business. "Majette is withdrawing."

Jay slumped in his chair. "I'm really sorry to hear that."

"Her husband's lobbying is killing us, and his connection to Wildfire is a big problem because of the antitrust case." Hector sighed. "Penneymounter was about to issue a subpoena for Charles Majette's billing records. His law firm didn't want that, and neither did he. I don't know what's in them, but apparently they didn't want them to see the light of day."

Jay wanted to ask who had been in charge of vetting Majette, but he bit his tongue. Why pick the scab. "It's so sad. She would have been a great justice."

"Well, we're moving on," said Hector. "The president doesn't want his nominee to be bogged down in a bloody confirmation fight. He's looking for someone acceptable enough to centrist Democrats so we can get at least some bipartisan support."

Jay could hardly believe his ears. If Long kept his campaign pledge and nominated a strict constructionist, it guaranteed a bloodbath. He guessed Hector had helped throw Majette under the bus, and he suspected racial politics: Hector had pushed for a Latino nominee all along.

"Let me know how I can help, Charlie," said Jay. "Now that I'm done with Brodi, I can lend a hand."

"Actually, that's the other reason I'm calling," said Hector. "The president wants you to quarterback the confirmation of the new nominee."

"Okay," said Jay with a hint of trepidation.

"Jay, the president wants you to come to the White House as his senior advisor."

"What?" asked Jay, stunned. "I don't think that's a good idea at all, Charlie. I'm much more effective on the outside."

"This is not an outside job," Hector said firmly. "This requires coordination of the press office, the counsel's office, public liaison, leg affairs, and the political shop. You have to be in the building to be in charge of the nomination, Jay."

Jay felt the breath knocked out of him. But he lived by the rule that you never say no to POTUS. "If that's what the president wants," he heard himself say. "But I want to talk to him first. And I'll need your 100 percent backing. I need to know you're fully on board."

"On board?" laughed Hector. "Heck, it was my idea."

Jay doubted that, but he shook it off. "I'll get there as quickly as I can," said Jay. He hung up the phone and walked off the balcony into the suite. Gabriella stirred under the sheets. She raised her head from the pillow and stretched her arms, her hair mussed. Even after a night of partying, she looked gorgeous.

"Who was that?" she asked, yawning and rubbing the sleep from her eyes.

"Charlie Hector," said Jay. "The president wants me to come back to DC and help out in the White House. I can't say no. He's been my friend and client for twenty years. I have to go."

Gabriella plopped her head back on the sheet and let out a low moan. Then, in a pique of anger, she threw her pillow against the wall. "I knew this weekend was too good to be true. I had a bad feeling the minute Brodi won that you'd have to go back."

Jay didn't have the heart to mention Page Six. He picked up the phone to call the airlines. He had to find a flight to DC.

YOLANDA MAJETTE WALKED THROUGH the first-class lounge at Reagan National Airport, trying to avoid eye contact. She clutched her purse in one hand and a Bloody Mary in the other. On the television she could not miss the cable anchor announcing her nomination's demise: "Battered by allegations about conflicts of interest arising from her husband's lobbying, plagued by opposition from Senate Democrats, and left twisting in the wind by a White House unwilling to defend her, Yolanda Majette withdrew her nomination to the Supreme Court today."

Majette flinched. She sought refuge in a back corner of the deserted lounge and, passing by a coffee table with a *Washington Post*, her eye caught the front-page banner headline: "Majette, Under Fire, Withdraws." Mercifully, it would soon be over. She was flying back to Sacramento and leaving her dream of serving on the highest court behind. Shell-shocked and embarrassed, she sat in a cubbyhole in the back of the lounge. She pulled out her cell phone and checked her voice-mail box. It was filled with encouraging messages from longtime friends. She found it strangely comforting.

Then, unexpectedly she came across a message from the president. He must have called as she went through security.

"Yolanda, Bob Long," the message began. "I'm calling to tell you that I will always, *always* be proud that I nominated you to the Supreme Court. You conducted yourself with grace, dignity, and honor. No one knows better than I do that it is possible to come back from a bitter, hard defeat. Hold your head high. I'm on my way to Chicago for a health-care event, but if you want to call me back, you know how to reach me. I will talk to you soon. And I will always be your friend. God bless you."

Majette reflexively began to dial the White House switchboard, which would patch her through to the president, probably on Air Force One. But then she thought better of it. It would be too painful.

Throughout the ordeal her plastic facade of calm had never cracked. But the president's voice message unleashed a flood of emotion. In the privacy of the cubbyhole, Majette doubled over and quietly wept, her tears falling in drops on the carpet, silent sobs racking her body.

JAY WALKED ACROSS THE floor of Gare du Nord, the cavernous train station that was a Paris landmark. Shafts of sunlight fell through the ceiling windows, creating a spectacular tableau of color, smoke, light, and human energy. His overnight bag slung over his shoulder, Jay moved quickly, dodging bodies that seemed to fly from every direction.

He stopped at the board displaying departure times and track numbers. He found his train: destination, Charles de Gaulle Airport, Track 9. His BlackBerry vibrated. Perhaps Gabriella saying a final good-bye?

"Hi, honey," he said impulsively.

"I hope she was good," said a deep voice. Jay recognized the voice as belonging to Truman Greenglass. Why would the president's national security advisor be calling him?

"Sorry, T. G. I thought you were someone else," stammered Jay.

"Jay, we need you to make a side trip on your way back to DC. Official business."

"Sure. Where?"

"Tel Aviv."

Jay was confused. "Okay," he heard himself say. He knew if the NSC was involved, it was sensitive. He felt a rush of adrenalin. He spied a coffee bar and cupped his hand over the mouthpiece of his cell phone, ordering an espresso.

"I assume you're on a cell phone?"

"Yes."

"Since you're not on a secure line, I'll fill in the details later," said Greenglass. "Exit the train station. There's a car waiting for you outside that will take you to the airport."

"Alright," said Jay. "I can't wait to find out what this is all about."

"You will soon enough," said Greenglass. "And Jay, one more thing."

"Yes?"

"Don't screw it up."

Jay downed the remaining espresso. The caffeine was a booster rocket. He bounded up the escalator and out the door where he found a black Mercedes sedan idling on the curb. The driver waved at him.

"Mr. Noble, I'm your ride to the airport," said the driver. "Please get in."

The door opened and Jay slid in the backseat. To his surprise there was another passenger. With jet-black hair and dark eyes topped by caterpillar-like eyebrows, deep circles enveloping his eyes, he wore a blue suit and had a trench coat folded across his lap. At his feet was a battered briefcase that had clearly accompanied its owner on multiple continents.

"Mr. Noble, my name is Jim Plant. I'll be accompanying you on your trip to Israel and debriefing you en route," he said, his hand outstretched.

Jay shook his hand. His grip was firm; their eyes locked. Jay scoped him up and down. He knew instantly that Plant was CIA. "Let me guess: you're with the government."

"Yes," Plant replied. "I work at the U.S. embassy in Tel Aviv." He said something to the driver in French. Then, turning back to Jay, he shared the plan. "This trip is highly classified. We can't risk detection en route to Tel Aviv. Your commercial flight has been cancelled and a government aircraft will be waiting for us at the airport."

"Okay," said Jay, holding up his hands. "This is getting weird. Ten minutes ago I was on my way to Washington. Now I'm picked up by a total stranger sent by NSC and ferried on a government jet to Israel. I'm not going any further until you tell me what's going on."

Plant shifted in his seat. "Iran has weaponized a nuclear device," he said, his gaze steady and voice lowered. "The Israelis are prepared to take military action and will act alone, if necessary. But that's assuming the right person wins the premier's office in the elections, which take place in thirty-seven days. As you can imagine, we have a lot on the line in the outcome. That's where you come in."

"So we're covertly trying to defeat a democratically elected government in a country that is one of our closest allies so we can elect a prime minister who will attack Iran?" asked Jay.

Plant ignored Jay's remark. "You'll be meeting the nominee of the Likud party and her advisors at a private dinner tonight."

"The right-wing party in Israel?"

"Correct. They want your help. This came directly from NSC."

Jay had heard about this kind of operation. He had a partner once who worked for the Agency in the former Soviet Union, conducting polls for various parties and candidates, making sure the remnants of the Communist Party didn't win the election. Jay had heard of similar black-bag consulting gigs in central and Eastern Europe. But Israel?

"Mr. Noble, the cloak-and-dagger stuff is for pulp fiction," said Plant. "Today the State Department, Pentagon, and CIA have political consultants on retainer all over the world. Back in the 1950s, we used military coups to effect regime change. We still resort to them in worst case scenarios. But we much prefer polling, focus groups, phone banks, and television ads." He paused. "How do you think we ended up with the right government in Iraq?" He leveled his gaze. "By the way, how do you think Brodi won? Those things don't just happen, as you know better than anyone."

Jay's eyes widened. "You guys helped Brodi?"

"Absolutely," said Plant, the corners of his mouth turned up suggestively. "The current foreign minister of the European Union is an Italian diplomat close to Brodi, and we need the EU's support for military action against Iran." For Jay it was a humbling revelation. He thought he had single-handedly pulled Brodi to victory.

"Alright, if this is coming from the White House, I'll do it," said Jay. "But I don't work for cheap."

"Money is not an issue," said Plant, eyes steady. "Just make sure Likud wins."

"Oh, is that all?" Jay looked out the window. They were outside central Paris, the Benz flying down a highway on its way to a remote airstrip. Peering in the distance, Jay could make out La Defense, the business district to the west of the city center, its modern skyscrapers and white Grand Arch rising in the distance. Jay was conflicted. Part of him wanted to jump on a plane back to Italy and hang out with Gabriella at her Tuscan villa, far away from the press attacks and the bitter partisanship roiling DC. But Long needed his help. He was fighting two wars at once, one with Iran and its funding of terrorists like Rassem el Zafarshan and the other with Joe Penneymounter and Sal Stanley over the Supreme Court. Jay was about to find himself at the center of both of wars, and it was right where he wanted to be.

TWENTY-THREE

"I've been saving this wine for a special occasion," said Joe Penneymounter, holding court from behind the bar in his apartment at The Watergate, a sweeping view of the Potomac and the twinkling lights of the city visible through the sliding glass door. He poured the wine. Light from the bar hit the red liquid, turning the crystal into glassy kaleidoscopes with revolving pinkish-red shades of color. He handed them to Christy Love and Natalie Taylor.

"This certainly qualifies as a special occasion," said Christy. She wore a black contrast jacket with white boot-cut jeans and black-toed patent leather pumps. Thin and athletic, she looked more like an Olympic volleyball player than a DC lobbyist.

"Wait. A toast," said Penneymounter. He raised his finger. "Here's to the team that forced Yolanda Majette to bail. Now on to victory."

"Here, here," said Christy, clinking her glass with Joe and Natalie.

"This is *excellent*," said Natalie, pursing her lips, savoring the taste.

"It's from a village in Alsace-Lorraine," said Penneymounter. "I bought a case when I was in Strasbourg on a codicil. Shipped it back on a C-130. It's almost impossible to get now. It's going for $800 a bottle on eBay."

Natalie's cell phone rang. She rummaged through her purse, pulling out the phone and glancing at the number. "That's the *Wall Street Journal*," she said. "They're under deadline on a story about the next Supreme Court pick." She flashed an evil grin. "I'm going to say that if Long moves to the right, the nominee is dead on arrival."

"You go, girl!" said Christy.

Natalie stepped into the dining room to take the call. "Christy, have you ever seen my photography collection?" asked Penneymounter.

"Where do you keep it?" asked Christy playfully. "The master bedroom?"

"No!" laughed Penneymounter. "It's in the study. Follow me." He grabbed her by the hand and led her to the study, desk strewn with papers, bookshelves bowed with books. Framed photographs covered two walls: celebrity images by Annie Leibovitz and Herb Ritts, a migrant woman by Dorothea Lange, landscapes by Ansel Adams, a self-portrait by Robert Mapplethorpe, Bill and Hillary Clinton captured by Tipper Gore during the 1992 campaign.

"This is incredible," gushed Christy. "It's one of the finest photography collections I've ever seen. I didn't know you were into art."

"It's an expensive hobby," sighed Penneymounter. "I don't recommend it. It's become very addictive."

He led her to a black-and-white print of a buxom Marilyn Monroe sheathed in a sequined dress, vacant eyes gazing into the distance. "This is by Richard Avedon. I got it at a gallery in New York." He pointed at her melancholy expression. "See how sad she looks?"

"You're trying to tell me you bought this for the expression on her face?" joked Christy.

Penneymounter ignored the dig. "She wanted fame and stardom. Of course what she really wanted was the approval of others," he said. "But it did not satisfy her. In fact, our adoration killed her. That's why we identify with Monroe, Elvis, or Michael Jackson. Because we also desire approval and applause . . . and, in the end, it destroys us."

"It's so true, isn't it?" replied Christy softly. "I had no idea you were so self-aware, Joe. I always took you for . . . I don't know, don't get mad, but a politician."

"There's a lot you don't know about me, Christy," said Penneymounter. He moved in closer, their bodies brushing. "I appreciate fine things. Good wine, art, intelligent conversation, a classy lady." he said, his breath against her cheek. "I'd like to show you that other side of me."

"Senator," said Christy, her posture stiffening. "I don't play in someone else's sandbox."

"I didn't mean to suggest otherwise," said Penneymounter, back-pedaling. He lowered his voice to a half whisper. "Look, I just think we could both really help each other. That's all."

Natalie walked in unaware, intending to report on her conversation with the *Wall Street Journal* reporter. Seeing Penneymounter and Christy in a near embrace, her eyes widened. "Sorry to interrupt," she said, backing out slowly and disappearing down the stairs.

Christy pulled away. "Just great," she said. ""You better go downstairs and take care of your girlfriend."

"She's not my girlfriend," Penneymounter lied.

Christy shrugged. "Joe, this isn't true confessions. But people are talking. Whatever she is, you better put a stop to it before you're the next John Edwards."

"Don't worry about her; she's fine," said Penneymounter. "Now what about the two of us working together? This could be the beginning of a formidable partnership."

Christy was not a novice when it came to fending off congressmen with wandering eyes and roving hands. "Joe, you deliver the goods on the Supreme Court," she said with a sly smile. "I'll make sure you're amply rewarded."

"Sounds tantalizing. And how exactly will I be rewarded?"

"I'll make sure you get a shot at our people when you run for president."

Penneymounter's face fell. "That's not what I had in mind."

"Too bad. That's the offer; take it or leave it," said Christy. She downed the remainder of her wine, setting the empty glass on the desk. She patted him on the cheek with the palm of her hand and dusted his shoulder, flecking away an imaginary piece of lint. "Thanks for the wine, Mr. Chairman. Good-night."

With that, she was gone.

FROM THE RESTAURANT JAY could see the walls of the old city, a tangible reminder of the thousands of years of history played out in Jerusalem. The gold dome of the Temple Mount glimmered against the black night. It was a warm evening, and someone had opened a window to let in a breeze. Ceiling fans spun overhead.

Jay felt queasy. It had all been too much: the flight from Paris, partying with Gabriella until dawn, the all-nighter in Rome celebrating Brodi's victory. He was no longer a kid, and politics, wine, and women across two continents now took its toll. To make matters worse, he felt like an idiot in the slapstick disguise Plant forced on him: wig, fake mustache, and baseball cap. *At least this will make for a good story in my memoir,* thought Jay. Safely ensconced in a private room in the restaurant, he removed the wig and moustache.

"Mr. Noble," said the Likud party's senior political advisor, "you travel incognito!" Everyone laughed.

"I only wish I had been smart enough to wear a disguise in Italy," Jay volleyed.

"Thank you for agreeing to meet with us," said the advisor. "We hope you can help us. We have only five weeks to claim the center the way you did in electing Bob Long."

"Like we did?" replied Jay. He tore into a mini-falafel appetizer. "My guy was a moderate who moved right. You guys are right-wing nuts. You need to move in the other direction!"

They all enjoyed a good laugh. The humor was an ice breaker.

The door swung open, and in stepped Hannah Shoval, the strikingly attractive Likud candidate for prime minister. With dark bangs combed to the side of a round face, penetrating brown eyes, and freckles flecking her nose and cheeks, she could have passed for an attractive, youngish college professor on her way to tenure. But her preternatural confidence, an effortless poise, and the security guards trailing her, said otherwise. She worked the room like a skilled pol, hugging necks and pumping hands before coming to Jay and extending her hand.

"Mr. Noble, your reputation precedes you," she said in flawless English.

"I do whatever President Long tells me to, ma'am," he said with a smile. "He told me to help you. So here I am."

"The president is fortunate to have such a loyal and discreet advisor," said Shoval. "So you are the cavalry then . . . kind of like in the westerns?"

"Something like that. I kill the bad guys."

Shoval sat down directly across from Jay. Sipping intermittently from a bowl of matzo ball soup, she spoke in crisp paragraphs, laying out the state of the campaign. "If this election had been held thirty days ago, I would have lost," she said with the detached professionalism of a physician diagnosing a patient. "The CIA leak about Iran obtaining a nuclear weapon has completely reshuffled the deck. When you combine that with Hamas launching raids from their sanctuary in Gaza, it's driving voters to me. The peace vote will stick with Labor. Kadima is stuck in the middle, which right now is no-man's land."

Jay nodded. "Kadima was a cult of personality," he said. "Once Sharon was gone, it lost its *raison d'etre*."

Shoval glanced around the table, pointing at Jay admiringly. "He knows more about Israeli politics than some of our own people," she said. Chuckles rumbled around the table. Her face turned serious. "The flip side of the coin is that if the election is about security, a woman is at a real disadvantage. Keep in mind I'm running against a former defense minister and a retired general."

"Push Labor further left," said Jay. "Your task is to build a center-right coalition. Can you pick off any Kadima party leaders by promising them cabinet posts?"

"I've made cabinet concessions already," replied Shoval with a wave of her hand. "Pretty soon I will have promised the same ministry to ten different people."

Jay smiled. "In terms of the security issue, for a woman candidate, it's all about clearing the toughness bar," he said. "You need to be an Israeli Margaret Thatcher. Give a major speech on the peace process and lay out a new proposal that transcends the failed policy of seeking a two-state solution."

Shoval nodded, listening.

"Campaigns are about the future and hope," Jay continued. "Israelis are weary of fighting and negotiating with no real change. Give them hope of a new day."

"That's hard when I'm hinting pretty strongly that if I'm elected I will take military action against Iran."

"It's hard, I admit," said Jay. "But now that you're in the general, you can move to the reasonable middle as long as you avoid the dovish left. That's what Long did. He actually got to the right of Petty on Iran. So it is possible to come off tougher than a general and more reasonable than Labor at the same time."

"Tough and moderate. Isn't that a contradiction?" asked Shoval skeptically.

"In a way, yes, but voters hold to contradictory views all the time. Consistency is one of the most overrated attributes in a leader," said Jay confidently. "Heck, my guy flip-flopped on abortion!" Everyone laughed.

"I want to loan you our pollster, Fred Edgewater. He's the best. I can also get our media team who did the closing ads for Brodi to come to Israel and shoot some footage that will give you a strong security image."

"Absolutely," said Shoval. "I want to meet them as soon as it can be arranged."

"The president needs you to win," said Jay.

"And not only President Long," said one of the Likud advisors. "The Arabs are secretly pulling for her. They want her to take care of Iran so they don't have to."

"So Mr. Noble, let me ask you a question," said Shoval. "If Bob Long is so tough, how come he's leaving it to a woman to deal with Iran?" She raised an eyebrow, clearly enjoying throwing the punch.

"We took out Saddam Hussein," said Jay slowly. "One good turn deserves another, don't you think?"

"Touché," replied Shoval, smiling. "Here's to victory at the polls for me and Long . . . and to a partnership in confronting Iran." She lifted her glass and clinked it with Jay's.

IT WAS JUST AFTER two in the morning when an unmanned, remote-controlled Predator drone dropped out of the clouds and floated above a safe house on the outskirts of Makeen, a small village in the Shakai region north of Wana in South Waziristan nestled in the mountains of Pakistan along the border with Afghanistan. The drone launched two laser-guided Hellfire missiles, lighting up the sky. They streaked to the target at a thousand miles an hour and exploded in a pillar of fire and smoke. Inside the house were several militants and family members, known associates of Rassem el Zafarshan, the mastermind behind the assassination of Vice President Harrison Flaherty. Everyone in the hut was killed instantly.

Long a refuge of Al Qaeda and the Taliban, the tribal region of Waziristan had become the refuge for Zafarshan after he lost the sponsorship of Iran, which deemed him too hot to handle after Flaherty's death. But in spite of its technological wizardry and firepower, the Predator attack failed. Zafarshan was not in the safe house. Unconfirmed reports indicated he had "gone rogue," snapping the leash of his Iranian handlers. Where was he now? No one knew, least of all the CIA.

TWENTY-FOUR

Ross Lombardy peered at the computer screen in the deserted offices of The Message Group, a political consulting firm on K Street. It was nearing midnight, and Ross stayed alert with a steady stream of caffeine, swigging from his third Diet Coke in two hours. He was joined by Sam Tayamo, a brilliant Filipino and Republican speech writer whose heroes were (in order): Jesus Christ, Abraham Lincoln, Ronald Reagan, Bobby Kennedy, and the Grateful Dead. Tall and dark, with a thatch of black hair and sad-sack eyes, Tayamo's fingers pecked away at the keyboard as his mind whirred.

"How about this?" Tayamo suggested. "'We will not bow to the counselors of retreat who insist that the path to victory is paved with the compromise of our principles.'"

Ross screwed up his face. "Too declaratory. Too subtle."

"A sentence can't be both declaratory and subtle."

"That one is." Ross stood up and began to pace the floor, waving his arms. "We need to throw a grenade! This has to make the nets and lead Fox News!"

"We want a riot," agreed Tayamo, working himself into an ideological froth. "This is pure, bloody red meat, and we're dropping it into a shark tank."

"Try this," began Ross. "'Let me offer a word of caution to those who seek our support. We will not follow those who cower in compromise or forget those who offer up our principles on the altar of political expediency.'"

Tayamo's body wiggled excitedly as his fingers flew across the keyboard. "It's not 'a word of caution,'" he said. "It's a 'word of warning'."

"Ooooh," said Ross. "This is too much fun."

"This may be the first time Andy has had to tone down our speech drafts!"

"He better not! This will land him on the front page of the *Times* and WaPo," said Ross. "If I have to, I'll distribute it as an advanced text."

"ANDY! ANDY! ANDY! ANDY!"

The Grand Ballroom of the Washington Hilton echoed with the primal screams of ten thousand right-wingers releasing the pent-up frustrations and grievances of forty years in the wilderness. They chanted the name of their fearless leader, the Reverend Doctor Andrew H. Stanton, stood on chairs, and waved American flags. On a back riser, the press corps surveyed the scene, horrified. They hadn't seen this many goobers from the backwoods of the Bible Belt since the Tea Party movement burst on the national scene. They worried: were these swamp fevers of bigots and Neanderthals the real America?

Andy bounded onto the stage looking like an aging game-show host. He wore gray slacks, striped tie, double-breasted blue blazer with gold buttons, and black spit-shined crocodile cowboy boots. Bouffant hair sprayed into a salt-and-pepper helmet, flashing a Pepsodent smile, he raised both arms in the air. He was a little too happy to be there.

"Andy! Andy! Andy!"

Andy motioned to quiet the crowd. They slowly took their seats.

"Ladies and gentlemen, as we gather in our nation's capital, an island of fantasy surrounded by a sea of reality . . ."

The crowd rumbled with appreciative laughter.

". . . America is at a crossroads. We face a terrorist foe committed to the destruction of America and Israel, the harassment of our democratic allies, and the defeat of Western civilization." Like a pitcher in a wind-up, he stared down his target. "Their desire is to create by violent means an Islamic caliphate stretching from the Arabian sea to the Adriatic. If they succeed, they will usher in the darkest period of human history since the Middle Ages."

The crowd fell quiet and somber.

"Here at home the consequences of moral decline are haunting. Our nation has presided over the murder of seventy-five million unborn babies. Men forsake wives and children while some seek to destroy the institution of marriage. Only one thing stands between them and their goal in redefining marriage: a single vacant seat on the U.S. Supreme Court."

BACKSTAGE, ROSS STARED AT the television monitor through squinting eyes, watching Andy's image on the screen. A clutch of staff gathered around him. Sam Tayamo appeared at his side and gave him a knowing wink.

"I thought you never went to hear the speeches you write," said Ross.

"I don't," said Tayamo. "But I wouldn't miss this for all the money in the world."

"This is going to land in the West Wing like a box of horse manure."

"Andy's burning every bridge behind him."

"And us. We're strapped to the mast with him," said Ross.

ANDY GRASPED THE PODIUM, body coiled with energy, leaning forward as if he were a lineman preparing to blitz. The crowd rustled. Andy was not known to mince words; everyone awaited the thunderclap. Then suddenly it happened.

"With Yolanda Majette's withdrawal, President Long faces a momentous decision," said Andy. "There are reports he will choose the path of least resistance, selecting a nominee who will not engender the opprobrium of Joe Penneymounter, Salmon Stanley, and the media."

The crowd hissed.

"It is my hope that President Long keeps his campaign promise to appoint strict constructionists who will interpret the law, not legislate from the bench." Scattered applause. He paused to reload. "But regardless of which course the president chooses, we will remain true to our values. We will not follow leaders who choose timidity over principle. If the president nominates someone to the Supreme Court who does not have the record and philosophy of a judicial conservative, we will oppose the nominee and the Faith and Family Federation will spare no resource in defeating their nomination in the United States Senate."

The crowd leapt to its feet. A guttural roar rose from the back of the room and built with ear-splitting pitch into a full-throated shriek. They stomped their feet, clapped their hands, waved white handkerchiefs, and raised fists. Andy smiled defiantly, chin raised, jaw jutted.

TO THE PRESS, ANDY was anathema, channeling Aimee Sempleton McPherson and Tricky Dick. Hunched on a chair on the press riser, Dan Dorman scribbled away on his steno pad, peering over his glasses. "Moses is calling down plagues on Egypt," he said with a chuckle.

Satcha Sanchez, covering the conference for Univision, leaned over Dorman's shoulder. "And just like Pharaoh, Long will blow him off."

"Which comes first, frogs or locusts?" asked Dorman.

"Rickets and scurvy," joked Satcha.

They both laughed.

JAY NOBLE SAT IN a small office on the first floor of the West Wing, staring at the questionnaire for new White House employees as if it were a bomb on its last few ticks. Were it not too late, he would back out of his decision to join the president's staff right then. Incredulous, he barreled down the hall and rapped on the door to Phil Battaglia's office.

"Got a minute?" he asked.

"Sure, what's up?"

Jay sat down opposite Battaglia, slumping low, his posture telegraphing his discomfort. "This questionnaire is nuts, Phil. Who wrote this?"

A smile spread across Battaglia's face. "Me. Why, you got a problem with it?"

"Did everyone answer these questions?" asked Jay, chagrined.

"Yep."

Jay squirmed in his seat. "Alright," he sighed. "But I think this holier than thou posture is getting us nowhere. Majette is Exhibit A. Nobody's really clean in this business."

"Fair enough," replied Battaglia. "But you can't win an election promising to clean up Washington and then treat the sewer like a sauna." He formed his right fingers into a pistol, pointing at Jay. "Just make sure you're not Exhibit B."

Jay frowned. "To that end," he said slowly, "Can you give me some advice about a business matter?"

"Sure. Fire away?"

"After I finished the campaign in Italy, I went to Israel to advise Hannah Shoval, the Likud candidate for prime minister," Jay explained, standing up from the chair and pacing the floor. "The CIA and NSA were involved in some way, I'm not sure how." He turned and made eye contact with Battaglia. "Likud agree to pay me a $250,000 fee. There's no problem with my accepting that fee since the work was done before I started at the White House, is there?"

Battaglia looked at Jay with hooded eyes. "Jay, the fact that you feel it necessary to ask the question should tell you the answer."

Jay's face fell. "I can't take it, can I?"

"No," Battaglia replied firmly. "Not unless you want to read about it on the front page of the *New York Times* and endure a congressional investigation led by Joe Penneymounter."

"What if I have them pay Fred's firm and then he makes me whole later?"

"So you propose to resolve a conflict of interest by adding the charge of deception and money laundering?" asked Battaglia sarcastically.

Jay let out a long sigh. "Well, you can't blame me for trying."

Battaglia's assistant opened the door without knocking. "Sorry to bother you guys. Jay, the president needs to see you in the Oval. Stat."

JAY WALKED DOWN THE hall and rounded the corner to the Oval Office. Long's assistant greeted him with a welcoming smile. They had worked together on the campaign, and he gave her a warm hug. "Welcome back, Jay," she said. "Go on in. He's expecting you."

Jay opened the door and felt a sense of awe. Even though Long was his friend of more than twenty years, it was still hard to get used to him as the leader of the free world.

Long sat behind the desk, face flushed. Lisa Robinson stood in front of the presidential desk wearing a pensive expression on her face. Jay made eye contact with Lisa, but she looked away. They had not talked since the inaugural. He meant to send her an e-mail making nice once he learned he was coming to the White House, but he forgot. He now paid the price.

"Did you see what Andy Stanton said this morning?" asked Long, clearly irritated.

Jay rolled his eyes. "No, what did the good doctor say now?"

Lisa's eyes scanned a piece of paper in her hand. "In so many words, if the president nominates someone for the Supreme Court he deems insufficiently conservative, the Faith and Freedom Federation will oppose the nomination."

Long's eyes were aflame. "What's with Andy?" He leaned forward, tapping the desk with his index finger. "This *guarantees* I can't pick someone to the right of Majette. Everyone will say I caved to the far right."

"So what?" replied Jay.

"I'm getting press calls," said Lisa. "I say we pop him."

Jay thought Lisa's suggestion was insane. "Am I missing something? Andy's an evangelical leader who is pro-life. What else do we expect him to say?"

"He could say he trusts my judgment," said Long.

"No, he can't," said Jay. "Andy has to maintain the loyalty of his constituency. He answers to them. If he is a mouthpiece for you, he loses credibility with his own people."

"So you think he's just genuflecting for the cameras?" asked Lisa skeptically.

"Of course," shot back Jay. "And predictably the media fell for it. He's protecting his street cred on the right."

"We can't let special interest groups threaten the president."

"Agreed. But Andy has a role to play, and it's different from ours," said Jay. "His job is to hold our feet to the fire. Our job is to do the right thing."

"He's over the line," said Long.

"Our response should be: thanks for the advice, but the president will appoint a Supreme Court nominee based on qualifications and judicial philosophy, not on who will support or oppose the nomination."

Lisa looked at Long, her eyes telegraphing skepticism.

"That's pulling a punch," Long observed, not entirely pleased.

"Maybe so. But Andy has twenty million followers, and if you hit him, it will blow this completely out of proportion," said Jay. "Besides, it's below your pay grade, Mr. President."

"It's not below my pay grade," snapped Lisa. "Let me pop him."

"What's our goal here?" fired back Jay. "It's to reaffirm the president's criteria for selecting a nominee." His face lit up. "Hey, here's an idea! Point out that we responded similarly when Christy Love and Pro-Choice PAC came out against Majette."

Long leaned back in his chair. "I like that." He pointed to Lisa. "Work that in."

"I like it because it makes the issue bigger than the religious right. If we pick a fight with Andy, it only elevates him," said Jay.

"Alright," said Long, calming down. He looked at Lisa. "Foul this one off. E-mail out a statement that says we appreciate the views of all citizens, including Andy, but my criteria in selecting a nominee is unchanged."

"So I should leave out your earlier comment that Stanton is an egomaniacal, self-appointed mullah?" joked Lisa.

"That's our little secret," said Long with a wink.

Jay and Lisa turned to leave. When they reached the door, Long called out, "By the way, Jay, welcome back."

"Thank you, Mr. President. It's good to be back."

"Don't lie to me," said Long. "You probably wish you were still in Italy with the wine goddess. What was her name?"

Ouch! How did the president know about her? Jay flushed with embarrassment. "Gabriella Fellissi," he said.

"Gabriella Fellissi? You can't make this stuff up!" exclaimed the president. "Why would she want a nerd like you?" He let out a loud, playful laugh. He never tired of ribbing Jay.

Jay and Lisa walked out of the Oval and headed toward the West Wing lobby. He waited for her to say something, but she walked silently, her legal pad pressed against her chest like a flak jacket. Jay felt as though he were walking beside an ice sculpture.

"You don't agree with me, do you?" asked Jay.

"No," replied Lisa, staring straight ahead. "Andy's a blowhard. Sooner or later we're going to have to take him down a notch. We should have done it when we had the chance over his inaugural prayer."

"Maybe, but not now, not over the Court appointment," Jay insisted. He suddenly brightened. "So, are you glad to have me back?"

Lisa stopped dead in her tracks, turning to him, their faces inches apart. Her cobalt blue eyes looked through him. "Not especially. You're a brilliant strategist. But you know what your problem is? You know it, and you don't wear it well." Blue veins showed through the skin of her neck. "Sometimes being smart and having the best strategy isn't enough, Jay. Sometimes there's no substitute for maturity and treating others with respect. Your sophomoric political-hack schtick is tiresome. You walk all over people, showing no concern for their feelings. You're harsh and disrespectful, including to colleagues busting their tails." She paused long enough to take a breath. "And one more thing: your adolescent amorous adventures are an embarrassment not only to you but to the president and this White House."

Jay just stood there, stunned by her blast.

"Have a nice day." Lisa marched off, leaving Jay standing in the middle of the hallway. Several people passed, gazing at the exchange's aftermath.

"Sure, I'd love to have lunch later this week!" Jay called out. "How about Thursday?"

TWENTY-FIVE

Everyone expected Long to move quickly, probably naming an appellate court judge who had already been confirmed by the Senate. That was why Marvin Myers was surprised when he received a phone call the Monday after Yolanda Majette's withdrawal. His source was a high-ranking deputy to Attorney General Golden, calling from a pay phone at a Metro station.

"Mr. Myers, you don't know me, but I work at the Justice Department. I have some information you might find very interesting." He sounded jumpy.

"I'm listening," said Myers.

"The president has offered the Supreme Court nomination to Mike Birch."

Mike Birch! Myers almost spit out his coffee. If true, it was a bold stroke, even for Long, for whom audacity had become a trademark. Governor Mike Birch of Florida was the former attorney general and a former prosecutor in Tampa. A moderate (conservatives denounced him as a RINO, or Republican in Name Only) who governed from the middle, he enjoyed a 68 percent job approval rating. Media savvy and attractive, with wavy silver hair and a long-distance runner's build, Birch was a likely GOP candidate for president. Myers' first thought: was Long channeling Eisenhower, who appointed then-California Governor Earl Warren to the Supreme Court, thereby eliminating a major rival?

Myers tried to keep his cool. "When?" he asked, almost panting. He could hear the sound of the Metro announcer in the background.

"Not sure of the exact time, but this morning," replied the DOJ official.

"What did Birch's say?"

"He asked for twenty-four hours to think about it."

Too soon for Myers's next column; he would have to break this story on his Web site and on TV. His mind raced. *What's the source's motive?* he wondered. *Is he trying to torpedo Birch or build momentum?*

"It's an odd choice, isn't it? This is going beyond the short list, at least the ones I'm aware of," said Myers, prying. Myers was a master at bonding with sources by talking shop and whispering gossipy asides.

"Long's freelancing. Birch hasn't even been vetted."

"*What!?* Boy, Long is really pulling a rabbit out of the hat, isn't he?"

"I'm told he wants someone with life experience in the 'real world,' whatever that means," said the source, his voice dripping with disgust.

"And he removes a possible opponent in four years," drawled Myers.

"Bingo."

"This is good," said Myers, dropping into his best sleuth baritone. "Any ideas on who else I should talk to?" He needed a second source.

"I don't know," said the source in a halting, nervous voice. "It's a very tight hold."

"What's Golden's take?"

"He's outside the circle of love at this point," the source answered. "He shot his wad trying to block Majette. He's got no throw weight with Long anymore. A lot of people at DOJ are upset that Birch has not been vetted properly."

Myers wrapped his mind around the leaker's motive. The bureaucracy had a way of biting back, he reflected. He thanked the source profusely and hung up. Telling his secretary to cancel his lunch with some muckety-muck lobbyist looking to plant a story for a client, he closed his office door and began to work the phones. In a city filled with Woodward and Bernstein wannabes, he was the last of the Big Feet, always chasing the Next Big Story, and this time he had a whopper.

MIKE BIRCH SAT IN the study of his sprawling Mediterranean home on the water in Tampa. He wore khakis and a golf shirt, sockless feet slipped into Gucci loafers, hair sculpted with gel to reveal his stark widow's peak, emerald eyes a study in concentration. A legal pad rested on his lap. He had written two columns of words beneath the headings, "pros" and "cons."

No one was more surprised than Birch by Long's call. Neither he nor anyone in Washington figured him to be a factor in the Supreme Court sweepstakes. But like the selection of former Johnny Whitehead as vice president, Long relished surprises. He had already selected six Republicans to serve in his cabinet, including at Justice and Defense. Birch's elevation to the Supreme Court would be the ultimate gesture that Long would govern as a centrist.

Surprisingly Birch found himself intrigued. As he gazed out at the sun-speckled waves of the bay, deep in thought, he reflected that there was much to recommend returning to his roots in the law. When he raised objections on the phone call, Long had a quick answer for everything. Never been a judge before? Too many judges cloister themselves in their chambers and pursue the life of the mind, totally disconnected from the real world. Birch, Long implored, lived the law and saw its effects as prosecutor, state AG, and governor. A centrist who aroused the suspicions of the religious right? Good: it would help win confirmation in a Democratic-controlled Senate. Queasy about being the swing vote on *Roe*? Stop right there; there is no litmus test, period.

Birch glanced down at the legal pad. He was a methodical decision maker who approached his moves with a gimlet-eyed understanding of risk and reward. Under "pros," he wrote "opportunity to serve," "impact the country's direction," "historic time," "lifetime appointment," "collegial working environment." In the column headed "cons," he wrote, "job of thought not action," "controversial issues—abortion, marriage," "confirmation battle," and, most importantly, "presidential prospects end."

Long pressed skillfully, dangling the possibility of later elevating him to chief justice, but Birch knew he could not count on that. He was a man of action, a problem solver who as governor took on the sugar lobby and opened up Florida's outer continental shelf to environmentally sensitive offshore oil drilling. The presidency beckoned: Long's election was a fluke. Why settle for the Supreme Court if the White House was within his grasp? If he was the Republican presidential nominee, Birch was a dead cinch to carry Florida, and without the Sunshine State, Long's reelection was impossible.

On the other hand, Birch thought, if he went against Long, the contest would probably go to the House again. A presidential campaign was a crapshoot, a free-for-all with back-room deals, backstabbing, and logrolling. Nor was the GOP presidential nomination a cinch. In fact, it was decidedly uphill unless he tacked to the right, something he was not sure he was willing to do. Birch gave himself no more than a 40 percent chance of winning.

He wanted to serve on the Supreme Court; he just wasn't sure he wanted to go through the confirmation process. Presidents tended to appoint either stealth nominees (Souter, Bryer, Meiers) or ideologues (Scalia, Thomas, Alito). Birch was neither. A cottage industry of extremist groups would go after him, ideological bottom-feeders lurking in the dark eddies of American politics. To run that gauntlet could be more brutal and dehumanizing than even running for office, as Yolanda Majette had found out the hard way. The atmosphere in DC had become too poisonous, too partisan for rational debate.

Birch walked to the window, staring silently at the water dancing in the sunlight. He was supposed to give the president an answer in eighteen hours, and he had no idea what he would do.

"MARVIN MYERS ON LINE one," said Jay's assistant, sticking her head through the narrow doorway leading to his office.

Jay assumed Myers was calling to welcome him back and reconnect. He snapped on his headset. "Marvin!" he boomed. "So what am I today, source or target?"

"Always the former," replied Marvin in a friendly purr. "I thought you said you would never take a government job. What was your line again? 'The only thing I know how to run is my mouth'?"

Jay guffawed. "Great memory, Marvin," he said. He pretended otherwise, but Jay loved working the press. To him it was the ultimate Washington game: using someone else and being used at the same time, "Bob Long has been a client for twenty years. More than that, he and Claire are dear friends . . ." His voice trailed off. "What can I say? He love bombed me." The statement stressed both his loyalty and indispensability and was therefore entirely self-serving and always worked like a charm.

"Speaking of Claire, how is she?" asked Marvin, a hint of sadness in his voice.

"She's great," said Jay. "Her focus is on getting well. The president talks to her every day. They've never been closer." As always, Jay was disciplined and on-message. The tabloids were having a field day with Claire's visit to rehab, but the White House stuck to its script.

"Hey, I heard the strangest thing today," said Myers, shifting topics. "If it hadn't come from a good source, I would have ignored it."

"What's that?"

"I heard Long offered the Supreme Court nomination to Mike Birch of Florida."

Jay nearly fell out of his chair. Myers was maddeningly thorough, with sources burrowed all over town. "Not to my knowledge," he lied.

"Really?"

"No. I can't imagine Birch walking away from being governor, can you?" He was playacting, pulling out all the stops. He hoped it was believable.

"The president didn't talk to Birch this morning?" Myers pressed.

This source is going to die, thought Jay. The information was too specific. "Marvin, I don't know. What I can tell you categorically, and this is on background so deep that I'm wearing scuba gear, is no one has been formally offered the seat."

"Mmmmm," said Myers, absorbing the information. "You didn't deny the president spoke to Birch."

"I said I didn't know," said Jay firmly, his anger growing. "Even if he did, I wouldn't tell you." Jay paused. "Between us, Birch is a reach."

"Why?" asked Myers. "It's a two-fer, isn't it? You eliminate a formidable opponent and add gravitas to the Supreme Court."

"It's fantasy football," said Jay dismissively. "It's Bret Favre in a Vikings uniform."

"It would be a heckuva pick, though, wouldn't it?" asked Myers.

"Almost as inspired as Johnny Whitehead for vice president," Jay replied, laughing. He pushed hard for Whitehead, which allowed Long to pick up Kentucky and helped him carry West Virginia and southern Ohio.

"Keep me posted," said Myers. "My source is good and your denial is nondenying."

"It's a highly fluid process, Marvin. Lots of moving parts." He hung up, picked up the receiver and immediately dialed Phil Battaglia.

"I just hung up with Marvin Myers," reported Jay. "He knows all about Birch!"

"I know. He left me a message, which I have not returned."

"Where is it coming from . . . DOJ?"

"I doubt it," said Battaglia. "Birch is probably talking to his advisors. He's not going to resign as governor without talking to them. My guess is one of them is leaking."

"We need Birch to say yes," said Jay. "Otherwise, the president is left at the altar."

"The president promised to consider him for chief justice if there's a vacancy," replied Battaglia. "I don't know what else we can offer him."

Jay hung up the phone. He longed for the campaign, when only a few key people knew what was really going on. Now there were thousands, inside and outside the White House, in the alphabet soup of the bureaucracy— DOJ, CIA, FBI, DOD. And they talked.

STEPHEN FOX LOGGED ON to the *New York Times* Web site from his Powerbook as he did every day after his morning swim. He sat in a deck chair on the teak sundeck of his $16 million, 140-foot yacht, aptly named *Felicity's Pleasure,* floating in the gentle waters of the British Virgin Islands. He could make out the hilly outline of Virgin Gorda in the near distance and Richard Branson's private island (yours for only $25,000 a day) just beyond it. His eyes scanned the front page. "Birch reportedly offered seat on Supreme Court," read the headline, with its tantalizing subhead: "Long reaches for possible GOP presidential rival."

Fox was stunned. His consultants (he had an army of them) never mentioned Birch. *Why am I paying these guys so much money to play golf and go to lunch?* Fox's mood darkened. He might as well have flushed the $10 million he spent that year in lobbying and legal fees down the toilet. Needing to vent, he impulsively picked up his iPhone and dialed the DC offices of Hoterman and Schiff. G. G. Hoterman answered in his distinct gravelly baritone.

"G. G., why didn't we see Birch coming?" barked Fox.

"If it's any consolation, Stephen, no one did," said G. G., cocky as always. "This is like McCain picking Palin, or Long picking Whitehead. It's totally out of left field."

The comment partially pacified Stephen. "But I thought we hired lobbyists close to Keith Golden, plus we had Edgewater. Do they keep their own team in the dark?"

"Everyone's in the dark," said G.G. "Look, it was just as bad when he picked Majette, who was an affirmative action baby and ethically challenged lightweight. My sources tell me that DOJ is completely frozen out. Long has grabbed the joy stick and, he's flying the freaking airplane! No one knows what he's going to do."

"A guy like that is dangerous," said Fox.

"How do you think his wife ended up in rehab?" joked G. G.

"So are we covered with Birch?"

"As well as we could be," reported Hoterman. "Wildfire gave $25 thousand to the Florida GOP during his reelection and $50k for his inaugural. We hired a couple of his consultants to do business development. The good news is as state AG, he didn't join the antitrust suit."

"That's helpful," said Fox. "Is there a law firm close to him?"

"Finding that out as we speak."

"If there is, hire them."

"I'm all over it."

Fox hung up without so much as a good-bye. Orlando, his long-serving houseman, brought him an Arnold Palmer in a tall glass with a wedge of lemon and sprig of mint leaves floating on top. His eyes narrowed behind his silver Chrome Heart glasses. As the future of Wildfire hung in the balance, Bob Long was choosing a Supreme Court justice like he was firing a rifle at a shooting gallery. He shook his head in disgust.

Just then Felicity glided up the circular stairway wearing a fishnet bikini with a wraparound skirt, Chanel sunglasses and wedges. Her hair pulled up to the top of her head with a hair clasp revealed her long tanned neck, well-defined collar bone, and toned muscles.

"Hi, baby," Fox greeted her, flashing his pearly whites.

Felicity walked around behind him and leaned forward, jutting out her rear and wrapping her arms around his neck, hands draping over his chest. She placed her chin on his shoulder and looked down at the Mac. She begun to massage his shoulders gently.

"Turn it off, Stephen," she said. "You agreed no work on this trip, remember?"

"Can't help it, honey. Long offered Mike Birch the Supreme Court seat, and we're playing catch-up. All our expensive consultants got caught with their pants down."

Felicity slid into the deck chair next to him and crossed her long legs, bouncing one of her wedge sandals on the end of her toe. "Let's sail over to Little Dix Bay for lunch."

"Sure, babe, whatever you want."

"Good answer," said Felicity with a playful lilt. "I've trained you well." She leaned over, placing a hand on his knee to balance herself, and kissed him multiple times, her lips brushing his lips, nose, chin, and cheeks. "I'll get you to turn that computer off yet," she giggled.

TWENTY-SIX

It was 11:00 a.m. when Mike Birch walked to a podium covered with microphones at the sleek and modern Tampa Bay Convention Center, an antiseptic building with stark lines and mammoth windows offering spectacular views of the bay. The operatic drama surrounding Long's offer to Birch stretched to its third day, with the White House growing increasingly frustrated with Birch's Hamlet-like decision-making process.

The media had a field day. Marvin Myers kicked off the feeding frenzy with a column reporting that Long had practically begged Birch on bended knee to take the job. "Birch Ponders, Long Waits," headlined *Politico*. "Will He . . . or Won't He?" screamed Merrypranskster.com beneath a photo of the relaxed, unruffled governor reading a newspaper poolside. "Birch's Choice: Supreme Court or the Presidency?" shouted the *New York Post*. No national politician had engaged in such riveting indecisiveness since Mario Cuomo flirted with running for president as a private jet waited on the tarmac to take him to New Hampshire.

Into this storm stepped Birch, tanned, silver maned, deep-set eyes fixed in a dispassionate stare, a stoic mask plastered on his face like heavy makeup. Cool and controlled, he spoke without a note. "First let me say I am deeply grateful to President Long for the offer to serve my country as an associate justice of the U.S. Supreme Court. It is a rare, once-in-a-lifetime opportunity I have seriously considered in recent days," he began, emerald eyes steady, chin raised. Cameras flashed, capturing Birch against a cloudless blue sky. "I spoke with the president a few minutes ago and informed him I believe I can be more effective in advancing the issues I care deeply about as governor."

There were audible gasps from the throng, which filled the ballroom to near capacity. Having twisted the knife, Birch moved to soften the blow. "The president told me he appreciated my willingness to forego a tremendous personal opportunity in order to serve the larger good."

His brief, no-frills statement finished, Birch agreed to take a few questions.

"Governor, could you walk us through the process by which you reached your decision? Was it the most difficult of your career?" asked the *St. Petersburg Times*, in full pander mode.

"Tough decision, no question," said Birch, verbs apparently unnecessary in describing the state of his psyche. "In the end it boiled down to where I felt I could make the biggest difference. Serving on the Supreme Court would be a great honor. But I've learned a lot about the challenges facing America after serving as governor of the third largest state in the country. If I were a Supreme Court justice, I would be limited in my ability to speak out on the issues facing the country."

The press smiled knowingly, scribbling furiously on steno pads. "Speak out" could only mean campaigning for the presidency. Birch seemed to be saying to Long, *sotto voce, I don't want to squander my talent on the Supreme Court. I want your job.*

"Did President Long promise to elevate you to chief justice if that opportunity presented itself?" asked the Associated Press.

Birch scowled theatrically. "The only position the president offered was associate justice." He paused. "Regardless, my answer would have been the same. My decision came down to where I thought I could be most effective."

"Now that you've ruled out sitting on the Supreme Court, is there a possibility you will run for president in the next election?" asked the *Washington Post.*

"I thought that question might come up," said Birch, barely repressing a smile. "It's way too early to think about that. Any considerations of seeking higher office played no role whatsoever in my decision."

The press smiled again: he could lie with the best of them! As the news conference wound down, the chief political reporter for the *Tampa Tribune* turned to a colleague. "Book your flights to Iowa and New Hampshire," he said in a half whisper.

BACK AT THE WHITE House, disappointed but grimly determined staffers in the Office of Presidential Personnel gathered around the television, doing a slow burn as they watched Birch kick their boss in the teeth. Their mood ranged from maudlin funk to gallows humor. There was no denying Long was publicly spurned by a leading candidate for the Supreme Court on the heels of his first nominee going down in flames. The chattering class handicapped the White House the way the ESPN anchors on "SportsCenter" analyzed a hapless football team. People were down and the White House plagued by second-guessing.

As Birch ended his news conference, Charlie Hector stuck his head in the door. "The president is on his way," he announced.

Long came down the hall with a spring in the step of his polished wing tips, the jacket of his blue suit buttoned, looking jaunty. Hector and Jay Noble were glued to his side, moving stride for stride. The OPP staff spontaneously gathered around the president, giddy that he chose to grace their lowly cubbyholes with his presence.

"I know the past few days have been tough. First Yolanda Majette withdrew her nomination, a decision I regretted but respected. Now Governor Birch has decided he does not want to serve." His forehead creased, his lips pressed into a thin line, he looked determined and upbeat. "It is a sad commentary on the judicial confirmation process that so many find it is not worth the trouble." Murmurs of agreement. "Washington is a tough town, and when a new sheriff shows up, it has a way of fighting back. We always knew with a Democratic Senate and the Judiciary Committee divided, the confirmation of a new justice would be a challenge." His eyes narrowed. "This is a test of what we're made of as a team."

Several of the staffers nodded. Jay stood to the side, hanging on every word.

"I wanted you to hear it directly from the horse's mouth," he said. *"I don't want you to change a single thing.* We have chosen outstanding people for the judiciary, every cabinet department and agency, throughout the government. You should be *proud* of the quality and caliber of our nominees." He pulled his right hand out of his pocket and formed it into a karate chop, slicing the air. "I have clear criteria for those who serve in my administration and on the federal bench. Don't lower our standards one inch." He threw back his shoulders, puffed out his chest, and bounced on his toes. "If the Senate rejects them or filibusters or delays, so be it. But we are not going to lower our standards." He turned to leave, then stopped. "Thanks for all you're doing for your country. Let's occupy this building for the short time we're here in a way that you'll be proud of the rest of your life."

The staff applauded. "Thank you, Mr. President," someone said. A few staff members teared up. Long shook a few hands and then turned on his heel, Jay and Hector in tow.

"I hope that helped," said Long as they headed for the stairs leading to the first floor of the West Wing.

"Big shot in the arm, sir," replied Hector. "They will be on cloud nine for a week."

"Those people are working their tails off, and I want them to know that I for one appreciate it," said Long. "We need to win the next one." He shot Hector a worried look. "Three strikes and you're out, you know what I mean?"

"We'll win, Mr. President," said Jay.

"We better," said Long. "We need to put Sal in his place."

"I have one request, sir. After we roll Stanley and Penneymounter, let me at Birch," said Jay, smiling. "I want a pound of that guy's flesh."

Long turned to Jay, eyes twinkling. "Sorry, but he's all mine."

They enjoyed a good laugh at Birch's expense. The battle was joined, and the Long White House was not about to yield. The political cognoscenti demanded that Long cut a deal with Stanley and the Democrats and put forward a nominee who would be easily confirmed. But Long was not buying. It was what Jay admired most about Long: when everyone else was ready to throw in the towel, Long doubled down. Jay hoped that the president's sunny disposition would be enough as they entered a new and dangerous phase in what had become an all-out war for control of the Supreme Court.

JOE PENNEYMOUNTER WALKED THROUGH the reception area in the Senate Majority Leader's suite of offices like a peacock in full feather, blithely ignoring the tourists who were milling around like puritans in Babylon. Two attractive, young receptionists worked incessantly jangling phones, glancing up to return Penneymounter's easy smile. Moving through the reception room with its large marble fireplace, early Federalist period furniture, large oriental rug, and sweeping view of the Mall, Penneymounter stepped into the private office of Sal Stanley without knocking. Stanley sat alone in a large overstuffed chair, brow furrowed, reading glasses resting on the end of his nose, studying what appeared to be a staff memo. Portraits of Stanley's predecessors, Lyndon Johnson, Everett Dirksen, and George Mitchell, hung on the wall, staring down like celestial witnesses from a bygone era. As usual, Stanley had the thermostat set to the temperature of a meat locker.

"So, what's the word?" asked Stanley, snapping off his reading glasses.

"Did you catch Birch's news conference?" replied Penneymounter.

"No, but I heard about it. What did he say?"

"He broke Long's jaw." He let out a little-boy giggle. Penneymounter's body man, who usually blended in like a piece of furniture, tut-tutted in low wheezes, his shoulders rising and falling, his skull undulating like a bobble-head doll.

"It was tastier than a warm cinnamon bun," said Stanley. "I had my staff Tivo it! I'm going to dub in a laugh track."

Penneymounter cackled with laughter. Then he suddenly turned serious. "We got lucky with Birch. He would have been hard to stop."

"Impossible," agreed Stanley. "Long's no idiot. It was a good idea, but Bob underestimated Birch's presidential ambitions. We dodged a bullet."

"Long's imploding!" exclaimed Penneymounter, suck-up juices flowing.

"Just amazing," said Stanley. "So what's next?"

"From what I hear, it's back to the drawing board," reported Penneymounter. "They passed over some good candidates for Majette and Birch. They're going back to that short list."

"This empowers Golden and the far right," said Stanley.

"No question," agreed Penneymounter. "Golden's people were the ones who leaked Birch's name. They deliberately sabotaged him."

"Really!?" exclaimed Stanley. "Wow. The guy's got a rogue attorney general fragging his Supreme Court nominee. He can't control his own people."

"There's just one thing that concerns me going forward," said Penneymounter.

"What's that?"

"Jay Noble. He's smart and tough and mean."

"How well I know," sighed Stanley. "I despise that little weasel."

"Until now the White House resembled a soccer team of twelve-year-olds all trying to kick the ball at once. That's going to change with Jay in charge of Supreme Court strategy."

"Stanley rose from his chair, eyes narrowed to slits, tapping Penneymounter's chest with his index finger. He lowered his face until it was inches from Penneymounter's nose. "Make sure the next nominee ends up like Majette and Birch," he said, his voice lowered to a whisper, the smell of coffee breath pungent. "I think we've got them on the ropes."

"We knocked two out of the box without a hearing. Just wait until one survives long enough for me to *really* get my hands on them," said Penneymounter. "By the time I get done, Bob Long's going to wish he'd never taken you on."

A broad smile spread across Stanley's face. "My official position is this is a matter for the Judiciary Committee, and I have no involvement," he said. "You know what to do."

Penneymounter nodded and turned to leave, turning the knob on the giant oak door and exiting through the formal reception area. His body man trailed him, shoes shuffling on the marble floor, eyes darting, sweat beading on his forehead. Penneymounter paused at the receptionist desk and introduced himself to the two attractive female receptionists, asking where they were from and where they were living in DC.

TWENTY-SEVEN

Judge Marco Diaz sat in his private chambers in the E. Barrett Prettyman U.S. Courthouse on Constitutional Avenue, two blocks from the Capitol, watching Mike Birch's news conference on television. He could not believe Long had offered Birch the seat, much less that Birch had snubbed him. The entire scenario was surreal. Meanwhile Diaz sat helplessly waiting for the call that never came. After Peter Corbin Franklin's stroke, Diaz filled out the Justice Department's extensive questionnaire, met with Golden and his team at DOJ, then sat down with Phil Battaglia at the White House. Later he met with Long in the Oval Office. Then: deafening silence.

Just as he gave up all hope, the phone on the credenza rang. It was Phil Battalgia.

"Marco, can you come over here first thing tomorrow morning?" he asked in an officious voice, the request sounding more like an order. "The president would like to see you."

A pregnant pause followed. After watching the baton pass twice, Diaz jettisoned his ambition to serve on the Supreme Court. Ironically, Yolanda Majette's run through the confirmation cauldron left him relieved . . . at least he had avoided her fate. But now his ambition returned with a vengeance.

"Phil, I'd be honored," Diaz heard himself say, his heart pounding like a jackhammer. "What time do you want me there?"

"Eight sharp. We'll send a car to pick you up and bring you in a back way. Don't tell anyone you're coming."

"Got it."

"That includes your friends, colleagues, personal assistant. Not even your wife."

Diaz gulped. *This is beginning to sound like the real deal,* he thought. He felt perspiration spreading on his palms. Flop sweat began to form under his hairline. Items on his desk came into clearer focus, like he had taken an upper. "Okay," he said. "See you in the morning."

As he hung up the phone, Diaz wondered if he was being set up for another fall. He gamely tried to keep his emotions in check, but his stomach did somersaults. The only thing worse than being passed over again was being selected. If that happened, Diaz knew his world would be turned upside down.

"THE FIRST THING WE need to do is shoot all the lawyers."

Everyone around the table enjoyed a good laugh except Phil Battaglia. It was 7:45 a.m. and Jay was halfway through the morning senior staff meeting in the main West Wing conference room, joined by Charlie Hector, Battaglia, Lisa Robinson, political director David Thomas, and a handful of others. Across the alleyway, Marco Diaz was secretly ferried to the Treasury Department building and was at that very moment being escorted by an aide through an underground alley connected to the White House complex for his final meeting with the president. Among the senior staff only Battaglia and Hector knew about the meeting.

"No offense, Phil," Jay said with a wink.

"None taken," said Battaglia.

"We've been acting as if the confirmation of a Supreme Court justice is some high-minded exercise in constitutional prerogatives," Jay continued. "This isn't filing a brief with some court. It's a knife fight!"

Lisa visibly flinched as Jay's raised voice bounced off the walls.

"That may have been what the Founders intended, but they also wanted an electoral college of wise men to elect the president . . . and we know better than anyone that doesn't happen, don't we?" He glanced around the table with a mirthful expression as they all chuckled at the irony. "This is a campaign, folks. We need to start acting like it." Jay dropped his voice down to conversation level, inflecting the words with an almost musical intonation. "We need a lean, mean political machine utilizing the technology of a campaign. That means a war room, rapid response capability, messaging team, paid media, surrogates, and net roots."

"Now we're talking," said David Thomas, always up for a fight. His cherubic face, velvety brown eyes, and chestnut hair belied the scars he earned in battle. "That's how we won the vote in the House during the presidential campaign. We targeted the key delegations and swing members and got our supporters to deluge them with calls, e-mails, and visits."

"Exactly!" exclaimed Jay. "We need to go back to campaign mode."

"I buy into the premise of the permanent campaign," offered Lisa. "But it's more like William McKinley running a front-porch campaign in 1896."

"Historical analogy alert!" joked Thomas.

"I'm not sure that's the case anymore," Jay replied.

"What do you mean?" asked Hector.

"We should get the nominee out there preemptively, sit them down with a few broadcast and print interviewers who are tough but fair. Almost like rolling out a veep pick."

Battaglia looked as if someone hit him with a baseball bat. He shook his head back and forth, his fleshy jowls and double chin shaking like Jell-O. "Surely you jest. That would be a huge mistake. *Huge*," he said, mouth agape.

"Why?" asked Jay pointedly. "Majette took a bullet in the head from a snub-nosed revolver and never had the chance to defend herself. You think Pro-Choice PAC and the left-wing bloggers aren't going to do the exact same thing to the next nominee?" He looked around the table for allies. Other than Thomas, there were none.

"Interviews before the Judiciary Committee hearing will backfire," insisted Battaglia. "The nominee will be asked how they would rule on specific cases. Abortion, same-sex marriage, the Wildfire antitrust case, affirmative action, the works. If they dodge the question, they look evasive; if they answer, they prejudge a case."

Jay threw his hands up. "Phil, the nominee's going to be asked those questions anyway when they go before Judiciary . . ."

"And the Senate has an advice and consent function under the Constitution," fired back Battaglia, his face reddening. "If we go over the head of the Senate, the members of the Judiciary Committee on both sides of the aisle will eat the nominee alive."

"Who makes these rules?" asked Thomas. He had a law degree from Georgetown and could hold his own with Battaglia. "No Supreme Court nominee even appeared before the committee until the twentieth century. Now we have five days of hearings. It's search and destroy. They hit us; we can't hit back. Why don't we make some rules of our own."

"He who makes the rules, wins," said Jay, tapping his pen on his legal pad.

"You won't find a qualified nominee worth their salt who's willing to go out there and sell themselves on television in order to be confirmed," said Phil.

"Do they want to be on the Supreme Court or not?" asked Jay.

"Not if they have to sell themselves like a box of soap."

"Darn, then maybe I should resign now," said Jay, his lips curled into a sardonic smile. Everyone broke up. It eased the tension in the room.

"I'm not yet entirely convinced Jay's right," said Hector, who had hung back to act as the referee, as was his usual style at meetings. "We don't want to reduce the nominee to a city council candidate." He rested his chin on his fingers. "But I *do* think we need to quit playing defense and get on offense. That was our big mistake with Majette."

"The ABA rates federal judicial nominees," said Thomas. "Bush 43 came into office and said he was not submitting his nominees to the ABA. Boom! Just like that." He snapped his fingers. "That was the end of the ABA. My point is: the rules change, and we need to be the one changing them."

"The U.S. Senate is not the ABA," said Battaglia, scowling.

"I like the idea of being more proactive with earned media," said Lisa, joining in. "But I get indigestion about putting a Supreme Court nominee on *Nightline* or *60 Minutes*. When someone does that, they're usually dead. John Tower and Lani Guinier, call your office."

Jay shot Lisa a look of disapproval. Lisa just stared back, blue eyes unblinking. She was not backing down.

"Lisa, that's when nominees didn't fight back," said Jay. "I'm talking about pro-actively getting your message out before Penneymounter defines the nominee."

"I'm all for it," replied Lisa. "Use surrogates. Don't put the nominee out there unless it turns into World War Three."

"It's World War Three now," quipped Thomas.

Everyone laughed again. It was less painful than crying.

"Enough discussion, we're talking in circles." Hector pointed to Jay. "Jay, draw up the campaign plan for the new nominee. You'll have a chance to make your case. The president will make the call. Everyone on board?" Heads nodded.

Everyone got up from the table and filed out. Jay found himself sitting across from Lisa, who was still gathering up her papers, eyes glued to the table, ignoring him.

"You're not disagreeing with me just because you're mad at me, are you?" he asked.

"I'm not mad at you, Jay," Lisa replied, rising from her chair.

"Yes you are."

"Is that so?" she said. "So now you can read my mind?"

Jay did a double take, then fired back, "As a matter of fact, I can."

"Okay," said Lisa slowly, a sarcastic lilt in her voice. "What am I thinking right now?"

"You're thinking how good it is to have the gang back together." He glanced around the table. "The verbal jostling, the intellectual swordplay. We're a good team."

"Bzzzzzzz," said Lisa. "Sorry, that's not the answer I was looking for." She raised her chin and did her best game-show announcer impersonation. "Don Pardo, tell our contestant about his consolation prize." She twisted her face into a theatrical frown. "Lunch by himself in the White House mess!" She spun on her heel and left.

A SECRETARY LED ROSS Lombardy through a confusing labyrinth of narrow hallways deep within the bowels of the Capitol. Ross had no clue where they were. At last they arrived at the hideaway office of Senator Tom Reynolds. The assistant knocked gently. The door swung open to reveal a beaming and effervescent Reynolds, coatless, his tie loosened, striking a casual and confident pose. He looked smaller and more genial than he appeared on the cable scream-fests in which he was a regular and enthusiastic participant. In the Senate the joke was that the most dangerous place on earth was between Tom Reynolds and a camera.

"Ross, come in," said Reynolds. "Welcome to my humble abode."

"Thank you, Senator," said Ross. "It's all very cozy." He glanced around the tiny room, furnished unpretentiously with a small desk, a couch, a large ottoman, and a bare coffee table. He directed Ross to sit on the couch while he put his feet up on the ottoman.

"So what brings you to town?" Reynolds asked.

"Meetings. The pending Supreme Court nomination," replied Ross.

"I'm glad Mike Birch turned it down," said Reynolds, diving in without hesitation. "He would have been a *disaster*! I don't know what the president was thinking."

"What in the world is going on at the White House?"

Reynolds sighed. "I don't think anyone's in charge. Golden's a great guy. . . . I served with him in the Senate. But Justice is Siberia. Hector and Battaglia have their own agenda. Jay Noble's very capable, he's brought a strategic sense, but he's still finding his sea legs."

"They better get their act together, or Bob Long is going to be a one-term president," said Ross.

Reynolds placed his hands in his lap, linking his fingers in a thoughtful pose. "The president knows that. I've told Hector and the president they're running out of political capital. I was a good soldier on Majette." He sat up suddenly. "I was the best friend Long had here! But I told Hector she wouldn't be confirmed, . . . and that was before the stuff about her husband's law practice."

"We told them the same thing. Who are they leaning toward naming now?"

Reynolds placed his feet on the floor and leaned into Ross. "The president hasn't decided," he said, lowering his voice. "I'm working him hard. I told him Diaz and Hillman were both excellent." He paused for effect. "The president is listening to me. I think I'm having a real impact on him."

The phone rang. Reynolds answered it. "It's the White House," he said, his eyes apologetic. "I have to take this. Can you excuse me for just a minute?"

Ross stepped out into the cramped hallway, the brick walls, low ceiling, and concrete floor echoing with the sound of shuffling footsteps. A water pipe squeaked. He stood there awkwardly for about three minutes. The door opened and Reynolds waved him in.

"That was the president," said Reynolds, his voice lowered, self-importance radiating from every pore. "He calls me directly. I can't say exactly what I told him. I'm making progress." His voice became a barely audible hush. "I told him not to nominate Jan Cargo because I can't support her." Cargo was a centrist appellate court judge on Long's short list who was anathema to conservatives.

"Good for you," said Ross. "We can make a great team. If you work the inside while we work from the outside, we can really turn the screws."

"Keep the fact that I'm talking to the president between us," Reynolds instructed him, seemingly nervous. "If Long thinks I'm talking about our conversations, he won't call me."

"Are you giving any thought to running for president?" asked Ross.

Reynolds's eyes lit up like headlights on high beam. "I'm thinking about it seriously," he said in a half whisper. "Don't get me wrong. . . . I want Long to succeed. But he's a Democrat. He's off to a rough start. If it looks like he will not get reelected, I may have to run."

Ross nodded, saying nothing.

"When I was twelve, I went to the altar at a revival when a traveling preacher came to my hometown in Oklahoma," Reynolds said, his face growing animated at the telling. "The altar call was not for salvation. I had already been saved. I got down on my knees. I can still smell the sawdust to this day. I asked God for a clear understanding of his calling on my life."

When I was twelve, I was playing with G.I. Joe, thought Ross.

Reynolds leaned forward, placing his elbows on his knees, gazing into Ross's eyes intently. "I heard the Lord clearly. Not an audible voice, but it was like He was speaking right behind me. He told me I was called to public service." His eyes grew wider. "And he told me that someday I would be the president of the United States."

He apparently told the same thing to every other member of the Senate, thought Ross.

"If that's what God called me to do, I can't go to my grave and not be faithful," said Reynolds firmly.

"Of course not," Ross replied. He'd heard a similar story from three other senators and a governor.

"With your help I could win." He tapped Ross on the knee. "You and I would make quite a team. Me as the candidate, and you would be my Jay Noble."

Ross didn't quite know how to respond. He already had a job, and being Tom Reynolds's Jay Noble was not really on his list of things to do before he died. "We would indeed," he heard himself say.

"I'll stay in touch," Reynolds said. "If I go, I want you on my team."

Ross smiled wanly. The meeting over, the staffer appeared at the door to show him the way out.

TO MARCO DIAZ'S SURPRISE, his second meeting with the president took place upstairs in the second-floor living quarters in the long and airy West Reception Hall, which served as a living room of sorts for the First Family. Diaz's eye caught a Monet on the opposite wall. The place seemed deserted; the First Lady was still away at rehab. Diaz felt bad for the president, living alone in such a big house. Long settled into an overstuffed chair while Diaz took the couch. The sunlight flowed through the window, giving the meeting a bright, cheery overtone.

Long was remarkably relaxed and loose, which in turn calmed Diaz's frazzled nerves. If the president was at ease, he figured he could be, too.

"So tell me about your family," Long began informally.

"My family of origin or my wife and children?" asked Diaz.

"Both."

"Well, my father came to America from Mexico when he was nineteen years old," Diaz began. "When he arrived, he had fifty cents in his pocket. He worked hard, sometimes holding three jobs at once. He never took a dime of public support. Today he's worth $100 million dollars and has twenty-five car dealerships, including the largest Ford dealership in the state of Texas."

"What a great story," exclaimed Long. "That's the American dream."

"Yes, Mr. President," said Diaz, his voice catching. "Sir, I was the first member of my family to go to college. My parents spoke Spanish at home. But they insisted that all of us children, seven brothers and sisters and I, speak English. Every one of us went to college. I've got a brother with an MBA from Harvard, two brothers who are lawyers, and two sisters who are doctors."

"I'll forgive you for the lawyers," joked Long. Diaz laughed. "You've got a great mom and dad," said Long affectionately. "I talk a lot about the three Es: English, a good education, and excellence in doing a job . . . any job." It was one of his favorite riffs, a CliffNotes version of one of his stump speeches. He cocked his head. "Tell me about your own family."

"I met my wife when I worked as a summer intern in a Dallas law firm," Diaz said. "I was going into my final year at Yale Law. She was a junior associate. You might say it was love at first sight."

Long smiled. He seemed to warm to the story.

"We have two boys, six and eight, and my wife is pregnant with our third child."

"Terrific," said Long. He seemed to have not a care in the world. If Diaz had not known he was a candidate for the Supreme Court, they might have just as easily been shooting the breeze on the porch of a country store. *Long is one cool customer,* he thought to himself.

"Let me ask you a judicial question: which justice do you most admire?" asked Long.

It was a predictable question, and Diaz came loaded for bear. "For his passion and sense of justice, Thurgood Marshall," he said without hesitation. "For his first-rate intellect and understanding of the role of a judge, John Roberts. For the quality of his opinions, his rapier wit, analytical ability and overall judicial philosophy, Scalia."

"That's three," said Long. "I asked for one."

"I'm more conservative than Marshall, more collegial than Scalia," said Diaz. "I hope I'm as smart as Roberts, but I don't know if anyone is."

"You're too humble," said Long. "Don't sell yourself short. You're plenty smart."

"My father used to quote a verse from Proverbs to me all the time," replied Diaz. "Before honor comes humility."

Long nodded, his face brightening, seeming to sense an opening. "You're Catholic, aren't you?"

"Yes, sir."

"I like this pope. He's the real deal . . . a man of God. He wrote me a beautiful letter after I won the election. I'm going to meet with him in Rome next month."

Diaz nodded.

"Do you believe in destiny, Marco?"

Diaz froze. It was not a question he had prepared for. He searched for the right words. "Yes, God has a plan for all of us," he said. "But He also has a plan that's bigger than all of us."

"Well said." Long's eyes bore into him. "Majette's decision to withdraw and Mike Birch turning me down might have looked like setbacks to the chattering class. But I don't see things as the world does. I think God just had a better plan."

Diaz could hardly believe his ears. Was this a job interview? "I believe that, sir," he said as if on autopilot.

"Good." Long suddenly stood bolt upright, extending his hand. Diaz rose and took it, shaking his hand with a firm grip. "Thanks for coming. Very impressive."

An aide appeared, seemingly out of nowhere, to lead Diaz to an elevator that took him back to the passageway leading to the Treasury Building. He and the aide walked silently, exchanging few words. Diaz's mind ran at warp speed. Had the lightning bolt he had been waiting for his entire career finally struck?

TWENTY-EIGHT

At 9:00 p.m. every television network went live as two figures walked purposefully down the hallway toward the East Room. They strode shoulder to shoulder on the red carpet between the busts of former presidents. The White House scheduled the announcement in prime time for maximum impact, and amazingly nothing had leaked. The president turned to his companion, still shrouded in shadows, and stage-whispered an aside. He looked relaxed and at ease.

"Is it Marco Diaz?" someone in the front row whispered.

Indeed it was. The East Room crackled with anticipation as Diaz walked up the steps of the stage and stood on a tape mark. His expression earnest, dark eyes staring straight ahead, he wore a charcoal suit with a striped blue tie. As he and Long took their places on stage, a staffer assisted his wife, dark haired with espresso eyes, and the Diazes' two boys, aged eight and six years, dressed in suits and ties with Buster Brown shoes, as they came on stage and stood beside him.

Long moved directly to the podium. "Tonight I announce that I am nominating Judge Marco Diaz to be the one hundred and seventeenth associate justice to the Supreme Court of the United States," said Long. "Judge Diaz is truly the personification of the American dream. His father came to this country from Mexico forty years ago with only fifty cents in his pocket. He started out as a janitor at a Ford dealership in Dallas, Texas. Later he became a salesman and ultimately bought his own dealership. He retired as the largest Hispanic automobile dealer in North America with twenty-five dealerships in six states."

Battaglia and Hector exchanged knowing glances. A palpable sense of relief filled the staff section. Diaz had been ordered up from central casting.

Long continued, his baritone deep and commanding. "Marco was the first member of his family to attend college. He went to the University of Texas, so he's a Longhorn. He graduated with honors from Yale Law." Long glanced at the first row. "His father Manuel is with us tonight. Mr. Diaz, I know you are very proud of your son."

Jay sat between Battaglia and Hector, his eyes twinkling, his facial expression a mixture of relief and joy.

"Judge Diaz has served with distinction as a deputy attorney general, a district court, and an appellate court judge on the DC Circuit. During that time he has impressed colleagues and the attorneys who worked with him or appeared before him with his collegiality, fairness, and open-mindedness," Long continued on a roll. "His superior judicial temperament, personal integrity, and knowledge of the law will make him an outstanding addition to the Supreme Court." He cocked his head for emphasis. "I am confident the U.S. Senate will be as impressed with his remarkable judicial record as I was when I decided to nominate him."

Diaz came to the podium. Shorter than Long, he stood a little lower to the microphone, his facial expression serious, a shock of black hair combed perfectly. "Mr. President, thank you for the confidence you have placed in me," he said. "Serving on the Supreme Court of the United States is the highest privilege and honor that can be accorded in my profession and is one I approach with a love for the Constitution, a deep and abiding respect for the rule of law, and a recognition that for many the Court is the final arbiter of justice."

The younger of his two sons began to edge toward him. Diaz glanced down, smiling awkwardly. His wife reached out and grabbed the boy by the hand, pulling him back. He tried to twist away. The audience chuckled appreciatively.

The news conference ended, Diaz stepped toward Long, who shook his hand firmly, their eyes locked. As Long and Diaz stepped back down the hallway, flanked by his wife and children, the network correspondents scrambled to do their stand-ups.

"Tonight a beleaguered President Long sought to pacify his estranged social conservative base and rescue a Supreme Court vacancy plagued by fitful starts, ethically challenged nominees, and self-inflicted wounds. In so doing, he selected one of the most controversial and conservative appellate court judges in the nation," the NBC White House correspondent said into the camera. "Tacking right by choosing Diaz is sure to unleash a battle royale in the Democratic-controlled Senate. Senate Majority Leader Salmon Stanley has already issued a statement pledging to examine thoroughly Diaz's record and rulings." He held up Stanley's statement for the cameras. "And the Pro-Choice PAC joined the attack, denouncing him as an extremist with ultraconservative views." A barely controlled grin rose at both corners of his mouth. "After a series of miscues and mistakes, including the withdrawal of Yolanda Majette and an embarrassing rejection by Mike Birch, the White House is bracing for a firefight in the Senate, and they are going to get one."

G. G. HOTERMAN HELD court in his usual corner booth at The Palm, working his way through his second scotch (Macallan 25, two ice cubes only) on the rocks. An artist's caricature of his head (minus receding hairline) adorned the wall above his seat. Joining him at the power dinner were three of the hottest "It" girls of the moment in DC, Christy Love, Deirdre Rahall, and Natalie Taylor. Any man in Washington would have been happy squiring any one of them, but G. G. was just two short of a women's basketball team. The Palm was where the famous and powerful, or those who wanted to be famous and hungered for power, gathered to gaze at one another while pretending to eat. Waiters rushed to and fro past every table, the din of conversation loud, the room pulsing with energy. Popping corks, rattling plates, and clinking glasses created a cacophony of noise. Sizzling steaks hot off the grill arrived at tables. Hoterman noticed other patrons staring at his table. Others might find such gawking mildly irritating, but not G. G.

"I'm here with my harem!" said G. G. to the waiter with a laugh, rattling the ice in his glass to signal he needed another scotch. "What are people going to say?"

The waiter grinned embarrassingly. His body language seemed to say, *I'm not touching that with a ten-foot pole.*

"They'll say you're a very lucky man to be in the presence of such a combination of brains and beauty," laughed Deirdre, patting his fleshy fist with her long fingers.

"And they'd be right!"

"I'm concerned about people overhearing us plotting strategy," said Christy. "Everybody keep your heads on swivels. You never know who's in the next booth." She cast a suspicious eye at neighboring tables.

"Speaking of which: do you have the dirt on Diaz?" asked G. G.

"Do I ever," replied Christy. "There's a discrimination case where he ruled against three women who were sexually harassed by the same supervisor. The details are ghastly."

"Tell me more." G. G. loved gossip, the more salacious the better.

"The case involved a manager at a hedge fund," said Christy, going into lawyer-speak. "Lewd remarks, sexually explicit e-mails, fondling, lingerie left on women's desks during their lunch hour." She paused a beat, leaning forward and speaking in a quiet whisper. "One time he called a female trader into his office, and when she came in for the meeting, he was watching porn."

"That's incredible. How in the world could he rule against the women?" asked G. G.

"He said they failed to file their complaint with the Equal Employment Opportunity Commission within the time limit required under the law."

G. G. shook his head in disbelief. "This guy's out of touch with reality."

"Fortunately, G. G., you don't have to worry about me filing a sexual harassment complaint," said Deirdre, her eyes dancing. "I was a willing participant."

G. G. shifted uncomfortably in his seat. Christy and Natalie's eyes widened. Neither said a word. G. G.'s affair and pending divorce were the talk of the town. Deirdre grinned away, apparently either unconcerned or oblivious to the awkwardness of her remark.

"There's something else," said Christy, deftly getting the conversation back on track. "Diaz is a member of Opus Dei, the right-wing Catholic society."

"We can't oppose him because he's Catholic," said G. G.

"Not because he's Catholic. Opus Dei is commissioned by the pope to impose Catholic social doctrine," she continued. "It's very conspiratorial. Diaz can't be impartial on abortion and gay marriage when he's taken a secret oath to rule in favor of the views of the Vatican."

Natalie looked at G. G. He shrugged noncommitally.

"Anyway, we're going up with our first television ad in a few days," said Christy. "The message is Diaz is an extremist: antiwoman, antichoice, antiworker."

"What markets?" asked G. G. "Please tell me it's not a phantom buy."

"Oh, no," replied Christy. "We'll do news avails in DC. Plus national buys on CNN, MSNBC, Lifetime. In the states we're targeting soft Ds or soft Rs on Judiciary."

"How much are you spending?"

"Two million a week. A thousand gross rating points in the target markets."

"That's a lot of money," said G. G.

The waiter appeared at the table with a medium-rare filet for G. G., salmon entrees and salads for the women. He refilled wine glasses. G. G. tapped his glass with his index finger to indicate another scotch.

"Can you help me raise some from your clients?" asked Christy.

"Sure," said G. G. "I've got some guys in LA and Silicon Valley who will want to play. I assume this is a (c)(4) play and contributions are nonreportable?"

"Yep. It's a (c)(4). Donations are not disclosed."

"I wish I could go to Stephen Fox," said G. G. regretfully, shaking his head. "He's my best donor. But he's backing Diaz." He sighed. "I guess you can't blame him. After all, Diaz voted with Wildfire in the antitrust case."

"G. G.'s firm is lobbying *for* Diaz because of the Wildfire ruling," said Deirdre.

Christy and Natalie looked stunned. G. G. shot Deirdre a sideward look of disapproval, clearly embarrassed. There was an awkward silence. G. G. raised a wine glass to his lips. . . . He was now alternating between scotch and red wine.

"Oh, that? It's nothing," he said with a wave of his hand. "We have a Chinese fire wall built between me and the Wildfire lobbyists." It was a convenient lie, and he told it smoothly. "I may be the only guy in DC who's helping to lead the opposition to Diaz while his law firm is lobbying for his confirmation!"

"Only in Washington," joked Christy.

"It pays the bills, darling," said G. G.

"Guess who I hired to do our press?" asked Christy, perking up.

"Who?" asked Deirdre.

"Nicole Dearborn."

G. G.'s jaw dropped. "*The* Nicole Dearborn . . . the chick who moled her way into the Long campaign and passed intel to Stanley?"

"Yes, that Nicole Dearborn," replied Christy proudly.

"Aren't you concerned that will raise the whole issue of the scandal?" asked Natalie, screwing up her face.

"Are you kidding?" replied Christy, laughing. "Having Nicole on board will get us a Style section profile in WaPo and a 'where are they now' piece above the fold in the *New York Times*. Best of all, it will drive Jay Noble *bats!*"

"I love it . . . playing head games with Noble!" exclaimed G. G. "Scandal-tinged political operative makes comeback. Spurned romantic interest stalks Noble, seeks Diaz's defeat. Oh, that's rich. Positively rich!"

Christy cocked her head, gently flipped back her blonde hair and smiled as she took another sip of red wine. "Why, thank you, G. G.," she said, giggling. "I thought it was pretty clever, if I do say so myself."

MARCO DIAZ SAT TO Sal Stanley's left, his body coiled with nervous energy, one elbow on the armrest of the chair, eyes blinking rapidly as photographers blazed away. It was the morning after the announcement of his nomination to the Supreme Court, and Diaz was making his rounds on the Hill. The first stop: the Senate Majority Leader, who lost to Long in the previous election and blasted him in a news release just hours earlier.

"Senator Stanley, is your mind made up? Are you going to oppose Judge Diaz's confirmation?" asked *Roll Call*.

Stanley smiled smoothly. "Judge Diaz deserves the opportunity to make his views known to the Judiciary Committee and the full Senate," said Stanley, an empty statement belying his antipathy for Diaz. "I will not make a decision on how I will vote on Judge Diaz's nomination until after his confirmation hearings."

Diaz gazed into the white hot glare of television lights. The temperature in the room rose measurably. A press aide to Stanley stepped forward, shouting, "Sorry, but that will have to be the last question. That's all."

The press filed out, leaving Stanley and Diaz sitting in wing chairs, with deputy Attorney General Art Morris and Stanley's chief of staff on the couch.

"Judge Diaz," Stanley began slowly, measuring his words, "I think you know that I have some deep concerns about your rulings on the DC Circuit Court. But I want you to know that I'll keep my mind open."

Diaz knew the statement was a lie. Stanley was already burning the lines to members of the Democratic caucus, collecting commitments to oppose Diaz . . . and this before he had met with a single senator. It was a shocking breach of protocol.

"I appreciate that, Senator. I hope I can allay any concerns and answer questions you might have about my record. That's why I appreciate the offer to visit with you," said Diaz as though reading from cue cards.

"Judge, do you believe there is a constitutional right to privacy?" asked Stanley.

Art Morris visibly flinched on the couch. The exchange was fraught with hazard.

Diaz tiptoed through the minefield, choosing his words carefully. "Senator, the Supreme Court has ruled there is a right to privacy, and I have no quarrel with that finding," Diaz replied, his posture confident. He did not rattle easily. "To put it in perspective, Griswold as a precedent is only nine years younger than *Brown v. Board*. The Court has upheld and expanded on that precedent repeatedly. The principle of *stare decisis* requires that jurists recognize precedent and overturn it only with great reluctance."

Stanley sat impassively, looking at Diaz with hooded eyes as he delivered his canned answer. He reloaded. "And does that privacy right extend to a woman's right to an abortion?"

"Senator, with all respect, I can't comment with specificity because it involves prejudging cases that could come before me if confirmed," said Diaz, fouling off the pitch.

"That's a lot of caveats and academic jargon, Judge. It's a simple question. I would appreciate a straight answer. Do you plan to vote to sustain *Roe v. Wade*?"

"Sir, my answer on *Roe* is no different," said Diaz, nonplussed. "It's a long-standing precedent. It has been refined and clarified in a number of high-profile cases. As such, while the Supreme Court is certainly not prohibited from revisiting its findings, and it has done so, for instance, in *Webster v. Reproductive Health Services* and *Casey v. Planned Parenthood*, it should do so only in those rare instances when new facts warrant."

Stanley frowned. Seething with frustration, he glared at Diaz, hardly disguising his contempt. Diaz thought he might lunge at him. Then, after a seemingly endless pause, he asked: "You would be the sixth Roman Catholic on the court. I assume you know that."

Diaz bristled, drawing back. "I hadn't really thought about the Supreme Court in terms of the religious affiliation of its members, Senator," he said, doing his best to control his anger.

"Six Roman Catholics, two Jews, and one Protestant—do you think that is representative of the country?" Stanley pressed.

"Senator, one could just as easily ask whether it's representative for the Court currently to have no Hispanic, even though the country is 15 percent Latino," Diaz volleyed back. "And it would be just as wrong to confirm me because I am Hispanic as it would be to oppose me because I am Catholic."

The tension in the room thickened. Stanley's chief of staff sat impassively, jotting an occasional note on a legal pad. Morris's face twitched with anger.

Stanley held up his palms, shaking his head back and forth. "I didn't suggest that I would vote for or against your confirmation based on your religion," he said defensively. "Far from it. But I do believe it's healthy for institutions of government to reflect the full diversity of the country, and in terms of religion and gender, the Supreme Court does not. Wouldn't you agree?"

"Senator, I'm not sure I do," said Diaz firmly.

There were no more fireworks after Diaz and Stanley crossed swords over the questions of abortion and his Catholicism. The rest of the meeting proceeded pro forma, with Stanley probing and Diaz bobbing and weaving. Afterwards, to avoid the media, Diaz and Morris slipped out a side door to a waiting elevator, escorted by two beefy Capitol policemen.

When the doors to the cramped elevator closed, Morris turned to Diaz. "I wish I'd had a tape recorder for that," he said, the vena cava in his neck showing. "I can't believe he actually played the religion card. I don't know how you kept from slugging him."

"I've dealt with it my whole life," said Diaz calmly. "But who knew Sal Stanley was a bigot?"

TWENTY-NINE

Phil Battaglia took another swig of coffee, the hot blast of java burning his tongue as his eyes scanned the front page of the *New York Times*. It was 5:47 a.m., and he was being whisked to the White House in a government Town Car, his driver zipping through yellow lights flashing at barren intersections, amber reminders of his sleep-deprived, stress-filled existence. Battaglia shook his head in disgust. The *Times* was pulling out all the stops. "Diaz's Membership in Catholic Order Draws Fire," read the headline.

The four-thousand-word hit piece read like an excerpt from *The Da Vinci Code*, mixing innuendo with vaguely sinister rumors of alleged anti-Semitism, graphic descriptions of the mortification of the flesh (celibate members wore metal rings around their thighs), and church rituals. The objective: make Opus Dei sound like a frightening cult. The reporter hunted down the priest who recruited Diaz into the group at Yale, ambushing him at an Opus Dei retreat center in Spain and asking him if he screened Diaz's reading materials at Yale, "dictated which classes he could take and condemned certain professors as anti-Christian" at the law school, and insisted on approving Diaz's selection of a wife. The priest denied the charges.

Just as he finished reading the jump page, Battaglia's cell phone rang. It was Keith Golden.

"Have you seen the story on Opus Dei in the *Times*?" he asked.

"Reading it as we speak. Par for the course."

"They can't attack him for being Hispanic so they're going to attack him for being a devout Catholic," said Golden with disgust.

"It reads like a Ku Klux Klan pamphlet," agreed Battaglia. "This will backfire big time among the Reagan Democrats in the midwest." His wheels turned. "I think we put some nuns behind Diaz when he testifies."

"Great idea and make sure they wear their habits," said Golden. He paused. "Quick question: do we have an accountant who can do some work on Diaz's blind trust?"

"I'm sure we do," replied Battaglia. "Why?"

"I know you're sitting down. Diaz's blind trust owns $250,000 of Wildfire.com stock."

Battaglia felt blood rush from his head to his abdomen, an involuntary reaction to stress, leaving him suddenly light-headed. "How did that happen?" he stammered. "He was ruling on the antitrust case, for crying out loud!"

"I guess that's why they call it a blind trust," said Golden. "However it happened, it's going to be a flap. The Judiciary Committee staff has his financial records, and they're starting to leak. We're going to get a bad story, maybe as early as tomorrow."

"Do you think this is serious enough to endanger his nomination?" asked Battaglia. The thought of yet another Supreme Court nominee imploding sent a chill down his spine.

"I hope not," said Golden. "But we need a top-notch accountant so we know what we're dealing with. Right now we're flying blind."

"I'll get back to you this morning." Battaglia hung up the phone. As his car pulled through the iron gates to the West Wing parking lot, he dialed Jay Noble's cell phone. Jay was on his way to the office in his own car.

"I know you're not calling to wish me a good morning," said Jay drily.

"Get your tail in here," said Battaglia. "I just got a call from Keith Golden. Diaz's blind trust owns a quarter of a million in Wildfire stock."

Jay let out an expletive.

"When it rains, it pours," said Battaglia. "See you when you get in."

The door to the Town Car swung open. Battaglia took pleasure in the fact that the Wildfire story would overwhelm the *Times* Opus Dei piece. Diaz's confirmation had become a fire-free zone, with shots fired from every angle.

MARCO DIAZ TOOK THE call in the kitchen. His wife Frida was busy getting their boys off to school. Their housekeeper was at the sink, doing the breakfast dishes. The sound of dishes rattling mixed with shouted voices, the typical confusion of a house filled with young children.

"Marco, we've got another story," said Art Morris, Diaz's chief handler from the Justice Department. "I think it's manageable, but we want to get our ducks in a row."

"What now? Did they run down the priest who took my confession in college?" asked Diaz bitterly. He was livid about the *Times* piece on Opus Dei.

"It's your blind trust," replied Morris. "Apparently it holds Wildfire stock."

"It's a blind trust, for heaven's sake!" Diaz exploded.

"No one's suggesting you did anything wrong, Marco," said Morris. "But we need to talk to the trustees, and we're bringing an accountant in to go over everything with you."

"This is going to delay the hearings, isn't it?" asked Diaz, exasperated.

"We don't know," said Morris. "Penneymounter hopes so. But if we have a good answer, we may still be able to go day after tomorrow."

Diaz fell silent. He had a bad feeling about the hearings, like he was walking into an ambush. "Art, I just don't know how much more of this I can take," he said, his voice shaking. "It's like there's some evil force trying to destroy me."

"Hang in there, Marco," said Morris, trying to buck him up. "We're almost at the finish line. We just need to answer some questions about the trust. After that you'll do great at the hearings. Then we're on to the confirmation vote in the Senate, which looks very solid."

"No," replied Diaz, shaking his head, voice downcast. "Penneymounter will use this to delay the hearings, and they'll dig up more garbage. After the blind trust, it's going to be something else. It's never going to end until they kill me with death by a thousand cuts. I can feel it."

"It's going to be *fine*," insisted Morris. "No one here cares what the *New York Times* says. I'll bring the accountants by at noon. Can you assemble the statements from your trust account?"

"I think so," said Diaz. He hung up. For Diaz it was just the latest blow in a hail of punches. Between murder boards, meetings with senators, and rereading every opinion he ever wrote, he was exhausted and depressed. It was not going to be fine, he thought, it was not going to be fine at all.

THE STORY APPEARED ON the *Washington Post* Web site at 3:12 p.m. under the byline of Dan Dorman, the most feared investigative journalist in DC. "Diaz's trust bought Wildfire stock shortly before ruling on antitrust case," screamed the headline. It was an astonishing revelation. The trustees of Diaz's blind trust acquired ten thousand shares of Wildfire.com stock only twelve days before Diaz cast the deciding vote in the Internet giant's favor in what was the biggest anti-trust case since the breakup of AT&T.

Charlie Hector stared at a printout of Dorman's story in his spacious, airy office in the West Wing. Jay, Lisa, and Phil Battaglia sat on the couch looking shell-shocked.

Hector let out a heavy sigh. "This complicates things," he said.

"Penneymounter's going to the floor in twenty minutes," said Lisa. "He's calling for delaying the hearings."

"Figures," said Hector. "That's a Judiciary Committee matter. Beyond that we don't comment. Let Tom Reynolds respond."

"What?! No comment?" Jay jumped up from the couch like a jack-in-the-box, waving his arms. "We have to push back hard. Diaz is the president's nominee. We need to defend him forcefully."

Hector looked at the others impassively, his eyes soliciting opinions. He was a no-drama kind of guy.

"Diaz did nothing wrong," said Battaglia. "He fully complied with the guidelines for federal judges governing investments in blind trusts. Lisa should say that in the briefing today and put an exclamation point on it."

"I'm going to need the poop on the blind trust rules," said Lisa.

"We'll get you some talking points," said Battaglia. "But you can refer most of their questions on that to Justice."

"We should also pop the *New York Times* for the Opus Dei piece," said Jay. "Roll them together. This is a search-and-destroy mission against a man of faith. Shift the subject from blind trusts to anti-Catholicism."

"Normally I don't agree with starting a fight with someone who buys ink by the barrel," Lisa replied. "But the *Times* story is outrageous."

"I'll call Ross Lombardy. We need the Federation ginned up," said Jay.

"You might want to recommend that Andy Stanton book that guy from the Catholic Anti-Defamation group," said Lisa, her eyes lighting up. "He's a pit bull."

"Andy doesn't do guests," said Jay with a sardonic smile. "There's only one star and it's him."

"And Fox News," offered Lisa. "They'll love the anti-Catholic angle."

"I like it," said Hector, moving the meeting along. "Anything else?"

"Yes," said Jay. "What about my campaign plan? I hate to say, 'I told you so,' but we're now officially getting our heads handed to us. Pro-Choice PAC has ads up in twelve states and national cable. We've got a hatchet job running in the mainstream media every day. If we don't change the dynamic, Diaz is a dead man walking. We need to go to the mattresses . . . now."

Hector frowned. Lisa and Battaglia were silent. Jay could tell they were torn. Was it the optics of running a campaign for a Supreme Court pick out of the White House, or was Hector worried Jay would get the credit if Diaz won confirmation?

"You win," said Battaglia at last. "Let's do it."

Jay smiled. "Music to my ears."

"I only have one question," said Hector. "If we green light this, do you have everything you need to win the nomination?"

"Absolutely," said Jay without hesitation. "I'll bury Capitol Hill under an avalanche of e-mails and phone calls. They'll never know what hit them."

"Then go," said Hector.

Jay turned to Lisa, who sat next to him on the couch. "Lisa, I'd like your help on this. I'll coordinate the paid media and grass roots; you do earned media."

"Sure, okay," replied Lisa. The tension in the room was palpable. Everyone in the West Wing knew Jay and Lisa had flirted with romance, only to part in a messy breakup. But they had to get Diaz confirmed, and personal feelings had to be set aside.

The meeting broke up. Jay felt better. Hector finally dropped the leash, and he was free to do his job. Lisa would be his wingman. Who knew? Maybe he could rekindle the fire he once had with Lisa while he was busy trying to save Diaz's nomination.

SENATORS OF BOTH PARTIES parted like the Red Sea as Joe Penneymounter walked down the center aisle and took his place before his desk on the Senate floor, a desk once used by Daniel Webster. Looking for all the world like an actor in a Hollywood production standing on his tape mark, he clipped a lavalier microphone to his suit coat. In the press gallery, reporters scrambled to their seats and exchanged whispered asides. The word on the street was that Penneymounter was about to launch a bone-crushing attack on Diaz. Everyone braced for the fusillade.

"Article Two, Section Two, Clause Two of the Constitution explicitly stipulates that the appointment power of the president is *not* absolute. The president may nominate officers of the government, including justices of the Supreme Court, but they are confirmed with the 'advice and consent' of the Senate," Penneymounter began, his voice modulated and officious. His hair coiffed, his tie perfectly knotted, he was a study in control. "That means full consultation with the Senate, preferably in advance of the appointment, preferably on a bipartisan basis."

Several senators drifted in and sat at their desks. No one wanted to miss the fireworks. Tom Reynolds sat in the front row, shoulders hunched, game face on, lips pressed together, looking like a one-man truth squad.

"Sadly, Mr. President, that is not what happened in the case of Marco Diaz. The president named Judge Diaz without any consultation with me as chairman of the Judiciary Committee," said Penneymounter. "That is his prerogative. But had he done so, I could have educated him on the profound reservations I and other senators have about Judge Diaz's disturbing past statements and troubling decisions that might have caused him to reconsider this appointment of a judicial extremist to the nation's highest court."

Ouch! Penneymounter was just getting warmed up. "I could have told the president that Mr. Diaz's disrespectful treatment of women who suffered sexual harassment and sought redress before him raised questions about his judicial temperament," Penneymounter said, a scowl spreading across his face. "I could have shared the insights I gained as the ranking member of the Judiciary Committee when Mr. Diaz was confirmed for the DC Circuit Court of Appeals, when he was specifically asked about his investments and the potential for conflicts raised by those holdings. He promised at that time to take whatever steps were necessary to prevent such conflicts." He paused, surveying the faces of his colleagues. "We now know, Mr. President, that those promises were broken. Judge Diaz's trust bought stock in a technology company even as he presided over a case that affected the value of that company."

On the front row Tom Reynolds glared at Penneymounter, his eyes shooting darts. Only senatorial decorum (and C-SPAN's cameras) kept them from coming to blows.

"I do not take the confirmation of an individual to lifetime tenure on the highest court lightly," Penneymounter said, his voice rising. "Serious questions have been raised about whether Judge Diaz violated judicial ethics in ruling on the Wildfire antitrust case. Given the circumstances, I have no choice but to delay the hearings for Judge Diaz until further notice. We must review his investments, the legal agreements governing his blind trust, and who made the decisions about his portfolio."

Reporters bolted from the press gallery. They had their headline: "Penneymounter Calls for Indefinite Delay in Diaz Confirmation Hearing."

A look of supreme self-satisfaction spread across Penneymounter's face. "Mr. President, let me be clear: I am not passing judgment on whether Judge Diaz should be confirmed to the Supreme Court." It was a ruse, and everyone knew it. "I have a responsibility as chairman of the Judiciary Committee, and I intend to live up to it. Just because the president does not take the advice and consent clause of the Constitution seriously does not mean we do not."

Penneymounter unclipped the microphone from his lapel, methodically gathered up his papers, and exited the Senate chamber, his body man in tow.

A senator walked over to Tom Reynolds and leaned over, his arm on Reynold's shoulder. "What a piece of work that was. If this were the nineteenth century, Diaz would challenge him to a duel," he said.

"If this were the nineteenth century," said Reynolds in a half whisper, his lips curling into a sardonic grin, "*I* would challenge him to a duel. And I wouldn't be trying to give him a flesh wound, either."

THIRTY

Marine One fluttered down from the sky nose up, its wheels touching down on the South Lawn. A Marine guard rolled out a red carpet while another guard opened the door and stood at attention, snapping a salute. President Long emerged from the helicopter first, returning with his own brisk salute. Then, in the most anticipated moment, Claire Long stepped out into the afternoon sun.

All the cable networks interrupted regular programming to capture the riveting scene of the First Lady returning to the White House after six weeks at Hope Ranch, an alcohol and drug rehabilitation center in Phoenix. Hers had been the most public admission of chemical dependency by a First Lady since Betty Ford. Speculation about her condition roiled official Washington: how was she?

Bob and Claire walked hand in hand down the red carpet and across the lawn, their body language projecting the unrestrained, adolescent-like joy of a couple reunited, both smiling broadly. A rent-a-crowd of White House staff and the Longs' extended political family was conveniently arranged to cheer their arrival. The president stepped to a stake-out location not far from the entrance to the West Wing. Claire slid to his side, looking relaxed and comfortable in a St. John's navy blue pantsuit.

"Let me be the first of many to welcome Claire back to the White House," said Long, one hand in his pocket, voice tinny from nerves. "And more importantly I want to welcome her back home. I love her, we've all missed her, and we're thrilled she's back." He bobbed his head as if to say, "There, I got through it."

Claire stepped to the microphone, remarkably poised and confident. She smiled easily, her arms at her side. She looked, well, different somehow. Thinner perhaps?

"First of all, it is really great to be home," she said with a sigh mixed with joy and relief. "I'm honored you would all come out to welcome me back." The press tittered at the sarcastic reference to the stakeout. "Seriously, my time at Hope Ranch has been such a blessing. You might be surprised to hear that, but it was. I learned so much about myself, about life, and about the most important things in life. I now understand that your faith, your family, and your friends are more valuable than any career achievement or any public victory or defeat and more important than whether others approve of you or not." She stared past the press, seeming to speak over their heads directly to the American people. "Bob has been tremendously supportive, and for that I am very grateful." Her eyes widened with emphasis. "I'm sure I'll be able to share more in the days ahead, but I want to thank the people of this great country for their thoughts, their notes of support, and their prayers. I received thousands of letters and cards, and I read them all. They meant so much to me. Thank you."

Claire avoided the shouted questions from the press as the staff scurried to pull down the microphones. Bob put his arm around her waist, and they walked into the White House together.

As the door closed behind them, White House staffers streamed slowly back to their offices. A clutch of media Big Feet stood around on the lawn like pillars of salt, seemingly frozen in place by the evocative encounter. Dan Dorman sidled up next to the Associated Press reporter.

"This may be the first time in recorded history that a president has welcomed a story about his wife's stint in rehab," said Dorman with dry wit.

"How's that?" asked AP.

"It's better than the story of his third choice for the Supreme Court going down in flames over an ethical lapse."

"Boy, you've got that right," agreed the AP. "Diaz is on life support. What do you think . . . does he make it?"

"I sure hope not," said Dorman with a crooked grin. "I'm having too much fun."

ANDY STANTON, HEADPHONES STRAPPED to his gigantic skull, 240-pound frame nestled in a large leather chair, glanced up at the clock. Two minutes to air. His beefy hands flipped rapidly through "the stack," the news clips and backgrounders providing the raw material for his program. His leaned forward to the microphone of New Life Ministries, knowing that twenty million listeners hung on his every word, and popped a cough drop into his mouth to lozenge his golden vocal chords. In the semidarkness of the studio, he resembled a cross between Billy Graham, Sean Hannity, and Jabba the Hut. The phone in the studio jangled, breaking the silence. It was Ross Lombardy.

"Andy, I just got off the phone with Jay Noble," Ross said, his voice lowered to a self-important hush. "The White House would love it if you could pop the *New York Times* for its anti-Catholic smear of Diaz."

"Haven't you been listening, brother?" replied Andy. "I opened the show with it! In the next segment I'm reading Charles Krauthammer's column on how it reveals the secular elite's disdain for religion. It's brilliant!"

"That's . . . great," stammered Ross. "Sorry I missed it. . . . I was in a meeting."

"Always listen to the show, Ross," said Andy. "Standard operating procedure." Andy expected senior executives to have his program on in the background like Muzak, but he drove them so hard that most of them had to catch the podcast later in the evening. Not knowing what witty or incisive bit Andy had uncorked on radio or TV that day could get a senior vice president sent to the penalty box.

"What about booking the guy who's president of the Catholic Anti-Defamation League on the radio show?"

Andy turned the idea over in his mind. Then: "I've got a better idea. Have him blog about it on our Web site. Then I'll read it over the air and drive people to the site. I'll plug him and Faith and Family at the same time."

"Now you're talking," said Ross. "That'll get us fifty thousand hits on the Web site. Good thinking, Andy."

"That's why I'm the boss. E-mail me that blog as soon as it's posted. Gotta go." He abruptly hung up. A technician behind a glass wall held up five fingers and counted down silently, then pointed with his index finger. The red light in the studio lit up.

"Welcome back to the program, my friends," Andy began in a conversational tone. "We've been talking about the vicious attack on Marco Diaz masquerading as a news story in today's *New York Times*." He dropped his voice an octave. "Ladies and gentlemen, make no mistake, this is bigotry as detestable as that directed against John F. Kennedy when he ran for president in 1960. Remember the signs that used to hang outside homes that said, 'Irish Need Not Apply'? Remember the signs in my native South that once warned, 'Whites Only'?" He paused. "Well, the secular elite have hung a sign outside the Supreme Court building that reads: 'No Roman Catholic or Evangelical Need Apply.'"

Andy spun in his chair, whipping his head back and forth. "Imagine that! There is now a ban on Catholics and Evangelicals to preside in a room that has the Ten Commandments carved in stone over the justices!" He let out a theatrical guffaw. "Marco Diaz may have graduated first in his class at Yale Law School. He may have served with distinction on the most important federal appellate court in the land. But he's disqualified because . . . he *might* actually believe the Bible is the Word of *Gaaaawd*!" Behind the Plexiglas, Andy's producer rocked back and forth in his chair like a little boy, grinning from ear to ear, lips and gums flapping, clapping his hands together in a silent pantomime.

THE WHITE HOUSE RELUCTANTLY negotiated a one-week delay in Diaz's confirmation hearing. The truth was the administration had little choice. Diaz's Wildfire holdings blindsided the vetting team at DOJ, which splattered more egg on Keith Golden's face, as if he needed any. With Diaz's nomination in a tailspin, Washington whispered that it was only a matter of time before Golden was forced out at Justice. What looked like a marriage made in heaven between Long and his AG was souring with striking rapidity. Once again the Long White House hunkered down beneath a hail of second-guessing by columnists, bloggers, and pundits who asked: "How could the people who ran such a brilliant campaign just last year be so stupid?"

Seven days was an eternity in politics, as Christy Love fully grasped. But the left could only gain the upper hand if more dirt surfaced. The day after the White House caved on the delay, Christy took a call from an old law school friend that fell like manna.

"Christy, I know someone who might be able to shed some light on the real Marco Diaz," said the friend.

"I'm all ears," she replied. "Talk to me."

"Here's the story," the friend began slowly. "I'm good friends with the vice president of the Dallas Bar Association. She went to Yale Law with Diaz. She knows a woman who dated him very seriously. They almost got engaged."

"And?" asked Christy.

"According to her, Diaz got her pregnant and then paid for her abortion."

Christy felt the blood rush to her head. Her heart rate quickened. She got up from behind her desk and closed the door to her office. "He knocked her up and then forced her to have an abortion! What a creep. Who is the woman?"

"She's a partner at Lewis and Lapham in Dallas."

"Is she willing to go public?" asked Christy, hyperventilating.

"Honestly, I don't know," said the friend. "But if anyone can talk her into doing so, I know it's you."

Christy wrote down the woman's phone number, her heart pounding. "I'll give her a call." Then, after a pause: "Does anyone else know about this?"

"Not to my knowledge."

"Good. Keep it between us."

Christy hung up, her mind racing. She thought, *The Catholic altar boy paid his girlfriend to abort his child.* It was too good to be true. And that was precisely what worried Christy. This was not her first rodeo; she was the veteran of ten Supreme Court confirmations and over the years had grown skeptical of rumors that would allegedly sink a nominee. Most turned out to be phantasms. But what if this was real? If Diaz's old girlfriend was willing to talk and her story checked out, his nomination was dead.

G. G. HOTERMAN AND Deirdre Rahall walked across the tarmac of the Beef Island airport looking like they stepped out of the pages of *Vogue.* G. G. ambled along in the uniform of a Washington power player on holiday: white linen shirt, pressed khakis, Gucci loafers with no socks, blue blazer. Deirdre's outfit screamed wife number three: blonde hair whipping in the wind, Chanel sunglasses, diamonds sparkling from her neck and earlobes, and a white Chanel dress with a hemline well above the knee. The sun beat down on them, and the wind whipped their hair and clothes, and they still looked like a million bucks. As they rounded the corner, they caught sight of Stephen Fox waving on the dock, clad in cargo shorts and a Tommy Bahama shirt unbuttoned to mid-abdomen, revealing graying chest hair.

"Over here, mates!" he shouted. Stephen grabbed their overnight bags and loaded them into the dinghy. He held Deirdre's hand and helped her into the boat, showering her with effusive compliments for how nice she looked.

"Felicity's on board," Stephen shouted as he guided the dingy to his yacht. "She's got some appetizers. You must be hungry. If you're not, act like you are."

G. G. looked at Deirdre knowingly. Felicity was a born hostess.

As they pulled up to the yacht, Felicity, wearing a black bikini top and a denim mini skirt, leaned over the rail on the sundeck, her sun-streaked brown hair falling over her shoulders. "G. G. and Deirdre, darlings, you made it! Come up here!" she shouted. "We have food and drinks."

They feasted like kings on salmon pate, stone crab, jumbo shrimp, lobster, and raw vegetables, washed down with a California chardonnay. Deirdre nibbled on a single crab leg and celery sticks. G. G. went back for seconds, then thirds.

"I think we should do all our planning meetings down here, Stephen," G. G. said with a chuckle, his cheeks stuffed like a chipmunk.

"I'm all for that," said Felicity, her legs splayed across Stephen's lap. "Sometimes I think we should sell our houses and live on the boat."

"Hurricanes, dear," said Stephen. "Besides, where would you shop?"

"Shopping is never a problem," shot back Felicity. She glanced at Deirdre with motherly disapproval. "Eat something, dear."

"No, I'm fine," said Deirdre. "I'm not hungry."

"Let's have a painkiller," said Stephen with sudden inspiration. He turned to Orlando the houseman. "Four painkillers, Orlando."

"What's a painkiller?" asked Deirdre.

"Rum, coconut juice, pineapple juice, orange juice," said G. G. "But mostly rum."

"You need to get into the mind-set of the BVI," said Stephen suggestively.

"Don't worry, be happy?" asked Deirdre.

"That's Jamaica, honey," corrected G. G.

Within minutes Orlando magically appeared with a silver tray of towering painkillers. The rum hit Deirdre's bloodstream like a long pull of moonshine. She laughed out loud at every joke, giggled at every sarcastic aside. After they polished off the painkillers, G. G. shifted to ice water. He needed to stay alert for the business he had to discuss with Stephen. The men drifted to the back deck, pulling up chairs as the crew readied for the evening sail. Felicity gave Deirdre a tour of the boat.

"Give me an update," said Stephen, lighting a cigar. "Is Diaz going to make it?"

"It's a jump ball," said G. G. with clinical detachment. "The blind trust is a serious problem. If he comes out of Judiciary, even with a one-vote margin, he'll be confirmed. If he loses in Judiciary, he's DOA. If it's a tie in Judiciary, all bets are off."

"I've been turning over in my mind whether there's anything we can do."

"Not much," said G. G. "With the Wildfire stock story, we're in a delicate situation. I instructed our lobbyists to stand down. Right now we're in the mode of not saying or doing anything stupid."

"That's a tall order," joked Stephen.

"Tell me about it. But for now, the first rule is: do no harm."

Stephen's face grew serious. "Are any more shoes going to drop?"

G. G. shrugged. "Who knows? Rumors are flying."

"Like what?" asked Stephen.

G. G. leaned forward, dropping his voice. "The word is an old college girlfriend has some interesting stories to tell." He leaned closer, until his face almost touched Stephen's. "Diaz was apparently into kinky stuff."

"Really? I thought he was a Boy Scout."

"Apparently not," said G. G. "He beat her up, made her do things she didn't want to do, took her to nightclubs, and tried to get her to hit on other men." Actually, he made it up. But he knew it would entertain Stephen endlessly.

Stephen's face fell. "That'll kill him!"

"If she talks. Christy Love knows all about her. So does the Judiciary Committee staff. But she's apparently reluctant to come forward and testify."

"Can we hire her law firm?" asked Stephen. "Maybe that'll keep her quiet."

G. G. shook his head. "It's past that point. If we try to hire them now, it's radioactive." G. G. found it quixotic the way Stephen hired and fired lawyers and consultants, sometimes layering them like a cake, as if they were a panacea for whatever ailed Wildfire at that moment in time. It helped sink Majette, yet Stephen was still on a hiring binge.

"It's maddening," said Stephen. "I've got twenty-two billion dollars riding on this antitrust case, and I'm sitting here in the BVI drinking umbrella drinks, watching from the cheap seats." Suddenly he spun around and hurled his glass against the rail, shattering it. G. G. jumped. Orlando, who stood no more than ten feet away, never moved.

"Stephen, politics is like poker," said G. G., trying to calm Stephen down. "Sometimes you're dealt a bad hand, and you just play it. Hopefully Diaz's girlfriend keeps her mouth shut."

At that moment Felicity and Deirdre burst through the door to the yacht's back sundeck, looking relaxed and playful. Felicity spied the shards of glass on the deck. She put her hands on her hips and gave him a wifely, disapproving look.

"Did you throw a glass *again*?"

"Of course not, honey," Stephen lied. "I dropped it."

"He did," lied G. G. "I was a witness."

"Whatever. Orlando, please get that up before someone cuts their foot on the glass." Felicity clapped her hands. "Alright, everyone, time for afternoon naps."

"But I'm not tired," protested G. G. "We just got here."

"Well, Stephen and I are taking a nap," said Felicity, flashing a smile. "So everyone retire to their respective bedrooms. Read a book, or . . . whatever."

"Oh, I see," said G. G., chagrined at being slow on the uptake.

Stephen grinned at G. G. sheepishly, his eyes seeming to say, *Can you believe how lucky I am?* Felicity grabbed him by the arm and led him below deck.

CHRISTY LOVE AND NATALIE Taylor entered the bar off the lobby of The Mansion, the swanky hotel in the Turtle Creek section of Dallas. When they walked through the door, Christy saw three traveling businessmen knocking back drinks at the bar. Their leering eyes followed her and Natalie like barflies. In the back of the room, sitting at a table shrouded in semi-darknesss, were two women. One of them waved. Christy walked over and extended her hand.

"You must be Christy," said one of the women. "I'm Piper Duncan." Duncan was vice president of the Dallas bar and a prominent attorney. She had bleached hair, toasted skin, high cheekbones, and blue-shaded glasses that gave her an exotic look. A former member of the city council, she was a mover and shaker in the Democratic Party circles who ran a lucrative municipal bond practice. "Christy, meet my good friend, Maria Solis."

Maria had a round face, cropped black hair, and large, searching brown eyes. She shook Christy's hand. "It's a pleasure to meet you."

"Good to meet you, Maria," said Christy, smiling. "Please meet my associate, Natalie Taylor." She paused as they shook hands. "Natalie is with the Senate Judiciary Committee."

Solis visibly drew back. "I thought we were just talking confidentially," she said. "No one told me the committee would be involved."

"Natalie's my friend," said Christy. "She's not going to do anything without your explicit permission. She's here simply to hear what you have to say. I trust her. So can you."

Solis glanced at Duncan, whose eyes sought to reassure her. "They just want to hear your story," said Duncan softly. "I made it clear you've made no decision about whether you want to submit anything to the committee."

Solis seemed to calm down. She took another sip from her drink. Christy and Natalie waved over the waiter and ordered red wine.

"So Piper tells me you dated Marco at Yale," said Christy, grabbing a handful of mixed nuts from a dish on the table.

"Yes," said Solis haltingly. "We dated for about a year and a half. We were hot and heavy. He was my first real love. He was good-looking, smart, a big man on campus, going places." She paused, frowning. "Marco was torn about his Mexican heritage. He felt guilty about getting into Yale and worried he might be seen as an affirmative-action baby. He worked so hard to prove them wrong. He wanted in the club. That's part of why he was conflicted about marrying a Latino." She flashed a sardonic smile. "A lot of Latino men want to marry a gringo. They want to fit in. I think that doomed us."

Christy nodded. "So what happened between you two?"

"Marco was ambitious." She chuckled at the thought. "Everyone was . . . it was Yale Law, after all. But Marco stood out. He told me someday he would be attorney general, Supreme Court justice, or the first Hispanic president. But I wanted a normal life, whatever that is. We began to grow apart." She paused, taking a sip of gin and tonic. "But our physical attraction remained very strong." She smiled at the memory.

"So eventually you broke up," said Christy.

"Yes," said Solis. "He didn't want to, but my feeling was, if we were not going to get married, we should move on. I cared for him, but I knew I'd take a backseat to his legal career." Her dark eyes fixed on Christy's. "He was also moving to the right. It was the Reagan era, and it moved him ahead in those circles. We disagreed about politics." She looked down at the table. "Not long after we broke up, I missed my period."

"What did you do?"

"I took a home pregnancy test, and it was positive. I walked around in a daze for an entire day. I couldn't believe it. Hoping it was some kind of mistake, I went to the health clinic at Yale and took another test. It came back positive."

"Did you tell Marco?"

"I did," said Solis. "He was the father. I was young, I was scared, and I was confused. I was applying for jobs at law firms. I didn't know what to do."

"What did he say when you told him?" asked Christy.

Solis sighed. "At first he was speechless. Then he started pacing around the room, waving his arms, analyzing the situation. Typical male reaction to an inconvenient reality that hits him right between the eyes."

"Was he angry?"

"Not at me. I wasn't trying to manipulate him because I had broken up with him. I wasn't trying to trick him. He knew that. But it was what it was." She sighed. "It was a mess."

"I've been there," said Christy empathetically.

"I told him I might have the child and then put it up for adoption," said Solis. "I was raised a very strict Catholic. My mother never missed Mass. It was hard for me to imagine doing anything else."

"What did Marco say?"

"He told me he wanted me to have an abortion," said Solis quietly. Silence hung over the table. "So that's what I did. I've lived with that for twenty-four years." She began to tear up. "Don't get me wrong, I believe in a woman's right to choose. But I never really felt like I had a choice, not with him."

"So he definitely knew you were pregnant," said Christy. "No question about that."

Solis nodded. Her eyes were watery.

Natalie, who had remained silent up to this point, jumped in. "Maria, I know how difficult this is, and we really appreciate your courage in telling us," she said. "I'll respect whatever you decide to do. But it isn't right for the members of the Senate to vote on Marco's nomination without knowing this. She peered into Solis's eyes with a penetrating gaze. "If it would make you feel more comfortable, we can do it without anyone knowing who you are."

Solis bristled. "I can't do that," she said. "I don't want to be the next Anita Hill . . . making an anonymous charge and then getting outed. Even though I oppose what Marco stands for, there's a part of me that's rooting for him. I'm proud of him. Isn't that strange?"

"Not at all," said Natalie. "It's natural. You loved him. But this isn't about your feelings. It's about the country."

"I know," said Maria. "But I don't want to hurt Marco. And I'm not the black widow."

"I don't want to speak for Maria," said Duncan firmly. "But I don't think it's a good idea for her to try to remain anonymous. If she's going to tell her story to the Judiciary Committee, she has to do it for attribution."

"We're kidding ourselves if we think I won't be drug through the mud," said Maria. "Look at Monica Lewinsky. She was eviscerated, and Bill Clinton got a $10 million book deal. Clarence Thomas was confirmed. The men who take advantage of women always survive while the woman gets smeared. That's still the nature of our society."

Natalie reached across the table and placed her hand on Maria's. Their eyes locked. "Maria, this is different." She glanced at Christy. "Christy and I are as close to Penneymounter as any two people on earth. We will go to the wall for you. If the Senate votes to confirm Diaz, it's a miscarriage of justice . . . even more than what happened to you twenty-four years ago."

Solis remained silent for a full ten seconds. "I'll think about it."

Natalie and Christy pulled business cards from their purses and handed them to both Solis and Duncan. They paid the bill with a credit card and rose to excuse themselves. Duncan walked them to the door, leaving Maria at the table alone.

"Don't put Maria in the crosshairs without her permission," said Duncan in a whisper. "It's her life, not ours."

"We won't," said Christy. "She's our sister. Don't worry."

They went back to Christy's room and sat out on the large balcony overlooking the pool. Grey twilight faded to darkness as Christy pulled a bottle of Cabernet out of the minibar. For a few minutes they drank in eerie silence, absorbing the full weight of Solis's extraordinary tale. They held in their hands the key to defeating Diaz, . . . but they did not know if they'd be able to use it.

"Do you believe her?" asked Christy at last.

"Yes," replied Natalie. "I *want* to believe her."

"So do I."

"What could be her motive for lying?"

"Maybe he broke up with her. Maybe she wanted to be Mrs. Marco Diaz, but she didn't get to be because he dumped her. Maybe she's looking at Frida and grinding her molars every day, wanting to get even."

"That's a possibility," said Natalie. "Something real went on between them. She loved him once. I'm sure of that much."

Christy took a long sip of red wine and swallowed. "One thing's certain: if we can persuade her to come forward, her story better be true."

"That's what the FBI is for," said Natalie. "They'll interview her, and they'll interview anyone she has ever shared this with over the years . . . close friends, family members, maybe a marriage counselor."

Christy walked to the rail and leaned over, staring into the twilight. Then she turned back to face Natalie. "If she doesn't come forward, it may leak. Have you thought about that?"

Natalie raised her eyebrows. "I can't believe we're the only two people other than Maria and Piper who know about this. There *have* to be others. There are a lot of reporters who would die to get their hands on this story, starting with Marvin Myers." she said. "I just hope it doesn't come to that."

"If the Wildfire stock and blind trust issue don't sink him first," said Christy. "We may not have any other choice."

THE CONFERENCE ROOM ON the third floor of the Eisenhower Executive Office Building was turned into a war room, strewn with cans of Diet Coke, paper cups, rotting fruit and wilting sandwiches, whiteboards filled with illegible scribbles, and whirring laptops. Sitting around the table was the high command of the judicial confirmation team at the White House: Jay Noble, Lisa Sullivan, David Thomas, and the researchers Jay called "propeller heads."

"Okay, what's the next hit piece from the *Times*?" asked Jay.

"They've got a panel of public accountants who say the mistakes Diaz made in managing his blind trust were highly irregular," said an aide. "They accuse the trustees of lying."

Jay glanced at Lisa. Her eyes were glazed, her face pale, her skin sallow. The stress of her job was taking a heavy toll. "What's our response?"

"We've got our own team of outside accountants who have reviewed all the stock transactions within Diaz's blind trust," reported Lisa, flipping her black hair behind her ears with her long fingers. "They're issuing a report concluding that Diaz dotted all the i's and crossed all the t's when he established the trust. One of the accountants signing the report is the former chairman of Price Waterhouse."

"I know him. Great guy," said Jay.

"We also did a contribution history on the *Times*' accountants," Lisa added. "And guess what? Three of them wrote checks to Democratic candidates. Two of them gave to Stanley; one of them maxed."

A wicked grin crossed Jay's face. "*Liberal* accountants?!" he shouted in mock outrage. "Isn't that an oxymoron?"

"We also have fourteen retired federal judges who have signed a letter to Penneymounter saying that Diaz should not be punished for what the trustees did," said David Thomas.

"That works," said Jay. "What's our push back on Diaz's receiving written notices of all the stock trades?"

"He says he didn't open them," replied Lisa. Jay raised his eyebrows and dropped his chin, projecting skepticism.

"Wildfire was less than 5 percent of the trust's assets," said Thomas. "There's no way he'd risk his career over that. Besides, who doesn't have Wildfire stock? It's one of the most commonly held stocks in the country."

"Does Penneymounter own any Wildfire stock?" asked Jay.

"We're trying to find out," said one of the opposition researchers.

"Get the goods. He's chairman of Judiciary," said Jay. "He has jurisdiction over the antitrust division of DOJ. It would be a conflict." He leaned forward in his chair, jabbing the air with his finger, punctuating his words. "If not Wildfire, something that's a conflict . . . maybe stock in one of the Wall Street firms. Keep digging until we find something."

The researcher nodded, scribbling notes on a legal pad.

Jay got up from his chair and signaled Lisa to join him. When they left the room, he whispered, "Come here, I want you to meet the latest member of the team."

They walked across the hall, and Jay opened a large door with no name plate. To Lisa's astonishment, there at a plain wooden desk pecking away feverishly at a computer, was Taylor Sullivan, the famed opposition research guru and political hit man who had worked for the Republican National Committee in the previous election. His bald head glistened beneath the fluorescent lights, the worry lines on his forehead prominent, black eyes gazing out beneath bushy eyebrows. Clad in blue jeans and a button-down denim Oxford shirt, with his shaved head, beard stubble, and pumped biceps, he looked strangely like a prison inmate on furlough.

"Lisa, meet Taylor Sullivan," said Jay grandiloquently. "He's going to help us get Diaz confirmed."

Lisa gamely disguised her shock. Sullivan was a feared, even notorious Republican operative known for black bag jobs, nasty leaks to favored reporters, and backstabbing. Rumor had it that Sullivan was behind the most vicious attacks on Long during the campaign.

"Well, this certainly gives new meaning to the phrase, 'politics makes strange bedfellows,'" said Lisa, shaking his beefy hand warily.

"Glad to be here, ma'am," said Taylor. "Hope we can let bygones be bygones."

"Taylor's going to be in charge of rapid response," said Jay. "And keeping Penneymounter back on his heels."

"Sounds good," said Lisa, still shell-shocked.

"You're gonna need me," said Sullivan with characteristic brio. "Check this out." He handed Lisa a copy of a press release from the Pro-Choice PAC announcing the hiring of Nicole Dearborn, late of the Long for President campaign, to head its communications strategy.

Lisa read the release, shaking her head in disbelief. "This chick is shameless," she said. "She's cross-dressed more times than a transvestite."

Jay winced. "Christy Love's trying to play mind games," he said, shrugging. "It's pathetic."

"Here's our first salvo at Penneymounter," said Sullivan, handing Jay a document.

Jay stared at it. It was an article about a speech Penneymounter delivered three years earlier to a Chamber of Commerce in Minnesota in which he offhandedly referred to immigrants as "wetbacks" and said "You can't get your lawn mowed or your house painted anymore without speaking Spanish." Sullivan highlighted the offending passage.

"He's an anti-Hispanic bigot," said Sullivan.

"This is delicious," said Jay, smiling. "Let's see him defend this to La Raza."

"It's a twofer," replied Sullivan. "Diaz's confirmation hearings are the opening salvo of his presidential campaign. It helps confirm Diaz and hurts Penneymounter among the Latinos."

"No question," agreed Jay. "Penneymounter's a bad guy. If we face him in four years, I want him walking with a limp."

"I already got the 'wetback' story to Merryprankster," said Sullivan. "It's up on the home page." He spun around the monitor so Lisa and Jay could see the headline: "Penneymounter's Anti-Hispanic Slur!" "This will be the buzz on every talk radio show in the country tomorrow during morning drive."

"Well done," said Jay effusively. "This may even cancel out the blind trust story."

Lisa, her arms crossed over her chest, gave Sullivan a departing once-over. "Taylor, just don't do anything stupid. I don't mind the tough guy act, or even your insistence on wearing jeans around the White House. But this is important to the president. Don't screw it up."

"Don't worry," said Sullivan, unfazed by Lisa's cutting remark. He leaned back in the chair and placing his hands behind his head to reveal pools of perspiration at his armpits. "Things will happen mysteriously. Discretion is my modus operandi."

Jay turned to leave, with Lisa trailing a step behind. They left the room and began walking down the hallway back to the West Wing. Neither said anything for about ten paces.

"I can't *believe* you hired him," Lisa finally said, spitting out the words.

"We're at war. We need killers. Sullivan's the best in the business. Frankly, we're lucky to have him."

"It's not the way we operate," said Lisa. "And it's not how we won."

Jay felt his stomach flipping and not just because Diaz's problems were mounting by the day. The prospect of dealing with Nicole, including the tabloid coverage of their former romance, was an embarrassing and needless distraction. Like a ghost from the past, she continued to haunt him.

THIRTY-ONE

The head of White House public liaison, who reported to Jay Noble, led the delegation into the Roosevelt Room, where paper nameplates before each chair marked assigned seats, subtle reminders of the pecking order. Andy Stanton sat to the immediate right of the president; Jerry Patterson, pastor of Sonshine Church in Orlando and president of the Southern Baptist Convention, to his left. In front of the center chair, in simple handwriting, the nameplate read simply: "The President."

It was the biggest gathering of religious broadcasters, evangelists, and preachers since Long's inaugural. Everyone wore tight smiles and spoke in hushed tones. The purpose of the meeting was simple: the Diaz nomination was in triage, and the White House needed the black regiments that elected Long to ride in like the cavalry and save the day.

Andy sat down at his assigned seat and leaned over to chat with Patterson. "This meeting certainly is a sign that they're starting to get it around here," he said, cupping his hand over his mouth.

"When you're drowning, you don't care who throws you a lifeline," said Patterson, acid dripping from his voice, letting out a low belly laugh.

At that moment the door flew open, and Bob Long appeared at the threshold. Everyone bolted up from their seats. Long went around the table, shaking each hand and gazing into each face, his countenance filled with intensity. He was focused like a laser beam.

Long patted Andy on the back and squeezed his shoulder as he took his seat, shooting him a wink. Warm fuzzies passed up and down Andy's spine.

"Thank you all for coming," said Long earnestly. "I know you're all busy men with major ministries and important work to do, so please know my decisions to ask you to fly into Washington today was not made lightly." Heads nodded appreciatively as they reveled in presidential flattery. "We are in a battle over the Supreme Court vacancy, and the other side is going after Judge Diaz. I'm not at all surprised, given the stakes." His eyes scanned each face, measuring his words. "You are absolutely critical to this process. I need you. Judge Diaz needs you. The country needs you." Warm grunts greeted Long's suck-up. "Now, as you know, because we worked with your legal teams at the time, I laid out clear and unambiguous standards for the nomination of judges during the campaign." He paused, reloading. "They must be eminently qualified, possess character and integrity, and share my judicial philosophy. Judge Diaz is such a nominee."

He looked around the table, making eye contact. "Gentlemen, I wouldn't be in this office if it were not for the help of the folks in this room. Don't think I don't know it." It was a remarkable statement of Long's debt to the evangelicals. Twenty-eight eyes were glued to him. "But it doesn't do a lot of good to put me in this office if I can't move my agenda. Confirming Marco Diaz to the Supreme Court is critical to restoring respect for the rule of law and ensuring that the courts interpret the law rather than legislating from the bench."

His opening statement finished, Long paused, his eyes soliciting questions. "So thanks for coming. With that I want to open it up for questions, comments, and discussion. Please speak freely. You can't say anything the press hasn't already said."

Everyone chuckled at the sideswipe at the media. The others hung back, waiting for Andy to speak first. In a room full of big fishes, he was the whale shark.

"Mr. President," said Andy, "I truly believe we are here for such a time as this."

"Amen," seconded several of his colleagues.

"I've been beating the drum for Diaz three hours a day on radio and an hour a day on television for weeks. You've given us a truly outstanding nominee, and the second Hispanic, which is important as the country becomes more diverse." He paused. "We had a few hiccups along the way, but that's within the family." Long remained poker-faced at the reference to Majette, who Andy opposed. "But you came through. Now we've got to live up to our end of the deal and make sure the Senate hears from our supporters. Most of us have big audiences and constituencies, and we can mobilize them."

"Absolutely," said Long. "If they don't see the light, make them feel the heat." Chuckles rumbled up and down the boardroom table. People began to loosen up, reaching for some of the hard candy in crystal bowls in the center of the table. Hanging out in the White House and strategizing with the leader of the free world was fun!

"Mr. President, we appreciate your leadership so very much," said Jerry Patterson in a syrupy, soothing baritone. "Not only the courage of your convictions but your witness for Christ. We pray for you every day, sir."

"Amen," several of them said in a chorus.

Long nodded and smiled. "I feel your prayers. I really do. So does Claire, by the way."

Jay sat against the wall, watching the proceedings like an anthropologist observing a tribal ritual. It was always the same, he thought . . . everyone groused and complained until they came into the president's presence, then turned into blubbering sycophants.

"What I'd like from your staff, Mr. President," continued Patterson, "is a list of the targeted senators I can call. The Southern Baptist Convention has 18.3 million members. If 10 percent of them contact their U.S. senator, we can have a major impact. I will call all of them myself."

"We'll have that list for you before the end of the day," said Long, pointing his index finger at the head of public liaison. "Let's circulate it to everyone here."

"Mr. President, I just have one request of you," said Paul Parker, the president of Trinity University, the largest evangelical college in the nation. All heads turned. "We will go to the wall for Judge Diaz. Whatever happens, sir, don't let him withdraw. Make the Senate vote. If we lose, we lose. We need every senator on the record so we can take them on next year at the polls."

"Hear, hear!" the pastors said, a few of them rapping knuckles on the tabletop.

"We're not only gonna make 'em vote," said Long, his eyes flashing, punching the air with his hand like a blade. "We're going to win. By God's grace and your hard work, Marco Diaz is going to be on the Supreme Court when it hears the California marriage case this fall."

The evangelical leaders broke into spontaneous applause. Long had the eye of the tiger. He was up for the fight.

The White House arranged for conservative radio and television hosts to broadcast from the grounds that day, reaching an audience of millions with the message that Diaz was the victim of a liberal smear campaign. Administration stars like Jay, Charlie Hector, Phil Battaglia, Lisa Robinson, David Thomas, Vice President Whitehead, and even the president were granting interviews throughout the day. It was the Jerry Lewis telethon meets Court TV.

Lisa caught the president's eye, signaling she was bringing the press for a quick photo, known as a "spray." No questions allowed.

Long leaned over to Andy. "I asked them to sit you next to me for a reason," he whispered. "This is going to drive Joe Penneymounter up the wall."

Andy laughed. "Anything to help, Mr. President."

Lisa limited the pool to AP, *Politico*, *USA Today*, and Fox News. Once they were in position, Long made a brief statement.

"I've just finished meeting with faith-based leaders from across America representing tens of millions of my fellow citizens," said Long, jaunty and confident, his arm stretching to the evangelical leaders in a sweeping motion. "I reiterated to them the quality and caliber of Judge Diaz. He is *superbly* qualified. He is a good man, a man of integrity, and he has the wisdom and temperament to be an outstanding justice." He looked directly at the reporters, pounding the table with an open palm. "It is now the Senate's responsibility to give Judge Diaz a fair hearing and a vote in the full Senate with all due and deliberate speed."

"Thank you all very much!" shouted Lisa.

"Mr. President, why didn't your vetting team know about the purchase of Wildfire stock by Mr. Diaz's trust?" shouted *USA Today*. "Isn't this an embarrassment after having two nominees withdraw?"

Lisa glared at the reporter. The faces of the evangelical leaders were twisted with contempt.

Long shook off the question. "Judge Diaz followed the appropriate guidelines required of federal judges," he replied. "He had no involvement in and no knowledge of the stock transactions to which you refer." He leaned forward, his face animated. "This is one of the things we need to change about Washington, playing 'gotcha' with people's lives, and turning the personnel process into blood sport. The confirmation process has become a search-and-destroy mission, and it is discouraging good people from serving. I'm tired of it, and the American people are tired of it."

"Thank you!" shouted Lisa.

The reporters filed out, looking sullen. Their disdain for the evangelicals (and Long for sucking up to them) was boundless.

As the meeting broke up, Andy clasped the president by the arm and pulled him into a power clutch. "Mr. President, I want you to know we've been praying for Claire. She looked great the other day when she came home."

Long's blue eyes misted. "Thank you, Andy," he said. "I think the good Lord has answered those prayers. She is doing well, and our marriage has never been stronger."

"I heard she has come to the Lord," said Andy. "Is that true?"

"She did," said the president, his face lighting up. "Hope Ranch has a faith-based counseling program, and God used it to touch her heart." His voice caught. "She gave her life to Christ while she was there. It's a major answer to prayer."

"Please give her my love," said Andy. "Tell her that if she ever needs anyone to talk to, I'm just a phone call away. We love her." With that, Long broke away to greet the others before heading to another meeting.

Ross Lombardy, who accompanied Andy to Washington, sidled up to Jay. "You got a minute to talk?"

"Sure," said Jay. "Follow me." He led Ross out the door and down the hall to his office, which was next to the president's private dining room. Once used by George Stephanopolous under Clinton and David Axelrod under Obama, its proximity to the Oval declared its occupant's power. Jay closed the door. "That was a good meeting, don't you think?"

"Home run," said Ross. "Jay, I've been in meetings with politicians trying to engage in God talk for twenty years. I've never seen anybody better than Long. Ever."

"He's unbelievable," agreed Jay. "It's like watching Ted Williams take batting practice every single day." He shifted to the topic at hand. "So what's up?"

"We're launching a two million-dollar television buy in six targeted states on the first day of the hearings."

"Fabulous," said Jay. "Where?"

"Louisiana," Ross answered. "We're going after Rhoades." Rebecca Rhoades was a DLC, centrist Democrat and a Roman Catholic from the Bayou state who was still undecided.

"She's vulnerable," said Jay. "She's up next year. Good. Where else?"

"Pennsylvania, Ohio, Colorado, North Carolina, Virginia. We're bypassing Minnesota. We're wasting money targeting Penneymounter."

Jay nodded. "Totally. Stick with red-state Democrats and squishy Republicans. Start with Judiciary Committee members. Coordinate with David Thomas. He's the one driving the target list with coalition groups."

"Will do," said Ross. "Listen, I have a business matter I need to take up with you."

"What is it?"

"The IRS has been auditing New Life Ministries for seven years."

Jay nodded. He knew about it. He seemed to know about everything.

"They have agents camped out on campus. Andy finally moved them to a trailer with no air conditioner. The general counsel of the IRS is totally hostile and keeps moving the goalposts," said Ross, his voice lowered. "We don't think he's going to revoke the ministry's tax-exempt status, but he may hit Andy with a big fine. Can anything be done to restore some sanity to the process?"

"Let me look into it," said Jay ambiguously. He walked to the door, putting his hand on the knob, then stopped. "We've been hearing about problems at the tax-exempt division from a lot of people. It's a mess we inherited, and it's taking longer to fix than I would prefer."

"Andy's at wit's end," said Ross. "He said he's being harassed more under Long than he was under the Democrats."

"On the case, pal. Check back in with Thomas in a couple of weeks for a status report." Jay opened the door and coincidentally nearly ran into Andy, who was standing in the hall holding court with the other preachers. Jay held up his wrist and tapped his watch, then pointed dramatically at Andy. "Dr. Stanton, I believe you're due in the radio studio!"

Andy grinned. "I wonder what I'll be talking about?" Everyone laughed.

THREE BLOCKS AWAY, IN a cavernous room at the National Press Club, reporters jockeyed for position at a news conference sponsored by the

Pro-Choice PAC. The room's temperature rose from the swelling crowd, the walls lined with those who arrived late; others spilled into the hall, unable to get in. Tempers were short and everyone was drenched in sweat. Fire marshals ordered the doors closed.

The ostensible purpose of the press conference was for female victims of employment discrimination and sexual harassment to voice opposition to Marco Diaz. But the reason for the mob scene was the first public appearance of Nicole Dearborn, former girlfriend of Jay Noble and campaign spy for Senate Majority Leader Salmon Stanley, since Michael Kaplan's indictment for perjury and obstruction of justice the previous January.

Nicole kept a low profile for six months. Her flowing black hair feathered at her shoulders, she walked to the podium to flashing strobe lights of dozens of still photographers. In a smart Dior black dress with a gold belt accentuating her waist, legs sheathed in lace hose and Ferragamo stilettos, she did not disappoint. Christy Love stood to the side, fairly beaming. Hiring Nicole was a hat trick . . . among the credentialed press attending the press conference were *People* magazine and *Us Weekly*. It took an unusually savvy leader to step away from the limelight; Christy was no garden-variety DC hack.

"Good morning and thank you for coming," said Nicole, her head barely reaching over a mountain of microphones. "Pro-Choice PAC is dedicated to protecting the right of all women to make choices in their lives, including career, marriage, family, and reproductive health." Cameras clicked and whirred. "The nomination of Marco Diaz to the Supreme Court is a dagger aimed at the heart of women's rights. Today we will hear from women who have been victims of discrimination and harassment of the worst kind: victims whose plea for justice has fallen on deaf ears before Judge Diaz."

Nicole called the women to the podium one at a time. Each recited their own tale of gender discrimination or lewd conduct by superiors. All opposed Diaz because of his ruling upholding the statute of limitations on filing sex discrimination complaints. Ten minutes into the proceedings, Nicole called an attractive Hispanic woman to the podium.

"My name is Dona Cruz," she said. She had dark hair parted down the middle, black tresses framing her long, narrow face, and wore a form-fitting red dress. "I came to America eleven years ago and got my green card. I worked as a receptionist for an engineering firm in Richmond, Virginia. At first I liked my job, but then the head engineer began to make sexual advances at me." She spoke in a quiet, tentative voice. "When I reported this to my boss, I was moved to a clerical position that paid less money." The press corps fell silent. "By the time I realized that I had rights and found an attorney, the period to file a complaint had expired. The wrong done to me can never be made right. And Marco Diaz is the reason."

She folded up the paper on which she had written her remarks. Her almond eyes were dark with pain. "As a Latino and a woman, it is not easy for me to oppose a Hispanic nominated to the Supreme Court," she said, her voice quavering with emotion. "But Marco Diaz's hostility to the rights of the poor, women, and minorities is more important than our shared Hispanic heritage. Thank you." She stepped away from the podium.

Nicole returned to the microphone. "Questions?"

"Do any of the women speaking today plan to testify before the Judiciary Committee?" asked the *Wall Street Journal*.

"We are in contact with the committee, and these women are prepared to tell their stories if asked to appear," said Nicole.

"So have you asked that they appear?"

"We have made the committee aware of these women and their stories."

"Nicole, your presence adds a twist to these proceedings," said Reuters. "I wonder if you would respond to the charge by some that you're simply doing this to get even with Jay Noble and the White House for firing you from the Long campaign."

Nicole's lips pressed into a thin line of red lipstick. Her jaw hardened. "I'm here because I believe these women should not be denied their day in court and because I do not believe Marco Diaz should be confirmed as a justice on the U.S. Supreme Court."

"Are you concerned that your own personal soap opera and legal drama, for lack of a better term, will distract from the issue?" asked Reuters in a nasty follow-up.

Nicole kept her cool. "If you're talking about what transpired during the presidential campaign, I've moved on. I'm only answering questions today about the Diaz nomination. But if the question is whether I'm helping or hurting this effort, if my presence encouraged any of you to come to this press conference, I guess I'm helping."

Knowing laughter rose from the press throng as they scribbled on their steno pads. After the news conference Christy and Nicole rode down the elevator and walked out on to the sidewalk on Fifteenth Street. Riding high at their success, they headed down the block to the nearest Starbucks and ordered a couple of skinny lattes.

"That was fabulous," said Christy effusively. "I teared up when Cruz told her story. And you were *great*. The media ate it up . . . just like I knew they would!"

"If you're happy, I'm happy," said Nicole. "To be honest with you, I'm still not so sure. I just don't want to be a liability to the pro-choice cause."

"Come on, Nicole, this is where you belong. I knew you'd be back," said Christy.

"How did you know that?" asked Nicole, her eyes filled with pain and searching.

"Because you've got *it*, kid, whatever *it* is," said Christy. "We had eighty-five credentialed reporters today. You should be high-fiving your way to the champagne bucket." She laughed.

"They were only there because of the scandal," said Nicole, her voice tinged with regret. "I'm a freak show. I guess it's going to follow me the rest of my life."

Christy leaned forward, cradling her latte in her lap. "Nicole, stop feeling sorry for yourself. You didn't get indicted. Trust me, this is *good*. You're famous. *How* you got famous is irrelevant." She raised her latte in a toast. "Tip 20 percent and enjoy the ride, honey."

Nicole shook her head. She thought: on some strange level, politics was a game, a reality show where everyone tried not be voted off the island and, if they were, at least become rich and famous in the process.

THIRTY-TWO

In the black waters off Diego Garcia, a tiny spit of land in the middle of the Indian Ocean, twelve speedboats raced across six-foot choppy waves as they approached a Canadian-flagged vessel. Each motorboat carried a crew of eight men armed with AK-47 machine guns, machetes, and pistols. Pulling beside the ship, they hurled hooks on the end of ropes to the deck and shimmied up the side of the hull.

The invaders were Somali pirates, and they looked like sea-bound vagabonds, thin and suffering from malnutrition. But their emaciated appearance was misleading. They were not exiles seeking refuge. Nor were they demanding ransom. Their objective: 650 tons of high-grade enriched uranium known as "yellowcake," the raw material for building a nuclear bomb.

Once aboard, the crews moved with lethal efficiency. Climbing up ropes and assembling on deck, the pirates broke into three groups: First, the sailors who would handle the ship's navigation and keep the speedboats ready for a hasty escape. Second, the militiamen, many hardened veterans of ethnic clashes in Somalia and Ethiopia, providing the muscle and firepower. The third group was engineers who knew how to identify the yellowcake and safely transport it. As soon as the first pirates clambered onto the deck, security cameras captured their shadowy figures.

In the crow's nest, the ship's head of security saw them immediately. "Pirates!" he shouted into the ship's public-address system. "All security personnel to stations. Stat!"

Fifteen armed security guards came charging up a ladder from quarters below, pistols held in the air. Several carried sawed-off shotguns and Uzis. The first three men to burst through a door to the main deck were greeted with a hail of gunfire. One of the guards took a fatal shot to the chest and dropped to the deck.

"Cover fire, I need cover fire now!" shouted one of the guards as he fell to the floor, dodging bullets.

The doorway was impossible to exit through, their position under intense enemy fire, the ugly *ping-ping* of bullets ricocheting off metal in their ears. One of the guards signaled to his comrades to go back down the ladder and find an alternate route to the deck.

"Which way?" asked one of them.

"To the stern, exit there, then we'll climb up the back of the crow's nest to pin them down with fire," ordered the senior guard.

"Roger that," came the response.

At that moment one of the pirates dropped a phosphorous grenade through the door. It exploded, killing two of the men instantly and setting the uniforms of several others ablaze in a chemical fire. Their hideous screams filled the corridors that fanned out below deck.

In the crow's nest the ship's crew locked the doors, ignoring the banging from the butt of one of the pirate's guns. They heard the pirates shouting back and forth at one another in another language, trying to figure out a way in. One seaman looked into the eyes of another, exchanging a nervous glance.

At that instant a concussion grenade hurled by one of the pirates shattered the glass windshield that provided a view from the crow's nest. One of the pirates climbed in, wielding a pistol.

"Down on floor!" he shouted in broken English. "Heads down."

He turned the latch and let in his fellow hijackers. Below deck the crackle of gunfire indicated sporadic fighting. But the battle over the ship was over: the pirates had taken control in less than ten minutes.

One of the pirates carried a satellite phone into the crow's nest, placing it on the counter. He flipped it on, checked the signal, and dialed the number of the man who had hired them: Rassem el Zafarshan. "The vessel is secured," he said into the receiver. "We are moving to the cargo hold to obtain the package."

BEHIND CLOSED DOORS IN Tom Reynolds's private office on the fifth floor of the Dirksen Senate Office Building, a small group gathered. This was no legal strategy session; it was a prayer meeting. Joining Reynolds and Marco and Frida Diaz were Father Frank Henkel, a priest in DC, Andy Stanton, and Ross Lombardy.

"Marco, before we go to the hearings, I want us to pray for you and ask for God's protection and blessing," said Reynolds.

"I'd be most grateful," said Diaz in a scratchy voice. He was thoroughly exhausted, running on fumes. Two FBI agents showed up at his house around dinnertime and asked questions about Maria Solis and her lurid allegation that he pressured her to have an abortion twenty-four years earlier. Unable to eat, he tossed and turned all night, getting only three hours sleep.

"Marco, why don't you and Frida kneel down, and we'll lay hands on you and pray," suggested Reynolds.

"I better not," laughed Frida, who was six months pregnant. "I might not be able to get back up again." Everyone laughed. Marco got down on his knees and closed his eyes.

Father Henkel placed a hand on Diaz's shoulder and led them in prayer. "O God, you know that from dust we have come and to dust we shall return. Be mindful of the frailty of our bodies. We confess our weakness and ask for your strength, O God." To Marco, it seemed a particularly fitting prayer given his state of physical and mental exhaustion.

"Amen," muttered Andy.

"Protect our brother Marco from evil, bind the devil, and shield him from the lies and distortions that are the work of hell. Keep him humble and repentant, and may he hold no root of bitterness against those who unfairly malign him."

The room became strangely quiet and filled with emotion. A strange peace infused Marco. Frida began to weep quietly.

"Lord of heaven and earth, deliver Marco from those who would seek to do him harm. Grant him your protection and favor. Guide and direct him and give him your transcendent peace through Jesus Christ our Lord."

Diaz rose from his knees, his eyes watery.

"Marco, before you go to the hearing, I'd like to anoint you with oil and ask God's blessing," said Andy.

Diaz nodded affirmatively. "I'll take all the prayer I can get, Reverend." There was nervous laughter.

Andy pulled a small vial of oil from his pocket and opened it, dabbing it on his index finger. He drew a cross with oil on Diaz's forehead and began to pray, his eyes squinting closed.

"Father, we come before You and ask You to surround Marco and Frida and their family right now with Your grace and Your love. May he experience the peace that surpasses all human understanding. In the name of Jesus, we dispatch angels to go before him and even now wage war on his behalf with those evil forces in the spiritual realm that would seek his harm." Andy drew out the vowels, so the name of the Son came out as "Jeee-zuuhs." Andy filled his prayer with martial language and Manichean imagery. Given the political conflict enveloping the Diaz family, no one demurred.

"Lord, I pray even as You sent an angel into the lion's den to shut the lion's mouth and deliver Your servant Daniel, so too you would defang those who would seek to defeat Marco in these hearings."

"Amen, Father," said Father Henkel.

"I ask even as You promised that You would give words to be spoken by those who were dragged before courts and tribunals in the end-times, so too You would give Marco the words to speak today." Andy raised his voice, punching the syllables for emphasis as he reached an emotive crescendo. "Give him calm, confidence, and eloquence beyond his own natural ability. Give him *victory* and elevate him to the Supreme Court where he can bring honor to You and justice to the oppressed. We ask all this in the mighty name of Jesus, *Amen!*"

The prayers finished, everyone hugged, their eyes teary, their voices choked with emotion. Reynolds began singing the opening stanza of "Amazing Grace" a cappella. Everyone else joined in. As they sang, tears streaked Marco's cheeks. Andy walked over and put his arm around him, pulling him close.

When the song finished, everyone was crying. Reynolds walked over to his credenza and grabbed a box of tissues, passing it around. Andy reach for a handkerchief from his pocket and leaned over to dab the oil off Marco's forehead.

"No, leave it there," said Marco. "I want to sense the anointing when I go before the committee." He shot a sly sideward glance at Father Henkel. "Is it alright if a Catholic boy wears Southern Baptist oil?"

"Entirely appropriate for the occasion," smiled Henkel.

Andy laughed. "Marco, you've been anointed by an evangelical and prayed over by a priest. You're fully covered!"

"All I need now is a rabbi to pray for me," said Diaz.

"I can arrange that later," said Reynolds, laughing. He held up his wrist and glanced at his watch. "But we better go."

"Let's do it," said Diaz. "I'm ready."

Diaz felt an infusion of inner strength. He came to rely on prayer to get him through the ordeal. And there was something else. He saw in the attacks, criticism, and personal smears not his doom but rather God's favor. A thought struck him: perhaps the reason for the ferocity of the opposition was God's desire to show His delivering power. Diaz was at peace, whatever the outcome.

THE PRESIDENT WAS ON the phone when his secretary walked in slowly, carrying a note in her right hand. The late afternoon sun broke through the goldenrod curtains framing the window behind Long's desk. She stood in front of his desk wearing a pensive expression on her face. He nodded to acknowledge her, and she handed him the slip of paper.

Opening the note and reading it, Bob Long's face went white. He wrapped up his call.

"Who told you about this?" he asked.

"The secretary of defense," she answered. "I just hung up with him. I told him you were on the other line, and he told me to interrupt you."

"Get Truman Greenglass and Bill Jacobs over here," said Long, his voice rising. "And get the chairman of the joint chiefs on the line. Right away."

The president's secretary hustled out of the office, closing the door behind her, her steps hurried and slightly stumbling.

Long looked down at the note: "Somali Pirates Hijack Ship Carrying Iraqi Yellowcake." Long had been president for eight months now and was used to getting bad news. He was not easily rattled and his mind raced through the various scenarios, what he liked to call "thinking around the corner." But this time none of the options were good.

TOM REYNOLDS'S CHIEF OF staff's BlackBerry vibrated repeatedly in his pocket. He was ignoring it. The senator was in a holding room just down the hall from Room 216 of the Hart Building, huddling alone with Marco and Frida Diaz.

Capitol Hill was under siege. The phones in every Senate office rang off the hook, with hundreds of calls and thousands of e-mails an hour landing from both sides in the confirmation struggle. The right-wing talk jocks, led by Andy Stanton, were in full froth, giving out the switchboard number and jamming phone lines to the point that normal work was impossible. The *Post* reported that 750,000 calls had hit the Capitol switchboard in the previous twenty-four hours. Protestors ringed the Capitol building, holding signs aloft and shouting slogans with bullhorns. Everyone was on edge.

A White House lobbyist walked over. "Jay Noble is trying to reach you," he blurted.

"What about?" asked the chief of staff.

"Here he is," answered the White House lobbyist, handing him his own BlackBerry.

"Jay, what's up?" asked the chief of staff. "The senator's about to walk into the hearing room with Judge Diaz."

"I need to talk to Tom right away," said Jay.

"Now?"

"Right now. It's urgent."

The chief of staff knocked gently on the door to the holding room. He walked in to find Diaz and his wife seated at a table, holding hands anxiously. Reynolds stood to the side.

"Senator, it's Jay Noble."

Reynolds nodded and took the BlackBerry in his hand. He stepped into the hallway to take the call, an aide by his side. "Hi, Jay," he said.

"Tom, sorry to bother you right now, but we have a new development."

Reynolds felt his heart skip a beat. "What is it?"

"The accountants found that Diaz's blind trust owned stock in an Internet holding company called THN, which stands for The Heat Network," said Jay. "It's based in LA. It was a roll-up of Web sites. One of the sites was a site that promoted better sex for married couples. The problem is the site sold pornographic videos."

"Okay," said Reynolds slowly. "It sounds like a very small piece of a big Internet holding company."

"That's right," said Jay. "But the CEO of the company was indicted on pornography charges in Oklahoma twelve years ago."

Reynolds shook his head. "Terrific."

"Pro-Choice PAC is issuing a press release denouncing Diaz for making money off the degradation of women. They've got a list of videos the site sold. It's not pretty."

"Alright," said Reynolds calmly. He was beginning to get shell-shocked from all the incoming charges. "Thanks for the heads-up."

"You need to tell Diaz."

"Right now?" asked Reynolds.

"It will come up," pressed Jay. "I don't want him to be blindsided."

"Alright, I'll take care of it," said Reynolds. He hung up and handed the BlackBerry back to his chief of staff, who handed it back to the lobbyist. Reynolds rolled his eyes and shot his chief of staff a knowing glance that said, "You can't make this stuff up." He stepped back into the holding room.

"Who was that?" asked Diaz, a troubled look on his face.

"Jay Noble checking in to see how things were going," Reynolds lied.

Diaz smiled. He turned to Frida. "That was nice of him. See, honey, the White House isn't wavering. They're behind me." Frida, who looked slightly pale and as if she were carrying a basketball under her dress, allowed herself a relaxed smile.

Reynolds didn't have the heart to tell Diaz about the Internet holding company. He feared the news might send Diaz, already fragile after the FBI interview about Maria Solis, into a tailspin. That was the last thing they needed before Diaz stepped in front of the cameras and a national television audience estimated at fifty million people.

THIRTY-THREE

Mercifully the opening statements finally ended. Each senator on the committee burned up the maximum allowable time, droning on for a combined six hours and twenty-eight minutes of hot air, self-congratulation, and on-camera genuflection. Diaz's sons had long since been escorted from the hearing room, while the adults wore plastic masks of barely disguised boredom. At last, it was Diaz's turn.

"Judge Diaz, thank you for your patience. If you would now stand so I can put you under oath," said Joe Penneymounter, as he rose to his feet, his facial expression grave. "Please raise your right hand."

Diaz rose. Dozens of photographers clicked away. The "money shot" would appear on the front page of every newspaper in the country the next day. Diaz wore a determined look as the camera shutters clicked and whirred, the noise like a controlled explosion.

"Do you solemnly swear that the testimony you are about to give before the Committee on the Judiciary of this United States Senate will be the truth, the whole truth, and nothing but the truth, so help you God?"

"I do," replied Diaz.

"Very well, you may be seated," said Penneymounter. "Judge, the floor is yours."

As Diaz leaned forward to the microphone and prepared to speak, loud screams split the air. Three protestors in the back of the room unfurled a white sheet that one of them had hidden under her dress. It was spray-painted in black letters: "DIAZ HATES WOMEN."

They rose in unison, clutching the sheet, eyes flashing with indignation. The leader, a middle-aged woman with a bony frame, an unkept tangle of graying hair, and a piercing voice, shrieked like a wounded animal. "Diaz is antiwomen! Diaz is antiwomen!"

"Order, order!" shouted Penneymounter, banging his gavel. "The committee will not tolerate any verbal outbursts of this kind."

Three Capitol policemen hustled to the row where the women stood, grabbing the leader by the arm and pulling her forcefully.

"Defend Women, Defeat Diaz! Defend Women, Defeat Diaz!" they shouted.

Diaz refused to turn around to face his accusers. He remained stoic as the women were dragged from the room, arms and legs akimbo, still shouting as the doors closed behind them.

"I apologize for the interruption, Judge Diaz," said Penneymounter. "Please proceed."

"Mr. Chairman, Senator Reynolds, and other members of the committee," said Diaz, shifting in his seat. "Let me first say it is a profound honor to be nominated to the Supreme Court of the United States. I thank President Long for the confidence he has placed in me."

"My father came to this country a half century ago with only fifty cents to his name and possessing a desire to build a better life for himself and his future family. He married, had a family that included me and seven siblings, and built a successful automobile dealership business. I was the first member of my family ever to attend college."

Diaz's father sat behind him, on the front row, along with Frida and other extended family members. It was a powerful moment.

"My point in relating this is not to celebrate my father's sacrifice and success, admirable though it is, but to underscore how much I owe this country," Diaz continued. The emotion in his voice was palpable. The senators in Diaz's corner smiled, while the others met his words with poker faces. It was hard not to be moved by his story. "No one has benefited more from the opportunities that flow from America's constitutional system and its guarantee to liberty, justice, and equality for all than I have. It necessarily requires humility as I have served as an appellate judge and now aspire to the Supreme Court and makes me mindful of a burden to ensure that the same opportunity is afforded to others."

Diaz held the room in the palm of his hand. Every eye was on him. No one moved.

"I pledge to represent no special or vested interest. I will be fair. I will approach each case with an open mind. I will seek to uphold the rule of law and the Constitution, mindful of the fact that within the rows of musty law books and court cases and written opinions are found the lives, the hopes, and the aspirations of a free people."

Several of the senators leaned forward, sensing an oratorical high point.

"The law is the ultimate arbiter of justice. In our country it has been the final refuge of a diminutive, soft-spoken woman in Montgomery, Alabama, ordered to the back of the bus by a system of segregation that outlasted slavery by a century; the child forced to attend a substandard school that delivered a second-class education because of the color of his skin; the person accused of wrongdoing who has been denied due process and the right to review the evidence against him. When the legal system fails, America does not work. Therefore, if confirmed, I will seek to defend the Constitution so every American can be confident that all are equal before the law and no one is above it. Thank you very much."

Joe Penneymounter did not look pleased. Diaz used his opening statement to make an argument in the form of biography. Everyone knew if the battle over Diaz turned on his humble origins and personal story, he would win. The hour was late. Penneymounter wisely decided to cut his losses.

"The Committee on the Judiciary stands in recess until tomorrow at 9:30 a.m.," he said, banging his gavel. A crowd of supporters rushed to Diaz's side, slapping his back and pumping his hand. Frida pecked him on the cheek.

Diaz felt no sense of triumph. He knew the counterassault would begin the next morning.

Reynolds came down from the dais where the members of the committee sat, a broad smile on his face. He extended his hand in triumph. Diaz grasped it, and Reynolds pulled him in tight. "You hit it out of the park," he whispered, leaning into Diaz's right ear.

"You really think so?"

"I *know* so," replied Reynolds. He bobbed his head in the direction of Joe Penneymounter, who stood at the center of the dais, gathering up his notes, exchanging worried looks and whispered asides with a clutch of aides. They looked like they were hit by a truck. "Look at Joe. I've never seen him so flustered in my life."

Art Morris came over to join in the fun. "You stripped Penneymounter to his skivvies," he said, chuckling. "Score this one for the home team."

Diaz allowed himself a nervous smile.

"What do you say?" asked Morris. "Anyone up for dinner?"

They formed a wedge of bodies in front of Marco and Frida and pressed slowly through a mob of reporters outside the entrance to the Caucus Room. The hallway was jammed, the surging crowd eerily illuminated by glaring television lights.

"Judge Diaz, how do you feel after today's hearing? Are you encouraged?" shouted *Roll Call*.

Diaz raised the corners of his mouth in a restrained smile, saying nothing.

"Please, everyone, make way for Judge Diaz!" yelled Morris.

At that moment Diaz heard a female voice through the pandemonium. "Judge Diaz?"

He turned and caught the eye of a troika of women who had been sitting quietly just behind his family throughout the day's proceedings. Their faces telegraphed a somber, determined empathy.

"Yes?" asked Diaz as a DOJ staffer pulled him by the coat, trying to yank him through the crowd. Frida held on tightly to one of his belt loops as the crowd jostled her.

"We've been praying for you and wanted to give you this," one of the women said, handing him a folded piece of paper. She smiled. "Read it later."

"I will, I will," promised Diaz. They hustled him to the elevator.

CHRISTY LOVE SUCKED ANOTHER blue point oyster out of its shell and chased it with a shot of vodka. Tucked in a back booth at Oceanaire with Natalie Taylor and her communications director, she licked her wounds in one of DC's top power lunch locations. There was no denying the obvious: the day was an unqualified disaster.

"Why in the world did our guys have to drone on for hours like that, pontificating like a bunch of windbags?" asked Christy, spitting out the words. "The contrast between a bunch of pasty white guys staring down at a handsome Hispanic guy with two boys in Brooks Brothers suits and his pregnant wife over his left shoulder was devastating!"

"And don't forget the nuns," said the communications aide.

"That was just over the top," seethed Christy. "As if being against Diaz means you're anti-Catholic. What total baloney." She sucked in another oyster. "But the White House is smart. What is the problem with our team?"

"They've all got senatoritis," replied Natalie. "They're inveterate blowhards. They can't help themselves."

"I talked to Dan Dorman," said Christy's communications director, a thin, raven-haired woman with television-anchor looks and a sarcastic outlook on life in general. "The *Post* is playing it as a defeat for Penneymounter and us. He doesn't have the headline yet, but the lead is 'Diaz deflects attacks, disarms critics.'"

Christy rolled her eyes as she scanned the appetizer plate for any remaining oysters. There were none. "Someone's got to tell Joe to quit giving *speeches* and hit this guy." Her eyes shot darts. "Hit him high and hard!"

"We told him," said Natalie. "He knows what is at stake. Joe will rise to the occasion tomorrow."

Christy shot her a skeptical look.

"We're leading with the right to privacy and *Roe*," said the grimly determined committee aide, who sat next to Natalie and was halfway through his second glass of red wine. "We've got a memorandum he wrote when he worked in the Justice Department under Bush 43 where he argued for using a partial-birth abortion case to revisit *Roe*."

"I want to see him talk his way out of that," said the communications director.

"Senator, my father came to this country with fifty cents in his pocket and gave me a better life. I love this country," said Christy, mocking Diaz. She shook her head. "What a load!"

"We concede that his personal story is compelling. We hit him on his *record*, his *rulings*, and his *rhetoric*. It's the three Rs," said Natalie.

"I like it. That will work," said the committee aide.

"It's not going to be enough," said Christy cryptically.

"What do you mean?" asked Natalie.

"He'll foul those fast balls off like he's at batting practice," said Christy. "Diaz is no idiot. He's read every single word of every memo, every opinion he ever wrote, every speech he ever gave. He's been through murder boards until he's been reduced to tears. He's ready. That much was clear today."

"He's a very good witness," agreed the committee aide.

"There's only one way to rattle him," said Christy. "Maria Solis."

A silence hung over the table. Natalie stared into her wine glass.

"Where are we on her?" asked the communications director.

Natalie let out a long sigh. "The FBI interviewed her," she said quietly. "They don't have sufficient corroboration of her story. It's a mishmash of raw interviews."

"What!?" asked Christy, her ire up. "Since when do we let a bunch of white guys at the FBI run a committee investigation? They tried to cover up for Clarence Thomas."

"Joe says the FBI report is weak and she's a reluctant witness," said Natalie.

"This is unilateral disarmament," exclaimed Christy in disbelief. She leaned across the table, her face etched with anger, lowering her voice to a jagged-edged whisper. "The guy paid for his girlfriend's abortion. Not that I have a problem with that, by the way. But for him . . . he's a *total* hypocrite."

Natalie shrugged. "Christy, you can't take somebody's raw FBI file and dump it into a Judiciary Committee report. There's no corroborating witness."

Christy put down her vodka glass with a thud and bolted from her seat, nearly shoving her communications director to the floor.

"Where are you going?" asked Natalie.

"I'm calling Joe," said Christy.

Their eyes followed her as she marched out of the restaurant, pulling her cell phone out of her blue Chanel purse. Some restaurant patrons recognized her and turned their heads. The maître d' nodded as she barreled through the lobby. Stepping out on the sidewalk on F Street, she dialed the number of Penneymounter's Watergate apartment. He answered on the second ring.

"Joe, Christy," she said quickly. "What's this about not calling Maria Solis? We *agreed* that if I could get her to cooperate, you would call her. Please tell me you're not rolling over on this." She turned away from a couple getting into a taxi, her hand on a jutting hip.

Penneymounter did not appreciate the invasion of his jurisdiction as committee chairman. "We've not made any final decision on that," he said firmly. "But I'm warning you, Christy, she's a reluctant witness. My staff talked to her and it was like pulling teeth. There are serious problems with her story and with her."

"If this is how you plan to run the hearings, Joe, we can wave the white flag right now," fired back Christy. "I talked to Maria personally. She's telling the truth."

"Maybe she is," said Penneymounter. "But her lawyer says she'll only appear if subpoenaed. Those are bad optics. It makes it look like we're dumpster-diving instead of her coming forward voluntarily."

"Fine. But if you don't call her, there's more than one way to skin that cat," said Christy, seething. "What if someone leaks to the *Huffington Post* or *TMZ* that Diaz paid his girlfriend to abort his love child and you refused to call her? How do you think that will affect liberal support for you when you run for president?"

Penneymounter was taken aback. "Christy, I respect you as a leader of the pro-choice cause, but don't even think about taking me on. I was in this town before you got here, and I'll be here after you're gone. If you threaten me, you'll live to regret it."

"If you don't call her, it's going to leak," said Christy. "Every member of the Judiciary Committee has seen the FBI report. Every staffer knows about it. It's not a question of if it comes out, only when. Protect yourself, Joe. Call her as a witness."

Silence hung on the phone for a minute. "Believe me, if I can, I will," Penneymounter said at last. "But if I can't, I'm not going to try to jam her down the committee's throat. That will backfire. You do your job. Leave running the committee to me."

"Alright," said Christy softly, backpedaling. "It's just there's a lot on the line here, and we're not going to win if we don't pull our punches."

"Don't you think I know? Message delivered. Good-night," said Penneymounter abruptly, hanging up.

Christy walked back into the restaurant, ignoring the stares of the DC crowd who knew she was at the eye of the storm in the Diaz confirmation. Returning to the booth, she slid back into her seat.

Natalie stared at her as if to ask: "And?"

Christy raised her eyebrows and batted her eyelashes. "No comment," she said mysteriously.

IN A PRIVATE ROOM at Old Ebbit Grille just around the corner from the White House, Marco Diaz cut into a ten-ounce portion of filet mignon.

While the others (minus Frida) unwound with wine, Diaz drank iced tea and Pelligrino. . . . He wanted to stay mentally sharp. He pulled out his BlackBerry and scrolled through the congratulatory e-mails he was receiving after his opening statement. When he did, the note the woman handed him as he left the hearing room fell out of his pocket. He opened it.

"Cursed will be your going out and your coming in," read the note, the letters written in block letters. "Cursed will be your rising in the morning and your going down at night. Cursed will be your body with fatigue, illness, and disease. Cursed and confused will be the thoughts of your mind and the words of your lips. Cursed will be your home, your family, and your children. Cursed is the fruit of your wife's womb. Your unborn child will never see life on this earth."

Diaz stared at the note in shock. His mouth dropped open.

Morris saw the expression on Diaz's face. "What?" he asked.

Diaz passed him the note. "Some woman gave this to me as I left the hearing. I think she must be a witch or something."

Morris read the note. He rolled his eyes. "What a whack job," he said dismissively.

"Let me see it," said Frida, reaching for the piece of paper.

"No," said Marco.

"Honey, it's nothing," said Frida. "She's a nut. Just let me read it."

Morris glanced at Marco, who nodded reluctantly.

Frida read the note. Her face went white. She tore up the note and threw it at the base of the lamp in the middle of the table. "These people are sick," she said. "Excuse me." She got up hurriedly and left the table.

"I shouldn't have let her read it," said Marco.

"It's nothing. I don't believe in witches. Do you, Marco?" asked Morris, his voice laced with skepticism.

"I believe in heaven and hell. I believe in the existence of God and the devil," said Marco. "So, yes, I suppose on some level I believe there are witches. The efficacy of their curses is a different matter. Now, were these women really witches? I don't know."

"Well, after today's testimony, I like our chances," said Morris, smiling, trying to lighten the conversation. "They can bay at the moon all they want."

Diaz glanced over his shoulder in the direction of the restrooms, his mind focused on Frida. He hoped that she—and their child—would be alright.

THIRTY-FOUR

"Ladies and gentlemen, join me in welcoming a man of courage, integrity, and character, the president of the United States, Robert W. Long," bellowed Attorney General Keith Golden, almost shouting the words into the microphone. Long glided across the stage in the cavernous atrium of the Ronald Reagan Building, basking in the rousing welcome from hundreds of members of the Federalist Society. He pumped Golden's hand firmly and patted him on the back affectionately. Whistles and cheers could be heard over the applause.

Long's appearance was rich in symbolism. Introduced by Golden, hero of the Federalist Society, in a building named after Reagan, he stepped behind the bullet-proof podium with the presidential seal and smiled beneath the warm glow of the crowd's nearly worshipful reception. In the back of the room, a press contingent of camera operators and reporters hunched over laptops studied his appearance with professional detachment mixed with skepticism.

"Thank you for that generous introduction, General, and thank you all for having me," said Long, warming up. "I was going to breakfast anyway, and I heard you had an opening for a speaker. (Appreciative laughter) Incidentally, Keith Golden is doing a superb job as attorney general, and he has been a fantastic addition to my administration." (Loud applause) Everyone knew that Golden's stock had fallen; Long's public praise was an attempt to deny the obvious. "I'm here to talk with you about a timely and vital topic, namely the importance of the rule of law, the separation of powers, and the vision of our founders to have a judiciary that upholds the law rather than legislating from the bench."

Behind the curtains Jay Noble observed Long's performance with gimlet eyes, his arms crossed over his chest. Jay had been unable to persuade the lawyers, he called them "pettifoggers losing as slowly as possible," that Diaz should give some media interviews to answer critics. But Jay still controlled "the body": where the president went, who he spoke to, and what he said. To that end the White House scheduled the speech to the Federalist Society at 8:30 a.m., one hour before Diaz appeared for his second day of hearings before the Senate Judiciary Committee. It was a howitzer fired across Joe Penneymounter's bow.

"When litigants believe a case is decided not by the application of the law passed by a state legislature or Congress but by the personal views of a judge, not only does the individual litigant suffer, but respect for the rule of law suffers," Long asserted to loud applause. "It strikes at the heart of our common faith in democracy. This state of affairs is not a hypothetical matter. In a recent survey a majority of the American people said they believed judges were more likely to rule based on their own opinion than enforcing the law as written." Long glanced away from the teleprompter, ad-libbing. "On the day I was inaugurated, I took an oath to protect and defend the Constitution of the United States, so help me God. That included the separation of powers. Congress cannot undermine the independence of the judiciary by reducing a judge's compensation or punishing him or her for unpopular rulings. Nor are judges to supplant Congress by legislating from the bench. Judges are bound by an oath as sacred as the one taken by presidents, and it is long past time to restore respect for the law, the restraint of power, and humility in its exercise to the judiciary." In the back of the room, reporters scribbled down the words, which appeared nowhere in the text. Long was on a roll.

"Judicial activism is what has transformed the confirmation process into the theater of the absurd. Why? Because senators assume they are confirming de facto legislators with lifetime tenure," Long continued, his eyes intense and jaw firm. "Advice and consent has become search and destroy, with philosophical differences rendered disqualifying, and with no smear or character assassination out of bounds." The crowd fell silent, hanging on every word. "I have nominated Marco Diaz, a fine man and an outstanding judge, to the Supreme Court of the United States. He has not been immune from these unsavory tactics. But the American people are tired of confirmation by kangaroo court in which honorable men and women must sacrifice their good name, their reputation, and their families in order to serve on the

Supreme Court." Long paused, gazing across the adoring sea of faces. "My friends, it is time to restore the judiciary to its proper place in our constitutional system of government. The Senate can begin by swiftly confirming Marco Diaz to the Supreme Court." The crowd jumped to its feet as one, exploding in thunderous applause.

"Marco! Marco! Marco!" the crowd shouted in unison.

Long let them calm down, retaking their seats. "As long as half of you don't start shouting, 'Polo,' we're alright," he joked to loud laughter. Long flashed a wide, relaxed smile.

The speech, twenty-one minutes in length and salted with hard-edged rhetoric, was sure to dominate the news. Jay's strategy was to "bracket" the committee hearings in the Senate at the beginning and end of every day, stealing Penneymounter's thunder. When Long finished working the rope line, he came through the blue curtain backstage, catching Jay's eye.

"Well?" he asked, his eyes searching.

"Outstanding, Mr. President," said Jay.

"You sure?"

"What do you want to hear?" replied Jay. "You laid an egg?"

"I want the truth," Long fired back.

"Sir, the truth is we have this crowd," said Jay. "We need the vote of one Democrat on Judiciary. If we don't get it, we fought the good fight, but we'll lose."

Long walked briskly to the presidential limo in the underground garage as they talked. "A lot of people think the presidency is state dinners, Camp David, and flying around on Air Force One. In fact, it's all about the math. Fifty percent plus one on election day, 51 in the Senate, 218 in the House. Simple as that."

"Or in our case, 37 percent on election day," joked Jay.

Long chuckled. "Touché," he said.

JOE PENNEYMOUNTER TOOK HIS seat and banged the gavel at 9:30 a.m. on the dot with theatrical flair. Everyone scrambled to their seats. "This hearing of the Committee on the Judiciary of the U.S. Senate will come to order," he boomed. "We will begin with questions in thirty minute intervals in order of seniority." He stared down at Diaz, who took his seat alone at the witness table. "Judge Diaz, good morning," he said with a weak and hollow smile.

"Good morning, Mr. Chairman," replied Diaz.

"Judge, thirty minutes may seem long, but the time will fly, especially for a witness as learned and well informed as you," Penneymounter said smoothly, hoping Diaz would drop his guard if he showered him with flattery. "With your permission, Judge, I'd like to dive right into the heart of a matter on the minds of millions of Americans. We have a right to know what you believe. So let me ask you directly: do you believe there is a right to privacy in the Constitution?"

Everyone's back straightened and ears perked up. Reporters made sure their Pearlcorders were turned on.

"I do, Senator," replied Diaz, his eyes steady. "That right to privacy extends across a wide range of areas in the law and the Constitution, and it is protected in a variety of ways. In the *Loving* case, the Court found it protected the right of persons of different races to marry. In the *Lawrence* case, the Supreme Court held it governed certain sexual conduct within private, consensual relationships. In *Griswold* and *Eisenstadt*, the Court ruled it covered access to a full range of reproductive health options, including contraception."

Penneymounter, wearing reading glasses, scanned a piece of paper with questions. "Do you believe the right to privacy is found in the liberty clause of the Fourteenth Amendment?"

"Yes," said Diaz. "The right to liberty involves more than restricting the government's ability to place restraints on physical freedom and personal property. It also involves what might be called less tangible forms of privacy."

"You've cited *Griswold*," said Penneymounter, impatient with Diaz's lecture. "As you know, the *Roe* court relied heavily on *Griswold* in holding that privacy protection extended to a woman's right to all reproductive health options. Without committing to how you would rule on abortion cases, do you have any reservations or concerns related to that sequence in the development of the court's precedent from *Griswold* to *Roe* to *Casey*?"

"Senator, those are the court's precedents," said Diaz in a professorial tone. "I have no *a priori* agenda to modify them. I have previously stated my strong belief in the importance of *stare decisis*. But to comment on a specific case, in my view, would be inappropriate."

"Judge, this is fascinating. You've spoken about a number of cases, including *Brown v. Board* and *New York Times v. Sullivan*, and the lineage of those precedents," pointed out Penneymounter. "Yet when anyone asks about a woman's right to choose, you seem to suffer from a selective attack of judicial conscience. With all due respect, I find it unconvincing."

Diaz visibly bristled. "Senator, future litigants have a right to know that if confirmed to the Supreme Court, I will decide cases on the facts, the rule of law, and the governing precedents, not my personal views." His face hardened.

"No one's asking you to do otherwise, Judge," fired back Penneymounter. "But you had a different view when you served in the Justice Department, didn't you?" He shuffled through some papers. "I have a memorandum over your name to the attorney general." He turned to an aide. "What exhibit is this, please?" The aide leaned forward and whispered in his ear. "It is Exhibit 11-B. In this 2003 memo you urge that a case involving partial birth abortion be used to challenge *Roe v. Wade*. So this unwillingness to address abortion is a rather convenient memory lapse for you, isn't it, Judge?"

"Senator, that memorandum summarized possible litigation strategies for the Justice Department," said Diaz. "I pointed out that the case provided a timely opportunity for revisiting the framework of *Roe*, but I did not recommend overturning it."

Penneymounter threw up his hands. "Judge, why would you revisit *Roe* for any reason other than overturning it? Whatever else would be the point?" He whipped off his reading glasses, holding them to his side, his facial expression telegraphing he believed Diaz was dissembling or lying.

Diaz was unfazed. "Senator, I wrote the memo to the attorney general, who held the view that *Roe* was wrongly decided. I served at his pleasure, and my job was to advance the views of the administration—"

"So you're blaming John Ashcroft?"

"No, Senator," shot back Diaz, his jaw muscles tightening. "I'm stating that I wrote that memo in my capacity as a deputy to the attorney general, whose views on the subject were well known, who in turn worked for a president whose views were well known. Those views were not necessarily my own."

"Judge, I would remind you that you are under oath," said Penneymounter gravely, wagging his gavel. He paused for dramatic effect. "Is it your testimony that the memo in question, written August 18, 2003, Exhibit 11-B, in no way represented your views on *Roe*?"

Diaz glared back, doing his best to control his indignation. "Senator, my duties as a judge are entirely different from those of a political appointee—"

"It's a yes or no answer, Judge," said Penneymounter, cutting him off.

"Senator, to impute my views to that memo is simply inaccurate."

Penneymounter sighed loudly into the microphone. He placed his black reading glasses back on the end of his nose. After a long pause: "Judge, you're a member of an organization called Opus Dei, is that correct?"

"Yes, Senator."

"And Opus Dei is a Roman Catholic organization with a papal prelate, which is to say it is directly commissioned by the pope, correct?"

"That is correct." Diaz was sticking to script. His handlers at DOJ and the White House urged him not to be defensive about Opus Dei. Keep it brief, they instructed.

"Given the teachings of the Catholic Church on abortion and its doctrinal position that abortion is the taking of a human life, how can you rule on abortion cases given the strong views associated with your faith?"

"Senator, my faith concerns my personal beliefs and has never prevented me from deciding cases on the merits," said Diaz, refusing to take the bait.

"Ah, the merits," Penneymounter said, jumping at the phrase. "Is faith meritorious? Is it irrelevant to your duties as a judge? My understanding is that Opus Dei teaches the application of Catholic social teaching in one's lay work is a moral imperative."

"My faith teaches me to exercise prudential judgment in the application of justice," said Diaz. "As for my Catholic faith, to paraphrase John F. Kennedy's remarks before the Houston Ministerial Association in 1960, it would be tragic if I or any other Americans lost their right to sit on the Supreme Court on the day they were baptized." His eyes flamed with indignation.

"Of course," said Penneymounter, clearly deflated. "No one is suggesting a religious test here. Article X, Section X of the Constitution forbids it." He looked at the clock in the back of the room. "Quoting John F. Kennedy may make for a good sound bite, but frankly that is a straw man. But my time is up. I yield to Senator Reynolds."

Diaz maintained a stoic gaze. The abortion memo nicked him, but the damage was far from fatal. There was only one problem: without the support of a Democrat, Diaz's nomination would die in committee.

CHRISTY LOVE WAS HAVING lunch with a Democratic leadership aide at The Monocle on the Senate side of the Capitol, not far from Union Station, when her cell phone went off.

"Ms. Love, I'm calling from Senator Joe Penneymounter's office," said a woman's voice. "Please hold for the Senator."

Christy felt her mouth go dry. She knew what the call was about, and she feared an explosion. Holding up an index finger to signal she needed privacy, she got up from the table, walking upstairs to a private room and closing the door.

"Penneymounter here," came the senator's voice, frosty and distant.

"Hello, Mr. Chairman," said Christy, bracing herself.

"Have you seen Merryprankster?"

"No. Why?" She feigned surprise and hoped he was buying

"They've outed Maria Solis," said Penneymounter. He read from the web page: "Diaz's College Girlfriend Claims He Forced Her to Have Abortion."

"Ouch," said Christy.

"Any idea who might have leaked this?" asked Penneymounter accusingly, his voice jagged.

"No clue. If you're asking if I did it, the answer is also no," lied Christy. Technically she was telling the truth. Christy slipped it to a friend at Democratic Study Committee, who had passed it to Merryprankster.

"It's an amazing coincidence," said Penneymounter, unconvinced. "You're the one who told Natalie. She didn't leak it. Then you threaten to leak it if I don't call her. Two days later it's all over the Internet." He paused. "Rather ironic, wouldn't you agree?"

"Joe, I *swear* on my mother's grave I didn't leak it," protested Christy. "I hate Merryprankster. They're thugs. If I did leak it, I would give it to the *Huffington Post*." It was a plausible denial. "Once the FBI got involved, too many people knew." Christy was so nervous her hand holding the cell phone was shaking.

"I better not find out you're lying. If I do, you're finished in this town."

"For the last time, Joe, it wasn't me."

"Well," said Penneymounter, shifting gears, "I have to call her now. My staff is trying to reach her, but we haven't made contact. Can you reach out to her lawyer?"

"Sure," replied Christy. "I'll call her right now."

"Tell her we need her client here by 10:00 a.m. tomorrow."

"I'll charter a plane and fly her up here myself if I have to."

"Make sure she's ready to sing for the cameras. Talk to you later," said Penneymounter, hanging up.

Christy hung up the phone and collected herself, checking her hair and blouse. She walked down the stairs and rejoined the Democratic staffer at the table.

"What was that about?" asked the leadership aide, curious.

"Penneymounter's calling Diaz's old girlfriend to testify," said Christy matter-of-factly. "She's gonna drop a bombshell."

"How's that?"

"Totally between us, she's going to say he got her pregnant while they were at Yale Law, and he pressured her to have an abortion," said Christy. "Bob Long's Hispanic altar boy turns out to be a creep."

The staffer's jaw dropped. "You can stick a fork in Diaz. He's done."

Christy signaled the waiter to bring the check. "I hope you're right. Sorry I have to go," she said apologetically. "My afternoon is now shot."

Christy regretted she was forced to leak Maria's story. She felt a twinge of guilt about it. But then she shook it off. She simply could not let Diaz be confirmed, and throwing Maria to the wolves was a small price to pay.

THIRTY-FIVE

The West Wing went on high alert when Merryprankster posted its story about Solis. In the war room the rapid-response team swung into action, decrying the leak of unsubstantiated rumors "spread by far-left interest groups," the illegal disclosure of "uncorroborated material from a raw FBI file," and "the politics of personal destruction." The White House leaned into the storm. Jay put the word out there would be no more Majettes, no withdrawals; they would attack the attackers. Abandoning Diaz was not an option.

A media feeding frenzy erupted. Cable television and the blogosphere degenerated into a shouting match of accusations and insults hurled by angry partisans. The White House deployed Johnny Whitehead to do radio interviews with Andy Stanton, Rush Limbaugh, Sean Hannity, and Glen Beck. As he made the rounds, Whitehead delivered the administration's message: Penneymounter and the far-left could not defeat Diaz on substance, so they rummaged through his garbage and smeared him with a twenty-four-year old unproven rumor. A high-stakes scramble among the networks ensued for the first televised interview with Solis. Her attorney fielding calls from the *Today* show, Oprah, and Marvin Myers.

At 2:00 p.m. Taylor Sullivan crossed the alley from the Eisenhower Executive Office Building (EEOB) to the West Wing, ducking up the narrow stairwell to the second floor. He was joined by Lisa Robinson. She rapped her knuckles on the doorway to Jay's office and walked in. They stood silently in front of his desk as he spun a reporter.

"Be careful," Jay warned, dropping his voice with mock suspense. "When have I ever steered you wrong? Trust me: when all the raw FBI interviews come out, they will be highly exculpatory. There's zero proof that Diaz was the father." Jay paused, listening to a question. "Her motive? I don't know and I wouldn't want to speculate." He paused again. "This is on very deep background. And please don't say 'White House source.' Say 'administration source.' That way it could be coming from here or DOJ. Okay?" He hung up.

"Who was that?" asked Lisa. "You're spinning like a top."

"Marvin Myers," answered Jay. "I think we've got him to a good place. He's skeptical. He thinks the fact Solis dropped at the eleventh hour is fishy."

"Taylor has something to share with you," said Lisa.

"Mind if I close the door?" asked Sullivan, glancing about nervously.

"No, go ahead," said Jay. Sullivan pulled the door closed.

Sullivan returned to the desk and took a chair, letting dead air hang. "Turns out Joe Penneymounter's got a girlfriend," he said matter-of-factly.

Jay raised his eyebrows. He looked at Lisa. Her expression telegraphed concern. "I've heard that, too," said Jay. "But I never got anything specific on it."

"I have. Her name is Natalie Taylor. She's the communications director at the Judiciary Committee," he said. "He hired her last year and jumped her over three other candidates with more seniority and stronger qualifications."

"Looks like he jumped her in more ways than one," Jay said, the edges of his mouth rising as he reached for a can of Diet Coke. "Who knows?"

Sullivan shrugged. "Everybody. It's an open secret on the Hill. Frankly, I'm surprised it hasn't come out already."

Jay turned to Lisa. "How did it get out?"

"I'm told he had a girlfriend behind the back of his girlfriend."

"Oh, that's a problem," said Jay, nodding. "You can't ever have a mistress on your mistress." He turned to Lisa. "Well, what do you think?"

"The press knows, but they're sitting on it. No one wants to be the first to run with it. I also think they're protecting him until after the Diaz vote," she said cautiously. "If it ever got out we leaked it, the repercussions would be . . . well, I don't want to think about it."

"Who says we're leaking it?" asked Jay.

"It gets better," said Sullivan, leaning forward, the veins in his bald head visible. "After she graduated from the University of Pennsylvania and before

Penneymounter hired her, she had a page under an assumed name on a Web site called MySugarDaddy.com."

"What the heck is that?" asked Lisa.

"It's a Web site where women advertise themselves to men with big bucks," said Sullivan, a crooked grin spreading on his beefy face. "The sugar daddies are looking for hot babes. They advertise themselves for three to ten grand a month." His cheeks puffed up like a chipmunk, his mouth curled into a boyish smirk. "It's capitalism at work!"

"How utterly *pathetic*," said Lisa.

"What was her price?" asked Jay.

"Seventy-five hundred a month," said Sullivan.

"Her page isn't still up, is it?"

"No, but we have the screen shot," explained Sullivan. "They're archived."

"How did you find out about this?" asked Lisa in amazement.

"A little bird told me," deadpanned Sullivan.

"This has to come out at some point," said Jay. "I can't believe Penneymounter would be this reckless. It's like he has a death wish."

"The guy is a notorious skirt-chaser," replied Sullivan. "But it doesn't do us a lot of good if it doesn't get in the water in time to help Diaz. We've got a narrow window here."

"I'd be careful," instructed Jay. "It can't come from here or the Hill. Maybe a blogger? Or, better yet, *TMZ* or the *National Enquirer*."

Sullivan nodded. Lisa pursed her lips in disapproval.

Jay read her thoughts. "Lisa, no one's suggesting *we* do it."

"Watch your step," Lisa warned. "If there are any fingerprints, I'm on the record saying this is a bad idea. And I didn't bring Taylor in. You did."

Jay seemed taken aback by Lisa's brushback pitch. "Lisa's right," he said. "Sit on this for now. If it starts to seep out, maybe we help it along. But for the time being, stand down."

Sullivan's face fell. He leaned forward in his chair like a Doberman pinscher straining at his leash. "Fine," he said with passive-aggressive resignation. "But sooner or later, if we're serious about confirming Diaz, the other side has to feel pain."

Jay knew Sullivan was right. It was only a matter of time before someone dropped the dime on Penneymounter. Would it be them . . . or someone else?

ROSS LOMBARDY WAS IN his office in Alpharetta, Georgia, on the campus of New Life Ministries, when his assistant stuck her head in the door. "There's a man claiming to be Stephen Fox on the phone. He says he needs to talk to you," she said. "He says it's important."

Ross's eyes widened. "*The* Stephen Fox?"

"I couldn't believe it either. But it's him."

Ross picked up the phone. "Mr. Fox? Ross Lombardy here."

"I've been watching you on television," said Fox without even saying hello. "You're good. I may not agree with you, but man, you're good. You're as smooth as they come."

"Thank you, sir." Ross could hardly believe his ears. Fox was one of the wealthiest men and biggest liberal funders in the country. He stroked a $10 million check to Movon.org, $15 million to the Committee for a Better America, and he hosted a fund-raiser for Sal Stanley at their palatial Palo Alto estate. What was Fox doing reaching out to him?

"Please, call me Steve," said Fox slickly. "Listen, I have a business proposition for you. But I need to discuss it with you in person."

"Sure," said Ross with slight hesitation. "Can you tell me what it's about?"

"It's about Diaz," said Fox. "Look, I'm a Democrat, but I'm also an American, and I think what's going on is disgusting. I'm ashamed of my party. This attempt by Penneymounter and Stanley to lynch a fine man is anathema to me." He paused. "So it seems we have a shared interest here."

Ross's mind raced. He almost wanted to take notes of the bizarre conversation for his memoir. No one would ever believe him. "That's good to hear," he said.

"Listen, I'm going to be down at my house in Bermuda for the next couple of weeks. I'd like to sit down when I get back, but by then I'm afraid this might all be over," said Fox. "If you can break away, I'll send a plane up and bring you down here and we can visit."

"Okay," Ross heard himself saying.

"Do you play golf?" asked Fox hopefully. "Bring your clubs if you want."

"A little," said Ross. "I work too hard. I don't have the time to play."

"You need to change that," said Fox. "Did you know that the lower someone's handicap is, the wealthier they are?" They both laughed. "Jack Welch was a scratch golfer. Duffers are losers. Just remember this, Ross: no one ever got ahead by working themselves to death. You get ahead by getting other people to work themselves to death."

"I guess I haven't figured that part of the business world out yet," said Ross. To his surprise he found himself *liking* Fox. His Donald Trump-like self-parody, his Master-of- the-Universe affectation, and his complete lack of self-awareness were somehow endearing. *So this is how the other half lives,* he thought.

"Andy Stanton has," joked Fox. "He's getting all the glory, and you're killing yourself. If you worked for me, it would be different."

"I don't think that would be advisable for either of us," said Ross.

"Probably not," said Fox breezily. "But it sure would give the *New York Times* a bad case of whiplash!" He laughed at his own joke, then reloaded. "I'll have my girl call your girl and set it up. See you soon."

"Look forward to it, Stephen," said Ross.

"Me, too. Who knows . . . maybe we can make some beautiful music together."

Ross tried to get his bearings. Fox wasn't a big fish . . . he was a whale! Worth $10 billion, he was a living legend. Given Fox's left-wing politics, it would be dicey. But Ross found himself intrigued, even excited. As he picked up the phone to tell his secretary to set up the meeting, he felt a jolt of adrenalin.

THE DINING ROOM OF the Diaz home in Alexandria was thick with tension. The curtains were closed, fastened with safety pins to block the view of TV crews that maintained a twenty-four-hour vigil on the sidewalk outside. They were prisoners in their own home. Present for a meeting were Art Morris and Diaz's handlers from DOJ and Phil Battaglia from the White House. Diaz sat at the head of the dining room table, looking thunderstruck. Frida sat beside him, her face etched with anguish.

"How's Penneymounter going to handle Solis?" asked Battaglia.

"It's a highly fluid situation," replied Morris. "Rumors are flying and no one knows the actual truth. But we're hearing that Solis is on her way to DC on a private jet paid for by Pro-Choice PAC. Judiciary staff will depose her tonight at her hotel and, assuming the deposition goes smoothly, she'll testify tomorrow."

"That's quick. Make sure minority counsel is present for the deposition and can ask questions," directed Battaglia. "I don't want any closed-door sessions."

"Agreed. That's what Tom Reynolds worked out with Penneymounter, but they're still ironing out details," said Morris. "Things are happening fast. We'll double-check it."

"Okay," said Battaglia. He let out a long sigh. "Marco, we don't know yet whether you will go before the committee to rebut her testimony, but I think for purposes of tonight's meeting, we should assume you will. Let's get your side of the story straight." He turned to Frida. "Mrs. Diaz, I know this isn't easy. If you'd like to be excused, we understand."

Frida raised her chin, her facial muscles twitching with emotion. "No," she said firmly. "I know Maria's lying. I want to be here."

"If she accuses me of forcing her to have an abortion, I'm definitely going back before the committee," said Diaz, his voice ragged. "You won't be able to hold me back with a team of horses."

"Let's set that aside for now," said Battaglia calmly. "Just tell us what you remember about what happened during the time frame of her allegations."

Diaz stared at the ceiling, collecting his thoughts. "It happened late in our second year at Yale," he said. "We'd dated since the second semester of our first year, when we were in the same contracts class. The relationship became physical." Battaglia took notes on a legal pad as Diaz spoke. "Late that second year, in the spring, we began to drift apart. She started hanging out with the Caesar Chavez types, who were protesting the lack of minority professors. They staged a walkout, and she participated. I was moving in the other direction, getting more active in the Federalist Society."

"Did you argue about your political differences?" asked Battaglia.

"I wouldn't say we argued," replied Diaz. "But we talked about it. We knew we were growing apart and going in different directions."

"Then what happened?"

"It was gradual," said Diaz. "She became distant. We saw each other less frequently. I was busy lining up my second-year internship, writing for the law review, and so forth."

"But you were still having sex?"

"Yes."

"How often?"

Diaz glanced at Frida, embarrassed. "A lot. We were kids."

"And when did you become aware she might have become pregnant?"

"We broke up near the end of the semester. My internship was in DC and hers was in Dallas and that forced the issue," said Diaz. "It was somewhat mutual, but I precipitated it. A few weeks after we broke up, she came by my apartment and told me she was late. She was afraid she might be pregnant."

"What did you tell her?"

"My reaction was mixed. I loved her, so part of me thought, 'Okay, let's go ahead and get married.' But another part of me knew it wouldn't work. I told her I'd support her whatever she decided. But we didn't know yet if she was pregnant or not." He paused. "The timing of it was very awkward in that we were breaking up at the time."

"Marco, were you or Maria using birth control at the time?" asked Morris.

"I wasn't. I was under the impression she was."

"Alright, after she came by the apartment and told you she thought she might be pregnant, when was the next time you spoke to her?"

"A couple of days later. She was on her way to the health clinic on campus and was going to take a pregnancy test. I still remember standing in the window of my apartment watching her walk away."

"What did she say when she stopped by?"

"She just wanted my support," said Diaz. "I held her in my arms. She teared up a little bit. Then she left."

"And then what happened?" asked Battaglia.

"She called me a couple of days later and said the test came back negative," said Diaz. "We were both relieved, as you can imagine. I think we both knew when the pregnancy scare ended in a false alarm, we were probably done as a couple."

"I know there's no way to know," said Battaglia. "But did you ever suspect she was faking her pregnancy in order to manipulate you into marrying her?"

"No," said Diaz. "I thought the stress of exams, the end of the semester, and our breakup might have just caused her to be late or miss her period."

"Any chance she was pregnant and had an abortion without your knowledge?" asked Battaglia. The question struck like a fastball at the head.

"I don't know. If so, she didn't tell me." He paused, glancing around the table. "I was so relieved when she said she wasn't pregnant, I didn't ask questions."

"My point in asking the question is, she might have had an abortion," said Battaglia. "That doesn't prove you were the father or approved of it, much less pressured her to do it."

"I would never have done such a thing," said Diaz.

The room fell silent. The lawyers seemed to have run out of questions. Diaz looked like he had just stepped out of the ring after twelve rounds in a heavyweight fight. Frida appeared pale and drawn. It had been a brutal but necessary cross-examination.

"Now what?" asked Frida.

"We wait," said Morris. "The next move is Penneymounter's."

The lawyers got up from the dining room table and headed for the front door. Before they left, they hugged Marco and Frida and urged them one more time to hang in there, offering words of encouragement, telling them the nightmare was almost over. But Marco could tell from the looks of the White House lawyers even they didn't believe it.

THIRTY-SIX

The G-5 carrying Ross Lombardy banked left as it made its final descent into Teeterboro airport, thirty minutes outside New York City. The sky was overcast, the Manhattan skyline shrouded in mist. The plane belonged to Internet magnate and equity-fund impresario Stephen Fox, who had moved the meeting from Bermuda to New York City at the last minute. As the wheels hit the runway, Ross felt a twinge of excitement. The truth? He longed to play with the big boys and run with the masters of the universe on Wall Street. As an evangelical whose nose had been pressed against the glass of elite culture his entire life, Ross dreamed of being ushered past the red velvet rope that had long been closed to his kind.

When the jet taxied to a stop, Ross ducked into a Town Car for the ride into the city. Always on the go, he whipped out his laptop and watched the latest pro-Diaz ad from the Faith and Family Federation, running in seven states targeting six centrist Democrats and one moderate Republican, at a cost of $625,000 per week. The media buy was both expensive and profitable. The Federation bombarded its three million supporters with daily e-mails asking for contributions, and the money was pouring in at a rate of $1 million a week.

When the Town Car pulled up in front of the Four Seasons, Ross walked to a house phone and dialed the operator. She rang Fox's suite. An aide answered. "Hello, Mr. Lombardy," he said. "Mr. Fox is waiting. Come on up."

Ross rode the elevator up to Fox's floor and knocked on the door. An assistant to Fox, a striking brunette wearing a black, silk, low-cut blouse and charcoal grey skirt opened the door, ushering him into a massive suite. Fresh fruit, cheese, and assorted soft drinks lay on the dining room table. Fox glided in from the adjoining bedroom, sans coat and tie, trailed by two other men, and extended an outstretched hand.

"Ross, thanks for coming. Pleasure to meet you," said Fox smoothly, his voice low and inviting. "You had a good flight, I hope?"

"Very good," said Ross.

"Sorry we couldn't meet in Bermuda," said Fox apologetically. "Felicity and I would have loved to host you at our house, but business called." He smiled. "Another time, I hope."

Fox introduced Ross to his colleagues. One was the bright-eyed, thin vice president for global public affairs at Fox's private equity firm, the other a smarmy Republican lobbyist, wrapped in a pin-striped suit with a loud tie and a custom shirt with French cuffs and presidential cufflinks, who boasted a shallow and dated background in GOP circles. Ross knew them both. The GOP lobbyist was a right-wing Uncle Tom who had been recruited by Fox and paid an embarrassingly large monthly retainer to influence-peddle for his liberal paymaster in DC. Everyone grabbed a soft drink or coffee, ignoring the expensive spread of food, and sat down in the living room.

"Ross, you're a smart guy, and I know you're plugged into the Long administration," said Fox, diving right into the business at hand. "I've got more lobbyists than Carter has liver pills"—he glanced at the GOP lobbyist—"and they tell me your views are highly regarded at the White House."

Ross nodded and allowed himself a self-satisfying smile. It was good to know that his importance had filtered up to Silicon Valley and Manhattan boardrooms.

"You and I don't see eye to eye on everything politically," Fox continued. "But I'm a businessman. I buy and sell companies and create value for my investors. That's what I'm about." He paused, his eyes twinkling. "If you ever want to come work for me, let me know."

Everyone laughed, Ross a little more nervously than the others.

Fox stood up and paced the floor, walking over to the dining room table. "I don't share Long's politics, but that's neither here nor there," said Fox, chopping the air a dismissive wave of his hand. "Five years ago I became the largest single investor in Wildfire.com, which is doing for the Internet what Bill Paley did for broadcast television and Ted Turner did for cable. That bet has paid off handsomely for me. Wildfire created the first workable online advertising model for the Internet." His face lit up. "Wildfire makes Google look like the Model T Ford. With Google, money tipped the scales of their search engine. With Wildfire, you follow the eyeballs. So wherever someone goes—any search engine, Web site, or news site—Wildfire finds your customers, tracks them, and advertises your product on the pages they visit. They sell pages by individual impression, which was unheard of even a few years ago."

"It's an amazing technology," said Ross. "How much of Wildfire does your firm own?"

"Twenty-three percent," said Fox. "The company is currently valued at $92 billion."

Ross let out a whistle.

"Wildfire lost the antitrust suit at the district court level, then won its appeal to the DC Circuit. Diaz ruled in our favor. That decision has been appealed by the Department of Justice," Fox said. He paused, picking up a single blueberry and popping it in his mouth, chewing. "All we want is a fair hearing. Diaz understands that the marketplace, not bureaucrats, should determine the future of the Internet. We want to see him confirmed, and I understand you're generating support for him."

"Big time, Mr. Fox," said Ross, brightening.

"Please, it's Stephen." He pointed to the GOP lobbyist. "Except for Fred here. He has to call me sir." Everyone laughed again.

Ross nodded. "We're sending out millions of e-mails a week, dropping hundreds of thousands of pieces of mail, organizing over 100,000 churches, and advertising on television and radio in seven states, including Pennsylvania and Ohio."

"How much does all that cost?"

"It varies from week to week, but about $750,000 to one million a week. We estimate that when it is all said and done, we will spend $5 million to get Diaz confirmed."

Fox looked impressed. "You're a pro," he said. "You know how to get things done. I like that." He paused. "I want to help you. Not Wildfire—I think that's too close for comfort—but I have some other entities that can support your efforts."

"I don't think we should accept a contribution from Wildfire or its executives," said Ross. "We don't need the headline, and neither do they."

"A hundred percent," agreed Fox. He pointed to his vice president. "My team can iron out all the details. We have a number of entities we can use." He shook his head. "I own more companies than I can keep track of. We could give it to another group that we work with, and then let them give you a grant." He glanced at the VP. "What's the name of that (c)(4) again?"

"Citizens for Technological Innovation."

"Right," said Stephen, snapping his fingers. "That's permissible, isn't it?"

"Yes, sir," said the vice president. "The Federation will have to report the contribution to the IRS, but all they will show on their 990 is CTI. Perfectly legal." He smiled.

"Good!" Fox smiled. He walked over to Ross, extending a hand generously. Ross pumped it enthusiastically.

"How 'bout I give you a million dollars?" asked Fox. "How does that grab you?"

Ross looked like he had just won the lottery. "Fine, sir," he stammered. "That's . . . terrific!"

"That probably makes me the largest donor to your group, doesn't it?" asked Fox.

"Yes, sir, I believe it would."

Fox burst out laughing. "Super!" he exclaimed, seeming to enjoy lavishing his largesse on the unsuspecting. "Go get 'em, champ." He slapped Ross affectionately on his shoulder, then turned and disappeared into the bedroom.

Ross walked back to the elevator, head swimming. He had heard of people who played both sides, but Stephen Fox was in a class by himself. He wondered: was it too good to be true?

THE BLACK CADILLAC ESCALADE carrying Maria Solis and her entourage shot past the Mayflower Hotel on Connecticut Avenue, where an unruly mob of reporters and camera crews gathered. The scene was pandemonium. News vans and satellite trucks were parked three deep in front of the hotel's motor entrance.

"It's a total cluster!" shouted Christy Love from the backseat. "Find another way in," she ordered the driver. "We can't walk Maria into an ambush."

In the backseat Solis glanced out the dark-tinted window nervously. "How did they find out where I was staying?" she asked, her soft voice plaintive.

"Who knows?" replied Christy. "Probably the minority staff. They're total jerks."

"Make a right on DeSalles Street," Natalie Taylor said, leaning forward from the backseat and pointing to her left. "Try the service entrance."

Christy called the head of security at the Mayflower on her cell phone and worked out a diversionary tactic: while the hotel security staff gathered in front of the building, pretending to prepare for their arrival, they would duck in a side entrance and take a service elevator. The driver steered down a narrow alleyway. Halfway down, they pulled up to an open door where a man in grey slacks and blue blazer holding a walkie-talkie waved at them.

"That's the entrance. Go! Go!" shouted the driver.

Natalie and Christy bolted from their seats, pulling Solis along with them. As they clambered up the stairs, they caught sight of two camera crews jogging down the alley.

"Block them!" yelled Christy.

The driver threw the Escalade in reverse and gunned the engine, careening backward down the alley, nearly running the cameramen over. They dove to the asphalt to avoid being struck, spewing profanity.

The security guard pushed them into the building and closed the door. They walked into an elevator, its door held open by a second guard. Climbing aboard, the group was silent except for the sound of their labored breathing. Solis looked like she had seen a ghost.

Christy turned to the security guard. "I want a hotel guard at the elevator to her floor 24/7 and a DC cop guarding her room. No one gets in except people on a list I give you. Everyone has to show a photo ID. Can you do that?"

"Yes, ma'am," he replied crisply.

Once they were safely inside the suite, Maria went to a back bedroom to freshen up. The others gathered around the bar where they grabbed bottles of water and soft drinks.

Natalie walked over to Piper Duncan, Solis's Dallas attorney, who had first contacted Christy about her story. "Is she going to be okay?" she asked quietly. "She seems pretty rattled."

"Wouldn't you?" asked Duncan. "She's been carrying this secret for twenty-five years, and now it's plastered on the front page of every newspaper in the country. Forty-eight hours ago no one outside of Dallas knew who she was. She's overwhelmed."

"Can she handle the pressure?" pressed Natalie. "We're out on a ledge here. If she's not going to be able to go through with it, we need to know now."

"I don't think you're really in a position to question her commitment," said Duncan. "*Someone* leaked her story. It wasn't me, and it wasn't her." She glared accusingly.

Solis walked into the living room area of the suite. Their conversation abruptly stopped.

"Maria, feel better now?" asked Christy affectionately.

"A little," said Solis haltingly. "There were a hundred reporters out there. I hope it's not going to be like that tomorrow when I testify."

"It won't be," Natalie lied. "We'll take you in the back way. The Capitol is very secure." In fact, it would be a complete circus.

"We should probably go ahead and call the committee lawyers and tell them to come on up to the suite," suggested Christy. "That way we can get the deposition out of the way, and Maria can get some sleep."

"Fine by me," said Duncan. "Maria, you okay with that?" She glanced at Maria, who appeared to hesitate for a moment. She bit her lower lip, her eyes searching.

"Sure," she said at last.

Christy reached over to the phone to dial the committee counsel. As he did, she wondered if Solis was really ready. Were they riding a three-legged horse?

PHIL BATTAGLIA AND JAY Noble stood outside the Oval Office, cooling their heels. The president was wrapping up a meeting with Truman Greenglass and the chairman of the Joint Chiefs of Staff. The shocking story of Rassem el Zafarshan hijacking a shipment of yellowcake from Iraq led every news broadcast, threatening to eclipse even the latest bizarre twist in the Diaz confirmation struggle off the front page. And why not? Zafarshan had already masterminded the assassination of a U.S. vice president, and now he had the raw material for a dirty bomb that could be exploded in a major American city.

The door opened and the Joint Chiefs chairman walked past them with a nod, his head down, face somber. Long hung back, talking in a low voice with Greenglass. When he caught sight of Jay and Phil, he waved them in. "Get in here guys," he said wearily. "And you better have some good news."

"Good is a relative term, Mr. President," said Battaglia with morbid humor.

"So I'm finding," said Long.

Jay noticed the strain on the president's face, the worry lines on his forehead like crevices in granite. He knew the meeting with Greenglass and the chiefs had been about Zafarshan and Iran. But as Long's political advisor, national security was not in his portfolio. As the pressures on Long increased, Jay sensed he was drifting away, consumed by Iran and foreign policy, growing more distant. Jay was helpless to stop it.

"Phil has an update on Diaz," said Jay.

"Fire away," said Long. He sat behind his desk, leaning back in the chair and slowly exhaling. Jay and Battaglia took the chairs on either side.

"We've debriefed Diaz," reported Battaglia. "His story is straightforward. He says that Solis was late and feared she might be pregnant. She went to the campus clinic to take a pregnancy test. The test came back negative. End of story."

"You believe him?" asked Long, his eyes boring into Battaglia.

"I do, Mr. President," said Battaglia. "We've got good facts. Solis has no extant medical records in her possession from the time period in question. The FBI has interviewed all the doctors and nurses who worked at the clinic at the time who are still alive. They're coming up empty."

"Sounds open and shut. Now what?" asked Long.

"She testifies tomorrow, Diaz rebuts her testimony. A day or two later, the committee votes."

"Where do we stand?"

Jay let out a sigh. "We're still short by one vote, sir," said Jay. "Reynolds has done his job. We've got all the R's, but we still don't have a Democrat."

Long arched his eyebrows. "Should I work the phones?"

"Not yet," answered Jay. "We want to get past Solis tomorrow. But we've got two lined up for meetings in the Oval. We need to give them the full treatment."

"Penneymounter's playing hardball," explained Battaglia. "He's twisting arms."

"So is Stanley," added Jay. "He's making it very tough on any Democrat who votes for Diaz. Everything's on the table: committee assignments, fundraisers, earmarks, you name it."

"I'm amazed they're falling in line with Stanley," said Long, shaking his head in wonderment. "They're kicking thirty million Hispanics in the teeth. What gives?"

"Two things," observed Jay dispassionately. "First, their liberal base won't stand for a pro-Diaz vote. Their assumption is this is the fifth vote to overturn *Roe v. Wade*."

Long nodded. He got it.

"Second," Jay continued, "Stanley's running for president again. If he stops Diaz, he's probably the Democratic front-runner, in spite of Dele-gate. But if he fails, he's done. The Diaz nomination is literally the first primary for the Democratic nomination."

"Stanley's never gotten over the campaign. It consumes him." He stared into the middle distance, his expression reflective. "What's the bottom line?"

"Unless something changes in the next forty-eight hours, Diaz will not be reported out of the committee favorably," said Battaglia slowly.

Long nodded slowly, absorbing the blow. "And that'll be it, won't it?"

"Yes," said Jay quietly. "We can force a floor vote, but we'll lose."

Long rubbed his chin, deep in thought. "You were supposed to bring me good news," he joked. They chuckled, rising to leave. As they walked to the door, Long stopped them. "Keep fighting," he said with a determined look. He wagged his finger. "If they crucify the first Hispanic nominated to the court in decades, we'll carry the Latino vote by a landslide in four years. One way or the other, we're going to have the last laugh."

They nodded and left. Walking back to their offices, Jay turned to Battaglia. "Assuming Diaz doesn't make it, what's the plan?" he asked, whispering under his breath.

"There isn't one," Battaglia replied.

Jay gulped. They were staring into the abyss.

THIRTY-SEVEN

 It was 11:30 p.m. when the den phone in the Diaz family home rang. Marco leapt for it, an instinct developed from having young children who went to bed early. He wondered who could be calling so late.

"Marco?" asked a familiar voice. Even after a quarter century, he recognized it instantly.

"Maria?" he asked.

"Yes."

"I sure wasn't expecting to hear from you of all people," he said.

"I just wanted to call and tell you I'm sorry all this happened." She paused. "I never meant to hurt you. I still don't." Her speech was slightly slurred.

His initial reaction was to be careful—he might be being taped. The woman who was going to accuse him publicly in less than ten hours of forcing her to abort their child was expressing affection for him. In an odd way he understood. They once loved each other. On one level he believed her— the entire confirmation had spun out of control, and they were both trapped on the roller coaster.

"I . . . I don't know what to say," said Diaz. "I never meant to hurt you either. I never wanted anything but the best for you, Maria. That's always been the case. I just wanted you to be happy, that's all."

"I know," she replied solemnly. There was a long silence. Then she spoke. "Marco, I aborted our baby. I did it. . . . I had an abortion. I never told you."

Diaz was floored. "Why?"

"I wanted something else for myself," said Maria. "I knew someday you'd be where you are right now. I knew that in the future you would either run for president or be nominated to the Supreme Court. I didn't want that. I made a different choice."

Diaz's mind raced. Should he say something designed to protect himself in case he was being taped? Instead, he threw caution to the wind. "You made the choice, but someone else paid the price. And now you're trying to make me pay the price."

"That's why I'm calling," said Maria. "To tell you I never meant to hurt you. I just wanted you to know that before tomorrow."

"I appreciate that," said Marco. "I will pray for you tomorrow, Maria."

"Thank you," she said quietly. She hung up the phone.

Diaz put the receiver down. Had he said anything incriminating? He didn't think so. He hoped the conversation might cause Maria to pull her punch the next morning.

ROSS LOMBARDY WAS BACK in his Alpharetta, Georgia, office, inhaling his second black venti bold Starbucks of the morning, losing the battle to calm his jumpy nerves. He was mainlining so much caffeine his wild eyes reflected his internal turmoil. And for good reason. Maria Solis was scheduled to testify before the Senate Judiciary Committee in less than two hours. The Faith and Family Federation was now blanketing eleven states and national cable with pro-Diaz ads, and its phone banks buried Senate offices beneath thousands of calls a day. One could not turn on Fox News without seeing the triple-F ads, which were running every five minutes. In the midst of this full-court press, at 8:04 a.m., Ross's cell phone went off. On the line was Dick Land, dean of the law school at Trinity University and prominent evangelical legal eagle.

"Ross, I know you're up to your armpits in the Diaz nomination," Land said, getting to the point straightaway. "Let me be brief. I have a friend who wants to help. Based on what he's told me, I think it might be the breakthrough we're looking for."

"Really?" asked Ross excitedly. "Tell me more."

"My friend, David Kenworthy, is a professor of law at Pepperdine," said Land. "Before that, he was dean of the law school here at Trinity.

We've been friends forever. I've known him for more than twenty years."

"Yes?"

"David was at Yale with Solis and Diaz," Land continued. "David dated her for a while after she and Diaz broke up. He caught her on the rebound. He says Maria was infatuated with Marco. She was still in love with him and wanted to get him back."

"No kidding," said Ross. "That certainly shows a motive."

"No question. Now, this was in David's BC days," said Land, using evangelical-speak for "before Christ," meaning Kenworthy had not yet become a believer. "He was in a period of his life when he was enjoying wine, women, and song."

"I get it."

"Anyway, a couple of months after they started dating, Maria was late. She told David she might be pregnant, and if she was, he was the father. But she told David she was going to tell Marco he was the father just to get a rise out of him."

Ross was thunderstruck. "Dick, that's damning," he said. "She lied!"

"Kenworthy remembers it just like it was yesterday," said Land. "After all, a guy doesn't forget when a girl tells him she might be pregnant. In the end it didn't matter. . . . She wasn't pregnant after all."

"Will Kenworthy put this in an affidavit?" asked Ross. "If he does, he's stepping into the eye of a hurricane."

"He understands," said Land.

"Give me his number. I'll call him right now."

Ross scribbled down the number and reached for the phone on his desk. He had to get Kenworthy in touch with Tom Reynolds's office and get him to prepare an affidavit within the hour. If he could pull it off, he might be able to blunt Solis's testimony.

THE BLACK LINCOLN NAVIGATOR carrying Marco and Frida Diaz turned left off Constitution Avenue and disappeared into the parking garage of the Hart Senate Office Building, rushing past television crews on the sidewalk. The lead SUV was trailed by a chaser car of Secret Service agents and a staff car carrying Deputy Attorney General Art Morris and other aides from the Department of Justice. Slowing to a stop, the cars pulled up to an underground elevator, disgorging their passengers in a blur.

A crowd of reporters ambushed Diaz as soon as he stepped off the elevator, walking briskly to Senator Tom Reynolds's office.

"Judge Diaz, did you father a love child with Maria Solis?" asked Roll Call.

Diaz, clutching Frida's hand and surrounded by a phalanx of Capitol police, kept his gaze straight ahead, ignoring the shouted question.

"Was it hypocritical to force Maria Solis into an abortion while opposing that right for other women?" shouted CNN.

The press scrum moved in step with Diaz, photographers running ahead to snap pictures. Arms and elbows flew. The Capitol police acted like cowcatchers, spreading the mob as Diaz and the entourage kept moving. The door to Reynolds's office opened and they disappeared.

"What a bunch of jackals," muttered Morris.

"I've never seen such a feeding frenzy," said Reynolds. He offered everyone coffee. Their nerves were on edge like a team huddled in a locker room before the Super Bowl. A clutch of pasty-faced Senate aides in nondescript suits stood around trying to look important, scrolling through their Blackberries, their postures hunched and mouths mum, eyewitnesses to history practicing their anonymity. Occasionally Reynolds's assistant would walk in and hand him a folded note. He would unfold it, read it, and nod.

Diaz's face was a mask of grim determination. "They've tried to take me down for months," he said calmly. "But I'm not going down. Nothing they have tried has worked. So now they're going to try Maria." He seemed almost energized by the intensity of the fight.

Frida was another matter. Her face etched with pain, her skin sallow, she seemed dazed. When they came into Reynolds's private office, she closed her eyes tightly and struggled to sit down, maneuvering her distended belly with obvious difficulty. As she sat on the edge of the couch, she let out a low, barely audible moan.

"Honey, are you okay?" asked Marco.

"I think so," said Frida slowly. "I—I—I think I might be having contractions. It happens sometimes when I'm tired . . . or stressed." She smiled weakly. "As I am right now."

"Are you sure you're okay?" he asked, his voice rising.

"No, I'm not sure, but . . ." Her voice trailed off. "The pain is coming in waves."

Diaz glanced around, his eyes panicked. "Can we get her a doctor?" he asked. "Frida thinks she might be having contractions."

Reynolds turned to an aide. "Call the clinic," he ordered. "Tell them Judge Diaz's wife needs medical attention." The aide bolted from the room.

Marco rubbed Frida's lower back to ease the pain and discomfort. Reynolds brought her a glass of water. Morris took a call from the White House, which was monitoring press reports about Solis's testimony. Details about her deposition from the previous evening were leaking. After a few minutes of hushed back-and-forth, he hung up.

"Penneymounter's leaking Solis's deposition," he announced. "There's nothing new."

"Is she here yet?" asked Reynolds.

"No," said Morris. "She's still at the Mayflower. ETA twenty minutes."

Frida doubled over and let out a louder moan. Diaz crouched down to comfort her, whispering, "It's going to be alright, honey. The doctor is on his way."

Reynolds and Morris exchanged nervous glances. Just then a doctor and a paramedic burst through the door, both wearing street clothes beneath white coats.

"Mrs. Diaz, I'm Dr. Paulk with the Capitol Hill medical clinic. I understand you're experiencing contractions?"

"Yes," said Frida, nodding her head.

"How long have you been feeling discomfort?"

"About twenty minutes. They started in the car on the way over here."

"How far apart, ma'am?"

"I haven't been timing them. Maybe every five to seven minutes."

The doctor checked Frida's vital signs, gazed into her pupils with a pen light, and took her blood pressure. After a brief examination he rose to his feet and turned to Marco. "Judge Diaz, I'm fairly certain this is false labor brought on by a lack of rest and stress. But just to be safe, I recommend we should take your wife to the hospital. It's a precautionary measure. But if she needs medical care, I'd feel a lot more confident if she was in a hospital. This is not the place for a pregnant woman experiencing her symptoms." He put his stethoscope back around his neck. "I recommend we take her to George Washington University Hospital's OB-GYN unit and let them examine her."

"Are you sure she's alright?" Marco stammered.

"I think so, but we should err on the side of caution," the doctor replied, sounding confident. He glanced at Frida. "Alright?"

Frida nodded.

"Should I go with her?" Marco asked the doctor.

"No, you stay here," Frida replied. "I'm okay. I'll call you from the hospital."

A wheelchair materialized, and the doctor and paramedic helped Frida into her seat, careful to place her feet firmly in the foot rests. They wheeled her out of the office, surrounded again by Capitol police, and steered her toward the elevator. The press scrum degenerated into a surging blob of humanity, craning necks, snapping photos, and jogging into better position with television cameras.

Within minutes, Merryprankster headlined the breaking news. "FRIDA DIAZ RUSHED TO HOSPITAL," the Web site's banner screamed. "DID GIRLFRIEND'S UGLY CHARGES CAUSE HER TO GO INTO LABOR? WILL HEARING BE DELAYED?"

JAY NOBLE SAT IN his office watching the breaking news on television about Frida Diaz being rushed to the hospital. He was on the phone with Ross Lombardy.

"Are you watching this?" he asked.

"Yes," said Ross. "Penneymounter has to delay the hearing, don't you think?"

"Not him," said Jay. "Solis is on her way to the Capitol." He paused. "Hold on while I patch in Phil Battaglia." He called out to his assistant, who got Battaglia on the line. "Phil, I have Ross Lombardy on the line. He's got some information about Maria Solis. Ross, tell Phil what you just told me."

"Okay," said Phil. "Go ahead but make it quick. I'm under the gun."

"Phil, I got a call this morning from a friend of mine who's the dean of the law school at Trinity University," Ross began. "He has a friend named David Kenworthy, who's a law professor at Pepperdine. Kenworthy dated Maria after she and Marco broke up. My friend said that Kenworthy had some information about Maria Solis, so I called him."

"OK. What's the punch line?" asked Phil.

"Right," replied Ross. "After they started dating, Solis told Kenworthy she might be pregnant and she thought he was the father. But she was mad at Diaz for breaking up with her, so she went to Diaz and told him that *he* was the father."

"Is he willing to submit that as sworn testimony?" asked Battaglia. "He'll say that under penalty of perjury?"

"Yes," said Ross. "He's preparing an affidavit right now. I just hung up with him. He said he's willing to come to DC and testify if necessary."

"To his knowledge, was she pregnant at the time?" probed Battaglia.

"According to him, she came back a few days later and said it was a false alarm," said Ross. "He didn't go with her to the clinic, but he said that's what she told him."

"I'll call Tom Reynolds right now," said Battaglia. "You call Kenworthy back and tell him to get that affidavit to you, me, and Reynolds ASAP."

"Where's he going to find a notary at 5:30 in the morning Pacific Time?" asked Jay.

"Don't worry, we'll find him one if he can't," said Battaglia, hanging up.

Jay and Ross were still on the line. "Good work, Ross," said Jay. "Can you call him and work with him on the affidavit? Just the facts, no embellishment."

"I'll call him right now," said Ross. "Where should we e-mail the affidavit?"

"Don't e-mail it," ordered Jay. "Fax it to my office, to Phil's office, and to Tom Reynolds's office. We'll take it from there."

"Got it."

"And Ross?"

"Yes?"

"Do it right now. We don't have much time."

"I'm on it," said Ross. He hung up and immediately dialed the home number of David Kenworthy.

NATALIE TAYLOR, CHRISTY LOVE, and Piper Duncan sat in the coffee bar in the lobby of the Mayflower Hotel, waiting for Maria . . . or so it appeared. Christy warily eyed the clutch of reporters gathered in the lobby, hoping to catch a glimpse of the woman of the hour.

"How do we get Maria past the press?" asked Christy.

"I've got that all worked out. We're a decoy," whispered Natalie, leaning forward to prevent being overheard. "While the press is shadowing us, hotel security will take Maria out a service entrance. We're meeting her at the Hart building."

"By the time the press figures out what's going on, she'll be gone," said Duncan, a smug expression on her face.

Christy scrolled through e-mail on her BlackBerry, killing time. Her eyes widened and she let out an expletive. "Merryprankster is reporting that Diaz's wife has been taken to the hospital."

"My God, we need that like a hole in the head," said Natalie. "Did she have some kind of panic attack? Do you think it's a plea for sympathy?"

"They say she's having contractions." She shook her head. "Let's hope it's false labor. If she has to be hospitalized, I can hear Andy Stanton and the right-wing talk jocks now."

Natalie's cell phone rang. "That's probably security," she said. "This may be our signal to go." Some reporters standing nearby pretended to shoot the breeze, all the while keeping an eye on the female troika so they couldn't slip away undetected. To avoid being overheard, Natalie stepped to the corner to take the call.

"Good morning, Ms. Taylor," came the voice on the other end of the line. It was the head of security for the Mayflower. "Are you in the lobby?"

"Yes. Is it all clear? Can we head on over?"

"No ma'am. I need you to come upstairs."

"Why?" asked Natalie. "Is there some kind of problem?"

"Yes, ma'am," replied the head of security. "I'll meet you in Ms. Solis's room."

Natalie hung up and returned to the table, grabbing her purse. "Something's up. We need to go meet up with the head of security. Let's go."

They headed to the elevator, causing a rustling among the press corps. When they arrived on the eleventh floor, there were two Capitol police-men at the elevator, grave expressions on their faces. Natalie and Christy exchanged worried glances. They walked down the hall to Solis's suite. The door was ajar. The head of hotel security stood in the foyer, hands clasped behind his back.

"Is Maria ready to go?" asked Natalie.

"No," he said. "Ma'am, she's gone."

"What do you mean, gone? Where?"

"She's dead."

"What?!" exclaimed Duncan, her voice ragged. "How?"

"We don't know. It looks like she passed away in her sleep," he said. "We don't know the time or cause of death. That will have to be determined by the medical examiner."

"I don't believe it," said Natalie, her face draining of color, eyes filling with tears.

"Come with me." The head of security led them through the living room to the back bedroom. He paused when they reached the door. "Don't touch anything," he instructed. "We are treating this as a crime scene."

Natalie shot Christy a look that said, "Crime scene?"

He opened the door slowly. Solis's body was sprawled on the bed, her legs turned to the side, her head tilted at an impossible angle. She wore a hotel bathrobe partially open at the torso. One arm lay at her side, the other dangled off the edge of the bed. Her face was pale and splotchy, the skin dark on her right side where her blood pooled. Her lips were blue. A half-empty glass of red wine was on the nightstand, lipstick smudges visible at the edges.

"My God," whispered Natalie. "Please tell me she didn't kill herself."

"She had prescription medication in her personal effects," said the head of security. "There's no suicide note. If the medicine killed her, it looks like it was an accident."

They stumbled out of the bedroom, stepping back into the living room of the suite, flopping on chairs and the couch.

"I can't believe it," said Christy softly. "This is a tragedy."

"I have to call Joe," said Natalie. "The hearing is in an hour. We have to war game how we're going to alert the media."

"I have to call her family first," said Duncan. "I don't want them hearing about this from the media."

"Sure, of course," said Natalie.

Christy nodded. She slouched in a chair, a devastated look on her face.

As Natalie dialed Penneymounter's number, Christy stared into the distance, her eyes glazed. Glancing back, she made eye contact with Duncan, who shot her an icy stare.

"How are you doing?" she asked.

"I'm not well at all," said Duncan, voice cracking. "You gave me your word no one would know about Maria unless she gave her explicit permission." The veins in her neck began to show. "You broke your word, and now an innocent woman is dead. I hope you're happy."

Christy said nothing in response. She got up and walked to the restroom, closing the door behind her, and began to sob.

THIRTY-EIGHT

Joe Penneymounter sat in his office in the Russell Building, flipping through the Solis deposition with the trained eye of a prosecutor, making notes on a legal pad. Next to the deposition lay a sheet of paper containing a list of questions prepared by his staff. But Penneymounter didn't need coaching. He knew the material backward and forward.

Penneymounter's BlackBerry vibrated. He answered it.

"Joe, it's Natalie," she said, voice catching. "I'm afraid I have some very bad news. Maria Solis is dead."

Penneymounter felt the breath knocked out of him. "How?"

"We don't know," replied Natalie. "The head of security for the hotel says it looks like an accidental overdose, but we won't know until the autopsy."

"Overdose of what?"

"Antidepressants," said Natalie. "And wine."

"Dear God," said Penneymounter, shattered. "I don't want to sound like a conspiracy nut, but do you think there's any chance there was some funny business?"

"I don't think so," replied Natalie. "It was a common prescription antidepressant. There are still pills in the bottle. If she took it with wine, the combination would slow her breathing and, in rare cases, stop her heart."

"At the risk of stating the obvious," said Penneymounter, beginning to panic, "if the police inquire about her state of mind, you and Christy need to make it clear there was no indication she wanted to harm herself." He was horrified at the prospect of Solis's death being ruled a suicide. It would make him look bad.

"Already talked about it," replied Natalie. "We're in agreement that she seemed to be fine." She paused for a moment. "I'm shocked."

"I'm just sick. I feel partially responsible. I knew I shouldn't have let Christy talk me into calling her as a witness."

"Christy blew it," said Natalie bitterly. "I know she's the one who leaked the story to Merryprankster. But she won't get blamed . . . we will."

"Count on it. They'll twist the knife. We would, too, if the shoe were on the other foot." He let out a sigh. "We have to let people know she's gone."

"Piper asked us to wait until she notifies her next of kin."

"Of course."

"I'm going to stay here at the Mayflower. I'll keep you posted as I find out more," said Natalie.

"On second thought," said Penneymounter, "we should wait until the ambulance takes Maria to the hospital and let them announce her death. The more I think about it, I don't think we want to get anywhere nearer to this than we need to."

"Agreed. Piper can call her family from the hospital."

Penneymounter hung up the phone and glanced back down at Solis's deposition. The words moved on the page, fading in and out of focus. He had never wanted to call Solis in the first place. Now he had a dead body on his hands.

JAY NOBLE SAT IN his office, reading the affidavit of David Kenworthy. "In early December 1998, Maria Solis came to my apartment and told me she might be pregnant. She informed me that if so, she believed I was the father. I specifically asked whether there was any possibility she might have been with other men during the period she might have become pregnant. She said there was not. She said she previously dated Marco Diaz, but they had not had sexual intercourse in some time."

Jay's eyes darted across the page, rereading the words. His leg bounced under his desk excitedly. Ross Lombardy had come through again.

His direct line on the phone on his credenza rang. No one had the number except the president. He reached to pick up the receiver. "Mr. President?"

"How's our man Diaz?"

"Doing well, sir," answered Jay. He scrolled through his BlackBerry as he talked. "Reynolds says Maria Solis's allegations have him fired up with righteous indignation."

"Good," said Long. "We need to give Marco a line like Clarence Thomas had when he said his hearing was 'a high-tech lynching for uppity blacks.'"

"Great idea."

"What's the Hispanic equivalent of that line?" asked Long. "Can you huddle with the smart guys in the speech-writing department and come up with something?" The president loved testing Jay's famous brainpower.

Jay's wheels turned. "You could say drive-by shooting, but that has gang overtones. I'm fine with saying a high-tech crucifixion, given the way they've attacked his Catholicism."

"Having a line like that is important," said Long. "We need to call this what it is. We need to put the Senate on trial."

There was a long pause. "Mr. President, I just got a news flash on my BlackBerry. If it's true, things just got a heck of a lot more interesting."

"What is it?"

"It's a *Wall Street Journal* news alert," Jay said, his voice shocked. "Let me read it to you. 'MARIA SOLIS FOUND DEAD IN DC HOTEL.'"

"Good Lord."

Jay continued reading. "'Maria Solis, ex-girlfriend of Supreme Court nominee Marco Diaz who was to testify this morning that he once forced her to have an abortion, has been found dead in a Washington hotel room. Sources say she appears to have died from an overdose of prescription medication. No further details about her death are yet known.'"

"So sad," said Long. "God bless that poor woman."

"We're piling up quite a body count," said Jay. "What does Penneymounter do? Does he release Maria Solis's deposition to the public?"

"He'll look like a grave robber if he does," said Long.

"Yeah, but on the other hand, if he doesn't use her deposition, the feminists will go bats. He's between a rock and a hard place."

"Couldn't happen to a nicer guy," said Long. "He's played this cheap and below the belt from the get-go. He's not an adult. He's not serious. Everything for him is 'my way or the highway.' Look what he did to Yolanda Majette."

"Outrageous," agreed Jay. "I don't know who's more evil, him or Stanley."

"Have Lisa work up a statement of condolence," said Long. "Nothing political. Everyone knows who's responsible for this. I don't need to say it."

"Yes, sir," said Jay. He hung up the Bat Phone, as the staff called the red phone on his credenza. He bolted from his desk to find Lisa. They needed to put together a statement quickly and come up with a Latino version of the "high-tech lynching" line.

IN A HOLDING ROOM off the Senate Caucus Room, Senator Tom Reynolds, Diaz, and Art Morris waited for the hearing to begin. What was the delay? At that moment Reynolds's assistant walked in and handed him yet another note. He unfolded it and read it silently, his eyes widening, his jaw going slack.

"What is it?" asked Morris.

"Maria Solis is dead," said Reynolds, still in shock.

Diaz slumped back against the couch. Morris sat wide-eyed, speechless.

Reynolds's assistant returned. She walked over to Reynolds and leaned over, whispering quietly in his ear. He jumped up from his chair and walked behind his desk. As he put his hand on the phone, he said, "It's Penneymounter." He picked up the receiver. "Joe, Tom here. I just heard." He paused, listening. "No, it's tragic, really tragic. I'm so sorry for her and her family. Let me know what I can do. Whatever you think is best." A longer pause. "Sure, I'll be glad to do that. Let me know." He hung up.

"What did he say?" asked Morris.

Reynolds walked back to his chair and sat down. "He said they're going to let the hospital make the official announcement of her death. Then he plans to make a brief statement for the cameras. He asked me to stand with him as a bipartisan gesture."

"So that's it?" asked Diaz, his face twisted in anger. "They bring Maria into town to tell a pack of lies, force her into the national spotlight, she kills herself, and then it's over? I don't get to refute the charge that I forced her into having an abortion?"

"I don't know yet what will happen, Marco," answered Reynolds sympathetically. "But Maria is dead. She obviously can't testify. An affidavit from an unimpeachable witness says Maria told him you were not the father. I think this is over and we won."

"But I'll never be able to face my accuser," said Diaz, his voice rising. "Even if I'm confirmed, this will hang over me like a cloud for the rest of my life. It will taint every ruling I make and every opinion I write, especially anything related to abortion. Tom, I can't go on the Court under those circumstances." He looked away.

Reynolds looked stunned by the emotional ferocity of Diaz's statement. "Marco, you'll have plenty of opportunity to answer the charges. Once you're on the Court you can grant an interview to a reporter who will treat you fairly or write a book."

"We can't back out now, Marco," urged Morris. "We're on the five-yard line."

"No, you're on the five-yard line," said Marco, shaking his head. "I've lost my good name. My reputation is ruined. My name is worth more to me than a seat on the Supreme Court. I'm sorry, Art, but that's the way it is."

"Marco, it's your life, and I wouldn't presume to tell you what to do," Reynolds said quietly. "But I believe you're supposed to be on the Court. If you step aside now, they win in the worst possible way—with a lie. And a damnable lie at that."

"They've already won, Tom," he said. "Don't you see that? Maria's dead. My reputation will never recover. Nothing can restore my good name—not now, not ever."

"Yes it will, Marco," said Morris. "But only if you're confirmed to the Court and can show who you really are." He walked over to Diaz and grabbed him by the shoulders, pulling his face close. "*That's* your revenge."

"I'm not interested in revenge." Diaz stood up and walked to the window, looking out over the Mall. "I probably should have told you guys this before, but Maria called me."

"What? When?" said Morris.

"Last night. It was bizarre. She said she was sorry, that she never meant to hurt me. She basically apologized." He turned around to face them. "She said she was pregnant with our child and that she had an abortion. She never told me. She probably knew I'd want to keep the baby. Can you believe it?"

"So she admitted you never forced her to have an abortion," said Reynolds.

"Yes."

"Well, she took that admission to her grave," said Morris.

"I guess we'll never know if she would have told the truth when she testi-fied, but I kind of got the feeling she would," said Diaz. "I didn't want to tell anyone because frankly I didn't want to jinx it."

Morris shook his head in disbelief. "She still loved you. All these years later."

Diaz buttoned his coat and walked briskly to the door, placing his hand on the door knob, suddenly filled with energy. "Speaking of love, I need to be with Frida. You guys don't need me here anymore. Can someone take me to the hospital?"

"Of course," said Morris. He opened the door, sticking his head out into the reception area where several FBI agents sat. "Can you guys please take Judge Diaz to the hospital so he can be with his wife? On the double?"

"Yes, sir," one of them answered.

Diaz exited the room. Reynolds and Morris stood there, numbed by the news they had just absorbed.

"What do you think?" asked Reynolds. "Have we lost Marco?"

"I hope not," said Morris. "It would be a big mistake to bow out now. As sad and unnecessary as it was, Solis's death gives us the momentum."

"No question," agreed Reynolds. "Everybody's got a limit of how much pain they can take. Solis obviously reached hers. Marco may have reached his."

Morris shrugged. "Well, I should get back to the office. There isn't going to be a hearing today." He shook Reynolds's hand firmly. "Thanks for all you've done, Tom." He exited the same way as Diaz.

Reynolds shook his head in disbelief. He couldn't recall a day this crazy in his Senate career. He hoped Diaz would hang in there. If not, they'd be on their fourth nominee.

THIRTY-NINE

A black SUV with tinted windows pulled up to the emergency room entrance at the George Washington University Hospital, disgorging two dark-suited FBI agents wearing shades. One of the agents opened the rear door for Marco Diaz. A clutch of reporters on a deathwatch looked on, mouths agape. By a gruesome coincidence, the ambulance bearing the body of Maria Solis had arrived at the same entrance fifteen minutes earlier.

The FBI agents escorted Diaz into the emergency room waiting room and cleared a path in the crowded hallway, opening the door of a service elevator. "What floor?" one of them asked. Blank stares; no one knew.

An agent stuck his head out of the elevator and asked a nurse on which floor they could find the OB-GYN unit.

"Four."

Diaz reached over and pressed the button, punching it repeatedly even after it lit and the doors began to close. He was anxious to get there and see his wife. *How was Frida doing?* he wondered. *Had she heard about Maria?*

The service elevator stopped on the second floor to let off a janitor pushing a mop bucket. To Diaz's frustration, the janitor pressed the button to the third floor, then disembarked.

"I'm just glad we're not going to the eighth floor," cracked Diaz. The FBI agents chuckled.

When they finally reached the fourth floor, the doors opened. Stepping out of the elevator, Diaz nearly bumped right into Father Frank Henkel, one of his closest priest friends in the nation's capital. Father Henkel stood by the nurse's station between the elevator and the nurse's station, wearing a gravely serious expression on his face.

"Father Frank, I'm so glad you're here," said Diaz in an excited voice. "How's Frida?"

"She's doing fine. But before we go into her room, I need to tell you something," said Henkel.

"Sure, what's up?"

"Frida's fine," Henkel repeated. His eyes were dark with sadness. "Marco, she lost the baby."

Marco let out a low, guttural yell. It was the scream of a tortured soul that echoed in the hallway, bouncing off the walls and the linoleum floor. Instinctively Father Henkel grabbed him and hustled him into an empty hospital room, where Marco's knees buckled, his body crumpling to the floor. "No! No! No!" he screamed, his body racked with sobs. He fell forward, his elbows on the floor, his face planted on the linoleum. "Oh, God! Dear God, no!"

Father Frank went down on one knee, whispering words of comfort. "God knows you're in pain, Marco. He understands. Let it out," he said. Diaz's sobs melted into a quiet weeping. After a couple of minutes, he composed himself. Slowly he got to his feet, wiping the tears from his eyes with a handkerchief he pulled from his pocket. He began to pull himself together.

"Frida needs your strength and support right now," said Henkel. "This is going to be very difficult for her especially. It's common for the woman to blame herself at a time like this. You need to be prepared for that."

"I know, I know," said Marco. "How is she holding up emotionally?"

"As well as can be expected under the circumstances." He paused, his eyes downcast. "Marco, she won't let the nurses take the baby."

"Take me to her."

Father Henkel led the way down the hall and slowly opened the door to Frida's room, stepping back. Marco stepped across the threshold, his eyes adjusting to the semidarkness. The room was eerily quiet. Frida was in the bed, sitting up, holding the baby in her arms, lovingly stroking the little head, which had a surprising patch of black hair, and gazing into the face. She seemed lost in her own world.

After a long silence, Frida finally spoke. "It's a girl," she said softly, her voice barely audible. "I named her Anna."

"It's a lovely name," said Marco. They had wanted a girl for years, a daughter they could dote on and Frida could dress up. Now she was gone.

"She's beautiful, don't you think?"

"Yes, she is," said Marco. He began to weep, standing alone in the middle of the room, feeling utterly helpless.

"Look at what they've done," said Frida, her voice barely audible. "They killed my baby."

"It's too much," said Marco said, choking back the sobs. "Nothing is worth this . . . not even a seat on the Supreme Court."

"No, it's not."

"I'm calling Phil. I'm telling him I'm withdrawing."

Frida looked up, her eyes ablaze. "I know how you feel, Marco. I have felt like quitting for most of the past two months. But not now, not after what they've done. We have to go on, if only for Anna's sake. I don't want her to have died in vain. I want her life to mean something." She raised her chin, her ire up. "I want the whole world to see what they did."

Marco was taken aback by Frida's desire to fight on. He was spent, his tank was empty, and he was an emotional and physical wreck. He didn't even care if he was confirmed anymore; he just wanted it to end. "Are you sure?"

"Yes," replied Frida without hesitation. "We can't let them win after what they've done to us. All of us, especially Anna."

"Alright, if that's what you want to do," he heard himself say. "Can I hold her?"

"Sure," she said. "Be gentle."

He took Anna, swaddled in a maternity blanket, and cradled her lifeless body in his arms. He walked over to sit in a chair. He was struck by her features: her bow mouth, pug nose, her mother's feline eyes. She was perfect. He began to cry again, the tears burning his skin as they streaked down his cheeks and fell on the cotton blanket. A resolute purpose, stoked by Frida's maternal wrath, boiled inside him. He dedicated his nomination, win or lose, to Anna.

JAY NOBLE HOVERED OUTSIDE Phil Battaglia's door, waiting for him to wrap up a phone call. From behind the door he could hear Phil's low, hushed voice. Then silence. The door opened, and Battaglia waved him in without a word. He made eye contact with Jay, his eyes pained.

"Frida had a miscarriage," he said. "She lost the baby. I just told the president."

"No!" he exclaimed. He looked up at the ceiling, his emotions welling up.

"It's bad, pal."

"How's Marco?"

"Devastated. And yet when I talked to him, he was stoic. Numb might be a better word. My guess is the full impact won't hit him until it's all over."

"Does he still want to quit?"

"Oddly enough, no," said Phil. "Frida wants him to tough it out. He told me, 'They took my daughter from me. I'm going to spend the next forty years on that court paying them back.'"

"Wow," said Jay.

"They lost their baby, but I think they got some of their vinegar back."

They sat in silence for a moment, contemplating the carnage. Two people were dead, one by suicide or accidental overdose, the other by homicide as far as Jay and Phil were concerned. The Diaz nomination appeared lost, then won, then withdrawn, and now back again, all in the space of a single day.

"Oh, one other thing," said Battaglia. "You're not gonna believe this, but the preliminary autopsy finding by the DC coroner shows no cause of death for Maria Solis."

"I've never heard of such a thing. Is that possible?"

"Apparently it is," said Battaglia. "She was taking an antidepressant and diet pills. She drank a couple of glasses of wine. But they can't or won't say the combination stopped her heart. Maybe they're trying to protect her family."

"This is going to start a cottage industry of conspiracy theorists," observed Jay.

"Probably. It's sad. That witch at Pro-Choice PAC—what's her name—should have left her alone."

"Christy Love. She would back over her own mother to stop Diaz from getting on the Court. And the media was complicit in her sucking Solis into the whole mess." He shook his head. "What happens now?"

"Unclear," replied Battaglia. "I assume this will delay the hearings for a few days, maybe a week."

"Okay," said Jay. "Just keep me posted."

Jay, still in a daze, left Phil's office and headed down the hall toward the West Wing lobby and walked up the stairs to the second floor. Passing his assistant without a word, he closed the door to his office. Picking up the phone, he dialed a number.

"Taylor, Jay Noble. Listen, Frida Diaz just lost her baby."

Sullivan let out an expletive. "I guess the attacks got to her. It makes me want to puke. The left has blood on their hands on this one."

"Big time. I'm done pulling our punches. It's time we hit back. Where are you on that thing you've been working on?"

"Locked and loaded," said Sullivan proudly.

"Good. Go ahead and get it in the water . . . carefully."

"Now we're talking," Sullivan replied excitedly.

"Be discreet," Jay instructed.

"Don't worry. There's a lot of duct tape on the gun. There are no fingerprints."

Jay hung up the phone. Part of him regretted giving the order. But the loss of the Diaz baby had pushed Jay over the line. It was time to win at all costs.

SAL STANLEY'S HANDS GRIPPED the armrests of his chair, his legs crossed, his face stretched into a surgical mask of senatorial stoicism. The Democratic leadership spread out on two couches before the fireplace and several end chairs. The ticktock of the grandfather clock had the disquieting effect of increasing the tension in the room.

"Well, everyone, it appears Maria Solis died from a mixture of prescription drugs and alcohol," said Stanley. "By all appearances it was accidental. Our thoughts and prayers go out to her family. It is difficult at a time like this to dwell on political implications, but I'm afraid we have no choice. Our main witness against Diaz has died. Pursuing the allegations she made will be problematic at best." He turned to Penneymounter, who sat on one of the couches. "Do I fairly summarize our situation vis-à-vis the Diaz nomination?"

"I'm afraid so, Sal."

"What's your assessment of where we stand on the committee?" asked Stanley, sliding to the bottom line.

"I don't sense much movement. We've got one undecided on our side, the rest committed to vote no on the nomination. We're thinking of footnoting Solis's deposition in the majority report and including it in the appendix. Beyond that we let it lie."

"Anybody got a reaction to that?"

No one offered an opinion. Besides, anyone who questioned Penneymounter's leadership of the committee was liable to be decapitated.

"So the committee votes on the nomination . . . maybe day after tomorrow?"

Penneymounter frowned. "That was my original plan," he said. "But my staff heard from someone at DOJ that Frida Diaz went into premature labor and had a miscarriage."

Stanley sunk lower in his chair, his face going white. "You're kidding."

"I wish I were."

"If that report turns out to be true, it's very bad."

"Fox News and talk radio will blame us," said Craig McGowan, chairman of the Democratic Senatorial Campaign Committee. The junior senator from New Jersey was Stanley's protégé and designated hitter (some said lackey) on all matters political.

"When will we know?" asked Stanley, growing visibly agitated.

"Soon," said Penneymounter. "Should be any minute now."

"Assuming the committee votes this week, how does it look?"

"I've got ten votes. The only wobbly on our side is Rebecca Rhoades. The Republicans have eight in favor and one undecided, but I think we should assume they'll vote for Diaz."

"What's up with R-squared?" asked Stanley, using Rhoades's nickname. She was a centrist Democrat from Louisiana, ever mindful of the conservative sentiments of her Catholic and Cajun constituents.

"Who knows? She won't return my phone calls. She's up on the mountaintop, praying." Penneymounter rolled his eyes.

"Whenever she prays about a vote, that usually means one of two things: she wants more money for New Orleans levees, or she wants more subsidies for sugar," joked McGowan. Everyone chuckled appreciatively.

"There's a 'dear colleague' calling for a filibuster of Diaz," said Leo Wells, the Democratic whip. Wells was a true liberal who made no secret of his desire to replace Stanley as Majority Leader, a fact that caused no small amount of tension between the two. "If Rhoades announces she's voting for Diaz, I'm inclined to sign it."

Penneymounter moved to the edge of the couch, leaning forward. "I saw that letter. It's way too soon to be discussing a filibuster. It plays right into the hands of the White House and scares the daylights out of the blue dogs."

"No one in leadership should call for a filibuster," said Stanley declaratively.

"Sal, with all due respect, if we get forty-one signatures, it gives us leverage," said Wells insistently. "It doesn't mean we necessarily filibuster. But it allows us to operate from a position of strength. R-squared is less likely to vote for Diaz if she knows he's dead on the floor."

"No, it does the opposite," said Stanley, swatting aside Wells's self-serving suggestion like a fly. "Threatening to filibuster weakens our position because it's an admission we don't have the votes to stop him in committee. It lets R-squared off the hook."

"I won't belabor the point," said Wells, throwing in the towel. "But Diaz is the fifth vote to overturn *Roe*. Our base expects us to defeat him or die trying."

"What do you think I've been doing?" fired back Penneymounter, his eyes narrowed. "I know Rebecca. She's prickly to a fault. If she thinks we've given up on her and are counting her as a yes vote, we'll lose her." He shot Wells a withering look. "You keep doing MSNBC and leave counting the votes to me."

It was a vicious shot at Wells, a notorious camera hog. Stanley jumped in to stop the fight. "Settle down, everybody. Here's the deal: Joe's going to make a final run at Becky. If we don't get her, we discuss the filibuster option at that time. Alright?"

No one said a word. No one had the stomach to argue the point any further.

Penneymounter's BlackBerry went off. He got up from the couch and walked across the room to the window facing the Mall to answer it, talking quietly. After about a minute he returned to the group, his face somber.

"That was Phil Battaglia," he said. "He just confirmed what we heard: Frida Diaz had a miscarriage." He paused. "I have to talk with Tom Reynolds, but this means the committee won't vote until next week."

Everyone rose and began to file out. Penneymounter hung back, grabbing Stanley's arm in a power clutch, the two speaking in hushed voices. Whatever they were discussing, Penneymounter didn't want to share with the rest of the leadership.

FORTY

The sun hung high and hot as Marco and Frida Diaz and their friends and family gathered in a cemetery in Arlington to bury their daughter Anna. The air was thick. The memorial service, featuring a beautiful homily by Father Henkel, was held at St. Benedict's, their parish church in Alexandria. The graveside service, by contrast, was brief. People sought shelter from the blazing sun beneath a green funeral tent.

A woman sang "It is Well (with My Soul)" a cappella. Father Henkel said a prayer committing Anna's body to the earth and her soul to God. "Father, your Son instructed His disciples not to hinder the little children from coming to Him. We surrender our own desires for Anna's life and submit to Yours, allowing her to sit in the lap of Christ, surrounded by angelic majesties and by Your glory. Amen."

The casket was slowly lowered into the grave. Women seated in the front dabbed wet eyes, sniffling noses with tissues.

The memorial service sparked a raging debate on talk radio, cable, and the blogosphere. Some viewed a graveside service for a child not carried to term as morbid, others creepy, while still others called it political exploitation. But to Diaz partisans, Anna was the victim of a confirmation process poisoned by partisanship and the take-no-prisoners modus operandi of the far left. She deserved a proper burial. Even in death Diaz divided the country.

As the mourners began to drift away from the grave, greeting one another with hugs and handshakes, Jay Noble and Phil Battaglia walked up to Marco to pay their respects. When he saw them, his eyes lit up.

"Thank you for coming," Marco said with muted enthusiasm.

"The president asked us to convey his condolences," said Battaglia in official-speak. "He's pulling for you."

"He called me, you know."

"Did he?" asked Jay. He pretended to be surprised—it made the call look more spontaneous and a greater encouragement to Diaz, who the White House desperately needed to stay in the fight.

"Yes," said Diaz. "I told him he didn't have to. I know how busy he is. With all on his plate right now, it meant a lot."

Jay and Phil walked across the cemetery's grassy lawn back to the government sedan they rode from the White House. The driver pulled away from the curb and proceeded slowly out of the cemetery onto a busy road that led back to I-395.

"I'm glad we went," said Phil.

"Me, too," said Jay. "Golden, too. It was a statement."

"Frida looked like she has been through it."

Jay's BlackBerry went off. "It's Dan Dorman," he said, somewhat surprised.

"I wonder what he wants."

"Let's find out." Jay answered the phone. "Dan, to what do I owe the honor?"

"Your office said you were at the funeral for the Diaz baby. I hope I'm not catching you at a bad time."

"No, we just left. It was a very moving service. I'm headed back to the White House. What's up?"

"What do you know about Penneymounter having a fling with a Judiciary Committee staffer?"

Dorman's question landed like an artillery shell. "Not a thing," he lied. "Why?"

"Just asking. We're hearing fairly specific rumors. I don't know yet who's pushing it. Supposedly it involves a press aide on the committee."

"Mmmmm," said Jay. Sullivan's black-bag operation was underway.

"Everyone knows Joe likes the ladies," said Dorman. "But this is pretty specific information, and its coming right before the Judiciary Committee votes on Diaz's nomination. Pretty interesting timing, don't you think?"

"Dan, I can't comment on that. I'm staying as far away from this as possible."

"Okay, just checking," said Dorman, skeptical lilt in his voice. He hung up.

"What was that about?" asked Battaglia.

"Oh, just the rumor de jour. It's the day before the judiciary vote, and everyone is chasing rabbits." Jay paused. "What's the hard count on the committee?"

"Ten votes against, nine votes for," said Battaglia matter-of-factly. "It's all down to Becky Rhoades. No one knows what she's going to do. She's gone dark."

Jay shook his head in disbelief. He whipped out his BlackBerry again and dialed a number. "Ross, Jay here."

"What's shaking?" asked Ross.

"Listen, I'm sitting here with Phil Battaglia. We just left the funeral for the Diaz baby. Our count is nine yeas and ten nays, with R-squared undecided. Where are you on Louisiana?"

"I'm carpet-bombing it," said Ross with undisguised pride. "A thousand gross rating points on statewide TV, eight frequency on radio, and phone banks lit up like a Christmas tree. We're hearing Rhoades is getting two thousand calls a day, and they are running 80 percent in favor of Diaz."

"Fantastic," said Jay. "Keep it under the radar. Don't have Andy go after her on the air."

"Don't worry. Andy's on a short leash."

Jay hung up, satisfied with Ross's report. The sedan pulled up to the entrance to the West Wing. Jay turned to Phil. "If we don't get Rhoades, it sure won't be for lack of trying."

"If we don't get Rhoades, I'll be back to California making a living by handling DUI cases," dead-panned Battaglia.

Jay laughed. He stepped out of the car, greeted by one of his assistants, who stood on the curb clutching a leather-bound legal pad. "Senator Bottoms is here to see you," she said. "He's in the lobby."

"Again? What's he want this time?" asked Jay.

"The same thing he always wants. I'll tell you while you walk," she said. "We're late."

Jay power walked through the side door to the West Wing lobby, head down, his eyes straight ahead.

REBECCA RHOADES SAT IN a wing-back chair in her office in the Hart Senate Office Building, her chief of staff and her Judiciary Committee aide seated on the couch. Even at this late hour, no one knew how she would vote. Her office was ground zero in the battle over the Diaz nomination.

Rhoades, thin and intense, possessed the fading beauty of a former homecoming queen at LSU. Primly clad in a patterned blue dress with D & G heels, her dirty-blonde hair was streaked with highlights and cut at her shoulders, accentuating a high forehead, lush eyebrows, and piercing blue eyes. With smoldering looks mellowing with age, her skin had softened to reveal high cheekbones and an angular jaw.

"What's the latest call count?" she asked.

"Through noon today, twelve thousand calls," said the chief of staff. "Ten thousand five hundred in favor of Diaz, fifteen hundred against."

"How much of that is Astroturf, and how much is real?" asked Rhoades.

"No way to know," replied the chief of staff. "I'd say half and half. The Andy Stanton brigades are in full battle gear, as you can imagine."

Rhoades nodded. As a Catholic herself, she understood religious voters even though she thought they were too easily manipulated by con men and demagogues.

"There's something else, Senator," said the Judiciary Committee aide. "The NRA just announced they're scoring the Diaz vote."

"What? On what basis?"

"Diaz voted on the DC Circuit to overturn the DC gun ban," explained the aide. "So they're claiming that a vote against Diaz is a vote against the Second Amendment."

"That's crazy. Who got to them?"

"The White House. Jay Noble told the NRA if they wanted Long to slow-walk the assault weapon ban, they not only had to come out for Diaz; they had to score the vote."

"I'd hate to lose my A-plus rating from the NRA going into the re-elect."

"We need it," agreed the chief of staff. "There are 200,000 NRA members in Louisiana. And they vote."

A secretary stuck her head in. "Senator, Sal Stanley is on the phone."

"Again?" sighed Rhoades. "Tell him I'm out."

The secretary nodded and closed the door.

"Well, what's the verdict, boss?" asked the chief of staff, pressing the issue. "We need to make an announcement, and I don't recommend you wait until the day of the vote."

"Your advice is duly noted," said Rhoades. "But I'm going to watch a movie."

"Come again?" asked the chief of staff.

"I have to get out of here. A movie theater is dark and safe with no cell phones, and no one can find me."

The staffers chuckled. Rhoades picked up her purse and headed for the door. Before she exited, she turned back. "No calls until 9:00 a.m. tomorrow. That includes Stanley. Tell any press I'll announce my decision tomorrow."

"Yes, ma'am," replied the chief of staff.

With that she was gone.

SAL STANLEY HUNG UP the phone and turned to his chief of staff, the crow's feet at his eyes crinkling. "Joan of Arc is missing in action."

"If she doesn't get with the program soon," replied the chief of staff, "Her MIA status is going to be downgraded to KIA."

"It's unbelievable," said Stanley. "R-squared is pro-choice, and she may vote for a guy who is against choice and voted to sustain employment discrimination against women."

"I can sum it up in two words," said the chief of staff. "God and guns."

"You're right," said Stanley with a sigh. "The NRA announcement has to give her pause. They'll pay for that stunt, by the way. A Supreme Court nomination is now a gun vote?" He screwed up his face. "Come on!"

The chief of staff's face became somber, his eyes heavy. "What are we going to do about Penneymounter?"

"We wait it out. I made him chairman of the committee. I can't stab him in the back."

"Word is the *Times* has the story, and the *Post* is playing catch up," said the chief of staff. "Best case scenario, we've got two or three days before the story breaks."

"Check in with Joe's press secretary," said Stanley. "I can't imagine the *Times* would want to go before the story is fully baked."

The chief of staff nodded and got up to leave the room.

Stanley walked behind his desk and turned to look out the window, gazing down the Mall toward the Washington Monument and the Lincoln Memorial. The Diaz nomination had already claimed too many victims. Would Joe Penneymounter be next? The thought made him shudder.

IT DIDN'T TAKE LONG for Stanley to get his answer. Ninety minutes later news of Penneymounter's affair with Taylor rocketed across the Internet. Merryprankster posted its story at 4:32 p.m. under the lurid headline: "THE CHAIRMAN AND HIS MISTRESS: PENNEYMOUNTER STAFFER TARGETED DIAZ . . . SOUGHT SUGAR DADDIES ON SEX-FOR-CASH WEB SITE." The story featured links to Taylor's page on MySugarDaddy.com, which had been taken down ten months before. As if anyone needed another reminder that the news media now set the national agenda, Merryprankster's post attracted eight million people to the site in the first half hour. The *New York Times* had no choice but to post its own still-evolving version a little after 5:00 p.m. Every evening news broadcast led with the riveting story.

On Capitol Hill the Penneymounter scandal landed like a bomb. A crowd of reporters and camera crews gathered outside his office, hoping to catch a glance of him. About ninety minutes after the story broke, a harried press aide appeared in the hallway and was quickly surrounded by boom mikes and cameras.

"Senator Penneymounter will have nothing to say tonight about press accounts that first circulated on the Internet regarding an alleged relationship with a member of the Judiciary Committee staff," he said, reading from a piece of paper. "The senator has always endeavored to serve the people of Minnesota by advancing the values of the state. He is confident he has violated no law and no rule of the U.S. Senate. We will have no further comment this evening."

The statement was filled with legalese and nondenying denials. It only whipped the press into a bigger frenzy.

"So you are not denying that Senator Penneymounter had a sexual relationship with Ms. Taylor?" asked *Roll Call*.

"I am not confirming the unsubstantiated accounts that first circulated an Internet rumor site regarding a woman who works on the Judiciary Committee staff," replied the press aide, his pale face contorted with stress and anguish.

"To your knowledge, is Ms. Taylor still a member of the staff?" asked Dan Dorman of the *Post*.

"I don't know," replied the press aide.

"Will the committee still hold its vote on the Diaz nomination tomorrow morning as planned?" asked the *Washington Times*.

"Yes. If there is any change, you'll be the first to know. Thank you all for coming." With that the press aide disappeared into the office.

The reporters stood at the door, stunned. Dan Dorman broke the silence. "Penneymounter has no comment on his girlfriend?" asked Dorman aloud, his voice dripping with sarcasm. "I'll bet his wife does."

"I hear he's huddling with his advisors trying to figure out if he can survive as Judiciary chairman," said *Politico*.

"He's been huddling with people alright but not his advisors," joked Reuters. "Supposedly there's more than one girlfriend."

"What is it with these guys?" asked *Politico*. "Why can't they keep their pants on?"

"I don't know," answered Dorman. "But it's hard to beat for sheer entertainment value. It's like watching a car crash in slow motion."

The reporters closed their steno pads and turned off their tape recorders and iPhones, ambling down the hall like a mob in search of more victims. Dorman loitered around the elevators leading to the underground subway to the Capitol, hoping to grab a senator or two on their way to the floor for a vote and ambush them. An offhand comment or two from senators on the Penneymounter sex scandal would add a little spice to the next day's front-page story.

FORTY-ONE

The temperature in the Caucus Room of the Russell Senate Office building resembled a sauna from a combination of body heat and television lights. The room was packed, with bodies lining the wall, the press corps buzzing with rumors flying across the Capitol like stray bullets. Chief among the scuttlebutt: Penneymounter would stonewall, vigorously denying an "inappropriate" relationship with Natalie Taylor, parsing words and wagging a finger like Bill Clinton when the Monica Lewinsky scandal broke. Still others claimed Taylor had resigned and Penneymounter would fall on his sword for the good of the Democratic caucus. Which rumor, if either, was true? No one knew. Even Sal Stanley was in the dark.

At 9:00 a.m. sharp Penneymounter entered the room and strode purposefully to the podium, his wife in tow. The press corps rustled. His face was lined with exhaustion. His wife stood by his side, her face wan and stricken. Penneymounter pulled a statement from his coat pocket.

"Good morning. For seventeen years I have worked hard to uphold the trust that the people of Minnesota placed in me as a member of the U.S. Senate. I have tried throughout that time to conduct myself according to the highest standards of ethical conduct. However, I must acknowledge I have failed to live up to that standard. I have come here this morning to admit publicly and accept responsibility for a personal indiscretion." Just like that, Penneymounter admitted the affair, with all the usual euphemisms. "I apologize to my wife Anne,"—he turned in her direction and acknowledged her with a bob of his head—"to our three wonderful children, and to the people of Minnesota. As painful as this is, it is a reminder that some things are more important than politics. For now my priority must be to heal my family and my marriage. I ask respect for our privacy as we do so, and I will have no further comment regarding this personal matter." Penneymounter paused, clearing his throat, appearing to brace himself for what came next. "To that end, I am stepping down as chairman of the Judiciary Committee, effective immediately."

Audible gasps went up from the crowd. For Penneymounter, who reveled in his role as chairman and loved it more than anything, it was like having his right arm wrenched off.

"The issues at stake in the nomination of Judge Marco Diaz to the Supreme Court," he continued, "are too important for the Senate to be distracted by a purely personal matter." In his humiliation Penneymounter was still a skillful litigator, asserting he committed no official transgression. (A Senate Ethics committee investigation loomed; Penneymounter was lawyered up.) Raising his eyes from the paper, he made eye contact with the press corps for the first time, his gaze intense. "Serving as chairman of the Judiciary Committee has been the highest honor of my public life. Out of respect for the Senate I love so much, I relinquish it for the greater good of this institution and the nation. Thank you very much."

Penneymounter grabbed his wife's hand and hustled through a door that led backstage, ignoring an explosion of shouted questions from the restless press mob. The act of public humiliation complete, the media bolted for the door to file their stories and do stand-ups. Some Twittered from cell phones or blogged on laptops in the hallway. The effect was feverish, ritualistic, tribal sacrifice mixed with *schadenfreude*—oh, how the mighty had fallen!

The vote on Diaz's nomination in the Judiciary Committee loomed. Penneymounter's announcement unleashed a flood of questions: Who would succeed him as Judiciary chairman? Would he remain on the committee, pulling strings from the sidelines? His statement left open the question of whether he would even show for the vote. If he did not, the committee could deadlock 10 to 10, or, if Rhoades voted for Diaz, the nomination would go to the floor with a favorable recommendation, all but ensuring Diaz's confirmation. With only three hours left before the vote, confusion reigned.

CHRISTY LOVE WATCHED JOE Penneymounter's news conference at Pro-Choice PAC headquarters surrounded by senior staff. The mood was maudlin. Christy and Penneymounter had crossed swords—most recently over calling Maria Solis as a witness—but she found his egotism and wandering eye endearing in a way. There had even been talk of a presidential bid. But now Joe was done. Natalie Taylor was collateral damage; the Judiciary Committee had already announced her resignation.

"I wish I could say I was surprised," said Christy. "But everybody knew Joe had a zipper problem. I went to him and warned him about Natalie. He wouldn't listen."

"How about Natalie's double life as an Internet-trolling sugar babe?" asked one of her legal eagles. "You can't make this stuff up!"

"Now that did shock me," replied Christy. "You could have knocked me over with a feather. It just goes to show, you never really know people the way you think you do."

Scandal-mongering gossip preliminaries dispensed with, the group turned to the matter at hand: How would all this affect the vote on Diaz? Everyone was just guessing. But the conventional wisdom was it helped Diaz. His main nemesis fell on the field of battle.

"The timing is horrible," said one of Christy's aides, slumped on the couch, looking like he crammed all night for an exam. "Three hours before the vote!"

"It's very suspicious," agreed Christy, hands on hips. "I see Jay Noble's fingerprints. He's evil and he'll do anything to win."

"Well, now what?" asked the staff attorney.

"Joe has to show up and vote, and then we have to get lucky and get R-squared," replied Christy. "If we don't get both of them, it's over."

"Joe didn't say anything about stepping down from the committee."

"He better not," said Christy. "He's done enough damage as it is. If he's AWOL on the Diaz vote, he might as well resign from the Senate now." She glanced at her communications director. "Work up a statement praising the new chairman of Judiciary and urging a continued fight against Diaz."

"Who's the new chairman?"

"How do I know?" snapped Christy. "I can't do your job and mine. Just get it done." She stood looking at them. They stared back. "Well, what are you waiting for? Go!"

They hurriedly filed out to get to work. Pro-Choice PAC staffers were used to Christy's volcanic explosions. She was in the bunker, stressed out, and one vote short.

AT 11:00 A.M. THE members of the Senate Judiciary Committee filed into the hearing room in the Hart Senate Office building to cast their votes on Diaz. Joe Penneymounter was among them, his presence unavoidably awkward and a clear sign of the high stakes. In the hours since his news conference, Sal Stanley named his replacement, Chuck Hurley of Iowa, the next-highest ranking Democrat on the committee by seniority. Hurley was not the sharpest pencil in the box, but Stanley decided this was no time to upend seniority.

Hurley, pale and dough-faced, sharply parted helmet hair combed to a perfect pitch, took his seat and banged the meeting to order with the gavel. His facial expression was the pained, muted exuberance of a back-up quarterback called off the bench in the Super Bowl: nervous and giddy. Tom Reynolds of Oklahoma sat to his left, Penneymounter to his right.

Hurley cleared his throat and leaned into the microphone. "Ladies and gentlemen, the Committee on the Judiciary will now proceed in executive committee to a vote on the nomination of Judge Marco Diaz for associate justice of the United States Supreme Court." He raised his chin, bracing himself as he prepared to address the elephant in the room. "Before we do, I want to express my sincere appreciation to Senator Penneymounter for his leadership of this committee. No one in recent history has led this committee more ably. He has been an effective legislator at a time of great national challenge. Senator, you are a tough act to follow." He smiled weakly. "Thank you for your leadership and friendship, and please know I will be counting on you to continue to be an important voice on this committee." The members of the committee applauded in an obligatory, joyless manner. Penneymounter managed a weak smile.

"I am going to be brief in my comments on Judge Diaz's nomination. I hope other Senators will do the same," said Hurley. "In spite of the reporters and cameras joining us this morning, I don't believe there is a great deal of suspense about how each of us plans to vote"—he paused for effect, staring straight ahead—"with one possible exception." Nervous chuckles filled the air as all eyes fixed on Rebecca Rhoades. "I will vote against Judge Diaz's nomination. I do so reluctantly. He is a fine individual and a man of enormous talent and accomplishments. His story is the fulfillment of the American dream. But a seat on the highest court does not go to one with the most compelling biography. It goes to the person with the right judicial temperament and philosophy who will uphold the law and protect individual rights." His eyes narrowed. "On issues of gender and racial discrimination, antitrust law, a woman's right to choose, and the separation of powers, Judge Diaz fails that test. This nomination will be pivotal in deciding a number of issues pending before the court, including a woman's right to choose. I vote against Judge Diaz not because I do not share his *opinion* on these matters but because I have concerns about his *temperament* and judicial philosophy."

Hurley leaned back in his chair, satisfied he had pushed all the buttons for the liberal groups without committing any gaffes. He turned to Reynolds.

"Mr. Chairman, thank you," said Reynolds in a firm voice. "Let me say that I look forward to working very closely with you so the committee can move forward in an efficient and hopefully bipartisan basis. In just the few short hours since you assumed the chairmanship, you have been unfailingly courteous and professional in your dealings with the minority, and for that I want to thank you publicly." (Another knife in Penneymounter, which Reynolds twisted with glee.) "Ladies and gentlemen, I am saddened by the state of affairs in this body as we cast our votes today on the nomination of Judge Diaz. I am saddened not only as a member of the U.S. Senate; I am saddened as an American."

People rustled in their chairs. Reynolds was not taking Hurley's cue that everyone mail it in before the vote. He was doing what he did best: posturing before the cameras.

"Have our differences over contentious issues like affirmative action, marriage, and abortion reached such a low we no longer treat one another with decency and respect as fellow citizens? I fear that is the case. The manner in which this nomination has proceeded is frankly a disgrace to the Senate and our nation." His eyes were aflame, his hands shaking with rage as he glanced down at his notes. "Judge Diaz is a man of integrity, honor, and personal rectitude. He has been endorsed by Democrats who served with him, progressive and liberal attorneys who appeared before his court, and Democratic clerks who served him. They have all testified to his character, his fairness, his open mind, and collegiality."

Like an NFL player looking to make the highlight reel, Reynolds moved in for the kill. "Judge Diaz has been subjected to the most vicious, sustained campaign of personal attacks and smears I have witnessed in my entire career. A good man and his wife have almost been ruined." Hurley began to squirm in his chair. Reynolds ignored him. His audience was in front of him—the cameras. "Two people are dead, one a baby, the other a witness subjected to her own tabloid-like news coverage. The confirmation process bears no resemblance to the vision of our founders for our nation. It is search and destroy, smear and fear, the worst kind of politics of personal destruction." Reynolds was putting the committee on trial. No one made a sound. "The Diazes lost a child. But we have lost something, too. We have lost the sense of fairness central to America."

Hurley sat silently, stone-faced. "I will vote yes on this nomination not only because Marco Diaz is eminently qualified to sit on the Supreme Court but as a symbolic rebuke of the campaign of lies and smears that plagued previous nominations and has brought this one to such a disgraceful and ignoble conclusion. *Shame on us,* Mr. Chairman. *Shame on us.*"

The entire room exhaled. Penneymounter glared at Reynolds, eyes mere slits. The rest of the statements were anticlimactic, droning on along predictable lines. Then it was Rebecca Rhoades's turn, the woman of the hour.

"Senator Rhoades?" said Hurley expectantly. The entire room snapped to attention.

"Mr. Chairman, thank you for the job you and Senator Penneymounter have done conducting a thorough and fair process," she began ambiguously, declining to signal her intentions. "I have listened to the arguments of both sides. I paid close attention to Judge Diaz's three days of testimony. I have now reread that testimony twice. For me the question boils down to a simple one: Is Judge Diaz the most qualified person the president could have nominated to be an associate justice of the Supreme Court."

Diaz's opponents' hearts leapt: *Of course he wasn't!* Rhoades raised the bar high. For this fleeting moment in time, she was the most important person in the world, and she clearly intended to milk her fifteen minutes of fame. Washington was a parallel universe, an inversion of reality in which an anonymous politician from a small state with more oil derricks or cows than people held the fate of the nation in her hands. Was Rhoades up to it? No one knew, including her.

"I am pro-life in my personal views," Rhoades declared. "But I have never believed I have the right to impose those beliefs on others. Whatever one's personal views, *Roe v. Wade* is the law of the land. Judge Diaz said as much during these hearings. To paraphrase him, *stare decisis* requires respect for precedent, imposing on both policy makers and judges a prudential reticence to vitiate the social contract for women explicit in its ruling. Given his responses to these questions, I found Judge Diaz's judicial philosophy to be well within the mainstream."

Diaz supporters allowed themselves a smile. Such big words—*reticence, vitiate*! She did her homework and declared Diaz to be a mainstream nominee.

"My reservations about Judge Diaz arise from his tendency to side with powerful corporate interests against plaintiffs, which I find troubling." Sitting next to her, Penneymounter nodded slowly, almost imperceptibly. "His rulings on gender and racial discrimination, sexual harassment, and shareholder lawsuits leave little doubt he believes corporations are persons for purposes of Fourteenth Amendment protections, a controversial view with which I strenuously disagree." Rhoades turned over a page of her remarks, the suspense building. "My concerns about his views are deepened by his participation in the Wildfire antitrust case at a time when his blind trust held stock in that company. I believe the evidence shows Judge Diaz did nothing intentionally unethical. But the fact remains that if he is confirmed, the appeal of his ruling on the Wildfire case will await his judgment. This is critical not only for the technology industry but for our economy."

"My reservations were so profound I submitted written questions to Judge Diaz on the Wildfire case," said Rhoades. "I asked him if he would recuse himself from ruling on the *United States v. Wildfire* case should he be confirmed. In a written response Judge Diaz pledged seriously to consider recusal but declined to commit himself to that course. He felt to do so would subject future judicial nominees to legislative proscriptions on appellate jurisdiction. I found this response to be intellectually honest but ultimately unpersuasive."

The room fell completely silent. No one moved. "I continue to believe Judge Diaz should recuse himself from the Wildfire case. But to reject an otherwise qualified nominee for the Supreme Court of the United States in the absence of clear evidence of unethical conduct over a single case, even a case as important as the Wildfire antitrust litigation, is unduly harsh. Therefore, with reservations, I will vote to confirm Judge Diaz."

The room exploded in applause from Diaz supporters, who jumped to their feet. Hurley glowered at them, banging his gavel. "There are to be no outbursts of any kind during this session!" he shouted. "Marshals will remove those who disrupt these proceedings!"

The Democrats on the committee slumped in their chairs. They would pay Rhoades back for breaking ranks with a thousand slights, snubs, and public shunning. But that was all in the future. For now Rhoades had resurrected Diaz's nomination from certain defeat, giving him a tie vote in the committee, and he was on his way to the Senate floor. The White House would live to fight another day.

SATCHA SANCHEZ BREEZED INTO the lobby of the Four Seasons in Georgetown like she owned the place. She looked smaller than she did on television, weighing 110 pounds soaking wet. Her form-fitting red dress— subtlety was not her style—with mid-thigh hemline, plunging neckline, matching lipstick and rouge, and a peek of black La Perla drew gazes. Jay Noble waited at a back table. When she reached him, they embraced. Her personal assistant gravitated to the bar.

"Hello, darling," said Jay.

"Hey, baby," she replied, planting fire-engine red lips on his cheek, then wiping the lipstick off his cheek with her hand. A male waiter appeared. "Do you have a mango martini per chance?" she asked.

"I'm sorry, ma'am, we don't."

She frowned theatrically. "Mmmmm . . . bring me a dry chardonnay, honey," she said. "Very dry." As the waiter left, she turned to Jay, crossing her deep brown legs to reveal red six-inch Ferragamos. "Congratulations on Diaz. That was a close one."

"Thanks," said Jay with a slight smile. "R-squared sure made it interesting. It was a near-death experience, but we got the tie in committee, and now we move to the full Senate, which is better terrain for us."

"How about Penneymounter blowing up in a sex scandal? There goes his presidential campaign!"

"Unbelievable."

"Any truth to the Democrats mounting a filibuster?"

"We can't rule that out," said Jay. "It's dicey . . . the moderate Democrats tell our guys they won't go along. But Stanley and Penneymounter will fight until the last dog dies. They view stopping Diaz nomination as our Waterloo."

"They're right, you know."

"We know." Jay took a sip from his vodka on the rocks as the waiter brought Satcha's wine. "So what brings you to town? I know it's not me."

"Actually, it is you," Satcha said with a low, feminine purr. Jay's ears perked up. "I want to interview Diaz." She batted her eyes. "I need your help."

"Boy," said Jay, leaning back on the couch, his body language projecting his wariness. "That's tough," he replied. "We're running out of time. The Senate is scheduled to begin debate on the nomination in two days."

Satcha leaned forward, lowering her voice to a seductive whisper. "Jay, think about what we can do together," she said. "The second Latino nominee to the U.S. Supreme Court in a prime-time, exclusive interview on the number one Hispanic television network in the world." She paused. "I'll be tough but fair. I'll give Diaz a chance to speak directly to the American people. The ratings will be off the charts, and Diaz's support among Hispanics will go even higher!" She tapped Jay on his knee. He felt a tingle run up his leg. "What's wrong with that picture?"

Jay looked at her in wonderment. "You never quit, do you?"

"No. Come on, Jay, this is the 'get' of the century. So . . . are you game?"

"I'm game," replied Jay. "I think Diaz is, too. The president gets it. My problem is Phil and the lawyers."

"Is the problem Phil or Lisa?"

Jay winced. His on-again-off-again pseudo-romance with Lisa was a sore subject. "Both. Phil thinks it might turn undecided senators against us if we try to go over their heads. Lisa thinks we should leave it to surrogates. She's concerned about putting Diaz in the crosshairs."

"Lisa hates me. It's personal. I'm the star she wants to be." She shrugged her shoulders and took another sip of chardonnay. "It is what it is. But don't let that cloud your judgment on getting me the interview."

"Don't worry. I'll take care of Lisa. If I have to roll her, I'll roll her."

"I don't doubt your abilities," replied Satcha. She leaned forward again, her knee brushing against Jay's beneath the table. He felt a surge of sexual tension run through his body. "Jay, Diaz needs this interview. Look, I don't pull punches for anyone. But I will be fair. I don't cut people off, and I don't interrupt. I let them talk. It's not about me." She smiled wickedly. "Which is how I get it to be about me, if you know what I mean."

"It doesn't hurt that you've got a great set of legs."

Satcha raised her eyebrows knowingly. "Why do you think I don't have a coffee table on the set?" Jay laughed. "Speaking of great legs, are you over the Italian hottie?"

"I think so. I had fun with Gabriella. She's quite the accomplished businesswoman and very sharp. But when the president called, well, I couldn't turn him down." It was Jay's way of highlighting his symbiotic relationship with Long. "It's hard to maintain a relationship when you're six thousand miles apart. It's just not practical, you know?"

"Any regrets about coming back?"

"No. I walked away from a lot of money. But I'm serving a guy I really believe in. We're doing important things, historic things. I know it sounds corny, but I get excited every day when I go to work."

"I can relate," said Satcha. She looked down at her glass; it was empty. She glanced at her watch. Jay noticed it was a diamond-studded Cartier, almost identical to the one he bought Gabriella in Paris. Did all the divas shop at the same stores? "Have you had dinner?"

"No," replied Jay.

"Well then let me take you to dinner. I want a big fat steak to celebrate my getting the interview with Diaz."

"Whoa—hold on. That's not a done deal. I only said I would try."

"Quit trying to lower expectations, honey," said Satcha. She reached across the table and playfully patted his cheek. "The word *try* is not in your vocabulary. You're Jay Noble."

Jay laughed. The waiter brought the bill. He reached for it, but Satcha would have none of it. "Let Univision pay for this," she insisted. "I pitched you." She signed the bill hurriedly and grabbed her purse. "Come on. I've got a car and driver out front."

"Why don't you ride with me?" Jay replied. "I've got a White House car out front."

"Well, look at you, big shot!"

Jay just smiled.

FORTY-TWO

The weekly Senate Democratic caucus luncheon was usually a sedate affair, but this day was different. Tension among senators thickened as the oversized personalities crammed into an oak-paneled room in the Russell Office Building, bruised egos and frayed nerves on display. Penneymounter, the wounded lion, sat at a rear table licking his wounds, shaking hands with well wishers. The senators made small talk over salmon and rice served on U.S. Senate bone china. Sal Stanley tapped a water glass with the edge of his knife, calling the meeting to order.

"May I have your attention, please? The first order of business is the Diaz nomination," he said. "Two senators have asked to say a few words. First, our new chairman of the Judiciary Committee, Chuck Hurley."

Hurley rose to polite applause. "As all of you know, the Diaz nomination was reported out of committee yesterday with a 10 to 10 tie that was, with a single exception, a party line vote." He allowed a pregnant pause as icy stares settled on Rebecca Rhoades. "I don't expect the vote on this nomination in the full Senate to be any different. Long is playing to the religious right, the NRA, and the U.S. Chamber. It's a polarizing nomination."

"You think?" joked Stanley. Nervous laughter rumbled across the tables.

"Leo has a better feel for the vote count than me"—he pointed to Majority Whip Leo Wells—"but as of yesterday we counted forty-two votes in the caucus against the nomination, one in favor, and nine undecided or unannounced. This is going to be a close vote. By mutual agreement with the Republican leadership, we have set aside thirty hours for debate. I think that is more than enough time before we vote."

"There's a time agreement? Since *when*?" asked Wells pointedly. Stanley stared down at his plate. He had excluded Wells from the discussions. "I'm sure not on board with that. I think more than a few of us are not." His eyes scanned the room, looking for allies.

"That's right," said Dan Ratliff, who was circulating a letter vowing to filibuster Diaz's nomination. "A time agreement is unilateral disarmament. I've got thirty-six signatures on my dear colleague. That's only five short of forty-one. And all that was done, by the way, without the help of leadership." Knowing guffaws rose over the clatter of the cutlery on plates.

Ratliff had challenged Stanley, who never shrunk from a fight. "Dan, you'd have far fewer signatures had leadership opposed you," he said, his gaze steady. "I gave you every opportunity to circulate it; you're still not at forty-one signatures, and the debate on Diaz begins tomorrow." Stanley turned his scowl from Ratliff and faced his colleagues, his posture informal, relaxed. "I've never tried to dictate to the caucus, and I certainly won't start now. But a filibuster of a Supreme Court nominee has never occurred in the history of the Senate. I'm no Don Quixote. Unless we have forty-one solid votes, we're tilting at windmills."

Stanley's message was clear: put up or shut up. Wells, cheeks flushing, rose to his feet. "I have not signed Dan's letter yet because we agreed this should not look orchestrated by leadership. But we *must* stop Diaz. If he gets on the Court, he'll reverse a century of progress for women and minorities." He pulled out a pen. "Hand me the letter." Ratliff complied and Wells signed it with dramatic flourish.

"That's thirty-seven signatures," exclaimed Ratliff. "Four more and the Diaz nomination is dead." He turned to Stanley. "Sal, if you'll sign, it's thirty-eight."

Stanley's face went slack. "I don't think either I or Chuck should sign it . . . at least not yet. But if you get to forty, I'll be number forty-one."

Hurley jumped to his feet. "If you get to thirty-nine, I'll be number forty."

The room broke into applause. Wells sat in his seat doing a slow burn, realizing that Stanley had outmaneuvered him. By purchasing the last ticket on the filibuster train, a meaningless gesture, Sal protected his left flank.

Everyone wondered: could Ratliff and the diehards get two more signatures in the next twenty-four hours?

AT 9:00 P.M. THAT evening fifteen million people tuned in to watch Satcha Sanchez's interview with Marco Diaz, making it the highest rated program in the history of Univision and the largest audience in history for a cable news program not airing during a national convention. Fox and CNN went ballistic when they learned the White House granted the only precon-firmation interview with Diaz to Sanchez. Murmurs about Jay's romantic ties to Sanchez and professional jealousy drove the conversation that she would go easy on the nominee.

Diaz appeared on the screen looking slightly awkward, red tie slightly askew, eyes darting, his fingers fidgeting. Satcha sat opposite him wearing a tight, grey pinstripe, pencil-thin skirt above the knee with matching jacket. Her Latina sexuality smoldered just beneath the surface like the leather bustier beneath her jacket.

"Judge Diaz, thank you for joining us. You want to sit on the Supreme Court of the United States. It is a lifetime appointment. In order to give the American people some insight into your own judicial views, which Supreme Court Justice—and you can pick either a current or former justice—do you most admire?"

"Well, first of all, I will be my own person," replied Diaz, fouling off the pitch. "But in terms of who I most admire, I would say Louis Brandeis for his sense of justice, Anton Scalia for his intellectual courage, and John Roberts for his collegiality."

"Brandeis was a leading liberal, Scalia a vocal conservative," said Satcha. "Some might conclude that choosing such diametrically opposed role mod-els is incoherent. And you would say . . . what?" She cocked her head as if to say, *I've got your number.*

"Both possessed first-rate minds and brought passion to the bench," said Diaz. "That's what I so admire about them. Equally important—and it is why I mentioned Roberts—is the ability to build consensus. The Supreme Court works best when it achieves common ground. I've done that every-where I have served, and I will do so if confirmed as associate justice."

Satcha crinkled her nose, telegraphing she wanted more direct answers. "Let's turn to the issue of abortion. There is a restrictive abortion law in

South Dakota pending before the Supreme Court. In your opinion, when does life begin?"

"I appreciate why you ask the question and why so many people are interested in that topic. It's a deeply emotional issue involving one's personal values. But as a judge my personal views are irrelevant. My job is to apply the laws passed by Congress or another legislative body in light of prior court rulings." He gestured with his hands, growing more confident as he spoke. "*Roe v. Wade* has been the law of the land for almost a half century. Its core findings have been upheld in twenty-two separate Supreme Court decisions."

It was a well rehearsed and flawlessly delivered nonanswer. Satcha hunched her shoulders and narrowed her eyes. "I think what people want to know are *your* values. I'm not asking about your judicial philosophy. I'm asking when you believe life begins."

"I don't think my views or those of any judge in an area so deeply informed by one's moral beliefs are terribly instructive," said Diaz, not budging. "Nor are they dispositive. The same is true of other issues with a moral dimension, such as the death penalty. I have known judges who were personally pro-choice who upheld pro-life laws and judges who were personally pro-life who upheld pro-choice laws. The issue is not what I believe; it is what the law states as informed by the Constitution."

"In *Roe* the Court ruled that a woman had a fundamental constitutional right to privacy that included the ability to end a pregnancy," said Satcha. "If I hear you correctly, you are saying you take no issue with that ruling." She batted her eyes as if to say, *Gotcha*!

"That's a clever way of asking the same question, and my answer is the same. My general inclination as a judge is to seek predictability and stability in the law such that individuals can order their lives according to legal precedents."

"And as you testified before the Senate Judiciary Committee, that includes *Roe*."

"I wouldn't particularize it to a single case," said Diaz, his confidence growing with each question. "But as I noted in my testimony, *Roe* has been upheld for decades by multiple courts and dozens of decisions."

"I LOVE IT! PRO-CHOICE judges often uphold pro-life laws, and pro-life judges uphold pro-choice laws," exclaimed Jay. In his office on the second floor of the West Wing, he and other aides were glued to the television. Lisa chewed on the nubs of her fingernails. Jay swayed back and forth in his chair, occasionally swigging from a bottle of water. Taylor Sullivan stood in the corner, beefy arms crossed over his chest, sleeves rolled up to his elbows, rocking on his heels. For the White House, Diaz's interview was the field goal at the buzzer. If it went well, they felt good about their chances in the Senate. If it went poorly, they were finished.

"He's doing well," said Lisa. "She tried to pin him down, and he didn't take the bait. If he can handle abortion, he can handle anything."

Jay nodded. "He keeps going back to his testimony. That's the key. We need to play this like it's C-SPAN. Keep the temperature l-o-o-o-w."

"No one's paying attention to what he says," said Sullivan with a smirk. "They're too busy looking at Satcha's polished legs."

Lisa rolled her eyes. "That would be you and Jay. The women are listening to what he says."

AS THE INTERVIEW PROCEEDED into the second half hour, Sanchez ratcheted up the pressure. She knew the audience wanted fireworks, not Court TV.

"Judge Diaz, there has been a great deal of controversy about your Wildfire stock holdings and whether it influenced your ruling in the company's favor," Satcha said, setting up an uppercut. "Can you now acknowledge it was a conflict of interest?"

"No. A blind trust is exactly what it says: blind. I had no involvement in the investments made by the trustees. They made highly diversified—"

"But you were regularly informed of the Wildfire stock purchases, Judge."

"I received notices as required by law. I deliberately tossed them in the garbage. I didn't want to know where my retirement fund or 401K was invested."

"But if you were notified, the trust was not really blind, was it?"

"It was blind in that I had no involvement in the investment decisions and could not effectuate them either way—either a buy or a sell order. Had

I instructed the trustees to buy or sell a particular stock, it would have violated the terms of the trust. I never did so."

"Some have asked that you recuse yourself from the Wildfire antitrust case," said Satcha. "You have so far refused. Why?"

"I have not said I would not recuse myself. But I declined to commit to recusal as a condition of confirmation. To do so would set a dangerous precedent for future nominees, endangering judicial independence and violating the separation of powers. Under that scenario any senator could withhold their vote for confirmation until a nominee agreed to rule a particular way or not rule at all on a specific case. That's wrong."

"So you're still open to recusal in the Wildfire case?"

"I will seriously weigh that issue if confirmed. I will consult with the chief justice and ethics experts whose judgment I respect. I will do the right thing if confirmed, and those who have raised the issue will be satisfied with the outcome." He allowed himself a smile.

G. G. HOTERMAN SAT in his office spooning Chinese takeout, the empty containers and beer cans littering the coffee table, his lobbying team gathered around him. Beer, soda, and a bucket of ice filled the table, but G. G. drank Chivas on the rocks. The phone on his credenza rang.

"Did you hear what he just said!?" thundered Stephen Fox.

"I sure did," replied G. G., his voice steady, always unflappable.

"I can't believe I've spent millions of dollars getting this guy confirmed, and he throws us under the bus at the eleventh hour!"

"Welcome to DC," deadpanned G. G. "If you want a friend in this town, buy a dog."

"At least in my world, when someone gets bought, they stay bought."

"I'm not convinced he means it. Remember Noble's in charge. He's running this like a campaign, so Diaz is going to say whatever he has to in order to be confirmed. Once he's on the court and he doesn't recuse himself, what can they do . . . impeach him?"

"You're more cynical then me, G. G. I think he means it. But even if he doesn't, will floating the trial balloon work?"

"I dunno. The real question isn't whether the White House has fifty-one votes. The only question is: are there forty-one Democrats who will vote against cloture? Because if the answer to that is yes, then it doesn't matter how many votes Diaz has. He's dead already."

"What's your best guess? Can the Democrats muster forty-one votes against cloture?"

"I think it's right on the bubble. They've got thirty-eight hard votes but they're stuck. Stanley committed in front of the entire caucus at their weekly lunch that if they got to forty, he would be the forty-first vote. Hurley committed to being the fortieth vote. That still leaves them one vote short."

"I don't know what's worse," sighed Fox. "A filibuster that takes Diaz down, or Diaz getting confirmed and then recusing himself from our case."

"The latter. If he's rejected by the Senate, at least we get another crack."

"I agree. Keep me posted."

G. G. hung up the phone.

"Who was that?" asked one of G. G.'s line lobbyists.

"Stephen Fox. I had to talk him down off the ledge after Diaz all but promised to hit the eject button on the Wildfire case."

"He's probably shorting his own stock as we speak," joked the lobbyist.

G. G.'s assistant appeared at the door. "G. G., it's Christy Love to see you."

"What? On the phone?"

"No, she's in the conference room. I told her you were busy. She said she'd wait."

G. G. arched his eyebrows, surprised by Christy's impromptu visit. He kept the Wildfire lobbyists in the dark about the money he was raising for Pro-Choice PAC. He walked down the hall to find Christy in the conference room watching the Diaz interview on a flat-screen TV.

As usual, she looked striking, her blonde hair brushed back to reveal three-carat diamond earrings, a snug knit top flattering her figure, billowing white pants, and Christian Laboutin heels. She was a bundle of nervous energy.

"Christy!" exclaimed G. G. "How goes it?"

"Still fighting the wars."

"Are we winning?"

"I think so. I totally disagree with the CW on the Satcha Sanchez interview. I think it's going to backfire. The guy is overcoached, he's delivering talking points like an automaton, and the senators are not going to buy it."

"I sure hope you're right. What can I do you for?" asked G. G.

"What do I always need, G. G.? Faith and Family's up with a thousand gross rating points. We're at eight hundred. I have to match them. And I need more radio. Limbaugh and Hannity are killing us."

"How much do you need?"

"Two million. About 1.5 million for TV, half a million for radio."

"Wow," said G. G. slowly, wheels turning. "That's a lot."

"It's crunch time, boyfriend. I talked to Hurley. He says we're one vote away from being able to defeat cloture."

"So I heard. Let me see what I can do."

"Thanks, G. G. You're the best." Christy picked up her purse, giving him an affectionate hug and a peck on his cheek, then walked through the lobby to the front door.

"Hey!" shouted G. G. from behind her. Christy turned around to face him.

"I'm the money king, you hear me?" G. G. exclaimed, pointing at her with his index finger. "Other people talk big. *I* deliver! I've raised forty million bucks for this party in the past two years! I'm the second coming, for crying out loud!"

Christy looked at G. G. with disbelief and then walked out the door.

IN THE BOOK-LINED, OAK-PANELED den of Andy Stanton's well-appointed McMansion in a gated community in Alpharetta, Georgia, Andy and Ross Lombardy watched Diaz's interview with Satcha Sanchez like rabid fans watching a college football game. Andy sat on the edge of a large, leather upholstered chair, peppering the television with unsolicited commentary.

"Why doesn't he just tell the truth: *Roe v. Wade* was wrongly decided?" asked Andy in frustration. "Even Ruth Bader Ginsburg said that. She put it in writing!"

"It's mind-boggling," sighed Ross, sprawling his legs across an ottoman. "It's become mandatory for conservative nominees to deny the obvious."

"The Bible says if the bugle gives an indistinct sound, no one will rally for battle. You better tell our friend Jay that Diaz needs to quit playing around."

"I'm afraid it's a little late. The hearings are over. This is Diaz's only scheduled interview. The Senate begins debate tomorrow." Ross knew what Andy was really upset about—the White House gave the interview to Univision and not the God Channel. To Andy, it was the latest example of being taken for granted after putting Long in the Oval Office.

"What's the vote look like?" asked Andy.

"We're sitting at forty-eight. We need two more Democrats to come over. Whitehead will break a tie."

"What about cloture?"

Ross shrugged. "They're still one vote short. It's the nuclear option, and Stanley doesn't want to pull the trigger, but he's getting major pressure from the left."

"Keep after the centrist, red-state Democrats—the Rebecca Rhoades types. We'll either get their votes, or we'll defeat them in the next election."

Ross thought Diaz did well in the interview. He didn't care if Diaz took a powder on abortion and marriage, as long as he voted right once he was on the Court. Was it enough? He didn't know. But Ross knew how to count votes. And one thing was certain: win or lose, they were headed for the closest confirmation vote for a Supreme Court nominee in U.S. history.

FORTY-THREE

 Charlie Hector hung up the phone and immediately dialed Jay's extension. "Jay, come down to my office when you get a chance."

Jay appeared at the doorway minutes later. Hector motioned for him to close the door.

"I just got off the phone with Doerflinger," said Hector, referring to Senator Richard Doerflinger of New Mexico, one of the final undecided Democrats. "He's willing to vote for Diaz." He paused. "He wants a few things in exchange."

"Like what?"

"More money for Los Alamos. No surprise there. He wants an F-22 fighter jet wing relocated to Holloman Air Force Base." He glanced down at his notes. "That's a new one on me. I've got to look into it." He twisted his face into a scowl. "He also wants the president to do a fund-raiser."

Jay pursed his lips, thinking. "Los Alamos is a no brainer. The F-22 wing is a Pentagon call, but it's theoretically doable. The fund-raiser is a nonstarter."

"I need to run this by the president. We're running out of time and undecided senators. As much as I hate to say it, I think we need to cut a deal with Doerflinger."

Jay nodded. "There aren't a lot of good options at this juncture."

"Come with me," said Hector, catapulting out of his chair.

He opened the door, and they turned to the right, walking down the hall to the Oval Office. Hector looked through the peephole in the door, knocked gently, and opened the door. The president was seated at his desk, talking to Phil Battaglia.

"It's the Sanhedrin!" joked Long. "Come on in, guys. Do we have fifty-one votes yet?"

"Not yet. But we might have found a way to get there, sir," said Hector. He repeated the substance of his phone conversation with Doerflinger, including the list of demands.

Long shook his head in disbelief. "It never pays to be a man of principle, does it?" he sighed. "In this town, if you do the right thing, you get nothing. Someone like Doerflinger hangs back in the grass, asks for the moon, and gets it." He leaned back in his chair, staring at the ceiling. "We need his vote. And he knows it."

"All true. But we're negotiating from a position of strength, Mr. President. New Mexico has a huge Hispanic population," said Jay. "It's 47 percent of the population, 51 percent of registered voters. There are 624,000 registered voters in the state of Hispanic origin."

Long nodded. He never ceased to be amazed by Jay's recall of political facts.

"That's where the Satcha Sanchez interview really helped. It sent Diaz's numbers with Hispanics to 83 percent fav, 12 percent unfav. So we've got Doerflinger by the short hairs. He can't vote against Diaz without alienating Hispanics, which is death for him."

"Jay's just trying to take credit for the Sanchez interview because it was his idea," needled Battaglia good-naturedly.

"I think it's because he's got a crush on Satcha," joked the president. "I notice you didn't recommend that Diaz sit down with Marvin Myers, did you, Jay?"

Everyone enjoyed a chuckle at Jay's expense. Long loved putting Jay in his place, showing him that even if Jay had the brain power, Long was still in charge.

"It's all part of my Hispanic outreach strategy for the reelect," shot back Jay.

"I can't imagine giving him more money for Los Alamos would be a problem, do you?" asked Hector as the locker-room mirth drained away.

"I can't say I do," replied Long. "How much is he asking for?"

"He mentioned $400 million."

Long let out a whistle. "He doesn't sell out cheap, does he?"

"No. We can submit the budget request," replied Hector. "But will the authorizing committees and the appropriators go along with that much of an increase?" He shrugged. "I tend to doubt it. Frankly, in the end, it's a promise we can't guarantee we can deliver."

"My favorite kind," said Long.

"Where is the F-22 fighter squadron he wants?" asked Battaglia.

"It was at Langley in Virginia; now it's in Nevada," said Jay.

Battaglia looked at him as if to ask, *how do you know that?*

"Hey, it's twenty electoral votes, and they're both battleground states," said Jay sheepishly by way of explanation. "It's my job to know these things."

"The bigger problem is Holloway Air Force base already has a squadron, so he's taking from Nevada to beef up his own state's share of squadrons," said Hector.

"We can give him that or some reasonable substitute," said Long. "Run it by DOD to make sure there's not some logistical issue I'm missing."

"The fund-raiser's highly problematic," said Jay.

"I agree," said Long. "What if we offer him Johnny W?"

"He's not going to want Whitehead," said Jay. Everyone smiled knowingly.

"I shouldn't commit to the fund-raiser in exchange for his vote," said Long. "But I don't want to rule it out either." He narrowed his eyes, thinking. "Charlie, tell Doerflinger we're worried about getting deluged with other requests. What if he has a fund-raiser at a hotel somewhere and then we bring them over here for a briefing and I drop by and work the room?"

Hector nodded. "That's perfect." He scribbled notes on his legal pad. "He can't advertise the briefing in any printed invitations. There can't be a connection between the fund-raiser and an official White House event."

"Okay," said Long. "Reel him in. I'll call him after you seal the deal."

"Yes, sir," said Hector. He headed for the door with Jay in tow.

"Don't let him get away," Long said as Hector grabbed the door knob. "And don't give away more than we need to."

"Yes, sir," said Hector. With that he opened the door and they left.

As they turned the corner and headed down the hall, Hector and Jay nearly ran into Truman Greenglass, who was studying a piece of paper he was carrying and was not looking where he was going.

"Are you into your head or something?" joked Hector.

"No, but I think congratulations are in order for Mr. Noble," said Greenglass, smiling.

"How so?" asked Jay.

"We've been looking at the returns from Israel," said Greenglass, referring to the Israeli election. "All we have so far is Tel Aviv, but it looks like Hannah Shoval got over a third of the vote. She should be able to assemble a government with the help of religious parties and Labor."

"That's great," said Jay. "The nightly tracking started going our way the last week. The election was about three things: Iran, Iran, and Iran."

"I'm on my way to place a congratulatory call from the president," said Greenglass."

"And I bet that's not all," said Hector.

Greenglass just stared back. They all knew Shoval's election was the predicate to an Israeli military strike on Iran's nuclear facilities. Jay had begun his career working state legislative races, and now he elected prime ministers for the express purpose of starting a war in the Middle East. He hoped no one ever found out about his involvement.

ON CAPITOL HILL, TENSION over the Diaz nomination reached a snapping point. Attack ads lobbed by both sides ran in a dozen states, phones in Senate offices jangled off the hook, and cable television was a twenty-four-hour-a-day slugfest. Reynolds's accusatory speech in the Judiciary Committee had Democrats spitting nails. Meanwhile the liberal attempt to filibuster the Diaz nomination had Republicans threatening retribution, vowing to sink any judge later nominated with input from a Democratic senator. The Senate, which prided itself on its collegiality, threatened to come apart. A bipartisan group of senators appealed to their colleagues to hash things out before debate on Diaz began. They gathered in the old Senate chamber, the first such meeting since a similar gathering during the impeachment trial of Bill Clinton. Everyone agreed that the meeting was off the record—which meant the *New York Times* and the *Washington Post* would report the details within the hour.

Ed Bell, the Republican vice-presidential nominee from the previous campaign and the most influential moderate voice in the GOP, spoke first. "As we walked into this historic chamber, I thought of the giants who came before us," Bell said in a hushed voice. "Webster, Calhoun, Crittendon—the men who tried in vain to stop the Civil War and narrowly averted the conviction of Andrew Johnson in this very room." He walked from behind his desk, standing in the aisle, facing the presiding officer. "The apostle Paul spoke of being surrounded by a great cloud of witnesses. Well, we are surrounded by the memory of those who rose to the occasion in their own time. Now it's our turn." He cast a furtive glance in the direction of Sal Stanley, who sat at a desk in the front row. "Senator Stanley and I were on opposite sides in the last election. Neither one of us got what we wanted." The senator chuckled at Bell's use of humor. "Perhaps we lost so we could be in this place at this hour to ensure the Senate lives up to its traditions and our nation is not torn apart by this nomination."

Bell sat down to the loud applause. Stanley rose to his feet. He allowed the silence to hang.

"I believe the Senate's role of advice and consent is vital to our constitutional system of government," said Stanley. "It is the hinge point ensuring the proper balance of power between three coequal branches of government." The Democrats nodded with approval while Republicans listened impassively. "I oppose Marco Diaz's nomination. I will fight it vigorously on the floor." He paused, shifting gears. "But I hope all of us, in the zeal of advocating for our own position, do not do permanent damage to the Senate. Something more than a Supreme Court nomination is at stake. More even than Judge Diaz, I believe the Senate is on trial. May we not be found wanting."

The room fell deathly silent. Stanley was not known for self-reflection. It was a riveting moment for everyone, a rare instance when Stanley seemed to put his ambition aside. Was he finally recovering from his defeat for the presidency, finding his voice as a lion of the Senate?

"Unless we change the current trajectory of events, I worry that history will judge us harshly." He raised his arm, pointing in the direction of Penneymounter. "My friend Joe Penneymounter, one of the finest members of the Senate I have ever had the privilege of knowing, paid a heavy price for his stand on this nomination. One of the witnesses scheduled to appear before the Judiciary Committee has died. The Diazes have lost a child." He wheeled to face the Republicans, raising his arms. "Who is to blame? I supposed we can each point to the other. But the truth is, we're all to blame." His voice trailed off. "I'm prepared to meet the minority halfway. We can filibuster this nomination. Or we can discuss a range of options with the minority. If we can find agreement, I will recommend we proceed to a vote without unnecessary delay."

The entire chamber rose to its feet in a standing ovation. In truth Stanley was negotiating away what he did not have. Wells was stuck at thirty-eight votes against cloture, and the whip count was not moving. But Stanley's gallant move made for useful fiction in a Senate chamber riven by bitter partisanship.

Tom Reynolds raised his hand to seek recognition. He rose from his desk and cleared his throat, his eyes misty. "I am deeply moved by the Majority Leader's comments. I welcome his offer to seek a resolution to this dispute that does honor to this body." Everyone knew that Reynolds was emotionally involved, growing so close to Marco and Frida Diaz that he could no longer think dispassionately. "I have made no attempt to hide my revulsion at the way Marco Diaz has been treated. But I agree we all share the blame." His voice trembled. "Two wrongs don't make a right. The attacks on Joe Penneymounter were equally unconscionable. We have a higher calling. We must protect the Senate, and I pledge to do my part."

The meeting in the old Senate chamber became a cathartic exercise, with emotional speeches continuing for another ninety minutes. Senators bared their souls and normally bitter adversaries embraced. At the end the senators called in the U.S. Senate chaplain to close them in prayer. One member of the Senate remained strangely silent. In the back row Richard Doerflinger doodled on a pad of paper, saying nothing.

ROSS LOMBARDY SAT ON the bed in his room at the Ritz-Carlton on Grand Cayman, wearing nothing but a towel. It was his wedding anniversary, and he and his wife had flown down for a getaway weekend. He told no one where he was going, including Andy. The deep-blue Caribbean glistened in the distance, but Ross's eyes remained fixed on the television, watching the coverage of Hannah Shoval's remarkable election as prime minister of Israel. Ross had heard from his Israeli contacts about Noble's surreptitious assistance to Likud. He shook his head in wonderment; Jay had struck again. By his count Jay had now masterminded the election of three national leaders on three different continents in the space of eight months.

His BlackBerry, resting on the coffee table, vibrated. Who could be calling? Reluctantly, Ross answered it. The Senate debate on Diaz was scheduled to begin the following Tuesday, and he had to keep in touch.

"Ross!" boomed the voice of Andy Stanton on the other end of the line. "I hope I'm not catching you at a bad time."

Ross felt his heart skip a beat. "Not at all, Andy," he said effusively. "I'm sitting here watching the election returns from Israel. Can you believe it?" He chose not to mention the fact he was in the Cayman Islands. *Thank goodness for laptops and BlackBerries,* he thought.

"It's an incredible comeback for Shoval," agreed Andy. "Kadima blew it. It was theirs to lose and they lost it. And thank goodness. I just hope Hannah has the intestinal fortitude to take on Iran. If we're lucky, she'll turn out to be another Maggie Thatcher."

"You know the White House engineered her election," said Ross matter-of-factly.

"Really? How so?"

"Truman Greenglass short-sheeted the bed on Kadima with leaks about how their candidate was out of favor with Long. Then he forced the government to freeze settlements on the West Bank in exchange for the U.S. supporting the refined petroleum embargo against Iran. Kadima's support among settlers cratered."

"Wow. Greenglass did that? That's diabolical."

"It gets better. Jay Noble ran Shoval's campaign right out of the West Wing. Edgewater did the polling. The Shoval campaign was a White House operation from start to finish."

Andy let out a long whistle. "Well, it may have been unorthodox if not illegal, but I'm glad they did it. Israel has got to take out Iran's nukes."

"Shoval committed to Long she would do it. And Long is approving fly-over rights over Iraq in exchange for Shoval going back to the table and doing a deal with the Palestinians."

"Good luck with that, brother. Ross, I should probably fly to DC next week and meet with some of the senators before the Diaz vote."

Ross nearly dropped the phone. He knew Andy showing up on the Hill would turn into a circus. The Democrats would have a field day, claiming Diaz was a lackey for the far right. "Sure," he said slowly. "But just to manage your expectations, getting meetings set up with senators on short notice will take some doing."

Andy read the hesitation in Ross's voice. He knew he was a lightning rod. "I don't want to do any press. But we need to show the flag. Get me face time with the honorables."

"I'll get on it right away," said Ross. "But we need to be discreet. If you stick your head up, you're going to get shot. I don't want you to become a target."

"I know how to avoid that."

"How's that?"

"Bring our top grassroots leaders and pastors in from around the country," said Andy. "Go to the White House for a briefing, then head to the Capitol. That way it's not about me."

Ross felt his knees buckle. Andy was giving him forty-eight hours to organize a fly-in and a White House briefing. "Great idea," he said. His weekend was up in smoke.

"Terrific! Get our DC office on it. Debate on Diaz begins on Tuesday, so that would be the ideal day to fly up."

Ross hung up the phone. Andy's idea was both inspired and erratic. His wife came out of the bathroom, fresh from a shower, wearing a plush cotton bathrobe. She read the disconsolate look on Ross's face.

"What's going on?" she asked.

"That was Andy. He wants to go to DC next week and meet with senators. So I need to set up his meetings and organize a fly-in for all our state leaders and pastors."

"You can't blame Andy for wanting to do something. This is for the future of the Supreme Court. He's devoted his entire career to getting to this moment."

"I know. But it's so last minute."

"It'll work out. Don't let it ruin your weekend."

"I'll call the field folks and the lobbyists and get them moving. I also need to call Jay to set up a White House briefing." He picked up his BlackBerry and began to dial the White House operator, who could find Jay any time of the day or night.

"Jay can wait." She took the BlackBerry out his hand, tossing it across the room. Untying the sash, she dropped her bathrobe. "Happy anniversary, honey," she said as she fell on top of him, giggling.

FORTY-FOUR

The debate on the Diaz nomination dragged on, now in the sixth hour of the second of three scheduled days on the Senate floor. One desultory speech followed another for the benefit of C-SPAN and posterity. After the hearings and the deaths of Maria Solis and the Diaz baby, the debate had an anticlimactic feel. But nerves were still jagged—the Democrats remained one vote shy of a filibuster and the White House was stuck at forty-nine aye votes. Only two senators remained undecided. One of them was Richard Doerflinger.

On the floor Sal Stanley approached Doerflinger, who sat impassively at his desk. "Can I speak with you for a moment?" he whispered. Doerflinger nodded and followed him to the cloakroom. They huddled in the corner.

"What's this about you agreeing to vote for Diaz in exchange for more money for Los Alamos?" asked Stanley through gritted teeth.

"Sal, I didn't cut a deal. I had a conversation with Charlie Hector, and we discussed a number of issues. I'm looking out for my state. You don't look out for New Jersey?"

"Dick, this isn't about military bases in New Mexico; it's about the Supreme Court. If you wanted funds for Los Alamos, all you had to do is come to me. We're in the majority, remember?"

"That does me no good if the White House and the House Republicans oppose me. This is critical to my reelection, Sal. I've got to have it."

"Well, think on this," said Stanley, his voice lowering to half whisper. "If you vote for Diaz, hell will freeze over before you get more funding for Los Alamos. You will be a nonperson when it comes to appropriations. And I'll put the word out you sold your vote on Diaz in exchange for an earmark."

Doerflinger's eyes widened. "Are you threatening me, Sal?"

"I'm not threatening; I'm promising."

"Well, I don't scare easily, and I don't shrink from a fight."

"Me either. You're forewarned."

Joe Penneymounter loped in exuding sunshine, oblivious to the tense encounter. He saddled over to Stanley.

"Looks like it's time for Foreign Relations to subpoena Jay Noble and Truman Greenglass."

"How's that?" asked Stanley. Doerflinger stood there looking nervous and chastened.

"The *New York Times* is reporting Noble advised Shoval's campaign in Israel. Her campaign was run out of the White House and Langley. Labor and Kadima are up in arms. It's a total cluster. It's on the front page of tomorrow's paper."

"I've wanted to get that little weasel for a long time," said Stanley. "Now he's stepped in it. How could Long be so stupid as to fix an election in a foreign country using the CIA . . . and Noble! It's like a bad spy novel. This will spark a firestorm!"

"It's amateur night at the opera over there," said Penneymounter. "Noble traveled to Tel Aviv wearing a fake mustache and beard. There's probably a felony in this somewhere. We can tie him up for years with subpoenas. Long will have to defend him or cut him loose. Either way he's a one-armed paper hanger."

Stanley spun on his heel to return to the floor, now with a noticeable spring in his step after hearing Penneymounter's good news. He turned back, leaning toward Doerflinger. "Think long and hard about what we talked about," he said. "Dick, I'm your friend, and I'm telling you that you will be naked in this caucus if you vote for Diaz. Buck naked. So don't blow it."

Doerflinger stood there silently, absorbing Stanley's blast.

LISA STOOD IN FRONT of Jay's desk, her flowing jet-black hair resting on her shoulders, her cobalt eyes intense. "Jay, I've got a stack of messages on my desk six inches high about your consulting gig with Shoval. It's a feeding frenzy. What's going on?"

Jay averted his eyes. "I think some of it may be classified."

"Bull. Come clean. Besides, I can't say *that*."

"No, of course not," sighed Jay. "I wrapped up Brodi's campaign in Italy. The next day I flew to Paris for a little r and r—"

"What . . . with the Italian bimbo?"

"Whatever," said Jay dismissively. "Anyway, I get a call from Truman Greenglass. He says meet some guy in a sedan parked in front of the Gare du Nord. Turns out the guy's CIA. He puts me on a government jet to Tel Aviv. He tells me the Agency is working to make sure the next government of Israel is headed by Likud. I had dinner with Shoval and her political team. I suggested she hire Edgewater. That's it."

"All you did was have dinner with her?"

"That's it," Jay lied. In fact, he was on conference calls and e-mailed Edgewater multiple times a day.

"Did they pay you anything?"

"Nope. Not a dime."

"So we can say you met with her once in Tel Aviv—"

"Jerusalem. We drove there from Tel Aviv."

"Okay, Jerusalem, you met with her. You did so in your capacity as a private citizen before joining the White House staff," said Lisa, going into spin mode, her brain ticking off the talking points. "You were never compensated. You played no role in Shoval's campaign."

"I'd say no *formal* role."

Lisa glared at him. "Jaaaayyy . . . don't lie to me. If you do, I'll kill you."

"I'm the president's senior political advisor, and I talk to a lot of people. Did I talk to Edgewater? Sure. Why wouldn't I? He's *our* pollster. Did I tell them what to do? No, I did not. So you should say no formal role."

Lisa rolled her eyes. "How often did you talk to Fred?"

A sheepish look crossed Jay's face. "I don't know . . . um . . . occasionally." Lisa shot him a dirty look. "Okay, fairly often. But I was never paid, and I was just staying in touch."

"This better be protected by executive privilege. I'll work up a statement and run it by Truman."

"Lisa, I did this at the personal request of the president," said Jay, lowering his voice. "We need the Israeli government to be ready to take military action against Iran. I did what I was told."

Lisa nodded, taking notes. She sat down in a chair, crossing her long legs. "I've got something else I need to ask you about."

"What's that?"

"I got a call from Dan Dorman at the *Post*," said Lisa.

"What's he want now?"

"He claims you called someone at the IRS and pressured them to go easy on their investigation of Andy Stanton and New Life Ministries."

Jay stared back, his face expressionless.

"Well?" asked Lisa probingly.

Jay looked at the ceiling and let out a long sigh. "Andy and Ross Lombardy raised it with me," he said haltingly. "They said Andy was being harassed. I called the White House liaison at Treasury and passed on their concerns. It was a constituent request, pure and simple. We pass those on to agencies all the time."

Lisa's eyes grew wide and her mouth fell open. "Jay, you can't meddle in an IRS investigation of one of the most prominent evangelical leaders in the country, especially when said evangelist is one of the president's strongest supporters! Are you out of your *mind*?"

"Please, spare me the Common Cause nonsense. Dorman's a sleaze. I know he'll try to put it in the worst possible light. But my job is to pass on complaints from supporters of the president to the right person in a department." He leaned forward, palms down on his desk. "Did I call the head of the IRS on the carpet? Heck, no. Did I call the Secretary of Treasury? No. I called the White House liaison, for crying out loud. Big freaking deal!"

"What was the response? What action was taken?"

"How do I know? If they were smart, they did nothing."

"Wrong answer. Dorman says three agents on the Stanton audit team were reassigned. They claim the White House instructed the IRS to call off the dogs."

"That's garbage. Let 'em try to prove it."

"How categorical should I be in my denial?"

Jay shifted uncomfortably in his seat. Lisa stared at him, unblinking. He averted his eyes. "You can say I passed on concerns relayed to me by religious leaders about selective enforcement by the IRS. I made the IRS aware of concerns that audits appeared to be targeted at conservative ministries. I never asked anyone to treat Stanton differently or for the audit of his ministry to reach a conclusion based on anything other than the merits alone."

Lisa nodded, scribbling notes on a legal pad. "They're not going to buy it, but I'll give it my best shot."

"This is going to be ugly. This is why I didn't want to come to the White House in the first place. Between the media and the Democrats, it's a lynch mob."

"Look at the bright side. The flap over fixing the Israeli election may blow the flap over interfering with an IRS audit of Andy off the front page."

"Ha-ha-ha," shot back Jay sarcastically. "What's the latest on Diaz?"

"We're getting calls asking if we offered Doerflinger $400 million more for Los Alamos if he voted for Diaz."

"Not true," Jay lied. "That's Stanley trying to frame it as a bribe. The president has always supported more funding for Los Alamos. It's in his budget request. I was in the Oval when Charlie passed on Doerflinger's request. The president said no quid pro quo."

"I can swat that one away." Lisa's relationship with Jay was complicated. She was attracted to him and repelled all at once. She found his genius seductive, his sense of adventure intoxicating, but his immaturity and penchant for sophomoric trickery boorish. "So . . . are we going to win the vote on Diaz?"

"If we get Doerflinger, yes." He leveled his eyes. "Lisa, we've done all we can. It's out of our hands at this point."

Lisa nodded. "Alright, let me go jump in front of machine-gun fire for you."

"That's the Lisa I know and love!" bellowed Jay, standing up and raising his arms for dramatic effect. "You're my wingman! I'm sending you two dozen roses today!"

"Save the roses. Just stay out of trouble."

"Trouble is my middle name!" Lisa rolled her eyes and walked out.

THE MOTORCADE CARRYING ANDY Stanton—three black Cadillac Escalades with tinted windows—pulled up in front of the Russell Senate Office Building on Constitution Avenue, across the street from the Capitol. Two security guards wearing skintight black suits, wraparound Gucci sunglasses, and earpieces jumped out of either side of Andy's SUV, their heads on swivels, opening the car doors.

Traveling with Andy was like clubbing in Vegas with a rapper. The posse seemed to grow as the day went on. Besides the Prada-clad security guards (who had the caffeinated look of Marines in a firefight), there was a body man (whose main job was to carry menthol cough drops and say "yes, sir" a lot), three drivers, a vice president for communications, two Faith and Family Federation lobbyists, and Ross.

They trooped up the stairs (Andy rarely took elevators, claiming walking stairs was good for the heart) looking like a traveling circus, drawing stares. Andy trundled down the hall turning heads like a rock star. Occasionally an excited Senate staffer or tourist would stop the entourage and request a photo with Andy. The body man would take the camera or iPhone, and Andy would generously pose with the individual or group, enduring their giddy greetings and excited squeals with patient endurance.

"I hope there's no press," quipped Andy in a half whisper to Ross as they walked.

"No press?" replied Ross. "You might as well be Madonna at the MTV Awards."

Andy shot Ross a concerned look.

"I warned you. But we're here, so let's get in and out of these meetings and stay on message. We show the flag, rally the troops, and no gaffes."

"Agreed. We leave it all on the field on this one," said Andy.

They arrived at 453 Russell, the office of Senator Rebecca Rhoades of Louisiana. The first Democrat to announce support for Diaz, she had been subjected to a withering assault from Planned Parenthood, NARAL, Moveon. org, and the Pro-Choice PAC. They waited in the reception area, Andy admiring the awards and plaques on the wall, declining a seat, snapping photos with receptionists as the phones jangled incessantly.

"I guess those phone calls are our handiwork, eh?" whispered Andy.

"We've probably done eight million robocalls," replied Ross. Andy's eyes widened. "Your recorded message has done well. Our telemarketers patch the person directly into the Senate office, then solicit a contribution."

"I love it." He paused. "Now all we have to do is win."

Rhoades's chief of staff appeared suddenly, his deportment harried and solicitous. He greeted Andy and led him down the hall to Rhoades's private office.

Andy walked in, greeting Rhoades with a booming, "Senator! Good to see you!"

Rhoades smiled tightly. Wearing a proper white fluffy blouse buttoned to her throat and a navy wool skirt at the knees, she seemed both pleased and unnerved to be in the evangelist's presence. Incongruously, she held up a box of chocolates, offering one to Andy.

"Have a chocolate," she chirped. "These were a gift from my finance chairwoman. She was one of the civic leaders who helped bring back New Orleans after Katrina. Please!"

Andy, an exercise nut, was always watching his weight. But he played along, not wanting to offend Rhoades, and took a chocolate between his two fingers, holding it awkwardly.

Rhoades directed Andy to sit in the large chair next to her, as Ross, the lobbyists, and the chief of staff grabbed the couches to either side.

"I appreciate your coming, Reverend," she said.

"Please, call me Andy."

Rhoades nodded. "Alright," she fairly drawled. "But only if you call me Becky."

"Happy to. Becky, we're very grateful for your time, especially today, given all that's happening in the Senate. I wanted to come by and personally thank you for your support for Judge Diaz. It was a profile in courage."

"Thank you for your kind words." A pained expression crossed her face. "The labor unions and the left are threatening me with a primary. I may lose the primary because of my support for Diaz. But I probably would have lost in the general had I opposed him." She paused, her mouth curling into a smile. "The good news is I can only lose once."

Andy and the lobbyists tittered nervously. The chief of staff stared blankly.

"Well, if I have anything to say about it, you'll win them both," said Andy. "The far left may want to challenge you in a primary, and they may recruit a candidate. But Louisiana isn't Connecticut. I think you're going to do just *fine*."

Rhoades sat ramrod straight, her posture conveying her defiant attitude. "I'm not worried," she said, waving her hand confidently. "My staff is, but I'm not. I've never voted based on what the polls said. I think about what I believe is best for the country." She paused, allowing her point to sink in. "Not what's best for *me*, or what might get me reelected, but what's best for the *country*. That's rare in the U.S. Senate, I'm sorry to say."

Andy laughed appreciatively. "We need twenty more like you, Senator. I want you to know the Faith and Family Federation will go into Louisiana with everything we've got to help you get reelected. I've got a big audience.

I can't endorse on the radio or TV, but there's more than one way to skin that cat."

"Oh, I know. That's great to know. What exactly do you have in mind?"

"I'd like to have you on my radio show. Then do a conference call with some of the leading pastors in Louisiana. We will also highlight your vote for Diaz in our voter guides and congressional scorecards."

"Excellent," replied Rhoades, the tautness in her facial muscles suddenly relaxing. "Perhaps someone in your organization can share your plans with the RNC. They've targeted me for defeat."

Andy glanced at Ross. "We need to tell the RNC they're going to have to go through us to get to Becky."

After a few more pleasantries, the meeting came to an end. Throughout, Andy kept the chocolate cupped in the palm of his hand.

"Aren't you going to eat it?" asked Rhoades at last.

"I am now. . . . I've got your vote!" They laughed as Andy popped the chocolate into his mouth, chewing vigorously.

After the meeting Andy and Ross headed for the elevator, trailed by Andy's posse.

"Well, that certainly went well," said Andy.

"You realize you just agreed to help reelect a pro-choice Democrat. And you committed to try to get the RNC to back down from recruiting an opponent against her. We're going to have a hard time selling that one to the grass roots."

Andy glanced at Ross. "Is she really pro-choice?"

Ross nodded.

"Well, I traded one Senate seat we can't win anyway for a conservative, pro-life Supreme Court Justice, a devout Catholic, and a man who may be the deciding vote to overturn *Roe v. Wade*," he said. "Not bad for a day's work." Andy's face grew animated and he wagged his finger at Ross. "Tell our folks in Louisiana if that ain't good enough for them, they can take a hike! Tell them they better fall in line."

"Consider it done, boss."

They got on the elevator with the posse. As the doors closed behind them, Ross braced himself for the inevitable blowback when the grass roots learned about Andy's support for R-squared. Andy played chess while everyone else played checkers, and he was always one move ahead on the game board.

FORTY-FIVE

Every member of the Senate sat at their desks, a rarity reserved for the highest occasions: the impeachment of presidents, the censure of senators, the ratification of major treaties, and, in this case, cliff-hanger confirmations of Supreme Court justices. Sal Stanley sat stone-faced at his desk in the first row, his wiry frame folded into a dark brown suit with a red tie, his pasty face strained from exhaustion. Vice President Johnny Whitehead sat in the presiding officer's chair, his stooped posture and grave expression telegraphing the gravity of the moment. Everyone knew Whitehead was there in case he was needed to break a tie. The gallery was packed. Lines of spectators snaked down the stairs and through the Capitol.

Only one speech remained before closing comments by the chairman and ranking member of Judiciary (Chuck Hurley and Tom Reynolds) and the Majority and Minority leaders, who protocol dictated would close out the debate. The speech belonged to Richard Doerflinger. All eyes in the chamber turned to him as he rose at his desk.

"Mr. President, I rise to state how I intend to vote on the Diaz nomination," said Doerflinger, scanning the anxious faces of his colleagues. "Advice and consent is essential to maintaining the balance of power between the three branches of government. It is one of the few enumerated constitutional responsibilities of the Senate. It is one I take very seriously."

The civic lesson complete, Doerflinger plowed ahead. "I believe this is one of the most important votes, probably the most important vote, I have cast as a member of the Senate. The last vote that came close to this level of importance was when we elected my friend and former colleague Johnny Whitehead as vice president in this chamber this past January." He bowed out of respect in the direction of Whitehead, who acknowledged the mention by raising one corner of his mouth. "The Supreme Court is evenly divided along philosophical lines. Judge Diaz may tip that balance, and he may do so in a direction with which I disagree." He looked up from the paper on the podium before him. "But there can only be one president at a time, and presidents should enjoy the presumption that their nominees are qualified.

"Mr. President, I had concerns about Judge Diaz at the outset of this process. I addressed many of those in an hourlong meeting I had with him in my office shortly after he was nominated. Many of my concerns were addressed during the five days of hearings conducted by the Judiciary Committee." The tension in the chamber rose as Doerflinger conducted his own version of brinksmanship, waiting until the final moment to announce his vote. "Paramount among my concerns was the right to privacy. I support a woman right's to choose. Judge Diaz stated his belief that the Fourteenth Amendment to the Constitution included a right to privacy. While he declined to directly address how he might rule on a woman's right to reproductive freedom, his reluctance has been shared by all recent Supreme Court nominees. Judge Diaz's reticence in this regard is neither unique nor disqualifying."

Everyone held their breath as Doerflinger extended the drama of his decision. "I found Judge Diaz to be forthright, intellectually capable, and possessing the judicial temperament necessary to serve on the highest court. Therefore, while I do not share his philosophy in every respect, I will vote to confirm him as an associate justice to the Supreme Court."

The gallery exploded into a mixture of loud applause and throaty booing. Vice President Whitehead, mute in his chair until then, banged his gavel loudly.

"Those in the gallery will refrain from outbursts or expressing their sentiments either way," said Whitehead in a dull monotone devoid of emotion. "Violators will be removed from the chamber."

PRESIDENT LONG WATCHED THE Senate debate on television with a small group of aides in the study just off the Oval. The room was crowded, the tension thick. Jay Noble paced back and forth, blowing his nose into a handkerchief, nursing a stress-induced cold. Battaglia sat in a chair, dark circles under his eyes from lack of sleep. When Doerflinger announced his support for Diaz, Long's face broke into a broad, relaxed smile.

"We got him," said Long. "Wow, that was close."

"That's fifty," said Phil with a relaxed sigh. "Congratulations, Mr. President."

"Congratulations all around," replied Long. "It was a team effort."

"We did our part, that's for sure," said Jay. "But the real credit goes to Stanley."

"How's that?" asked Long, surprised.

"I've heard from two senators that Stanley told Doerflinger he would shaft him on funding for Los Alamos if he voted for Diaz. Doerflinger was so offended he came our way. He was sitting on the fence, and Sal pushed him into our arms."

"Sal is the gift that keeps on giving," said Long.

"Are we sure Rhoades won't jump ship?" asked Jay of no one in particular.

"She's stickin'," replied Charlie Hector. "Got confirmation from Tom Reynolds this morning."

"Now there's a woman with a pair of ovaries," said Jay.

"Speaking of which, I feel like I just gave birth to a bowling ball," said Long.

Everyone laughed. It was the first moment of genuine levity for Team Long in months. The White House had taken a beating over Iran's nuclear brinksmanship, a stagnant economy, the health care bill floundering on Capitol Hill—and, most recently, the flap over intervening in the Israeli election. It was a brutal few months.

For at least a day, everyone could savor a victory.

IN THE FRONT ROW, Stanley refused to look at Doerflinger as he plunged in the knife. His back to his colleague, his face pale and drawn, Stanley stared straight ahead. Doerflinger kept his head down, plowing ahead with remarks now plodding and uninspired.

"Mr. President, I do not think Judge Diaz—or any other Supreme Court nominee, for that matter—should be asked how he or she would rule on a given case," he said, flipping a page in a three-ring binder. "I have my differences with Judge Diaz in the area of employment discrimination. However, Judge Diaz has made clear that as a district and appellate court judge he could not legislate his own views on the statute of limitations for filing discrimination claims. While I disagree, I believe he was honest with me and the Judiciary Committee."

Tom Reynolds sat at his desk, his face like a headlight on high beam. Across the aisle, the Democrats were shell-shocked. To be betrayed by Rebecca Rhoades was one thing, but Doerflinger was one of the sharpest members of the Democratic caucus and a rising star. It was a bitter pill to swallow.

"I would be remiss if I failed to address the allegations against Judge Diaz by Maria Solis," said Doerflinger, his voice falling to a dramatic cadence. "I learned of her allegations from the chairman of the Judiciary Committee, Senator Penneymounter. At no time did the chairman treat Ms. Solis's allegations, at least in my hearing, as anything other than information of a highly personal nature requiring an answer from Judge Diaz. Nor did I have the impression Ms. Solis's deposition was dispositive or her charges proven." Several senators glanced down at the carpet. Solis's death hung over the chamber like a pall. "Due to Ms. Solis's untimely and tragic death, the issue is now moot. Differing and irreconcilable recollections by Ms. Solis and Judge Diaz will never be resolved in a way satisfactory to all. Judge Diaz should be granted the presumption of innocence in the absence of incontrovertible evidence to the contrary."

"THE ISSUE IS MOOT?!" Christy Love shrieked as she tapped the hardwood floor with her Jimmy Choos. "That's the first attack ad in the primary we're going to give this pathetic, spineless excuse of a sell-out."

"His party needed him to stand and fight and he caves," muttered one of Christy's lobbyists. "He's finished."

"Dick thinks this is a play for the Latino vote," said Christy. "I'll show him. I'll hire a Latina organizer to pass out flyers in Spanish saying he voted for a judge who ruled in favor of discrimination against Hispanics. If we don't beat him in the primary, we'll run an independent expenditure against him in the general. We'll do to him what we did to Lieberman after Iraq."

"He's toast," agreed the lobbyist.

"The guy caved for Los Alamos and an F-22 squadron!" shouted Christy. "That's what kills him—he sold his vote. The last time the Senate confirmed a wing nut like this was Clarence Thomas. It led to the Year of the Woman and a backlash at the polls. History is going to repeat itself."

"I hope you're right. And I hope Long goes down like Bush 41. Did you see where Noble sent an appeal to Long's e-mail list of twenty-one million supporters and activists and asked them to contribute to Doerflinger's campaign."

"Long's next on my list," replied Christy. "Trust me."

"MR. CHAIRMAN, JUDGE DIAZ is the embodiment of the American dream," Doerflinger continued on the Senate floor, reaching a crescendo. "As only the second Hispanic justice to sit on the Supreme Court, I believe he will bring a unique perspective based on his life experience. Judge Diaz has the character to be a very successful associate justice. I hope he will fulfill that promise. I will vote to confirm him."

Doerflinger unclipped the microphone from his coat pocket and sat down. Tom Reynolds rose from his own chair and walked over to shake his hand. No one on the Democratic side of the aisle moved. Most looked stricken.

About twenty feet away, Senate majority whip Leo Wells leaned over to Penneymounter. "Hold your head high, Joe," he said through a cupped hand. "You gave it your best shot. Don't let the SOBs get you down." He patted him on the knee affectionately.

"Thanks," replied Penneymounter. "Don't worry about me; I'll be fine. It's the country I'm worried about."

ROSS WAS IN HIS car listening to the Senate debate on the radio when Doerflinger made his announcement. He pulled off the road and dialed Andy's office.

"Are you watching the Senate vote?" he asked excitedly when Andy came on the line.

"No. What's up?"

"Doerflinger just announced he's voting with us. That's fifty votes, and Whitehead breaks the tie. We won, Andy!"

"Brother, this is huge!" boomed Andy. He let out a relieved sigh. "Millions of people were praying. It's the only way Diaz could have survived such a vicious onslaught."

"I agree," said Ross. "I don't think I've seen people pray this hard since the Florida recount in 2000."

"It took us a half century. We finally made it."

"It's too good to be true," said Ross. There was an incoming call beeping on his BlackBerry. He glanced down at the display. "Guess who's calling on the other line?"

"Who?"

"Stephen Fox."

Andy laughed. "He may be the only guy in the country happier than us."

"Big time," said Ross. "But he's holding his breath just like we are on the California marriage case and the South Dakota abortion case. It's 50-50 Diaz recuses himself from the Wildfire case."

"Not a chance," said Andy confidently. "That would be admitting he did something wrong on the blind trust. He's not going to give in to his critics."

"Who would've ever thought we'd be on the same side as Fox?"

"There's no chance that someone finds out about his contribution to the Federation, is there?"

"The check came from an account held by a law firm in LA, and the contribution was anonymous. Technically, I don't know who the donor is."

"It's not on our tax return, is it?" asked Andy.

"It's reported to the IRS, but we don't have to disclose it publicly."

"Good."

Ross shifted topics. "I would imagine you'll get a call from the president. He owes us big time."

"You said it, brother. Six million dollars worth of television and grass roots. It was well worth it. We now have a conservative majority on the Supreme Court. It's going to make a difference across the board: life, marriage, tort reform, religious liberty, you name it."

Ross hung up, feeling a greater sense of satisfaction in his work than he had in years. The truth? Sometimes he wondered if he wasn't wasting his life away beating his brains out with a right-wing group while others made the big bucks or had more power. But not today—he and Andy were in the catbird seat. Still a thought nagged him. Had he compromised his beliefs by taking Fox's money? He thought not: if it was the devil's money, at least it went to support a good cause.

Then a thought hit him. He clicked the Web browser on his BlackBerry, pulling up a stock-tracking Web site and typed in the stock symbol for Wildfire. When it came up on the screen, his eyes widened. Wildfire's stock had already jumped 18 percent. Apparently the Street didn't think Diaz would sit out the antitrust case either.

TWO THOUSAND PEOPLE GATHERED on the South Lawn waiting for Long and the newest member of the U.S. Supreme Court. The chief justice had already sworn in Diaz in a private ceremony in the Oval Office the morning after the Senate confirmed him by a 51 to 50 vote, with Vice President Whitehead breaking the tie. The White House released a photograph of the chief swearing in Diaz, but Jay was insistent they stage a public investiture ceremony for supporters.

In the Oval, Long, Marco and Frida Diaz, the chief justice, and the Diaz children gathered for photos. Long playfully scratched the tops of the heads of the two Diaz boys as the official photographer clicked away. He gave them a tour of his desk, showing them how to crawl through the trapdoor in its front, to Frida's chagrin.

Jay and Phil Battaglia hung back, admiring the scene. Long was a natural in such settings. He wasn't just posing for the cameras; he really liked people.

The door opened and Claire walked in, looking effervescent in a peach-colored Dior dress with matching heels, her hair and makeup exquisitely (and one guessed professionally) done, peach lip gloss gleaming on her mouth, complementing her fair complexion. Her strawberry blonde hair, high cheekbones, and blue eyes gave her a striking, if aging, beauty.

"Claire!" exclaimed Long. "So glad you could join us."

She rolled her eyes. "He's just teasing me for being late . . . again," she said. She turned to Marco and Frida and walked across the room, giving them both hugs. "Congratulations to both of you, and thank you for your willingness to serve. We're so proud of you."

"It is really we who should be thanking you," said Frida.

"Are you sure about that?" asked Long, chuckling.

"Now that it's over, yes," said Diaz.

"Had we known," said Frida with a bob of her head, "we would have said no."

"That's why we like to keep potential nominees in the dark," joked Long.

"We're glad you said yes," said Claire, placing a hand on Frida's shoulder. "Marco is going to do a terrific job. I hope you know how many people were praying for you." Her eyes grew warm with emotion. "I prayed for you two every single day. Millions of others did, too."

"We felt it," said Marco. Frida nodded, speechless, her eyes watery.

The door to the colonnade opened. "Time to go, Mr. President," said an aide.

Long opened his arms like a proud father and guided Marco and Frida out the door, their boys trailing like ducks waddling behind their mother. Claire and the chief justice fell in behind while Jay and Phil exited out a side door, not wanting to be within camera range of Diaz and Long when they reached the stage.

FOR DIAZ'S PUBLIC INVESTITURE, the White House staged a victory jig, inviting a euphoric crowd for what turned into a raucous celebration. It was homecoming for the vast right-wing conspiracy. Roman Catholic bishops, evangelical pastors, televangelists, conservative Hollywood types, Federalist Society lawyers, business lobbyists, and CEOs (Stephen Fox was conspicuous in his absence) shook hands, hugged and kissed, joked easily, signed autographs, and posed for photos. For them it was a dream a long time coming. For the press corps roasting on a riser, it was a freak show, the Tea Party crowd meets Barnum and Bailey.

"Ladies and gentlemen, the president of the United States and the First Lady, accompanied by the chief justice of the Supreme Court of the United States, Justice Marco Diaz and Mrs. Diaz," intoned an announcer. People scrambled to their chairs. Applause greeted Long and Diaz as they bounded onto the stage to the opening notes of "Hail to the Chief."

Long went directly to the podium as Diaz stood to his right, staring down at a piece of masking tape on the stage with his name on it. A roar went up from the crowd. Diaz's eyes glistened. Frida beamed.

Long hung back, letting the crowd revel in the moment. Their cheers were a lusty rebuke of Sal Stanley, Joe Penneymounter, Christy Love, and that perennial conservative bogeyman, the mainstream media. Andy Stanton sat on the front row with Tom Reynolds and Ross Lombardy on either side. In the calculus of Washington, Andy was the man of the hour. Hated and vilified by many, adored by millions, he was the Rorschach test of American politics: some saw a snake-oil salesman while others saw a modern-day prophet. For Andy's part, he did not care what others thought of him.

The president leaned into the microphone as people took their seats. "We already did this in private, but we wanted to make sure it took," he joked. (Loud laughter.) Long spoke extemporaneously, ignoring the prepared remarks on the podium.

"I really don't have much to add beyond what I have said many times before about this fine man. Judge"—he spun in Diaz's direction—"forgive me—Justice Marco Diaz . . ." The crowd applauded. Long cocked his head. "I kind of like the sound of that—Justice Diaz." More laughter mixed with applause. "Marco Diaz is going to make an outstanding addition to the Supreme Court. He demonstrated throughout his confirmation process what those of us who know him well already knew: this is a man of rare character, intellect, integrity, and honor." Long pointed at Marco. "We had a spirited debate. It was tough at times. But today we are all Americans. Wherever we might have been before, Marco Diaz is now justice for all of the American people, and we wish him God speed." He bobbed his head in the direction of Diaz. "Now the chief justice will administer the oath to Justice Diaz for his formal investiture."

The chief justice stood to the left of the podium while Diaz stood to the right, raising his right hand and placing his left hand on a Bible held by Frida, who stood between them.

"Please repeat after me," began the chief justice. "I, Marco Diaz, do solemnly swear that I will administer justice without respect to persons, do equal right to the poor and the rich."

Diaz repeated the line.

"And that I will faithfully and impartially discharge and perform all the duties incumbent upon me as associate justice of the Supreme Court under the Constitution and laws of the United States."

Diaz repeated the line, then added, "so help me God."

"Congratulations," said the chief justice, shaking his hand.

Marco approached the podium tentatively, his face reflecting the exhausted joy of a marathon runner crossing the finish line. The crowd roared, cheering and clapping for a full minute, shaking off Diaz's attempts to quiet them. Finally they fell silent.

"On behalf of Frida and our family, let me say thank you, thank you, thank you," Diaz began effusively, his voice a little hot. "My journey to this place began in a dusty little town in my father's native Mexico. He was a simple man who worked as a janitor when I was a boy. My dad taught me the value of hard work, honesty, family, and being true to myself. I would not be standing here today without all he and my mother invested in me." (Applause.)

"I want to thank the nuns at St. Christopher's in Dallas who believed in me when no one else did. They taught me that character is doing the right thing, even when no one is looking." Long allowed himself a slight smile as Diaz spoke. "Special thanks to Phil Battaglia here at the White House and Art Morris at the Justice Department, two of the finest public servants in government." (Applause.) "And finally, to my wife Frida—my best friend, the mother of my children, my wife who stood by me through thick and thin. Thank you, honey."

As Diaz turned to acknowledge Frida, the entire crowd stood to its feet in a thunderous ovation. It was an emotional moment. Frida stood motionless, tears welling in her eyes. Long walked over and put his arm around her. She buried her head in his shoulder and began to weep. News photographers scrambled to the stage, many of them going down on one knee, to capture the scene. Someone handed Frida a tissue. She wiped her eyes and waved to the crowd.

"Thank you," said Diaz, wrapping up. "Thank you all."

The ceremony finished, the crowd rushed the stage. They extended hands to shake Marco's hand or offer him a program to sign, shouting his name.

"Marco! Marco! We love you!" they shouted.

Long grabbed Claire by the hand and exited the stage from the rear; he wanted Marco to enjoy his day in the sun.

Andy Stanton stood to the side of the stage, shaking hands, embracing friends, and posing for photos when he heard a voice through the noise.

"Andy!"

Andy turned to see Diaz. Marco leapt from the stage and came over to Andy, wrapping him in a bear hug. They both dripped sweat. Andy felt the heat from Diaz's body, the sweat on their necks and faces mixing as they embraced. They seemed oblivious to the flurry of photos snapped by news photographers as they captured the moment.

"I wanted to catch you before you left and thank you for all you did," said Marco. "You were amazing. I was honored to have you in my corner, friend."

Andy beamed. "It was my pleasure, Marco. You're *my* hero."

"No, no," Marco protested. "Not me—you're my hero. You never gave up . . . ever. And I felt the prayers. No matter what happened, I was sustained by prayer."

"You're here because of the power of prayer," said Andy excitedly. "I believe that."

Diaz patted him on the back. "Stay in touch," he said. "I've got a great office at the Supreme Court building, and the door is always open. Come and see me."

"I will," Andy promised.

They broke from their clutch. Andy ambled back toward the White House, Ross at his side.

"What a great guy!" exclaimed Ross, still pumped.

"He's the real deal. That's why they wanted to stop him," said Andy. "They came close, but thank goodness they didn't. Every now and again the good guys win."

JAY RETURNED TO HIS office with a spring in his step. True, the IRS and Israeli election flaps trailed him, and Senate Democrats threatened to issue subpoenas and drag him before investigatory committees. Yet Jay somehow felt invincible. They won the Diaz battle, and, after a bumpy start, Long was in the zone. The mojo from the campaign was back.

He called his staff into his office, firing orders, ribbing people good-naturedly, running through the checklist of tasks. For Jay, it was compulsive and everyone knew it. He was mentally moving on to the next battle: the looming off-year elections, when he and Long hoped to gain control of the U.S. Senate and end Sal Stanley's political career forever.

Phil Battaglia appeared at the door, a satisfied smile on his face.

"Counselor!" Jay boomed.

"You got a minute?" asked Phil.

"For you, consigliere, of course," said Jay. He shooed the staff out of his office, the meeting now over.

Phil closed the door and pulled up a chair. "It was rough sledding out there, amigo. This wouldn't have happened without you," said Jay. "The president agrees."

"We blew a few tires, but I guess the third time's the charm, eh?" joked Battaglia, the satisfied smile on his face refusing to melt away.

"At least we didn't have to go to round four," said Jay, rolling his eyes. "Man, it got dicey there for a while."

Battaglia crossed his legs in a thoughtful repose. He pulled a manila envelope out of his legal pad cover and slid it across the desk at Jay. "Check this out."

Jay opened it and scanned the photocopied sheets of paper, flipping slowly through them. They looked like medical records. "What's this?" he asked, his brow furrowed.

"Maria Solis' patient records from the Yale student health clinic," answered Battaglia. "Look at the second page . . . about halfway down."

Jay looked intently. His eyes came to a notation: "D and C. No complications, no signs of hemorrhaging." His eyes grew wide. "*Holy smoke,*" he whispered. "So Maria had an abortion after all?"

"It sure looks like it. Either that or she miscarried. My guess would be she aborted the fetus."

"How come it never came out?" asked Jay.

Battaglia shrugged his shoulders. "The doctor who performed the procedure died in a freak automobile accident ten years ago. The only evidence is this notation. Believe it or not, the Judiciary Committee never asked Yale University for her medical records," he said. "DOJ had them." He shook his head. "All they had to do was ask, but they were so preoccupied with getting Maria ready to testify they forgot." He shrugged his shoulders. "When she died, that was the end of that."

Jay had a shocked expression on his face. "I guess we dodged a bullet." He put the manila envelope down. "What do we do with these now?"

"Nothing," answered Battaglia. "It's over."

"It doesn't prove anything either way, does it?" asked Jay. "We don't know for certain if it was a miscarriage or an abortion, and there's no way to prove Marco was the father."

"Maria called Marco the night before she was supposed to testify. She told him he was the father, she had an abortion, and she couldn't bring herself to tell him at the time," said Battaglia. "Was she telling the truth? Who knows?"

Jay handed the papers back. Battaglia slipped them back into the manila envelope and got up to leave. He put his hand on the door knob and opened the door. Standing in the threshold, he turned back. "This doesn't leave this room," he said.

"My lips are sealed."

"I can't believe with hundreds of reporters, lawyers, special interest groups, and sleaze merchants crawling all over Diaz, this never came out." Phil pointed the manila envelope skyward, his eyes glancing up. "Someone wanted him on the Supreme Court." He walked out, leaving Jay alone in his thoughts.

Jay turned and gazed out his window overlooking the South Lawn. The tranquility of manicured grass, sun-dappled gardens, freshly cut hedges, and blooming flowers contrasted with the carnage of the confirmation. Two people were dead—three if one counted Solis's (and Marco's?) unborn child. Penneymounter's presidential ambitions were torched in a bonfire of scandal, Natalie Taylor was being offered millions to pose for *Playboy*, and Sal Stanley's hopes for another presidential bid hung by a thread. Yolanda Majette's reputation was destroyed, the California Assembly was investigating her husband's law and lobby practice, and she would likely be forced to resign from the California Supreme Court. Long, who rode into Washington as a uniter pledging to heal the political breach, was now more polarizing than any president since Richard Nixon.

Jay shuddered. Diaz's confirmation was the culmination of a series of unthinkable, apparently random events. If Yolanda Majette's husband had not been so sloppy, Diaz never would have been nominated. If Mike Birch had said yes, Diaz would have languished on the appellate court for another decade or longer. If Maria Solis had lived, his nomination would not have been voted out of the Judiciary Committee. If Stanley had not played hardball and threatened Doerflinger, Diaz would have lost by a single vote. It was all in the bounce of the ball. Diaz's fate, like Long's before him in the campaign, was out of Jay's hands. As he gazed out at the flowers and the happy crowd filing from the South Lawn, Jay thought perhaps there was an angel in the whirlwind after all.

But there was no time to celebrate. He had to get ready for the off-year elections. That meant spreading the field on Stanley by recruiting a strong contingent of Senate candidates, raising a ton of money, and pulling up Long's job approval number, and fast.

ACKNOWLEDGMENTS

 This book began in 1991 when I was the executive director of the Christian Coalition and we mobilized support for Clarence Thomas's nomination to the U.S. Supreme Court. In many ways that episode changed my view of politics. Many scenes in The Confirmation have their roots in the struggle where I was privileged to have a front row seat to history.

I also drew from the experience of watching the filibuster in the U.S. Senate of Miguel Estrada and other appellate court nominees of President George W. Bush. In that sense, the inspiring as well as the haunting details of this story have antecedents in real life.

Resurrection, former U.S. Senator John Danforth's moving account of the Thomas nomination, showed the human toll of confirmations. I also am indebted to Stephen L. Carter, whose book *The Confirmation Mess* argued that the judicial confirmation process had become brutal, dehumanizing, and dysfunctional.

Rick Christian, my literary agent, convinced me to stick with fiction, for which I am grateful. I also want to thank Oliver North, Gary Terashita and the rest of the team at Fidelis/B&H. Gary did a terrific job editing the manuscript and helping me correct my many errors.

Jo Anne and our four children continue to allow the interference of my books in our lives. Jo Anne is the best sounding board any author could hope to have. She read and critiqued every chapter, and the final product is much improved as a result.

I owe a special debt of gratitude to my colleagues at Century Strategies and the Faith & Freedom Coalition. Having worked as outside consultants on the last four Supreme Court confirmations, my colleague Gary Marx and the rest of our team have seen firsthand how the process has changed from an inside to an outside battle.

In the end, this book is not just about politics. It is about men and women struggling to do the right thing under enormous pressure and for very high stakes. It is also about the spiritual dimension of the battle over our judicial system. Napolean said there were two forces in the world: the sword and the spirit, and the spirit is stronger. I hope that comes through in these pages.